THE INSURMOUNTABLE EDGE

Thomas H. Goodfellow

THE
INSURMOUNTABLE
EDGE

A Story in Three Books
BOOK THREE

CONTINUED FROM BOOK TWO

SPENSER PUBLISHING HOUSE

Spenser Publishing House, LLC
11661 San Vicente Boulevard, Suite 220
Los Angeles, CA 90049
www.spenserpublishinghouse.com

ISBN 978-1-7346130-2-5 (hardcover)
ISBN 978-1-7346130-5-6 (paperback)
ISBN 978-1-7346130-8-7 (e-book)

Library of Congress Control Number: 2020902683

Cover and interior design by Lisa Ham at spaceechoes.com
Image by peterschreiber.media

FOR J.A.G.

What is a fair lifespan for a human being? And if that life be taken by another before its natural end, what debt shall be owed?

Inscription on a stone tablet found on the island of Mykonos. Author unknown, circa 1200 B.C. Translated from the Greek.

PART V

THE VALLEY

Continued from BOOK TWO...

CHAPTER 93

Adelaide and I made a quick search of the bunker and identified where the air ducts came in. We then exited the bunker by squeezing between the side of the bunker's entrance door and the Slinky-like air hoses. We headed up the bunker's outside stairs to the base of the crater. I carried the Enigma machine under my arm.

"There's still one thing you forgot to ask me," Adelaide said.

"I didn't forget," I said.

"You didn't, huh?" Adelaide said. "What am I talking about then?"

"You realize the challenging tone of your question is just setting you up for embarrassment, don't you?" I said.

"Now I'm sure you have no idea what I'm talking about," Adelaide said.

"My mind is fine, Adelaide," I said. "I passed out down there. I didn't die."

"I thought you said you were taking a nap?" Adelaide said.

"Nap, pass out, no difference," I said.

"Right," Adelaide said. "You'll forgive me if I think you're full of shit, however, because it's obvious you're stalling as you still haven't asked me the thing you forgot to ask me."

"Okay," I said. "Just remember I tried to warn you. For the sake of argument, let's consider all workstations and desks as desks. How many desks were there in the bunker?"

"Goddamnit," Adelaide said.

"I got it right?" I said. "That's what you thought I had forgotten to ask?"

"Yeah, you got it right," Adelaide said.

"I told you you were just going to embarrass yourself," I said. "I included the vice president of dark programming's desk in my count and came up with 59 desks. Is that what you got?"

"Yes," Adelaide said.

"Freddy said the hazmat guys counted 56 dead, which is what I counted as well," I said.

"Me too," Adelaide said.

"Means three of the dark programmers weren't in the bunker when the carbon monoxide was pumped in," I said.

"So if the blond guy on the floor isn't Nemo, we have about a one in nineteen chance Nemo is still alive," Adelaide said.

"Assuming the explosion that created the crater didn't get him," I said.

"Forgot about that," Adelaide said.

"However, it's possible the odds actually might be better than one in nineteen," I said.

"They might?" Adelaide said.

"There's additional data to consider," I said. "For example..."

I was interrupted by the ringing of my iPhone. It was Haley attempting a FaceTime call.

"Hold on, Adelaide," I said. "I want to take this."

"I want to hear about the additional data," Adelaide said.

"Patience," I said.

I stopped where Adelaide and I were, which was then about halfway up the bunker's outer staircase, and answered the phone. Adelaide gave me a dirty look and continued up the stairs on her own. Haley's face was on my iPhone screen. She didn't look any less beautiful than the last time we had spoken despite the fact that she probably had been up for at least forty-eight hours.

"Haley," I said into the phone, "aren't you afraid that if you keep hanging around NORAD they might never let you leave?"

"They're treating me pretty nicely, actually," Haley said.

"They'd be fools not to," I said.

"Thank you," Haley said. "I'm afraid I've got some not so great news."

"You still haven't been able to find the second Doctors of Mercy plane?" I said.

"No," Haley said. "We found it. It's parked on an abandoned runway in the middle of the desert off Route 62 about thirty-five miles north of Blythe."

"They just left it there?" I said.

"Looks like they blew all the front landing gear tires when they touched down," Haley said. "Runway might have been in rougher shape than they thought."

"I assume you didn't find anyone on board?" I said.

"The thirty mercenaries who landed in Oklahoma City have vanished into thin air," Haley said. "Which is bad in and of itself. What's worse is there was also something else on the plane."

"A man-eating stewardess?" I said.

"If only you were so lucky," Haley said. "The team I sent out there was good. They tested for everything. They got a hit on the propellant used in the latest Soviet Igla surface-to-surface laser guided missiles."

"All we've seen are AK-12's so far," I said.

"Yeah, well, something else might be in your future," Haley said. "You have to watch your back now more than ever."

Hadn't Grace just warned me my life was in grave danger? How had she known?

"What's wrong?" Haley said.

"Wrong?" I said. "Nothing. I'm great."

"How come you look like you just saw a ghost?" Haley said.

"Must be the connection," I said. "We just left the bunker but we're still about twenty-five feet underground."

"If you say so," Haley said. "What's under your arm?"

I focused the iPhone camera on the Enigma machine.

"That what I think it is?" Haley said.

"Depends," I said. "What do you think it is?"

"I'm hopeful it's the property of the enigmatic Dr. Nemo," Haley said.

"I'm impressed," I said. "You remembered Nemo's voicemail."

"Hard not to," Haley said. "I've listened to it about a hundred times."

"I'm not sure 'hopeful' is the right word, though," I said. "The Enigma machine might actually make things more complicated. It's got about ten quadrillion possible combinations."

"I know that," Haley said. "But all our efforts to decode Nemo's message so far have left us stumbling in the dark. This might be a real lead. How fast can you get the machine to me?"

"How fast can you pick it up?" I said.

"Where you headed next?" Haley said.

"Back to Dr. Lennon's home in Malibu," I said.

"Bet she's missing you," Haley said.

"No comment," I said.

Haley shifted her gaze away from her computer's camera and I heard some keyboard clicks come over my iPhone. I assumed she was looking up something on another section of her monitor.

"I can have someone from MOM meet you in about fifteen minutes in the west San Fernando Valley," Haley said, turning her gaze back to me. "The name of your contact is Diana Armatrading. She'll be in a tan Prius at 22300 Serrania Avenue."

"That's quick," I said.

"You can thank U.S. Attorney Vandross," Haley said. "Vandross has people on standby. He figured since he already helped you three times in the last forty-eight hours it wouldn't be long until you called again."

Three times? I counted in my head. The Lancaster jail, Bobby and Timmy, and the VW bus man George Boole. Three was correct.

"I love Vandross," I said.

"What else did you find in the bunker?" Haley said.

"Fifty-six dead and fifty-nine workstations," I said.

"No thirteen or fourteen year old kids among the dead, please God?" Haley said.

"No one under eighteen," I said.

"Eighteen is bad enough," Haley said. "But I think I would have lost it if you told me there was anyone younger."

"You and me both," I said.

"You think any of the bodies could belong to Dr. Nemo?" Haley said.

"Don't know," I said. "At least there was no one sitting at the desk where I found the Enigma machine."

"We have a chance then," Haley said.

"God willing," I said. "I'll send you all the photos and ID's of the dead as soon as we get off this call. If you can get a list of the dark programmers from the NASAD files, you should be able to cross-check the list with what I send you and determine which three programmers weren't in the bunker today."

"I don't have a list of the dark programmers yet," Haley said. "NASAD's encryption of the dark programmers' info is much stronger than I thought. We should have a list soon, though."

"Great," I said. "I also think it's now reasonably certain that one of the dead is the NASAD vice president of dark programming, Rick Benavidez. Freddy said that upon Mr. Benavidez's death his top secret

NASAD records were unsealed. We have a photo of the vice president too. I think it would be a good idea for you to use the photo to try to fully confirm that the man in the bunker is really Mr. Benavidez."

"We'll do our best," Haley said.

"If you're successful in identifying the three dark programmers who weren't in the bunker," I said, "the next thing I'll need you to do please is send out some teams to find all three of them and keep them safe."

"Of course," Haley said. "I'll tell you immediately if we find any of the three."

"No news on Dragon Man or the donors behind Doctors of Mercy?" I said.

"Still working on it," Haley said. "I'm also still looking for footage from security cameras that were running outside the dark programmers' bunker, but I haven't found any yet."

"Parting is such sweet sorrow," I said.

"Sleep dwell upon thine eyes," Haley said.

"Other than we got the roles reversed," I said, "that wasn't bad."

Haley smiled and waved and my screen went dark. I uploaded the photos and ID's of the dark programmers to her.

I joined Adelaide where she was waiting for me at the top of the stairs. The generators were humming and the fans whirring. The air being sucked out of the dark programmers' bunker whistled through the hoses on its journey to the outside world. It was still warm, and the breeze soft. The night's stars, though partially obscured by haze and the light coming from the businesses, homes, and streetlamps of the vast San Fernando Valley, still twinkled at us from every direction. The smell of smoke continued to sting my nostrils.

I looked over at Jeff. He was lounging in the back seat of the police cruiser. The two cops were in the front seat munching on doughnuts.

"Sorry for the delay," I said to Adelaide. "Since it appears the cops are still occupied, we can take a quick look for the air intake vents we found in the bunker. After that we'll meet back up with Jeff."

"I want to hear about the additional data," Adelaide said.

"We need to focus on examining the vents and then getting back to the pickup point unseen first," I said. "I'll tell you everything once we're in the car again and on our way."

"Whatever," Adelaide said.

I pointed at an area about twenty-five yards away from us along the rim of the crater. "That spot over there seems to match up with where we estimated the bunker's intake vents would come out."

Adelaide and I, hunched low, silently picked our way through the rubble left by the building's explosion, and circled the crater's rim. We arrived at the spot at which I had pointed, then walked in opposite directions as we studied the ground for evidence that might support my theory that carbon monoxide had been pumped into the bunker.

"Got something," Adelaide said.

"That was quick," I said.

"How I roll," Adelaide said.

I walked over to where Adelaide was crouching and pointing at the ground. There was a strip of concrete that must have been a walking path. The path led up to the crater in one direction and back to the building's parking lot in the other. A swath of what had once been green lawn, but was now scorched dry brown, bordered both sides of the path.

What Adelaide was pointing at were two fresh tire prints in the grass between the concrete walking path and the building. The prints were about six feet apart from each other and were about a foot long, four inches deep, and nine inches wide. The reason the prints looked fresh was because, that while their sides were baked by the heat, their bases were still a bit damp.

I crouched down next to Adelaide and set the Enigma machine down beside me.

"What do you think happened?" I said.

"Truck pulled up here," Adelaide said. "Piped in the carbon monoxide."

"What kind of truck?" I said.

"If it were me, I'd have one from a heating and air conditioning company," Adelaide said. "Make it look like I was just doing repairs."

"What I'd do," I said. "Any security cameras that might have been out here went up in smoke with the rest of the building, but Haley is already looking for a digital record of anything the cameras might have filmed before that happened."

"Don't you think whoever did this would have disabled the cameras first, or at least covered up their lenses?" Adelaide said.

"Good point," I said. "They're evil, but they're not stupid."

I took out my iPhone and texted Jeff to tell him we were ready for pickup. I grabbed the Enigma machine and stood up. Adelaide and I moved rapidly to the hill upon whose crest we had earlier parked the Crown Vic. We scrambled up the hill's loose dirt and gravel and arrived at the top of the hill just as Jeff, who had the Crown Vic's lights turned off, slowly coasted to a stop. Jeff shut off the engine, opened the driver's door, and got out.

"How many calories in a doughnut?" Jeff said.

"Jelly filled or plain?" I said.

"We be eating both," Jeff said.

"Ten million filled, five million without?" I said.

Jeff shook his head.

"Nope," Jeff said. "Jelly be three hundred, plain be two."

"You sure?" I said.

"Posted right there on the walls of Winchell's Donut House," Jeff said. "New federal regs. Those boys in blue must have eaten seven thousand calories."

"Probably burn 'em off tonight," I said.

"Uh huh," Jeff said. "Sitting on your ass be hard work."

Jeff looked at the Enigma machine under my arm.

"Nemo's?" Jeff said.

"Could be," I said.

"You already try to decode Nemo's message with it?" Jeff said.

"Didn't work," I said. "Thought I'd let Haley give it a try. We're going to hand the machine off to someone who will get it to her."

"Don't envy Haley," Jeff said. "Ten quadrillion combinations."

"We might not envy the ten quadrillion," I said, "but we might soon be envying her safety within the warm and cozy confines of the NORAD bunker."

"You know something I don't?" Jeff said.

"Haley thinks the mercenaries have Igla surface-to-surface missiles now," I said.

"Laser or line of sight?" Jeff said.

"Laser," I said.

Adelaide said, "Hold on. Did you just say the mercs have missiles now?"

"Yes," I said.

Jeff said, "You got a problem with that little girl?"

Adelaide said, "You sure they aren't following us?"

I said, "I haven't seen anything. Jeff?"

Jeff said, "Not yet."

Adelaide said, "Not yet? That's very reassuring."

"We're in full combat mode, girl," Jeff said. "We don't deal in reassuring, we deal in the truth."

"You steal that from someone?" Adelaide said.

"Nope," Jeff said. "Just made it up myself."

"Why don't I believe you?" Adelaide said.

"Maybe you prejudiced against colored folk," Jeff said.

"That's the last thing I am," Adelaide said. "Anyway, shouldn't we be getting out of here? Seems to me the longer we stay in one place the easier we are to find."

"Out of the mouth of babes," I said.

Jeff said, "Now that be stolen."

Adelaide got in behind the wheel of the Crown Vic. Jeff and I got in after her. Jeff sprawled across the back seat and I sat in the front passenger seat with the Enigma on my lap. Adelaide drove slowly. She kept the Vic's headlights, roof light, and rear deck lights off until we got back on the southbound 5, whereupon she lit us up like a Christmas tree and gunned the engine.

It was a little after 11:00 p.m. and the traffic was light. Serrania Avenue, the street on which Haley had told me I was to meet Diana Armatrading for the Enigma pickup, was off De Soto Avenue. De Soto was an exit on the 101 Freeway. Under normal conditions it would take the average citizen about twenty minutes to get to De Soto from where we were, but with Adelaide doing over a hundred miles an hour, we would make it in under twelve.

"Inside of the bunker wasn't pretty," I said to Jeff.

"Death rarely be," Jeff said.

"Especially when the dead are all ours," I said.

"Especially that," Jeff said.

"They all had red cheeks," I said.

"Carbon monoxide?" Jeff said.

"Be my best guess," I said.

"Wasn't an accident, then," Jeff said. "At least they probably died quick. How many you find?"

"Fifty-six," I said. "But fifty-nine workstations."

"No thirteen or fourteen year olds?" Jeff said.

"Youngest looks to be eighteen," I said

"Good, Jeff said. "Sam and Lizzy plenty enough dead children for me."

"Agreed," I said.

"Problem is, with only three missing, odds are Dr. Nemo dead," Jeff said.

"Odds are," I said.

"Might be surface odds, though," Jeff said.

"Surface odds our only hope," I said.

Adelaide whipped around a red Ford Mustang that must have been doing seventy-five but from our vantage point looked like it was standing still.

"Surface odds?" Adelaide said. She turned her head to look at me. "That what you were talking about when you said there might be additional data?"

"Adelaide there's no question you're an excellent driver," I said, "but as we've discussed previously, I'd appreciate it if you keep your eyes on the road when you're going in excess of a hundred miles per hour."

Jeff said, "Not a bad concept."

"I have great peripheral vision," Adelaide said.

"I'm sure you do," I said. "However since your head is turned you can only see out of one eye. Therefore depth perception is an issue. Has it been your intent all along to take this vehicle under the tractor rig in front of us?"

Adelaide snapped her head forward. She deftly touched the brakes and wheeled into the next lane. We missed the cross-country eighteen-wheeler by inches.

"Good to put a little scare into you old folks every once in a while," Adelaide said. "Keeps the blood flowing. Save you from Alzheimer's. You gonna tell me what surface odds are?"

"What be surface and what be real," Jeff said. "Very deep question."

"Is this some sixties thing?" Adelaide said.

I said, "Why would you say that? Neither Jeff nor I were alive in the sixties."

"Could have fooled me," Adelaide said.

Jeff said, "Concept is much more ancient than the sixties, girl."

I said, "On the surface the odds are three in fifty-six, or about one in nineteen that Dr. Nemo is not among the dead back at the bunker. We're hoping Nemo had special knowledge that alters the equation."

"Special knowledge be good," Jeff said.

"What kind of special knowledge?" Adelaide said.

I said, "We can assume from Nemo's communications Nemo knows something is seriously amiss at NASAD and that it somehow relates to the Chinese invasion. Nemo has probably also figured out by now there is a reasonable chance the bad guys are onto him. He also likely knows the bad guys are escalating their activity, as it's hard to believe he doesn't know about the murders of Lennon's relatives and what happened at the site where NASAD is working on the drone submarines. So Nemo might not be subject to just surface odds, but might have created new odds with his special knowledge. The new odds would be much more in his favor."

"So maybe Nemo didn't come into work where he would be easily found?" Adelaide said.

Jeff said, "That be the hope."

"Seems like a long shot to me," Adelaide said.

"Long shot better than no shot," Jeff said.

"You think they killed everyone in the bunker just to get at Nemo?" Adelaide said.

"Nemo would definitely be the primary target, but Carter Bowdoin probably also planned on killing all the dark programmers at some point anyway," I said. "According to the VW bus man, George Boole, all the dark programmers likely knew that Carter was aware of their location. Carter's knowing their location was not only a huge breach of NASAD security protocol, but is also something that Carter would probably believe he had to cover up."

"Because Carter doesn't want to be linked to the dark programmers and what they may have done in relation to the Chinese's insurmountable edge?" Adelaide said.

"Correct," I said. "If I were Carter, I also might have been worried that the dark programmers might somehow leak something that might jeopardize the viability of the insurmountable edge. Killing the dark programmers solved all of Carter's concerns."

Jeff said, "Killing those programmers be what I would've done if I was Carter."

A green freeway sign with white lettering proclaimed the De Soto Avenue exit was three miles ahead.

"Adelaide, I know you don't like this much warning, but the exit is coming up in less than two minutes," I said.

Adelaide nodded. She was in the far left lane but made no move to get over to the right. I could have said something, but I have a policy against wasting my breath.

Jeff said, "You find anything else I need to know about?"

"If the Enigma machine really is Nemo's, he has good taste in movies," I said.

"Let me guess," Jeff said. "'Blow Up', 'Inception', 'Kill Bill', and 'The Matrix'."

Adelaide said, "How'd you know that?"

"Haley ain't the only person be profiling Nemo," Jeff said. "He young, he smart, and seeing's how he got his own Enigma machine, he hip."

"Well don't get a swollen head," Adelaide said. "Your profile is pretty shitty. You left out two movies."

"What are they?" Jeff said.

"'Babel' and 'The Conversation'," Adelaide said.

"Didn't say my profile be perfect," Jeff said. "Interesting though. I woulda thought 'The Conversation' be before Nemo's time."

I said, "How come you didn't say 'Twenty Thousand Leagues Under the Sea'?"

"If I had a code name Dr. Nemo," Jeff said, "I certainly wouldn't be advertising its source."

"Profile tell you that too?" I said.

"I just told you my profile says he smart," Jeff said.

The De Soto Avenue exit was then less than a hundred yards ahead.

"I hate to change the subject," I said, "but Adelaide, would you be so kind as to take the exit please?"

"What, you think I didn't see it?" Adelaide said.

"I don't know what you see or don't see," I said.

"That's for damn sure," Adelaide said.

She jerked the wheel hard right, cut across four lanes of traffic, slid through the V-shaped no drive zone lining the left side of the exit ramp, sideswiped the yellow water-filled collision tanks guarding the bridge that passed over De Soto, then sped down the off-ramp.

There was an intersection at the bottom of the ramp. De Soto's southbound lanes were on the side of the intersection farthest from us and De Soto's northbound lanes were directly in front of us. On the other side of the intersection was a westbound freeway entrance ramp.

When we reached the intersection, Adelaide would have the option of going either left and heading south on De Soto, right and heading north on De Soto, or straight, which would put us back on the freeway heading exactly the same way we were then going. Adelaide wasn't slowing down, even though she didn't know which way she needed to go. The intersection's light also happened to be red.

"You going straight, Adelaide?" I said.

"You tell me," Adelaide said.

"Straight takes us back up the westbound ramp onto the freeway," I said.

"Well I'm not going straight then am I?" Adelaide said.

I didn't say anything.

"What's your problem?" Adelaide said.

"Any normal person would not only be slowing down right now, but also would have asked which way to turn at the intersection a long time ago," I said.

"So now you think I'm normal?" Adelaide said.

"Heaven forbid," I said.

We were about fifty yards from the intersection and Adelaide continued to barrel down the ramp. I turned to look at Jeff. He was as calm as a snowman. He shrugged and smiled.

"You two seem to be playing your own version of chicken," Jeff said.

"I'm behaving that immaturely, huh?" I said.

"From my point of view, you are," Jeff said.

"Okay, Adelaide, you win," I said. "Right turn."

The intersection's light was still red. A blue Corvette and a black Honda Civic flew through the intersection heading north on De Soto. Adelaide, seemingly without looking in either direction, made the right turn. The Vic's right two tires came up in the air and the left ones screeched on the ground. Adelaide's maneuver had caused the Vic, for all intents and purposes, to completely block the intersection's northbound lanes. A late-model white Cadillac and a silver Hyundai heading north on De Soto - both cars again still having a green light to our red - were speeding toward us from behind.

The Cadillac's driver had to slam on the brakes to avoid hitting us. The Cadillac skidded left, then went barreling left across the southbound traffic and up the westbound freeway on-ramp. The Hyundai's driver also slammed on his brakes to avoid hitting us. The Hyundai skidded right, then careened up the exit ramp we had just come down.

Adelaide looked in the rearview mirror and chuckled.

"Looks like someone is gonna be going the wrong way on the freeway," Adelaide said.

Is there anything one can possibly say to someone like Adelaide when they behave as she just had that would do even a smidgen of good? I didn't know then and I don't know now. I did know that the meeting point was a few blocks to our north on Serrania Avenue, however.

I said, "Turn right when you get to Serrania and then stop at 22300."

When we got to the correct address I saw a tan Prius parked against the curb in the shadows between the hazy circles of light cast by two streetlamps. A woman was in the driver's seat.

"Park behind the Prius," I said to Adelaide.

She did.

"Flash your brights once," I said.

"That's the signal?" Adelaide said.

"Low tech," I said.

The Vic's lights bounced briefly off the rear hatch of the Prius. I got out of the car with the Enigma machine under my arm. The night air was still warm. There was the scent of jasmine, ozone, palm, and pine, a combination I'd never smelled anywhere outside Southern California.

Lights were on in most of the houses on both sides of the street. Televisions glowed in living room windows and the voices of late-night talk show hosts spilled out over front lawns.

The driver's door of the Prius opened. A tall, slim, good looking woman in her early thirties exited. Her hair was dark brown, straight, and fell to her shoulders, nicely framing her face. She had a wool two-piece grey tweed suit and black high heels. The suit's skirt stopped above a pair of nice knees.

The woman walked towards me. She had a nice walk. I moved towards her. We met at the back of the Prius. She smiled a pretty smile full of perfect white teeth.

"You're even better looking than they told me you'd be," she said. "Bigger and stronger too."

"I get that a lot," I said.

"Bet you do," she said.

She held out her hand. I shook it. Her hand was warm and dry and soft.

"Diana Armatrading," she said. "I'm an assistant district attorney for the City of Los Angeles. San Fernando Valley division."

"But part-time with MOM?" I said.

"Correct," Diana said.

"If I were a betting man, I'd say you used to be with military intelligence," I said.

"I was," Diana said. "With the Marines."

"You don't look like a jarhead," I said.

"Thank you," Diana said. "Is that General Bradshaw in the car?"

"Yes," I said.

"He's very good looking too," Diana said. "Is he also big and strong?"

"He likes to think so," I said.

She gave a little wave in Jeff's direction. He waved back.

"Who's the driver?" Diana said. "She looks too young to have anything but a learner's permit."

"Drives like it too," I said. "That's my ward, Adelaide Monroe. Be careful. She bites."

"I'll stay away from her then," Diana said. "That for me? It's an Enigma machine right?"

"Yes," I said.

I handed the Enigma machine to her.

"I'm taking this Enigma thingamajigee to Van Nuys Airport," Diana said. "A helicopter will take it from there to Pt. Mugu where a Navy jet is on standby. The jet will take it the rest of the way to Major Haley."

"Good," I said. "Hayley will know what to do with the thingamajigee."

Diana took a business card from the inside pocket of her suit jacket.

"If you have some time when this is all over, call me," Diana said.

"If I'm still alive, I most certainly will," I said.

Diana's cell phone rang. She looked down at the screen.

"Hold on," Diana said. "I think it might be for you."

"Me?" I said.

Diana held up a finger to silence me and answered the phone. She appeared to be listening to whoever was on the other end. After a moment she hung up and handed me the phone.

"That was Vandross," Diana said. "Within the next two minutes you'll be receiving a FaceTime call."

"From who?" I said.

"You know a couple of kids named Bobby and Timmy?" Diana said.

I smiled.

"I do," I said.

CHAPTER 94

I needed Jeff to participate in the conversation with Bobby and Timmy since Jeff was the expert on Chinese dragons and emperors. I signaled to him. Jeff exited the Crown Vic and joined Diana and me.

"Diana, this is General Jeff Bradshaw," I said. "Jeff, this is District Attorney Diana Armatrading. She's with MOM."

Jeff and Diana shook hands.

Jeff said, "Glad I'm not the only one who think so."

I had no idea what he was talking about. Diana seemed confused as well.

I said, "Uh, okay. Would you mind telling us what you're talking about?"

"That I's very good looking," Jeff said, smiling at Diana. "And big and strong too."

Diana turned beet red.

"I didn't think you heard that," I said.

"I didn't," Jeff said.

"Lipreading is a subset of 'heard,'" I said. To Diana, I added, "Jeff speaks dozens of languages, and he can lipread in every one of them."

Diana turned even redder.

Jeff said, "I'm available for private lessons if that something you might be interested in."

Diana appeared not to know what to make of that statement either.

"You mean lipreading?" Diana said.

"Yes," Jeff said. "But you seem the studious type and I do teach other subjects as well."

Diana smiled.

"Let me get you my card," Diana said.

Bobby and Timmy's FaceTime call came in just as Diana was taking out another of her business cards. She handed the card to Jeff. I accepted the call. The boys appeared on the screen.

"General Jack!" Bobby and Timmy said simultaneously.

"Boys!" I said. "I've missed you."

"We miss you too!" Timmy said.

Bobby and Timmy had been cleaned up since I had said goodbye to them the night before. Their freckled faces and red hair were free of grime and they had on clean, new white t-shirts instead of the tattered olive green ones they had been wearing.

"Let me introduce you to General Jeff Bradshaw and District Attorney Diana Armatrading," I said.

Jeff and Diana gathered on either side of me where the boys could see them.

"Diana's pretty!" Timmy said.

"Yes, she is, isn't she," I said. "Be careful what you say though. She can hear you."

Timmy blushed. Almost as red as Diana had earlier, but not quite.

Bobby said, "We know who General Bradshaw is."

"You do?" I said.

"We googled you and saw General Bradshaw too," Bobby said. "You played football together for Army."

Timmy said, "You both won the Heisman Trophy!"

I said, "Actually, Jeff and I both came in tied for second. But that's still very good research on your part."

Bobby and Timmy high-fived each other.

"Where are you two, anyway?" I said.

Timmy said, "We can't tell you!"

"Oh right," I said. "You're in witness protection."

"We're just like Henry Hill in 'Goodfellas'!" Timmy said.

I said, "You guys have watched 'Goodfellas'?"

"It's Foster Mom's favorite movie!" Timmy said. He scrunched up his face and, speaking in a high-pitched nasal whine, continued, "'What do ya mean funny? Let me understand this, cause, I don't know maybe it's me, I'm a little fucked up, but I'm funny how?'"

Diana seemed a bit taken aback.

Diana whispered to me, "How old is Timmy?"

"Seven," I whispered back. "But an advanced seven." Then to Timmy, I said, "Didn't Tommy DeVito say that?"

"Yes, General Jack!" Timmy said. "Tommy was trying to scare Henry!"

"As I remember it, he did a mighty fine job of it too," I said.

Timmy laughed.

"Henry was afraid Tommy was going to kill him," Timmy said. "But Tommy was just busting his balls!"

"What are you two doing up so late?" I said.

Bobby said, "Santiago let us have Coca Cola and we can't get to sleep."

"Santiago?" I said.

Timmy said, "He's a United States Marshal!"

Bobby said, "He's guarding us."

"Of course," I said. "I suppose Santiago doesn't have any kids of his own."

"How did you know that?" Bobby said.

"Lucky guess," I said.

"We're watching 'Harry Potter and the Sorcerer's Stone,'" Bobby said. "Santiago bought it for us on the hotel TV."

Timmy said, "Bobby, shhhh! You can't tell him where we are!"

I said, "It's okay Timmy as long as Bobby doesn't tell us the name of the hotel."

"Bobby, don't tell General Jack the name of the hotel!" Timmy said.

Bobby rolled his eyes.

"We need to ask both of you some questions about the man in the dragon mask," I said. "Is that okay?"

Timmy said, "He's a bad man!"

"Yes he is," I said. "General Jeff is going to ask the questions."

Diana whispered in my ear, "Who's the man in the dragon mask?"

I whispered, "Sorry. We're on a need to know protocol."

"You're kidding," Diana said.

"Nope," I said.

Jeff said, "Good evening, gentlemen. It is a pleasure to make your acquaintance."

Diana whispered again, "Wasn't General Bradshaw just speaking more like someone from the 'hood?"

I whispered back, "Jeff varies his patois depending upon the audience and occasion."

Timmy said, "What does acquaintance mean General Jeff?"

Jeff said, "It means it's nice to meet you."

"It's nice to meet you too!" Timmy said.

"Thank you, Timmy," Jeff said. "I also want to thank both of you for your father's service. I know he won the Medal of Honor."

"He was a hero!" Timmy said.

"He most definitely was," Jeff said. "Now, I would like to proceed with my questions, if I may?"

"You may!" Timmy said.

"First," Jeff said, "do you remember how many claws the dragon man's mask had?"

Timmy said, "Five!"

Jeff said, "Are you sure?"

Timmy nodded vigorously.

Bobby said, "Timmy told me it was a different dragon."

"From which dragon was it different?" Jeff said.

"The one in the Great Wall of China restaurant," Bobby said.

I said, "That's Timmy's favorite restaurant."

Jeff said, "Thank you, General Jack."

"Just doing my duty," I said.

Timmy said, "Barbecued spareribs! Shrimp with lobster sauce! Rumaki!"

Jeff said, "Sounds delicious. Now, Bobby and Timmy, I need you to think hard about the next question please. Did you see Dragon Man's socks?"

"Yellow socks! Yellow socks! Yellow socks!" Timmy said.

Bobby said, "His bow tie was yellow too."

Jeff said, "You're sure?"

"I'm sure, General Jeff," Bobby said.

"Very good," Jeff said. "Is there anything else you boys think I should know?"

Bobby and Timmy seemed to consider this for a moment.

"No," Bobby said.

"Me too," Timmy said.

Jeff said, "On behalf of the United States of America, I would like to thank you, Bobby and Timmy. You did an excellent job. Your father would be very proud."

Bobby and Timmy beamed.

"Do you want to come watch the 'Sorcerer's Stone' with us, General Jeff?" Timmy said.

Bobby said, "Timmy, how's he going to do that unless you tell him where we are?"

Timmy, "Oops! Sorry General Jeff!"

"How long are we going to be in witness protection?" Bobby said.

I said, "Shouldn't be more than a week or so. Would you like to come visit Jeff and me on our ranch when you get out?"

Timmy said, "Ranch! Ranch! Ranch!"

"I'll take that as a yes," I said.

We said our goodbyes to Bobby and Timmy and disconnected from FaceTime. I wished Diana good luck with the Enigma machine. Jeff and I headed back to the Crown Vic.

"Any doubt in your mind that Dragon Man and Carter Bowdoin's yellow sock wearing friend at the 'Save the Whales' charity ball are one and the same?" I said.

"I say we safe with that assumption," Jeff said.

"The five claws mean it's an emperor's dragon?" I said.

"Uh huh," Jeff said. "Chinese emperor only person allowed wearing yellow too."

"How is the House of Saud going to take it when Dragon Man becomes their new bossman?" I said.

"None too kindly, I suspect," Jeff said. "Only it ain't gonna happen."

"Because we're going to stop it?" I said.

"Yep," Jeff said.

"Despite any ambivalent feelings we may have towards the Saudi royals?" I said.

"We professionals," Jeff said. "Feelings don't be affecting our decision making."

"What about when someone stones little kids to death and blows up my good friend Milt Feynman?" I said.

"Feelings be good, then," Jeff said.

"Glad you understand," I said.

"Oh, I more than understand," Jeff said. "I'm what you call on board."

CHAPTER 95

Jeff and I climbed into the Crown Vic and took our usual seats. I quickly texted Haley the new information we'd learned from Bobby and Timmy about Dragon Man's yellow socks and his mask's five claws. I told her Jeff and I felt the yellow socks added further weight to our belief that Dragon Man was Carter's friend at the 'Save the Whales' charity ball. I also told her what Jeff and I had been thinking about Dragon Man having designs on being the Emperor of Saudi Arabia, and that the new information regarding the mask and socks also appeared to support our theories regarding this issue as well.

A few minutes later, Adelaide had the Vic roaring along the west-bound 101 at about a hundred miles per hour. The car's red roof light was spinning, its rear seat deck yellow lights flashing, and its bright headlamps cut through the nighttime darkness, splashing intersecting cones of silver light across the white cement of the freeway. We passed the Calabasas Parkway exit and then sped through a lonely canyon whose steep walls were black and devoid of life. The San Fernando Valley was left in our wake.

"Adelaide, keep an eye out for the Kanan Dume exit," I said. "We're going to get off there and take it back to Malibu."

Adelaide nodded.

As we continued west, I thought about the mercenaries having Russian Igla surface-to-surface missiles. A missile like that could easily be launched from the towering mountains that lay to the east of Kate's Malibu estate. Even an off-center hit could do a lot of damage. I decided I better bring Agent Ray Carpenter up to speed.

"Good evening, General," Carpenter said as he answered my cell phone call.

"Evening, Ray," I said into the phone. "I suppose I should have called you earlier..."

"Is this about the Iglas?" Carpenter interrupted.

"Actually it is," I said.

"I already know," Carpenter said. "Haley contacted me. She figured you were probably too distracted with everything else you were doing and took it upon herself to inform me. We've got men on the mountainside above the Pacific Coast Highway. No one will be able to launch from there."

"Good," I said. "That makes me feel a little better. But, given the circumstances, I really don't think we have any choice other than to get Dr. Lennon to a safe house."

"I've tried," Carpenter said. "She won't budge."

"Well, please keep trying," I said. "We'll be at the estate in under thirty-five minutes. If you still haven't made any progress by then, maybe I'll work on her myself."

"What kind of work would that be?" Carpenter said.

"Funny," I said. "Goodbye, Ray."

I hung up the phone.

Jeff stirred from where he was sprawled across the back seat.

"That Carpenter?" Jeff said.

"Yes," I said. "Haley told him about the Iglas."

"Good," Jeff said. "I been thinking."

"About how screwed we are if Dr. Nemo is dead?" I said.

"Uh huh," Jeff said. "I'm hoping there's a way to accomplish our mission that ain't so dependent on that boy."

"Maybe there is another way," I said. "You want to review what we know so far in case we missed something?"

"I'm down with that," Jeff said.

Adelaide, who seemed to have been ignoring us up to that moment, suddenly appeared to be all ears.

"Okay, here goes," I said. "We've got a lot of dead people. Milt Feynman is dead. Paul Lennon is dead. Most of Paul Lennon's family are dead, and the family members that are alive have been targeted. Twelve NASAD drone sub engineering project managers are dead. Seven FBI agents are dead. Eleven mercenaries are dead, but there are at least forty-eight mercenaries still running around, some of them with Iglas. Fifty-five dark programmers, some of NASAD's best and brightest young people, are entombed beneath the crater along with one of Milt Feynman's most trusted allies, Rick Benavidez, the NASAD vice president of dark programming. Dr. Nemo will almost certainly turn out to be a dark programmer and young and best and bright, and he easily could be down there in the bunker among the dead. Nemo, irrespective of whether he is alive or dead, however, most likely created, or along with the dark programmers, helped create, a doomsday software weapon for the NASAD war games, software that has probably already been inserted into the U.S. military's currently operating computer systems. As far as we know the military's systems are functioning normally right now, so there's nothing to suggest the software weapon has been activated yet. That software weapon is also likely to turn out to be what we've been calling the Chinese insurmountable edge - even though Hart is convinced the edge has to do with the drone subs. Haley's team is combing through the software programming for anything that could be the insurmountable edge, but with millions of lines of code, it's unlikely they'll find it in time." I paused. "I feel like I'm doing all the work here."

"You doing good too," Jeff said.

"Thank you," I said. "A little help would be nice, though."

"I'm happy to help," Jeff said. "I'll jump right in if you miss something."

We passed the Las Virgenes Road exit. To the south of the freeway was a shopping center with an Albertsons, a Jack in the Box, a McDonalds, and a Mobil station. The shopping center was well lit, but seemed deserted.

"Wonderful," I said. "Continuing then, we have a coded message from Dr. Nemo that Haley can't decipher even with the help of all her supercomputers. Haley should soon be getting the Enigma machine from Diana Armatrading, which might or might not help her. Haley is also looking for any connection between Dragon Man and Paul Lennon."

"A connection we know is there due to us finding the clue of the missing medal at Lennon's ex-wife's house," Jeff said.

"Correct," I said. "We also know Bryce Wellington had access to the GPS mislocating and radar evading technology that covered up the truth about Feynman and Lennon's plane crash. Wellington's access to the GPS and radar technology probably came through the NASAD military liaison at the time, Colonel Riley Whitelock, who also happened to be Wellington's godson."

"The death of Colonel Riley Whitelock be investigated by Pigeyes and deemed an accident due to alcohol even though Riley Whitelock don't drink," Jeff said.

"A miracle on a par with the immaculate conception," I said.

"Even more miraculous than that," Jeff said. "We better not forget Wellington also be the one that sent me on the mission to Sudan that wound up giving me this PTSD bullshit."

"Sudan mission is definitely important to you and me," I said. "But I don't see how it relates to the mission at hand."

"You mean you don't think Wellington sent me to the Sudan so I wouldn't be around to interfere with his plans for him and his buddies' insurmountable edge?" Jeff said.

I was momentarily taken aback. Was Jeff being serious? How could Wellington even know Jeff and I might be called on more than two and a half years in the future to try to thwart the edge?

"You really believe Wellington could have done that?" I said.

Jeff laughed.

"No," Jeff said. "That would be a crazy idea. I just said it as it go to Wellington's general assholic nature."

"It does," I said. "Next we come to Wellington's boss, Carter Bowdoin, the managing partner of Pennsylvania Avenue Partners. I believe Carter knew there was going to be an assassination attempt on Kate at the NASAD drone submarine plant. Our VW bus guy, George Boole, said Bowdoin knew all about the dark programmers and that Bowdoin was gambling with them. As a prerequisite of Bowdoin making his ten million dollar bet, he made the dark programmers convince him that their war games software program would defeat the NASAD defensive team in the upcoming war games."

"Such software program being one and the same with the insurmountable edge," Jeff said.

"Hopefully, yes," I said.

"'Hopefully' because otherwise we're on a wild goose chase?" Jeff said.

"Correct," I said.

"Of course whole reason Carter be proposing his gigantic bet in the first place, was to get the dark programmers stimulated to make the best possible war games software for beating the NASAD defensive team," Jeff said.

"Good point," I said.

"In fact, Carter don't even care who wins the bet, because all he was after is the insurmountable edge," Jeff said.

"Another good point," I said. "Now, we also know that Bowdoin went to Panama to sign some kind of deal with Dragon Man. That deal probably outlined how they would both profit together from the upcoming war in Saudi Arabia. As part of the deal, it is likely, that should the Chinese win the war, Dragon Man will become emperor of Saudi Arabia. Dragon Man himself is a child murderer who was watching the attempted assassination of Kate at the NASAD drone submarine manufacturing plant courtesy of one of the Kazakh snipers who was broadcasting the attempt over his cell phone. He is also the Chinese man that was with Carter Bowdoin at the 'Save the Whales' charity ball."

"How come you ain't mentioned Freddy yet?" Jeff said.

"I was about to," I said.

"What do you think?" Jeff said. "Is he a dumb, innocent, naive, feckless bystander or is he an evildoer?"

Whirling red lights and the sound of a siren caught my attention. I looked up to see an ambulance racing across the bridge at Chesebro Road. Chesebro seemed like an odd name. I fleetingly wondered if the locals pronounced it like 'cheese' or 'chess'?

"My take is that Freddy really was upset with Bowdoin when we saw them all at the crater," I said.

"Because he believe Bowdoin responsible for killing the dark programmers?" Jeff said.

"That's my guess," I said. "I think the realization that Bowdoin was most likely behind the massacre came as a total surprise to Freddy. Freddy might at this very moment be coming to the painful conclusion he was taken in by his hero."

"If that so," Jeff said, "it probably also mean Freddy in the dark about the insurmountable edge."

"Probably," I said.

"Might not hurt to grill Freddy, though," Jeff said.

"We can do that first thing in the morning," I said. "Damn, I should have thought of this sooner. If Bowdoin knows how Freddy's thinking..."

"Then Freddy might be next to die?" Jeff said.

"Uh huh," I said.

"We got any moral responsibility in that matter?" Jeff said.

"I suppose we could text Carpenter and tell him to try to get Burnette to take Freddy to a safe house," I said.

"Burnette so hardheaded he probably won't be doing anything Carpenter asks him to do," Jeff said. "But I think that would be enough to get us off the hook if Freddy die. I'm also worried about someone else though."

"Who?" I said.

"Professor Margaret," Jeff said. "I know they're guarding Margaret at her own home, and that no matter how hard we tried to get her to go to a safe house, she still refused to go. But I think she better off in one too."

"Good point," I said. "We'll also tell Carpenter to grind on Margaret until she agrees to go to a safe house."

"And that he gotta arrange for us to talk to Freddy tomorrow, too," Jeff said.

I texted Carpenter Jeff's and my thoughts on Freddy and Margaret Lennon.

"Alright, that's done," I said. "Anything we didn't cover yet?"

"We didn't mention that China about to start a war a week from Friday which be the same time NASAD war games be starting," Jeff said.

"You mean the same time the NASAD war games were supposed to start," I said. "Not sure they will go on now that the dark programmers are dead."

"Whether the games go on or not," Jeff said, "I think we got to stick to our belief it most likely be more than coincidental that the war games' start date, and the start date Hart provided for the beginning of the Chinese attack, both be ten days from now. Which means we have to keep looking at the NASAD dark programmers' war games software as the possible source of the insurmountable edge. Ten days also ain't a lot of time for us to figure out how the dark programmers' war games software work as the edge and put a stop to the bad guys' plan."

"I agree," I said. "The timing is most likely not coincidental, and ten days isn't long at all. Anything else?"

"Don't think so," Jeff said.

"Our review stimulate any new ideas on how we should proceed?" I said.

"Only ideas I got is that we better find Nemo or crack the dude's code," Jeff said. "And if we can't do that, then we gotta figure out who Dragon Man is and hope he somehow lead us to the insurmountable edge."

"Those ideas aren't new," I said.

"I know that," Jeff said.

"Guess that makes two of us," I said. "I don't have any new ideas either."

Adelaide said, "You idiots can't be serious. You made me listen to all that bullshit and we're right back where we started?"

"I understand it may be hard for you to accept this, Adelaide," I said, "but sometimes that's how it goes. And it's better to have an honest appraisal of your situation even if that situation isn't to your liking."

"Isn't to your liking?" Adelaide said. "Why don't you just say we're screwed?"

"I could have said that," I said. "I was just trying to put it in less vulgar terms."

Jeff said, "You catch more flies with honey than you do with vinegar, Adelaide."

Adelaide said, "That doesn't make any sense, you moron."

The car suddenly veered right and the centrifugal force was so great I was thrown against my seat belt. I almost blacked out and my head felt like it was going to be torn off my shoulders.

"What the hell, Adelaide?" I said.

"You told me to get off at Kanan Dume," Adelaide said. "We're at Kanan Dume."

Adelaide was correct. I had been so engrossed in my conversation with Jeff I hadn't noticed we had reached the Kanan off-ramp. Adelaide raced the Vic up the off-ramp's incline and sped toward a red light at the intersection of the ramp and Kanan Dume Road.

I braced myself against the dash as I didn't want my shoulder dislocated from what I knew was coming next. Adelaide hit the intersection without slowing down, whipped the Vic's steering wheel left, which caused the car, for the third time that day, to get up on two wheels as the tires screeched against the asphalt. My bracing did little good, as I was thrown against the passenger door. The door walloped my right shoulder and sent a rifle shot of pain up my neck and into my face. The pain made my eyes tear. Just when I was thinking that the pain was bad but not so bad as to be intolerable, the left side of the car crashed back down to the pavement, slamming my lower jaw into my upper and compressing whatever disks I had left in my lower back. Lightning bolts shot down my legs and I lost all feeling and movement below my hips.

"This thing handles pretty good for an American car," Adelaide said.

I didn't say anything. I was afraid to open my mouth lest my jaw would become unhinged or my teeth fall out. We flew west across the Kanan bridge. The feeling came back in my legs. I moved my right leg, then my left. I would live to fight another day.

We began the long climb into the mountains that stood between us and Malibu. The road was deserted other than for us. We were then far enough away from the San Fernando Valley and its dense population and millions of lights so that I was able to clearly see the stars in the sky for the first time that night. I rolled down my window. The air was dry and cool and there was the smell of dust and dry weeds. I could almost taste the dust.

Jeff said, "I been thinking..."

"God help us," Adelaide said.

"Even if Dr. Nemo is dead, he might still speak," Jeff said.

I said, "From the afterlife?"

"Guy like him maybe have something sent if he don't check in," Jeff said. "You know, like maybe a friend of his send something to some-body at NASAD."

I thought about that.

"Interesting," I said. "In today's world, however, Nemo wouldn't even have to check in with a friend, would he? I mean, George Boole knew his dark programmer friend, Hugh MacColl, was dead when he couldn't see MacColl's pulse on his app anymore."

"You think some app is tracking Dr. Nemo's heart?" Jeff said.

"Maybe," I said. I paused, thinking for a moment. "Who would Nemo send the message to?"

"Dr. Lennon be good," Jeff said.

"Yeah," I said, "that would be good. Be better if Nemo is alive, but, if not, hopefully the kid will have been smart enough to send us something we can use to take down the bad guys."

The Vic continued to hurtle up Kanan Dume Road's eastern incline. To our left was a residential neighborhood of large homes on big lots. Lights were on in the windows of only a few of the homes. A coyote howled in the distance. Three dogs barked their replies. On our right, the cliffs were steep and covered with dirt and scrub brush. The homes on that side were few and far between and they were all well off the road.

We passed a solitary narrow asphalt driveway that climbed steeply into the cliffside. A dark colored sedan was parked on the driveway about fifty yards from the road. The sedan's lights were off and it was facing downhill. It was too dark to see if anyone was inside the car. The house the driveway led to was nowhere to be seen. It seemed an odd place to park.

"See that?" I said to Jeff.

"Something wicked this way comes," Jeff said.

"Ray Bradbury?" I said.

"Bradbury done stole it from the immortal bard," Jeff said.

"Didn't know that," I said.

"Now you do," Jeff said.

"You and the bard wanna make a guess?" I said.

"If it is what we think it is?" Jeff said.

"Yeah," I said.

"Five seconds," Jeff said.

Up ahead, the road took a sharp turn to the right. If we made the turn, the side of the mountain would block my view of the sedan and I would have no idea whether the sedan stayed put or moved to follow us. I needed the Vic to slow down, but didn't want anyone inside the sedan, if indeed there was anyone, to see that we were doing so.

"Adelaide, take your foot off the gas a bit, but don't step on the brakes," I said.

"What is this?" Adelaide said. "Some new kind of test? Because honestly I've had enough testing for one day."

"This is not a test," I said. "Do it."

Adelaide slowed down. Maybe she heard something in my voice. Maybe if I knew what that something was, I could practice it. Practicing would probably be a waste of time, however. More than likely that voice would only work once. Adelaide would have inoculated herself against it by the time I used it again.

Just before we reached the curve, I saw the sedan, headlamps still off, start coasting down the driveway to Kanan Dume. Upon reaching the road, the sedan turned in our direction. Jeff, watching in the rearview mirror, saw what I saw.

"Damn," Jeff said. "That be five seconds on the nose. My perfect record intact."

I turned to Adelaide.

"What do you think, Adelaide?" I said.

"Jeff is far from perfect," Adelaide said.

"I wasn't asking about Jeff," I said. "I was asking about the tail."

"What tail?" Adelaide said.

Jeff said, "The tail tailing us."

Adelaide looked in the rearview mirror.

"I don't see anything," Adelaide said.

"You gotta pay closer attention, girl," Jeff said.

"How will paying closer attention help me see something that's not there?" Adelaide said.

I said, "It's there. A sedan parked by the side of the road slipped in behind us when we passed. It's keeping its distance with its lights off."

"I thought you said you guys were going to make sure we weren't followed," Adelaide said.

Jeff said, "We did. This one be lying in wait."

"Lying in wait?" Adelaide said. "Neither of you ever said anything about anybody lying in wait."

I said, "We mighta screwed up."

"Shit," Adelaide said.

Adelaide turned the wheel to the left and the Vic's rear end started to slide right as the car began to make a U-turn. I quickly leaned over, grabbed the wheel, and jerked the car back on course.

I said, "What the hell do you think you're doing?"

"We gotta go back and get them before they get us," Adelaide said.

"And run smack dab into an Igla?" I said.

"An Igla?" Adelaide said. "That's not one of those Russian missiles you were talking about, is it?"

"Yes," I said. "That's one of the Russian missiles I was talking about."

Adelaide's eyes opened wide.

"Jesus Christ," Adelaide said. "We're dead aren't we?"

"Panicking is not going to do us any good, Adelaide," I said.

"I'm not panicking," Adelaide said.

But her words, which were slightly slurred, belied her. I looked at Adelaide's hands. Even though they were gripping the wheel, they were quivering.

"With all due respect, I think you are," I said. "Nothing to be ashamed of. It happens to all of us. Just take some deep breaths."

Adelaide immediately began to breathe rapidly in and out. Too rapidly, in fact.

"Not that fast, Adelaide," I said. "I don't want you to pass out."

Adelaide took a deep breath and carefully let it out. She seemed to calm down a little.

"Good," I said. "Now, please bring the Vic down to the speed limit and we'll all figure out what we're going to do."

Jeff said, "Know what a speed limit is, girl?"

Adelaide said, "Shut up, Jeff."

Adelaide took us down to thirty-five miles per hour.

Jeff focused on the rearview mirror. I looked back. The car came around the bend behind us, then slowed down, keeping its distance from us.

"Not a good sign," Jeff said.

"No, it's not," I said.

Adelaide said, "What's not a good sign?"

Jeff said, "They're sealing up the rear."

"Sealing up the rear?" Adelaide said.

I said, "Sealing up the rear is similar to herding us as if we were cattle. Whoever is in the car is making sure we head into the ambush in front of us. By keeping their car behind us, they also have a second chance to take us out if the guys in front shoot at us and miss."

"Someone's in front of us?" Adelaide said.

"Someone, yes," I said. "But I'm more worried about the something that someone might have."

"The missiles?" Adelaide said.

"Yes," I said. "The missiles."

Whatever calm Adelaide had achieved a moment before seemed to disappear. Her eyes opened wide.

"Breathe deep again, Adelaide," I said.

Adelaide took some more deep breaths. They seemed to work as she appeared to start to calm down once more. I was impressed. I had seen highly trained special ops soldiers in similar situations be unable to get control of themselves as quickly as Adelaide seemed to be controlling herself at that moment.

"Jeff, your assessment, please?" I said.

"If they've got Iglas, they're up ahead," Jeff said. "Dudes in the sedan had them they would have fired when we went by, or closed the gap by now and done it then."

"You think the mercs finally decided we were too big of a nuisance?" I said.

"Maybe," Jeff said. "Could be revenge too. We did kill eleven of their compadres."

"Would they interrupt a mission just for revenge?" I said.

"If they Kazakhs they could," Jeff said.

"Okay," I said. "Question is how did they know we'd be here?"

"Probably just waiting," Jeff said. "Figured we have to go home to Kate's sometime."

"Makes sense," I said.

Just then we passed a trout farm on the corner of Troutdale Road and Kanan Dume where kids could visit and catch fish. We kept moving, quickly rolling through Kanan Dume's intersections with Sierra Creek Road and Triunfo Canyon Road. I punched up a map of Kanan on my cell phone. Too bad I hadn't done that earlier. Triunfo Canyon was the last street we could turn off onto before we reached the tunnel on Kanan Dume. It was the same tunnel I had traveled through on my way to Kate's house the night before and, at that moment, the tunnel was about a mile and a half ahead of us. Jeff could tell by my expression that I wasn't happy.

"What you got there?" Jeff said.

"We just passed the last street we could exit onto before we reach a tunnel," I said.

Adelaide said, "A tunnel? That can't be good can it?"

"No," I said. "Tell me why you think so, though."

"Really?" Adelaide said. "Another test? Now?"

"Yes," I said. "Another test. Right now."

"Once we're in the tunnel, we're pretty much trapped," Adelaide said. "We can't move side to side, only forward or back. Back is the tail car, front is a mercenary - most likely a Kazakh - aiming down the tunnel with a Russian surface-to-surface missile. We'll be incinerated as soon we enter the tunnel."

"That's pretty level-headed thinking for someone who was panicking a moment ago," I said.

"I'm fine now," Adelaide said. "So, what are we going to do?"

Jeff said, "Luckily our minds be a vast storehouse of experience."

I said, "Which experience you referring to?"

"Bogota," Jeff said.

"Which time?" I said.

"First and third time we in the middle of the town," Jeff said.

"So you're talking about the second time?" I said.

"Uh huh," Jeff said. "When we in the mountains."

Adelaide said, "What'd you do in Bogota?"

I said, "Slow down a little more and I'll explain."

CHAPTER 96

Adelaide brought the Crown Vic's speed down to under twenty-five miles per hour. Behind us, the dark sedan slowed down as well, keeping a steady distance from us. I told Adelaide about Bogota, converting Jeff's and my experience there into instructions for her. When I was finished with the instructions, I asked Adelaide to repeat them back to me. The instructions came back exactly as I had told them to her. It never ceased to amaze me how well Adelaide paid attention when she wanted to.

At that moment, we were still about a half mile away from the Kanan Dume tunnel and traveling through a part of Malibu's mountain range possessed of many high ridges. Deep valleys wound between the ridges, mostly in a north and south direction. I could see the very tops of the ridges, but the darkness of the night had made the valleys below nearly invisible.

I saw no houses. Indeed, the only man-made objects I was able to see were the road we were on, the telephone poles and wires that ran alongside the road, and an occasional streetlamp. The only sounds were the scissorlike clacking of crickets and the bass rumbling of bullfrogs. The only smell was the scent of the distant sea mixed with sage.

I had gotten a glimpse inside the dark sedan tailing us thanks to the light of one of those lonely streetlamps. There appeared to be four men inside, two in front and two in back. I couldn't tell if the men were Kazakhs, but we were about to find out.

"Ready, Adelaide?" I said.

Adelaide nodded.

"Floor it," I said.

Adelaide smashed down on the Crown Vic's gas pedal. The Vic's V8 engine roared like an angry grizzly and the car lurched forward, accelerating rapidly through the gears of its high-performance Police Interceptor transmission.

I turned to look at the sedan carrying the four men. We had gotten the jump on it and were quickly putting distance between the sedan and the Vic.

Thirty seconds later, we reached a portion of Kanan Dume where the road clung to the side of the canyon's mountain walls. On our left the walls rose steeply, while on our right there was a sharp drop to the valley below. Up ahead of us was a curve that I recognized from the night before. I knew that the tunnel was only about two hundred yards farther on.

I also knew that in another hundred and fifty yards we would reach a turnout on our left. The turnout had a dirt surface, fell away from Kanan at a slight slant, and went fairly deep into the brush that lined the rising mountain walls. The turnout also lay just beyond Kanan Dume's final bend before it entered the tunnel, and at a point where the mountain walls extended right up against the road and blocked any view of the turnout from the tunnel. Because of the turnout's location, once we parked in the turnout we wouldn't be visible to anyone in either the sedan carrying the four men or anyone coming out of our end of the tunnel. Our activities on the road on our side of the tunnel also could not be monitored by anyone on the other side of the tunnel since the tunnel had a slight curve to it. From the turnout we would, however, be able to keep a watch on the road. Bright beams from the powerful lights lining the interior of the tunnel spilled out of the tunnel's entrance and well onto the highway.

"Turnout is up ahead, Adelaide," I said.

"Got it," Adelaide said.

We passed the final bend. Adelaide killed the Vic's headlights and the rooftop and rear deck flashers. She kept the Vic barreling forward until the car was even with the turnout, then simultaneously slammed on the brakes and whipped the wheel sharply to the right. The suspension groaned as the car's rear end violently fishtailed left and the tires squealed searching for traction. Adelaide let the Vic slide through about ninety degrees of arc, and then, when the Vic's tail was directly lined up with the turnout, she released the brakes, jammed the transmission into reverse, and stomped again on the gas pedal. The rear wheels spun backwards, the tires screeching like a wounded eagle as they grabbed the pavement and pulled the Vic into the turnout. Adelaide slammed on the brakes and we came to rest in a cloud of dirt and dust inches from the sheer walls of the mountainside.

I looked back down the road. The four men in the sedan had not rounded the bend yet and so could have seen nothing of our maneuver.

"Good job," I said to Adelaide. "On my signal, yes?"

Adelaide nodded.

Jeff and I bolted out of the car, dashed across the road, and hurled ourselves over the steel guardrail on the opposite side of Kanan Dume. We landed on the downslope of the mountainside as it fell steeply away from the road and we slid about twenty yards down the slope's loose dirt. We stopped our fall by grabbing the branches of some of the low, threadbare trees growing on the slope. We hauled ourselves up to the road and peered under the guardrail. The air was dead still. The sounds of the crickets and frogs had intensified and the smell of asphalt and dust filled our nostrils.

The four men in the sedan were about a hundred yards away and closing.

"You sure you're up for this?" I said. "I can handle it myself you know."

"Immersion therapy good for the soul," Jeff said.

"What's that sliver of doubt I hear in your voice then?" I said.

"Doubt grow with knowledge," Jeff said.

"Goethe?" I said.

"Uh huh," Jeff said.

"So you're saying that the doubt is the sign of a rational mind at work?" I said.

"Yep," Jeff said.

"And reason overrides the irrationality of PTSD?" I said.

"I wouldn't be putting it exactly that way," Jeff said. "But you close enough."

Jeff took his Walther Tanto Tactical Folding Combat Knife out of his pocket and tried to hand it to me. I pushed it away.

"You keep it," I said. "If one of us has to be unarmed, it's better it's me. Besides, I got this..."

I showed him the large rock I had just picked up off the slope.

"That's mighty white of you," Jeff said. "However..."

Jeff took out a Kizlyar combat knife from his other pocket. Kizlyar knives are favored by the Russian Spetsnaz and this particular Kizlyar was quite a bit larger than the Walther Tanto.

"You get that off one of the dead guys in Professor Margaret Lennon's house?" I said.

"Uh huh," Jeff said.

"Why didn't you tell me about the Kizlyar before?" I said.

"You be so intent on telling Adelaide how we done everything in Bogota with just rocks and our bare hands," Jeff said, "I afraid you be insulted if I suggest it."

"We only used rocks and our bare hands in Bogota since we didn't have anything else," I said.

"That be true," Jeff said. "I suppose that mean you does want a knife?"

"Of course that means I want a knife," I said.

Jeff again extended the Walther Tanto to me. I took it.

"I don't want to appear ungrateful," I said, "but how come you get the bigger knife?"

"Don't want you to hurt yourself," Jeff said.

"Nice of you to watch out for me," I said.

"Be my job," Jeff said.

"Hard job?" I said.

"It certainly ain't no picnic," Jeff said.

The sedan continued to close in on us, the whine of its engine growing higher and higher in pitch. A moment later, the sedan reached the final bend before the turnout. Its headlights arced across the road from right to left as it took the curve.

I turned to look at Adelaide. The Vic's dimmed dash light illumined her face in the passenger cabin and I could see her staring at me, waiting for my signal.

I raised my arm above my head.

Adelaide nodded.

I waited until the sedan was only a few yards away from the down-hill edge of the entrance to the turnout...and...

Dropped my arm.

The Crown Vic's engine roared to life and its rear wheels threw dirt in the air like an erupting geyser. The Vic's front end lurched upwards and the car shot forward like it had been catapulted from a giant sling. Adelaide's eyes were fixed straight ahead, her face a tight mask of concentration as both her hands steadfastly gripped the wheel. The Vic hit the pavement perpendicular to the road just as the sedan was passing directly in its path. The driver of the sedan turned his head toward the Vic, but there was going to be little he could do. Adelaide, performing exactly as she had been instructed, swung the Vic hard left just before impact. The Vic's rear end spun violently around, generating centrifugal forces that exponentially multiplied the car's kinetic energy. The back fender of the Vic hit the driver's side of the sedan in an ear-splitting thunderclap of collapsing steel that blew the sedan ninety degrees off its intended course. The sedan flew into the guardrail inches from where Jeff and I lay concealed, crumpling more steel and setting off another thunderclap in the process.

Adelaide jammed the Vic in reverse. With the Vic's tires squealing once again, she pulled the right side of the Vic snug against the rear end of the Kazakhs' sedan and brought the Vic to a screeching halt. Adelaide's maneuver had put the Vic and the sedan into a formation that resembled a letter 'T' and the sedan was then pinned between the guardrail and the Vic.

Adelaide darted out of the Vic, jumped atop the Vic's roof, sprinted across both its roof and the roof of the Kazakhs' sedan, and then leapt over my and Jeff's heads into the valley below.

Adelaide's actions were not nearly as dangerous as they might have appeared to an untrained eye. I'd felt confident her parachute jump training would allow her to land safely despite the darkness, and I'd also had little fear her dash across the roofs would meet with any resistance. There was no way the four men, or any human for that matter, could possibly have reacted quickly enough to get a shot off from within the sedan after having suffered the violent ramming that Adelaide had meted out to them.

From Jeff's and my vantage point, we could then clearly see the men in the sedan were Kazakhs. They had the same bowl haircuts, sinewy build, and green windbreakers as did most of the other Kazakhs I had encountered over the last two days.

The four Kazakhs in the sedan looked like a bunch of caged, mean-spirited, rabid ferrets. All four of them seemed to be shouting at each other at once. I had been worried that one of them might take out a cell phone to call their cohorts on the other side of the tunnel and report what had just happened, but none of them did. If the Kazakhs had tried to make such a call, Jeff and I would have had to attack right then to try to stop the call from going through. Attacking the Kazakhs while they were still in the car, however, was a risky maneuver and one Jeff and I didn't want to have to execute. As to why the Kazakhs didn't make that call, no one will ever know - perhaps they were in too big a rush to decide what to do next, or they could have been worried about the security of their cell phone communications, or maybe they were just embarrassed at what had happened to them.

When the shouting was finally over, all four Kazakhs bolted from the car. The driver had to exit out of the front passenger door as his door had been sealed shut by the Vic's impact. Each man gripped a silenced AK-12 identical to the rifles the assassins had carried at Professor Margaret Lennon's house.

One of the Kazakhs ran to the guardrail and sighted his AK-12 down the valley. He swept his gun from side to side but there was no way he was going to see Adelaide - it was just too dark. Jeff and I were flat on the ground right beneath the Kazakh, our bodies parallel to the road. From that position the guardrail blocked us from his view. The only way he could have seen us would have been to bend down and look under the guardrail - something we thought was highly unlikely and had deemed a risk worth taking.

The other three Kazakhs surrounded the Crown Vic and pointed their weapons at its interior. One of them crept forward and opened the driver's door, sticking the muzzle of his gun inside as he did so. He then leaned his head into the car and seemed to be checking it for occupants. Apparently satisfied there were none, he pulled his head back out and shouted something to his comrades.

The Kazakh standing over Jeff and me turned away from the valley and toward the other three commandos. The Kazakh standing over us barked out what must have been orders, then watched as the other three men left the Vic's side and moved off carefully in different directions, I assumed in search of us. One of the three men went up the road towards the tunnel, another ran to the turnout, and the third ran back down the highway.

The Kazakh above Jeff and me remained with his back to us while his three comrades continued to fan out. I gave a small nod to Jeff. The two of us sprang into action. Jeff dove low under the guardrail and I leapt over it. Jeff grabbed the Kazakh around the knees while I wrapped my forearm around the Kazakh's mouth, ripped his head backwards, and slit his throat with the Walther Tanto. Jeff reached out with one arm and grabbed the Kazakh's falling AK-12. The two of us worked together to hold the Kazakh's dead body upright for a moment, as otherwise the noise of the body's fall almost certainly would have attracted unwanted attention. We then carefully laid the Kazakh's body down behind the guardrail.

Jeff handed me the AK-12 and we both looked out towards the highway. The three other Kazakhs were moving away from us, but all of them were clearly visible.

"I feel kinda bad shooting them in the back," I said.

"You wanna warn them so they can turn around and turn this into a real firefight?" Jeff said.

"No, but...," I said.

"We're in combat," Jeff interrupted. "Take the goddamn shots."

"Didn't you just say something like that to me yesterday morning?" I said.

"What if I did?" Jeff said

"It's like déjà vu all over again," I said.

"Take the goddamn shots, Yogi," Jeff said.

I sighted the AK-12 on the head of the Kazakh who was moving back down Kanan and squeezed the trigger. Since the rifle was silenced, the only sound was a soft 'pfft' and it came just as the Kazakh's head exploded in a pinkish spray of blood and bone. I swung the AK-12 to my right, killed the Kazakh who was moving towards the turnout, then kept swinging the gun right until I had sighted on the Kazakh who was approaching the tunnel. I killed him as well.

"Three bullets, three kills," said a voice behind me. "I'm impressed."

I turned around. Adelaide had crept up on Jeff and me.

"You were supposed to stay out of sight until I told you everything was clear," I said.

"I thought you and Jeff might need some help," Adelaide said.

"Adelaide, I need you to understand something," I said. "If I'm going to have to worry about you disobeying orders and possibly getting yourself killed, it's going to make it impossible for me to do my job. Unless you're going to do exactly as I say, I'm going to have to send you home."

Adelaide looked like I had hurt her feelings. She said nothing.

Jeff said, "Adelaide, I assume your disobeying orders was a cool and calculated heat of the moment combat decision and not just some knee-jerk antiauthoritarian adolescent reaction?"

Adelaide stared at him. Her hurt from a moment ago seemed to rapidly morph into annoyance.

"How many times have I told you not to speak like that to me, Jeff?" Adelaide said.

"Like what?" Jeff said.

"In goddamn perfect English," Adelaide said. "It spooks me out."

"Just answer the question, young lady," Jeff said.

"I'm a teenager," Adelaide said. "How the hell do I know why I do anything?"

Jeff and I looked at each other.

I said, "That's pretty psychologically profound, don't you think?"

Jeff said, "I didn't realize she was capable of such advanced introspection."

"Maybe we should let her off?" I said. "Just this one time?"

Jeff shook his head.

"I'd still like her to try and give us her best answer," Jeff said.

Adelaide said, "Would you two stop talking like I'm not here?"

I said, "Sorry. That was rude, wasn't it? However, I guess I'm with Jeff on this. Would you mind thinking about your answer a little harder?"

"What the hell difference does it make?" Adelaide said.

"Probably none," I said. "But you've got our curiosity up."

Jeff said, "Curiosity, yes. That's the word I would have used as well."

Adelaide said, "Oh my God! You guys are going to make my head explode!"

Jeff and I said nothing.

"Okay, fine," Adelaide said. "Let me think about it."

Adelaide was quiet for a moment.

"I suppose if I was being honest," Adelaide said, "it was a bit of both."

I said, "A bit of both?"

"What?" Adelaide said. "You don't like that answer?"

Jeff said, "It still seems too ambiguous."

"You're looking for certainty?" Adelaide said.

I said, "Yes. I suppose we are."

Adelaide smiled.

"Well, you can't always get what you want," Adelaide said.

I sighed.

"Mick Jagger," I said. "A little before your time."

"What happens when you hang out with old guys," Adelaide said.

Suddenly, shafts of light appeared on the road down the hill behind us. We heard the sounds of a car engine and tires rolling on the asphalt. Adelaide, Jeff, and I quickly scrambled behind the Crown Vic and took cover. I laid the AK-12 across the Vic's hood and sighted at a spot on the road just beyond the bend which I had calculated to be the first place the approaching car would come into full view.

A moment later, a large, late-model, white Mercedes luxury sedan rounded the bend doing about forty-five miles per hour. The car passed under a streetlamp and I could see that a man and woman, both of whom looked to be in their early eighties, and seemed to me like husband and wife, were in the front seat. There were no other passengers. Both the man and woman had well coiffed blond hair that I assumed had to be dyed. The man was driving and was wearing a black tuxedo. The woman was in an expensive evening dress. I guessed they were coming home from a party.

The Mercedes was headed directly at one of the dead Kazakhs where he lay in the road. The driver appeared to spot the body. He slowed down, then stopped. A look of horror came over his face, I assumed because he suddenly realized what he was looking at. He said something to his wife. She leaned over and looked at the Kazakh. Her expression became one of horror as well. Then, almost as if they couldn't help themselves, they scanned the surrounding area, their eyes appearing to stop briefly every time they alighted upon another dead Kazakh. They stopped scanning only after it looked like they had found every one of the dead bodies.

The man and woman talked to each other for a few seconds. They seemed to come to a conclusion. The Mercedes started moving toward the tunnel again and rapidly gathered speed. As the car passed the spot where Adelaide, Jeff, and I were huddled behind the Vic, the heads of the man and woman suddenly swiveled towards us as if they had somehow magically sensed our presence. Neither of them, however, acknowledged us in any way. Indeed both of them acted as if they had not seen us at all, as if we didn't even exist. They turned their heads back to face the road. The Mercedes continued to pick up speed and quickly disappeared into the tunnel.

"No way they coulda missed us," Jeff said.

"Especially since they looked right at us," I said.

"You'd think they stop," Jeff said, "seeing how it's clear we just had an accident and might be in need of assistance."

"And we have such nice friendly faces," I said.

"I bet if we in the Midwest they woulda stopped," Jeff said.

"Much nicer people in the Midwest," I said.

"They woulda stopped if we in Mexico too," Jeff said.

"Yes," I said. "But then they would've robbed and killed us."

Adelaide, who had been tapping her foot and impatiently holding her tongue throughout this exchange, could hold it no longer.

"Aren't we in a rush?" Adelaide said. "I mean what if those two old farts call the cops? Or if the Kazakhs on the other side of the tunnel start wondering where their buddies are?" She paused. "Actually now that I think about it..."

I waited for Adelaide to continue. She didn't.

"Now that you think about it what?" I said.

"Well, since we killed all these guys, maybe we shouldn't go through the tunnel after all," Adelaide said. "Maybe we should just turn around and go back the way we came. That way we can avoid dealing with the missiles entirely."

"If only it were all so simple," I said.

Jeff said, "Solzhenitsyn? 'Gulag Archipelago'?"

"Uh huh," I said.

Adelaide said, "Why isn't it that simple?"

I said, "Why don't you tell me?"

Adelaide again seemed unsure of herself. She appeared to think again.

"Because we don't know what's behind us?" Adelaide said. "I mean, there could easily be another team of Kazakhs with SSM's heading up the hill this very moment, couldn't there? If we go back the way we came we could run right into them."

"Correct," I said. "But it's not just what we don't know, is it? There's also things we do know about the Kazakhs or at least think we know, aren't there?"

"You want me to think combat strategy, like you taught me, right?" Adelaide said.

"Yes," I said.

Adelaide smiled.

"In that case we've currently got a big strategic advantage," Adelaide said.

"Which is?" I said.

"We know the enemy's who, what, how, when, and where," Adelaide said. "We know it's probably Kazakhs who are going to shoot at us with SSM's and they're going to do it as soon as we drive into the tunnel."

"And?" I said.

"We have a plan for how to deal with them," Adelaide said.

"Whereas?" I said.

"We currently have no idea what to do if any bad guys were coming up behind us," Adelaide said. "Especially if they actually do have SSM's."

"And?" I said.

"Another 'and'?" Adelaide said.

I nodded.

Adelaide smiled again.

"And we like our plan," Adelaide said. "We think it'll work."

Jeff said, "Why we be thinking it'll work, Adelaide?"

"Because, as you would say, when you aren't being an asshole and going all white on me, it done worked before," Adelaide said.

I said, "In Bogota?"

"In Bogota," Adelaide said.

CHAPTER 97

Adelaide, Jeff, and I climbed into the Crown Vic in order to begin Phase Two of our plan. We took our usual seats, Adelaide behind the wheel, me next to her in front, and Jeff in back.

"We have to move quickly," I said. "We can't give any reinforcements a chance to come up our rear. Even though it's late, and there's been no traffic on Kanan Dume, we've still been lucky the old couple in the Mercedes are the only civilians to pass our way so far. As we can't afford to screw up, it would be wise to take a moment, however, to review the details of the next phase of the plan. Adelaide?"

"Our working theory is that the Kazakhs have figured out by now that we're hard to kill," Adelaide said. "They aren't going to mess around anymore with half measures. We believe the most likely scenario is that there are mercenaries at the other end of the tunnel with an Igla SSM missile lined up at the tunnel's mouth..."

Jeff interrupted, "And that they be itching to blow the Crown Vic, with us in it, to kingdom come."

I said, "Thank you, Jeff, but it is still Adelaide's turn."

"Sorry," Jeff said.

"Go on, Adelaide," I said.

"Our plan is to let them satisfy some, but not all, of the itch Jeff just mentioned," Adelaide said. "The Kazakhs will annihilate the Crown Vic and think we have been killed as well, but it will only be the Vic they will get, not us."

"Excellent, please continue," I said.

"We believe the Kazakh Igla missile triggerman will fire at the Crown Vic almost immediately upon seeing the car coming through the tunnel," Adelaide said. "The triggerman will know that if he can see us, then we can see him, and that the first thing we'll try to do is look for a way to escape. He won't want to give us even an extra second to do that. We also think the Igla triggerman won't spend too much time trying to identify the Vic's passengers before he launches his missile."

"Why do we think that?" I said.

"According to you and Jeff, the rule is that people pretty much see what they expect to see," Adelaide said. "The triggerman's mind will be preprogrammed to believe the three passengers he sees in the Vic are Jeff, you, and me. But since we will not actually be in the Vic when the triggerman sees us exiting the other side of the tunnel, the Vic needs to be carrying three passengers that could at least be momentarily mistaken for the three of us."

"Which of the four dead Kazakhs lying out there on the street are we going to gather up and use as substitutes for us?" I said.

"That's a trick question," Adelaide said.

"Good," I said. "Why?"

"Because, while we're going to show the triggerman only three passengers," Adelaide said, "we're still going to pick up all four bodies so that we don't risk anyone seeing a body lying on the street while we are carrying out our plan."

"Which dead Kazakh are we going to put in the driver's seat?" I said.

"The one you and Jeff killed that is lying next to the guardrail," Adelaide said. "His head is the most intact of the four."

"Fantastic job, Adelaide," I said. "Let's get started."

Adelaide pulled the Vic away from where it was jammed up against the Kazakhs' sedan. We circled around the highway, picked up all three of the bodies of the Kazakhs I had shot, and threw them on the floor of the Vic's back seat. Jeff and Adelaide each took an AK-12 off the bodies for themselves and slung the rifles' straps over their shoulders. I already had the AK-12 from the first Kazakh we had killed, but I figured the more the merrier, and added the extra AK-12 to my arsenal. All three of us stuffed the Kazakhs' extra ammo magazines into our pockets.

We drove back to the guardrail and parked next to the body of the Kazakh Jeff and I had killed together. We hoisted the body into the driver's seat of the Vic and cinched it upright using the seat belt. We determined which two of the three other Kazakhs still had enough left of their skulls so that they would at least appear human on first glance, then lifted those two Kazakhs off the floor of the back seat and put one in the front passenger seat and the other in the rear passenger seat. We cinched both their bodies upright with seat belts as well. We left the fourth dead Kazakh where he was on the floor of the back seat. I took a quick look behind the ears of each of the bodies, at least the bodies that still had ears, and found what I was expecting to find - the cobra and crucifix tattoo of the Kazakh special forces.

Adelaide, Jeff, and I gathered outside the car and assessed our work.

"What do you think?" I said to Jeff.

"They ain't as good lookin' as us," Jeff said, "but they'll do."

"I'm a little worried about the driver," I said.

"Yeah," Jeff said. "Guess it kind of obvious he ain't Adelaide."

"Adelaide, any thoughts?" I said.

"The driver is all you're worried about?" Adelaide said. "What about the guy in back? Does he look black to you?"

Jeff said, "She got a point."

I thought this over for a moment.

"Okay," I said. "I know what to do."

I walked across the highway and up to the sheer wall of the mountainside. There were long strands of wild grass growing on the wall, and the ground below me was still muddy from the recent rain. I grabbed a few fistfuls of the grass strands and scooped up a handful of mud. I went back to the Vic. I plastered the mud on the face of the dead Kazakh in the rear seat. I walked around to the Vic's driver's door and cut a narrow swath of cloth from the pant leg of the Kazakh we had put behind the wheel. I tied the cloth around the Kazakh's head, stuffed the grass strands between the cloth and his skull, then carefully arranged the grass so it looked as much as possible like Adelaide's hairdo.

"How about this?" I said. "You think the Kazakhs will remember Adelaide wasn't wearing a headband?"

"Nah," Jeff said. "It looks like something she would wear. But now I be worrying about the shirt."

"Too masculine?" I said.

"Um-hmm," Jeff said.

Adelaide rolled her eyes.

"I knew you assholes would do anything to get me out of this dress," Adelaide said.

Jeff and I looked at each other. Our faces wore the horribly shocked expressions of the unjustly accused.

Jeff said, "What she talking about?"

I said, "Damned if I know."

"She's being so unfair," Jeff said.

"She certainly is," I said.

Adelaide said, "Screw both of you." She ripped off the tie-dyed hippie dress Margaret Lennon had given to her, leaving her clothed again only in her bikini. She threw the dress at me. "Take it asshole. I never liked it anyway."

I said, "Thank you Adelaide. Don't think I will forget your sacrifice."

"Ask me if I care," Adelaide said.

I was about to speak, but Jeff interrupted me.

"Don't be answering that," Jeff said. "It's a rhetorical question."

"I don't have to answer a rhetorical question?" I said.

"No," Jeff said. "The person asking it don't expect an answer. That why it's rhetorical."

"Adelaide," I said, "what do you have to say about that?"

Adelaide said, "Do you really want to know?"

Jeff said, "Don't be answering that either."

I said, "Why? Is it rhetorical too?"

"It worse than rhetorical, man," Jeff said. "It's an invitation."

"An invitation to what?" I said.

"You don't wanna know," Jeff said.

"What if I do?" I said.

"Trust me, you don't," Jeff said.

"I think I do though," I said.

"It's your funeral," Jeff said.

"Adelaide," I said, "I want to know."

Adelaide said, "You want to know what I have to say about whether or not I was being rhetorical when I said 'Ask me if I care'?"

"Yeah," I said.

"Okay," Adelaide said. "What I have to say about that is exactly what I said before. Screw both of you. You happy now?"

"Is that a rhetorical question too?" I said.

"Yes, it is," Adelaide said.

"So that means you don't care if I'm happy or not?" I said.

"I didn't say that," Adelaide said.

"You do care then?" I said.

"I didn't say that either," Adelaide said.

"What are you saying?" I said.

"I'm saying that I wouldn't mind at all if both of you were extremely unhappy," Adelaide said. "I'm saying that if I found the two of you lying in a ditch with knives stuck in your eyes and ears, and blood coming out your asses, I'd most likely get a warm and fuzzy feeling all over."

Jeff said, "See what happens when you don't listen to me?"

"Yeah, you were right," I said. "I don't know what came over me."

I carried Professor Lennon's dress back to the dead Kazakh in the Vic's driver's seat. I tore the Kazakh's shirt off his torso, inserted his head and arms into the appropriate holes in the dress, then shimmied the dress down and around his body. I stepped back so Adelaide and Jeff could admire my handiwork.

Jeff said, "Too bad he a guy and he dead, because otherwise I be asking for a date."

Adelaide said, "That's sick."

I walked around the Crown Vic closing both rear passenger doors and the front passenger door. I returned to the driver's side door. I unbuckled the pants belt of the dead Kazakh in the driver's seat and pulled the belt out of its pant loops. I wrapped the non-buckle end of the belt around the Vic's steering wheel, put the end through the buckle, and cinched it tight. I used Jeff's Walther Tanto Combat Knife to cut a hole in the driver's seat directly below the steering wheel. The hole went through and through from the top of the seat bottom to the underside of the seat bottom. I intended to put the free end of the belt through the hole when the time was right, but that time had yet to come.

Jeff said, "Seem a shame we gonna ruin a perfectly good car."

I said, "You got a better idea, tell it to me now. Time's a wasting."

"This idea already be mine," Jeff said. "I was hoping you the one with the better one."

"How is this your idea?" I said. "It was me who thought of it."

"In Bogota, yeah," Jeff said. "But I thought of it here."

"Really?" I said. "That's your position?"

Jeff smiled.

"Nah," Jeff said. "I just messing with you."

Adelaide said, "You know, I truly admire the incredible ability you two possess to squander massive amounts of time arguing over absolutely nothing, but is it really what you want to be doing right now?"

"We enjoying ourselves, girl," Jeff said. "Ain't no harm in that."

"What if one of the Kazakhs we think are at the other end of tunnel decides to come walking down the tunnel looking through the sights of an SSM?" Adelaide said. "Would there be any harm in that?"

I said, "Party pooper."

Adelaide made a show of tightening the shoulder strap of her AK-12, jerking the rifle up from her side, and placing her hands in a ready position. She started marching up the road toward the tunnel.

"I'm outta here," Adelaide said.

"AK won't be much good against an SSM," I said.

"Better than being a sitting duck," Adelaide said.

Jeff and I looked at each other.

I said, "Is that what we are?"

"Don't know about the sitting part," Jeff said. "But since she mention it, I am feeling kinda ducky."

"That's not good," I said. I yelled after Adelaide, "Come on back, Adelaide. We're ready to go."

Adelaide turned around.

"Ready now, as in right now?" Adelaide said. "Or now as in after we screw around some more now?"

"Now as in right now," I said.

Adelaide came back to us.

"Let's get you and Jeff set up in a spot behind the Kazakhs' sedan," I said. "You two can use the sedan as cover in case anyone coming out of the tunnel entrance intends to do us harm."

Adelaide, Jeff, and I walked over to the sedan. When we were up close to the car, I could see that it was a Hyundai and that its body, which I had earlier been referring to as 'dark', was actually blue.

"Would you say this is an arctic blue or a frost blue?" I said to Jeff.

Jeff said, "I think it's more of an aqua."

"I could see that," I said. "You know what kind of mileage Hyundais get?"

"Hear it pretty good," Jeff said.

Adelaide shook her head.

"Unbelievable," Adelaide said.

I said, "Why do you say that, Adelaide? It looks to me like it would probably get at least forty miles a gallon."

"I meant it's unbelievable that even though you and Jeff just told me you would stop screwing around, you can't do it can you?" Adelaide said.

Jeff said, "What's so unbelievable about that?"

"Arghhh!" Adelaide said.

Adelaide and Jeff crouched down behind the Hyundai and aimed their AK-12's at the mouth of the tunnel.

I climbed into the Vic through the driver's side door, sat down on the lap of the dead Kazakh we had cinched up behind the steering wheel, and started the engine. I shifted the Vic into gear, then drove slowly forward, turning just enough to aim the car's nose at the tunnel, then applied the brakes. Again, the tunnel had a slight curve to it so I couldn't see what was on the tunnel's other side and whoever was on the other side of the tunnel couldn't see me either.

I tugged on the Kazakh's belt to tighten it even more firmly around the steering wheel and slipped the belt's free end all the way through the hole in the bottom of the driver's seat I had cut earlier. I pulled on the belt to take out any slack, and, using a strong knot, tied the belt's free end to the portion of the belt on the top side of the hole.

My plan was to aim the Vic at the tunnel, set the Vic in motion, and rely on the Kazakh's belt to keep the Vic on course. I also hoped the belt would keep the Vic on course once it was in the tunnel. The slight curve inside the tunnel presented a potential problem, but I was pretty sure that since I planned on sending the Vic through at a low speed, the walls of the tunnel would nudge the Vic back on course if it brushed up against them. I also thought that the Vic was unlikely to sustain enough damage from any such low-speed collisions to keep it from completing its journey through the tunnel.

I turned on the Vic's headlights, released the brakes, and set the cruise control for twenty-five miles per hour. Maintaining a grip on the open driver's side door, I jumped out of the car and onto the asphalt. I ran beside the car for a short distance and, when I was sure of my balance, slammed the driver's door shut. I watched for a moment as the car slowly accelerated and continued on its way to the tunnel. Satisfied the

Vic would stay on course, I sprinted back to the Hyundai where I joined Adelaide and Jeff.

The three of us watched as the Vic entered the cone of light generated by the tunnel's interior illumination. The light reflected off of the Vic's body in thousands of pinpoint rays, so that the car looked like a sparkling diamond as it approached the tunnel's arched opening. The tunnel's inner walls had a smooth, almost antiseptic quality to them, and I felt as if I was looking down a long hospital corridor.

There was a chance that a civilian vehicle entering from either side of the tunnel just then could be blown up at the same time the Vic was blown up. We had decided, however, the risk of that occurring was low.

One, Jeff and I took turns keeping a careful watch on the road behind us and were ready to stop any vehicle coming from that direction.

And two, we thought it highly unlikely the presumed Kazakh mercenaries were currently letting any vehicles in from their end either. The mercenaries would do this not out of concern for any civilian's health or safety, but because they wouldn't want any other vehicle to potentially interfere with their ability to get a clean shot at the Vic. Jeff and I believed, that since the presumed Kazakhs had had some time to plan their attack, they had probably done what we would have done - acquired some detour and roadblock signs and deployed them as soon they had gotten word from their comrades in the trail car that Adelaide, Jeff, and I would shortly be in the tunnel. If the Kazakhs followed that plan, they wouldn't have to interrupt normal traffic for an extended period of time and interference from any local law enforcement authorities was unlikely.

There was also a chance that the presumed Kazakhs might not have behaved in a manner anywhere close to what Jeff and I had predicted. If they hadn't, then there might actually be a vehicle headed through the tunnel toward us even as the Vic continued its own progress into the tunnel's cavernous passageway. The headlights of any additional vehicles traveling in the tunnel would most likely cause a subtle increase in the intensity of the lighting within the tunnel. I studied the tunnel for such an increase, even though there was of course really nothing at that point I could have done if the lighting actually had changed.

Why would I do such a thing?

I'm not really sure myself.

But it was probably just compulsive behavior born of the fact I had spent most of my professional life studying my surroundings for similar clues.

The lighting, in any event, remained steady.

I turned to Jeff.

"Anyone coming up behind us?" I said to Jeff.

"If they is, they traveling with their lights off," Jeff said. "Canyon back there black like me."

"John Griffin?" I said.

"Yeah," Jeff said. "Not how I meant it though."

"Ah," I said. "You meant it was really black? Kinda like coal?"

"Uh huh," Jeff said.

"I think that's what one would call a simile," I said.

"One would if one be possessing more than a second grade education," Jeff said.

"You and me went to college," I said.

"That be you and I," Jeff said. "And yes we done gone to college."

"Together, as I remember it," I said.

"Yeah," Jeff said. "We be in college together."

"You think Adelaide should go to college?" I said.

Adelaide said, "How many times do I have to ask you two assholes to stop talking about me like I'm not here?"

"I don't know," I said. "Maybe a bajillion?"

Jeff said, "Bajillion be good."

Adelaide said, "You know what would be really good?"

I said, "No. But I have a hunch you're going to tell us."

Jeff said, "That ain't no hunch. That reality."

Adelaide said, "What would be really good is if you two were in the Vic right now riding along with the dead Kazakhs."

I said, "I don't think that's right, Adelaide. Especially since we believe the Vic is going to get blown up any second."

"Exactly," Adelaide said.

Jeff said, "She cruel."

We continued to watch as the Crown Vic pressed onward. But nothing happened.

We waited.

We waited some more.

Still nothing happened.

"Do you think we made a mistake?" I said to Jeff. "Is it possible there's no Kazakhs with Iglas on the other side of the tunnel after all?"

"Though patience be a tired mare, yet she will plod," Jeff said.

"Willie Shoemaker?" I said.

"Corporal Nym," Jeff said. "'Life of King Henry the Fifth.'"

"One would think I'd know that play by now," I said.

"One would," Jeff said.

Suddenly, the area of the tunnel above the Vic was lit by a new bright light, a light as bright as a small sun, a light we recognized as the light of the burning rocket engine of an Igla SSM. A moment later we heard the great screaming sound the burning engine was making as the rocket soared through the tunnel. Still another moment later, the screaming was followed by a terrible 'thwop' as the missile hit the Vic.

The light in the tunnel no longer resembled a small sun, but rather a supernova. The rocket and the Vic exploded together, sending molten metal hurtling in all directions. A cloud of swirling red, orange, and yellow gas rapidly expanded and filled the tunnel's interior. Razor-edged shrapnel flew out of the tunnel's mouth, the tunnel itself acting like a rifle barrel. The shrapnel looked alternately like multipointed spinning wheels flying end over end, or rotating murderous table saws freed from their mounts.

The shrapnel was followed by huge, ragged chunks of what had once been the Crown Vic tumbling through the air. The chunks crashed onto the road in front of us, skidded, and threw off flames. The chunks were followed by the hot whoosh of a pressure wave. The wave's scalding air blew by us making us feel like we were in a blast furnace. The wave was followed by an intense smell. It was a battlefield smell - the smell of melting metal, burning rubber, superheated gasoline, and finally, most distinctly, seared human flesh.

Adelaide, Jeff, and I shielded our faces from the heat with our hands. The Kazakhs' Hyundai sedan protected our bodies. Jeff stared out beyond the front of the Hyundai, his gaze seemingly taking in each and every piece of passing shrapnel and flaming chunk.

Jeff's eyes slowly took on a faraway look, as if he were somewhere else. His breathing became shallow. He took short breaths in and out between pursed lips, as if his body was avoiding bringing any air in through his nostrils, doing its best not to smell the odor of war. A moment later, Jeff's eyelids fluttered closed and his body slumped against the Hyundai.

Jeff looked so lifeless I was afraid he might have suddenly died.

I felt as if my own heart had stopped.

I took a deep breath and gently shook Jeff's shoulder.

"You okay?" I said.

I got no response.

I shook harder.

"Jeff?" I said.

Still nothing.

I shook him even harder.

"Jeff!" I yelled in his ear.

Jeff's eyelids fluttered open. His head slowly turned towards me.

"You alright?" I said.

"Why you always asking me that?" Jeff said, his words slurred.

"Sorry," I said. "But you don't look so hot."

"That's funny," Jeff said. "Because I feel like I'm in a goddamn Turkish sauna."

"So I take it you're going to be okay then?" I said.

"Yes, I gonna be okay," Jeff said. "Just give me a moment."

A wave of relief washed over me. I tried to hide my feelings from Jeff, however, because if he sensed how relieved I was, he'd also know how worried I'd been. If he knew how worried I'd been, he might have called me a fool - which I could have handled - but he also might have been embarrassed his PTSD had put him in so bad a state that it caused me such deep concern. There were plenty of things I didn't mind Jeff feeling embarrassed about - if only for my own amusement - but his disease was not one of them.

"What about you, Adelaide?" I said.

"Heat's not too bad," Adelaide said. "But what's that awful smell? Like someone's cooking rotten hamburgers."

I thought for a moment. I felt like I wanted to answer delicately, if that was possible. Before I found any words, Jeff spit out some of his own.

"That be barbecue," Jeff said, his speech still a bit slurred. He lifted his nose in the air, and took a deep inward breath through his nostrils. "Someone be grilling Kazakh, unless I miss my guess."

"Eeeeyouuuu," Adelaide said.

"Don't be knocking it if you never tried it, girl," Jeff said.

"You know what, Jeff?" Adelaide said. "You're disgusting."

As far as I was concerned, that exchange was proof enough that my comrades had made it through the second phase of our Bogota plan with their fighting spirit intact. It was time to commence Phase Three.

CHAPTER 98

The goal of Phase Three was to get through the tunnel and kill any mercenaries on the other side. Once we did that, we could continue on our way to Kate's estate in Malibu. I had every confidence in Ray Carpenter's ability to protect Kate. But the mercenaries' new escalation in hostilities, and the fact the mercenaries then possessed surface-to-surface missiles caused me to be particularly anxious to get back to Kate's side.

We were unable to immediately commence Phase Three, however. Dense, billowing smoke from the Vic's burning wreckage made it impossible to see inside the tunnel and discern our initial path through to the tunnel's other side. Adelaide, Jeff, and I were in the Kazakhs' Hyundai -Adelaide behind the wheel, me in the front passenger seat, and Jeff in back - waiting for the smoke to clear. The waiting, coupled with the depleted condition of my mind and body, nearly turned me into a basket case.

"It will probably take a few more minutes before the smoke dissipates enough so that Adelaide can see where she's going once we're inside the tunnel," I said. "While we wait, I believe it prudent to review the plan, especially since the stakes are so high."

Jeff said, "Few things are brought to a successful issue by impetuous desire, but most by calm and prudent forethought."

Adelaide said, "Genius."

"Thank you, Adelaide," Jeff said.

"I wasn't talking about you," Adelaide said. "I was talking about the dead guy you stole it from. 'The bravest are surely those who have the clearest vision of what is before them, glory and danger alike, and yet notwithstanding go out to meet it.'"

"How you know Thucydides?" Jeff said.

"What?" Adelaide. "You think I'm stupid enough to leave my entire military education to you fools?"

I said, "Heaven forbid. By the way, has your education caused you to cross paths with Sun Tzu yet?"

"Yes," Adelaide said.

"What's your impression of him?" I said.

"Sun Tzu is an idiot," Adelaide said. "'So in war the way is to avoid what is strong and strike at what is weak.' Any two-year-old could come up with that."

"Smart girl," I said. "Now, getting back to the problem at hand, I continue to have no reason to think our presumed Kazakhs on the other side of the tunnel believe we are anything but dead in a fiery explosion of their SSM's own making. Either of you disagree?"

Adelaide and Jeff shook their heads.

"I therefore don't believe they will have an Igla or any other weapon aimed down the tunnel," I said. "I also believe when they see the Hyundai they'll think it's their friends inside and so will have their guard down. Which should be to our advantage."

"What if they're getting worried they haven't heard from their friends yet?" Adelaide said.

"I think that's a possibility," I said. "But, again, as they just saw us die, and I know for a fact the cell service up here is very spotty, I am giving that possibility a very low probability."

Jeff said, "There's also a good chance, given how easy it be to intercept cell phone communications, the Kazakhs who were in this Hyundai weren't even supposed to call in unless there be an emergency."

"Excellent point," I said. "Now, once we get to the other side of the tunnel, Adelaide will pull a ninety degree turn which should line the Hyundai up broadside with the Kazakhs. We will then be positioned like an eighteenth century Royal Navy frigate engaged in a battle on the high seas. Jeff's and my AK-12's will be the equivalent of the frigate's cannons and we will empty them into the enemy."

Adelaide said, "What if the Kazakhs are not lined up across the road in a semicircle as we expect them to be?"

Jeff said, "Then we just gotta improvise. You understand improvise, Adelaide?"

"No," Adelaide said. "Why don't you spell it for me?"

"I...M...P...," Jeff began.

"Goddamnit, Jeff," Adelaide interrupted, "I know what improvise means."

"That ain't what you said," Jeff said.

"I was being sarcastic," Adelaide said. "You understand what sarcasm is?"

"No," Jeff said. "Maybe you should be spelling it for me."

Jeff cackled. Adelaide turned around in her seat and started to climb over it, apparently intent on getting at Jeff. I pulled her back down. Once I was convinced she would stay seated, I checked on the tunnel again. The smoke was still too thick to attempt a crossing.

I said, "It seems to me all this hostility you two have towards each other would be better put to use against the Kazakhs."

Adelaide said, "He started it."

"Yes, he did," I said. "And now you can be the adult and end it."

"I'll do that," Adelaide said. "If he shuts up."

"Jeff?" I said.

Jeff said, "What?"

"You going to stop giving Adelaide a hard time?" I said.

"You hear me saying anything?" Jeff said.

"No," I said.

"That's right," Jeff said. "Because I already being the adult before you be telling her she could be one."

Adelaide rolled her eyes.

"Jeff, do you really believe what you just said is helpful?" I said.

"Fine," Jeff said. "We'll call it a tie."

"A tie?" I said.

"Even though it's evident I be the first adult," Jeff said, "I'm willing to give up sole title and share it with the whippersnapperess."

"Is a tie okay with you, Adelaide?" I said.

Adelaide said, "Whatever."

"Great," I said. "Unless anyone has any other comments, we're ready to go."

Jeff raised his hand.

"You have a comment, Jeff?" I said.

"I think we got the same problem we had before only opposite," Jeff said.

"Explain," I said.

"Kazakh we lashed behind the Vic steering wheel didn't look like Adelaide before we give him some hair and changed his clothes," Jeff said. "Now Adelaide doesn't look like a Kazakh."

"Excellent point," I said. "Solution?"

"Adelaide be tying her hair back and wearing your shirt," Jeff said.

"Why my shirt?" I said.

"You think my Willie Shoemaker t-shirt look like something a Kazakh would wear?" Jeff said.

"That is pretty unlikely, isn't it?" I said. "If I give Adelaide my shirt though, what am I going to wear?"

"You just be slouching down under the dash so they only see your head," Jeff said. "I be slouching too so they can't see my face."

I took off my shirt and gave it to Adelaide. She put it on, then tied her hair back behind her head in a bun.

"That looks good," I said. "But I just realized something else."

Jeff said, "There are only three of us, but there were four Kazakhs in the car before we killed them all?"

"Yeah," I said.

"Spare tire might work," Jeff said.

"Really?" I said.

"You got a better idea?" Jeff said.

"No," I said.

I leaned over, reached under the steering wheel, and pushed the trunk opening button. Thankfully the trunk snapped open despite the damage we'd done to the sedan. I got out of the car, went to the trunk, unbolted the spare tire from its position on the bottom of the trunk, lifted the tire out of the trunk, then closed the trunk's lid. I went back around to the passenger side of the car and opened the rear door. Jeff got out of the car, and together we rolled the spare tire over the rear seat until it was behind the driver's seat.

"What do you think?" I said.

"It's better than nothing," Jeff said.

Adelaide said, "That's about all it's better than."

I said, "You're probably right, Adelaide. But the way I see it, we'll be so quick about shooting any Kazakh we see as soon as we exit the other side of the tunnel, even if any of them do figure out it's a tire and not one of their sleazeball friends, they'll be dead before they decide what to do about it."

Jeff said, "More likely they'll be dead before they even figure out it's a tire."

"Or that," I said.

Jeff and I got back into our seats. The smoke had dissipated enough for us to see the first half of the tunnel. It would have been nice if we had been able to see the second half of the tunnel as well, but the second half was blocked from our view by the tunnel's curvature. The Vic's blazing carcass was in the center of the tunnel.

"What do you think?" I said to Jeff.

"If we had the Maybach we could probably go right through the Vic," Jeff said. "I bet its armor hold up pretty good even in that inferno. We try that in this Hyundai though, we gonna be toast."

"Agreed," I said. "I think we're going to have to use one of those two channels."

"The ones between either side of the Vic and the tunnel's walls?" Jeff said.

"Yes," I said.

"Which one you wanna try?" Jeff said.

Adelaide said, "Hold on. You guys are kidding right? We go down one of those channels we're going to get burned to death."

"It'll be hot, but since we won't be exposed directly to the flames, we should be fine," I said.

"Don't you think hot is a little bit of an understatement?" Adelaide said. "It's like an inferno in there."

"Jeff, would you mind handling this?" I said.

"Happy to," Jeff said. "Adelaide, you ever run your finger really fast through a candle flame?"

"Yes," Adelaide said.

"Did you get burned?" Jeff said.

"No," Adelaide said. "You're not implying this is the same thing, are you?"

"That's exactly what I be implying," Jeff said. "We go fast enough, we ain't gonna get burned."

Adelaide looked at me.

"Jeff's full of shit, isn't he?" she said.

"We've tried it more than a dozen times," I said. "Always worked so far."

Adelaide appeared to study both of us. I assumed she was trying to decide whether or not we were out of our minds.

Jeff said, "It gonna work Adelaide."

Adelaide seemed to think for another moment. She rolled her eyes. "Alright, fine," Adelaide said. "It's not like we have any other options."

I said, "That's the spirit. So, which channel? Right or left."

Jeff said, "Right seem a little bigger."

"Right it is," I said. "Everyone ready?"

Adelaide and Jeff nodded.

"Let's go then," I said.

Jeff and I checked to make sure the safeties of our AK-12's were off and put a couple of extra loaded magazines in our laps. Adelaide started the engine and backed the Hyundai away from the guardrail. She continued in reverse, taking us back down the hill to get the running start we needed to avoid being fried to a crisp. When the Hyundai was about two hundred yards from the tunnel, she stopped, put the gearshift into drive, and floored the gas pedal. The Hyundai's tires spun for a moment, then gained purchase on the asphalt, and we shot forward.

One hundred feet before the tunnel's entrance we encountered the debris field of exploded Vic parts. Adelaide drove like a demon-possessed slalom skier, weaving a stomach churning, inner ear nauseating, zigzag course through the debris field. We zoomed past flaming metal that in its previous life appeared to have been one of the Crown Vic's doors, and then rocketed by, in turn, a charred fender, a burning rear bench seat, the Vic's melting steering wheel, two bent and twisted wheels with tires aflame, and finally, the Vic's nearly intact red roof police flasher.

I called Adelaide's attention to the flasher.

"I bet you miss that," I said.

"It was good while it lasted, but I'll make do," Adelaide said.

"Well, aren't we mature?" I said.

"New me," Adelaide said.

"Will it last?" I said.

"No," Adelaide said.

"I didn't think so," I said. "Right channel, yes?"

"On it," Adelaide said.

Adelaide swung around one last flaming, jagged, unidentifiable hunk of metal, and aimed the Hyundai at the right channel inside the tunnel.

It would have been nice to have been able to roll up all the Hyundai's windows before we entered the tunnel, but we had to keep Jeff's and mine down so that Jeff and I would have unencumbered fire lines once we reached the other side. Adelaide, Jeff, and I leaned as close to the left side of the car as we could to compensate for the open windows. We also would have preferred to have been able to douse our sleeves with some water so that we could cover our mouths and noses to protect them from the heat and smoke, but there was no water to be had. Our only choice then to protect our upper airways and lungs from being singed, was to take a deep breath at the last possible moment before entering the tunnel and then hold that breath during the entire journey through the hellish inferno.

That last possible moment came upon us.

We took our breaths.

And held them.

The Hyundai barreled into the tunnel doing over sixty miles an hour. I felt like the Pillsbury Doughboy entering an oven. The flames' heat dried out my eyeballs and the bright light nearly blinded me. A pressure wave of superheated air buffeted the Hyundai and lifted it off the ground. A thick cloud of acrid black smoke filled the top of the tunnel. The cloud moved with the jostling oscillations of a hurricane wind as it funneled out toward the canyon behind us. The booming sounds of rapidly oxidizing Crown Vic parts echoed against the tunnel's walls and hammered my ears.

Adelaide hugged the Hyundai tightly to the right tunnel wall. The Hyundai's body ground against the wall, and sparks, puny in comparison to the pyre on our left, spit into the air. Up ahead, a large, mangled fragment of the Vic's hood, its edges ripped into sharp points that looked like dinosaur teeth, suddenly appeared in our path.

"Go through the hood!" I shouted to Adelaide. My voice was hoarse, my throat dry and scalding. I had been forced to use the breath I had been holding to keep my lungs from being singed. My lungs emptied, it was going to take a great force of will to not breathe in again.

Adelaide didn't flinch or slow down, just gripped the steering wheel harder. The Hyundai's front bumper smashed into the Crown

Vic's charred hood. The hood caught under the Hyundai and stayed there, dragging and scraping along the pavement, journeying with us for a short while as it made its own terrible noise, a noise that sounded like a giant ogre rasping its massive claws against a Brobdingnagian chalkboard.

We passed a gnarled chunk of the Vic's incinerating fuselage, the heat nearly unbearable. We then sped by a charbroiled human thorax, the ribs white and the flesh a flaky black, the lumpy wad clearly the last remains of one of the Kazakhs. An explosion sent a molten sphere of metal like a cannonball through the back left passenger window, across the car's interior, and out the back right passenger window, barely missing Jeff's head.

Jeff cackled behind me.

"Great balls of fire!" Jeff yelled.

Unable to stop myself, I sucked in a huge breath of scalding air and shouted, "Scarlett O'Hara, 'Gone with the Wind'!"

"Yes, massah!" Jeff yelled back and cackled some more.

I chanced a peek at Adelaide. It looked like she thought we were insane. She wisely continued to hold her breath, said nothing, and kept to her task.

Suddenly we were past the worst of the inferno and I was able to make out the end of the tunnel through the multicolored flames and swirling smoke. Framed in the tunnel's arched exit, were three men. The men were thirty yards from the tunnel's entrance and facing us. They stood very close to one another in the center of the road and in front of some orange traffic detour signs. The signs blocked any approach to the tunnel from the road behind the men.

The three men again had the same build, bowl haircuts, clothes, and appeared even to have the same boots, as all the Kazakhs I had encountered over those last forty-eight hours. Since the man in the middle of the threesome was leaning on the empty firing harness of a Russian Igla SSM missile, and his two comrades beside him had silenced AK-12's with sniper scopes slung over their shoulders, I made a leap - I decided the men were Kazakhs.

All three Kazakhs were laughing. The Kazakh on the right was guffawing so heavily, he was doubled over at the waist. Clearly, they believed

Adelaide, Jeff, and I were toast, and that the blue Hyundai heading toward them was carrying their friends, not us. The three Kazakhs must have thought it the height of stupidity for their friends to be racing through the inferno. They laughed as soldiers the world over laugh at their comrades' foolhardy risk taking - and they would continue to laugh, just as all soldiers would continue to laugh, as long as, through the grace of whatever god they prayed to, those risks turned out well.

I didn't think it was going to turn out well for the three men, however. Mainly because killing them was going to be easier than expected. The fact they were standing so close together, rather than spaced widely apart in a textbook semicircle combat formation, was literally a grave error on their part.

"Adelaide, time to improvise!" I screamed, my lungs afire.

Adelaide glanced at me out of the corner of her eye.

"Abandon the frigate maneuver!" I yelled. "Mow 'em down!"

Adelaide appeared unsure of my meaning.

"Use the car!" I said. "Mow 'em down!"

Adelaide, her eyes fixed straight ahead, nodded.

We exited the tunnel. Adelaide, Jeff, and I deeply inhaled the cooler air. The Kazakhs remained positioned as they had been, but their merry expressions began to dissolve. Clearly, up until that moment, the fiery light of the tunnel's conflagration had allowed the Kazakhs to discern the familiar shape of the blue Hyundai, but not what was inside, behind its windshield. With us then only thirty yards away, however, that was changing. Discernment had become possible and their lizard brains began to sense something was not quite right...

A car traveling at eighty miles an hour doesn't take long to traverse thirty yards. In fact, it takes less than a second. An average human can react in about two hundred and fifteen milliseconds to a threat. The Kazakhs were not average humans, but trained warriors who, in all likelihood, started out with athletic skills far superior to average. At best though, the Kazakhs could perhaps react in one hundred milliseconds. That gave them nine hundred milliseconds to move after they reacted. The Kazakh in the middle, sandwiched as he was between his two comrades, had nowhere to go and never had a chance. The two Kazakhs on either side of him had a chance, but I calculated that chance to be near zero. Those two Kazakhs' hypothetical hundred millisecond reaction time was dependent on their minds being completely clear and possessing no conscious thoughts that might interfere with their ability to instantaneously react. But their minds were clouded, weren't they? After all, didn't they believe the Hyundai could be carrying no one other than their compatriots? They could not react until they overcame that belief, and that meant for them a hundred millisecond reaction was the stuff of fairy dust.

The three Kazakhs were not stupid men, just men who had not been trained as well as they could have been. Indeed, it was their less than adequate training that had helped keep me alive over those last two days. That was not to say their training, probably done by retired Russian Spetsnaz officers, had been awful by any stretch of the imagination. It simply had not been good enough to match the training the U.S. Army had given Jeff and me. Jeff and I had stayed alive for almost twenty years based on what the Army had taught us and there was no one more grateful than me for that fact.

The Hyundai continued to accelerate past the eighty mile an hour mark and bore down on the three Kazakhs. All three displayed the anticipated excellent reflexes, and I knew, having been there myself, that their minds were probably watching the scene before them unfold in slow motion. The Hyundai racing towards them through the ashes, flames, and smoke, probably seemed to have stopped in time. The sounds of the explosions coming from the tunnel and the Hyundai's straining engine had most likely transformed into bizarre, drawn-out, otherworldly moans, like a voice recording played so slow it was almost unrecognizable as having ever been spawned by anything human.

In those last fractions of a second, the Kazakhs' brains, analyzing everything they saw, felt, and heard, would have determined the men's bodies needed to leap and scatter, or die. Knowing thus, the men's brains sent their first messages back down the men's spines to the big muscles of the men's hips and legs. The muscles, active, strong, and with an intelligence of their own born of practice and repetition, bent knees, planted heels into the ground, and braced hips and cores until finally the men's bodies were placed in a powerful crouch. The crouch completed, the motion then reversed. The Kazakhs' weight transferred to the balls of their feet, their calves and quadriceps contracted, their knees straightened, their arms swung forward, and their bodies unwound and sprang. The Kazakh on the left leapt left. The Kazakhs in the middle and on the right leapt right.

There was just not enough time.

The Kazakhs had moved barely a foot when Adelaide hit the middle Kazakh in the dead center of his torso, the Hyundai's front end slamming into him at eighty-five miles an hour. The Kazakh's body collapsed into a U shape, his head smashed on the hood and cracked open, and his heels caught on the pavement causing his legs to tear from their hip sockets.

The other two Kazakhs were caught with similar blows, not dead center but more on the sides of their bodies. Their bodies bent in two at their flanks, their head and shoulders fractured on the car's hood, and their knees that were closest to the car ripped away from their femurs.

Adelaide held the steering wheel steady as the front and then the rear tires each ran over the Kazakhs' bodies. The Hyundai thumped, lifted and fell, thumped, lifted and fell, jolting us as we listened to the sound of cracking bones. The body of the Kazakh who had been in the center of the three-man formation was momentarily pinched between the car's metal underbelly and the asphalt and was dragged a few yards before the body finally slipped free and came to rest in the middle of the road.

"Good job, Adelaide!" I yelled, my lungs still aflame. "Frigate maneuver now!"

"Now?" Adelaide said.

"Now!" I screamed.

Adelaide executed a hard ninety degree right turn and slammed to a stop. The Hyundai was then broadside to the tunnel, leaving Jeff and me facing the tunnel and prepared to deliver a fusillade of fire. The smoke was less concentrated, but still acrid, and it burned our eyes and noses. The brilliance of the flames partially blinded our vision, and the continuing explosions of the Crown Vic's demise deafened us.

I peered through the telescopic sight of my silenced AK-12 and swept it from left to right. Jeff, in the back seat, mirrored my movements but in the opposite direction. I strained to see into the darkness of the canyon below the road, peered across the brightly illumined asphalt, and strained to see once again when I came to the black canyon walls above the road. I reversed my motion, my eyes and brain focused as a unit, my breathing as slow as I could make it, my concentration intense, scanning from canyon wall to road to canyon darkness. I repeated this two more times, each time slower than the one before it.

I saw no Kazakhs other than the three dead men in the middle of the road. The only vehicle was a white Ford Econoline van, windowless except for the passenger compartment, the kind of nondescript auto-mobile favored by painters, plumbers, serial killers, and, as I had seen over the last two days, by Kazakh mercenaries plying their trade in the United States. The van's lights and engine were off. Nothing was moving in or around it.

"Assessment?" I said to Jeff.

"Anybody who's anybody probably came out for the show," Jeff said.

"Got their money's worth no doubt," I said.

"Excepting they missed the finale," Jeff said.

"The finale was the best part," I said.

"Critics be agreeing with you," Jeff said. "Hear they say audience slayed by the finale."

"Ouch," I said.

"How about you, Adelaide?" Jeff said. "You hear that about the audience too?"

Adelaide said, "I know what I didn't hear."

"What that be?" Jeff said.

"Thank you, Adelaide," Adelaide said. "Nice driving, Adelaide. Thank you for saving us, Adelaide."

I swiveled around in my seat to face Jeff.

"Sounds like Adelaide wants us to thank her," I said. "Do you have any thoughts on that, Jeff?"

"Seem like she wanna be thanked for just doing her job," Jeff said.

"We don't want to set any bad precedents," I said.

"You're right," Jeff said. "We do it this time, we gotta do it every time."

"Wouldn't be good," I said.

"Not good at all," Jeff said.

Adelaide threw daggers at us with her eyes.

"Screw you guys," Adelaide said.

Jeff and I were silent for a moment as we nonverbally discussed the situation. I shrugged. Jeff shrugged back. I turned to Adelaide.

I said, "Then again."

Adelaide said, "Then again, what?"

"Thank you, Adelaide," I said.

Jeff said, "Ditto."

Adelaide said, "'Ditto'? You can't just say thank you?"

"I can," Jeff said.

"Then say it," Adelaide said.

"Thank you, Adelaide," Jeff said.

"That's better," Adelaide said.

I said, "Everyone happy now?"

Neither Adelaide nor Jeff said anything.

"Okay, I'm sorry I asked," I said. "I hate to change the subject, but can I have my shirt back now Adelaide?"

"You can have it back if you give me my dress back," Adelaide said.

"You mean Margaret Lennon's hippie dress?" I said. "Because if you do, you know full well it was incinerated in the tunnel along with the Vic."

"Not my problem," Adelaide said.

"Adelaide...," I said.

"Chill," Adelaide said. "I don't want your crummy shirt. Only an old fogey would wear a shirt like this. I wouldn't be caught dead in it."

Adelaide took off my shirt and handed it to me. I put the shirt on. Jeff and I opened our doors and stepped out onto the pavement. I left one of my AK-12's in the sedan and slung the carrying strap of my other AK over my shoulder. Jeff slung his AK over his shoulder as well. We pointed the weapons out in front of us in the ready position, fingers curled around the triggers.

Adelaide said, "Where you two going?"

I said, "We're going to check the bodies and then have a look in the van. Come along. We could use a hand."

CHAPTER 99

I was eager to look inside the van, but doing so without first being certain the three Kazakhs Adelaide had run over were truly dead would have been the height of unprofessionalism. Worst case scenario, if one of them was merely injured, he could have shot us all in the back while we were indulging our curiosity in regard to the van's contents.

I checked each of the Kazakhs' bodies where they lay in the middle of the highway. The bodies had been thrown about ten yards from each other and had come to rest in a triangular formation. Adelaide and Jeff, armed with their AK-12's, each chose a different body to stand over and thus each of them wound up at a different corner of the triangle. They kept a close watch on the van in case there were any Kazakhs hidden inside it - a scenario I sincerely doubted - and also surveyed the road up, down, and side to side, looking for any signs of movement, any potential threat. The light generated from the flames within the tunnel quivered upon the Kazakhs' bodies, casting flickering silhouettes in the shapes of their bodies on the asphalt. The oscillating glow seemed to animate the dead.

The three Kazakhs' necks and limbs were bent at odd angles and their ears and eyes dripped bright red blood. The skin of their faces, arms, and legs was streaked with the same red blood and abraded with ragged bits of asphalt. Their clothes were shredded.

I put my fingers on the neck of the Kazakh closest to me. The body was still warm as I felt for the carotid. There was no pulse. I pulled the ear back away from the skull. The cobra and crucifix insignia shone in the tunnel's light.

A breeze kicked up as I moved to examine the other two Kazakhs. The breeze, coming from the west, momentarily cooled the heat of the blaze and also ruffled the Kazakhs' hair which added to the illusion of animation. Kazakhs two and three were also pulseless and tattooed with the cobra and crucifix insignia. Just as I was about to stand up after checking the third Kazakh's tattoo, I felt a sharp jab just under my rib cage. I looked down and saw that the offending agent was Jeff's elbow.

I followed the elbow upwards as Jeff raised his arm and put a finger to his lips. I gave him a questioning look. Jeff gestured with his chin to his right and I turned my head to see what he was pointing at.

Adelaide was standing over the dead body of the first Kazakh I had examined. Adelaide's AK-12 was at her side and her eyes were locked on the Kazakh's face. She appeared transfixed.

I stood up. Jeff, holding his AK at the ready and still keeping a watchful eye on the surrounding area, moved closer to me. He spoke in a whisper.

"We forgot something," Jeff said.

I whispered back, "We did?"

"This is her first kill," Jeff said.

"You're right," I said. "You think she's okay?"

"Look like she in that spell that come over combat newbies when they be seeing first corpse they sent to the great beyond," Jeff said.

"Yeah," I said. "Looks just like that. Best to leave her alone then?"

"I believe so," Jeff said.

Adelaide slowly kneeled down and put her AK-12 on the ground next to her. She put her face close to the Kazakh's face.

"What's she doing now?" I said.

"I bet she looking in his eyes," Jeff said. "I hope they don't be moving. That spook the hell out of her."

"His eyes aren't going to move," I said. "I checked him. He's dead."

"You never been wrong?" Jeff said.

"Nope," I said.

"They think you dead this morning though," Jeff said.

"That's because it wasn't me doing the checking," I said.

"How could you be checking yourself if you was dead?" Jeff said.

"That's not the point," I said. "If I was doing the checking, I would have made it clear to everyone I wasn't dead. It was just that my heart temporarily stopped."

"'Tem-po-ra-ri-ly'," Jeff said. "I like that word. It moves trippingly on the tongue."

Adelaide reached her hand forward and touched the dead man's face. She put her fingers in the blood on his forehead, then smeared some of the blood on her own cheeks.

"Whoa," Jeff said. "That be weird."

"We better go over there," I said.

"You afraid like I am that she be cutting off his ear next?" Jeff said.

"Like some of our guys did in 'Nam?" I said.

"Yeah," Jeff said. "She start that shit we gotta stop her. Could be traumatizing to her soul."

Jeff and I walked over to Adelaide. Jeff remained standing and I knelt down next to her.

"How you feeling?" I said to Adelaide.

Adelaide didn't turn to look at me, just kept staring at the Kazakh's face.

"I've never killed anyone before," Adelaide said.

"Jeff and I were just talking about that," I said. "You okay?"

"It was him or us, I guess," Adelaide said.

"True," I said. "It still can be hard, however."

Adelaide turned to face me.

"It is hard," Adelaide said. "But I think I'll be okay. Otherwise, what kind of soldier am I going to be?"

"That's a very professional attitude," I said. "Promise me though that if you have any trouble handling this later you'll tell me, alright?"

"Okay," Adelaide said.

"Good," I said. "I'm curious why you put his blood on your cheeks?"

"It's an Apache tradition," Adelaide said.

Jeff said, "Apache do it when they kill a buffalo, not people."

I gave Jeff a sharp look.

"Sorry," Jeff said.

Adelaide didn't appear to notice Jeff's and my exchange. She said, "These men were our enemies. But they were also fierce warriors. I did it to honor them."

"That's a very noble sentiment," I said. "I'm proud of you."

Adelaide nodded very slightly.

The wail of approaching sirens suddenly became audible in the distance. It sounded like there were at least four vehicles racing toward us, coming up Kanan Dume from the west. One of the sirens sounded like it was coming from a very large vehicle, a fire truck in all probability.

"What do you think?" I said to Jeff.

Jeff said, "They'll be here, four, five minutes tops."

"Let's get out of here in two," I said.

The dead Kazakhs each had an MP-443 Grach semi-automatic pistol inside the waistbands of their pants and a Spetsnaz GRU combat knife in scabbards attached to their belts. I quickly removed the weapons from the bodies. I gave Jeff and Adelaide each a set and kept one set for myself. I took the AK-12's from the two dead men who had been toting them and also grabbed their extra ammo.

"This stuff's pretty good," I said, "but I got a hunch what's in the van will be even better. Let's go check it out."

The three of us cautiously approached the van. Adelaide took up a position in front of the van ten yards off the van's right side, and Jeff did the same on the van's left side. They both aimed their rifles at the van's windshield. I pointed my rifle at the driver's door, walked slowly up to it, then whipped open the door, and shoved the muzzle of the rifle inside the van. I sighted down the rifle barrel and swept the passenger cabin. The cabin was empty, but the keys were still in the ignition.

We hustled to the back of the van. Adelaide and Jeff took up similar triangulated positions to the ones they had taken at the van's front. The van's left rear cargo door was slightly ajar. I pulled it open, pointing my AK-12 inside the van's cargo hold as I did. There was no one inside.

The cargo hold, however, was not empty.

I gestured for Jeff and Adelaide to come to my side. I lowered my weapon and opened the van's right rear door as well. The three of us peered inside into the hold.

There were seven identical wooden crates. Each crate was about six feet long and eighteen inches high and eighteen inches wide. There was Cyrillic writing on the tops and sides of the crates. All the crates were sealed but one. The unsealed one was empty except for some packing material.

I said, "Adelaide, want to hazard a guess what was in the empty crate?"

"Is that a rhetorical question?" Adelaide said.

I smiled.

"Yes, I suppose it is," I said.

Jeff mimed drinking from a glass.

"A toast to Mother Russia," Jeff said.

"For the Iglas?" I said.

"For the Iglas," Jeff said.

I mimed drinking as well. We threw our imaginary glasses over our shoulders, listened as they imaginarily shattered on the asphalt.

Adelaide said, "We're taking the Iglas? What about that stuff you told me about not being armed?"

Jeff said, "We're adapting to new circumstances. Mercenaries be upping the ante. We can no longer afford to go weaponless."

I said, "Jeff's right. There's no way we're giving up our new AK-12's. So, the way I see it, in for a penny, in for a pound. Besides, I got a hunch the Iglas might come in handy later."

Adelaide said, "Sweet!"

She took out her SOG knife and started to pry open one of the crates. I pulled her hand away.

"We don't have time for that right now," I said.

The loud horn of a fire engine sounded just then. The timing could not have been better if I planned it.

"Into the van, everyone," I said, shutting the rear cargo doors. "Adelaide, you drive."

We ran around to the front of the van. Adelaide got in behind the wheel. Jeff climbed in through the passenger door and slid across the bench seat next to her. Just as I was about to follow Jeff in through the door, my cell phone rang. It was Haley and Hart. They were FaceTiming me and were coming in on a split screen.

I answered the call.

Haley was still in the NORAD bunker, and, despite probably having not slept for nearly 48 hours, looked fresh and crisp and beautiful, her hair lustrous and her eyes dancing.

Hart, who appeared to be in a command post in a desert somewhere, clearly had not slept either. He wasn't taking it nearly as well as Haley, however. Hart's uniform was disheveled, there was three days' growth of beard on his face, his hair was mussed, his eyes were bloodshot, and his lower eyelids were baggy and dark. But what really bothered me was the slightly florid cast to Hart's face. As much as I didn't want him to, Hart was growing old and his blood pressure had been an ongoing problem for him. The florid cast was a sign his pressure was up.

I said, "Ah, my two favorite people."

Hart glared. Haley smiled.

Hart said, "Can you hear me okay? We've got some important information for you."

"Sorry, it's gonna have to wait General," I said. "We're in the middle of a situation. Where are you, by the way?"

"I'm in goddamn Saudi Arabia," Hart said. "Where does it goddamn look like I am?"

"Doesn't look like you're getting much sleep, sir," I said.

"I haven't slept in seventy-two hours," Hart said. "Not that it's any of your business." Hart moved his face closer to the screen and appeared to be squinting to see better. "What'd you do, blow up something?"

"Indirectly," I said.

"I'm not even going to ask what that means," Hart said. "Those guys in the street dead?"

"Last time I checked," I said.

"Who are they?" Hart said.

"Kazakhs," I said.

"You kill them?" Hart said.

"Yes," I said. "Look, if we keep talking I'm going to have a problem." I pointed the phone's microphone in the direction of the oncoming sirens. "You hear that?"

"Local gendarmes?" Hart said.

"I believe so," I said.

"Alright," Hart said. "I don't want to be bailing you out of prison again. Do what you gotta do and call me back."

The screen went blank.

I slid in next to Jeff and shut the van's door.

"Arriba, arriba! Andale, andale!" I said to Adelaide.

Adelaide said, "What the hell does that mean?"

Jeff said, "That be what Speedy Gonzalez say."

"Speedy Gonzalez?" Adelaide said.

I said, "Yeah, Speedy Gonzalez. It means 'Get the hell out of here!'"

CHAPTER 100

We quickly headed west in the Kazakhs' van along Kanan Dume toward the ocean. The sirens grew louder and higher in pitch as the vehicles sounding them continued to approach. Adelaide was behind the wheel and Jeff sat on the bench seat between Adelaide and me, all of us squeezed together, my body also pressing against the passenger door. Adelaide drove at the speed limit, which was forty-five miles per hour, so as not to attract attention. Of course, if anyone looked in the van we might attract a lot of attention as Adelaide still had the Kazakh's blood on her face. Jeff and I could have told her to wipe the blood off, but we felt it was best not to revisit that subject for the moment. My window was down. I draped my arm on the sill and tilted my head out the opening, the flowing breeze making my eyes tear and my hair whip off my face.

I had two things on my mind. One was to get Hart and Haley back on the phone as soon as the siren-blaring emergency vehicles were safely past us. The other was to get back to Kate. The events of the last half hour had made it clear my war with the mercenaries and their overlords was rapidly escalating. I wouldn't feel comfortable Kate was completely safe until I was with her. If all went well, we would be at Kate's Malibu estate in less than fifteen minutes.

We crested a small rise in the road and started our descent to the Pacific Coast Highway. Three of the four vehicles whose sirens we had been hearing suddenly appeared and roared past us going up the hill on the other side of the road. The first vehicle was an L.A. County Sheriff's cruiser. It was followed by a fire captain's red sedan and then a highway patrol car. All three had their roof lights flashing. The fourth vehicle was as yet unseen, but its lights were strobing against the canyon walls and its straining engine was making sustained growls. The lights grew brighter and the engine growls louder as the vehicle came closer and closer.

The van started to speed up.

"Not yet, Adelaide," I said.

"They're not even paying attention to us," Adelaide said.

"I like it that way," I said.

"You worry way too much," Adelaide said.

"Do I look worried?" I said.

Adelaide turned to face me. I smiled at her. I projected calm.

"Yeah, you do," Adelaide said. "But, since you gave me my own scoped and silenced AK-12, an MP-443, and a GRU, I'll give you a break."

The van slowed down.

The source of the last siren finally appeared. A red hook and ladder fire truck raced toward us on the other side of the road. Adelaide didn't slow down or pull over and the fire truck blew its horn at us. The blast was so loud it sounded like it had come from a giant goose.

Adelaide gave the firemen the finger.

"You got plenty of room, asshole," Adelaide shouted at the fireman driving the truck.

Jeff shook his head.

"Girl knows how to keep a low profile," Jeff said.

The fire truck went past, its tailwind buffeting us. The pitch of the fire truck's siren dropped a notch and slowly died down. The canyon below us had become impenetrably dark and quiet.

I called Haley and Hart. They both instantly appeared on my iPhone screen. I angled the phone so that Jeff could see them as well.

Hart said, "You got seventeen and a half hours."

"Sir?" I said.

"Chinese moved up the start of their attack," Hart said. "War is set to commence at 4:00 a.m. Thursday morning, Riyadh time."

I checked my watch. It said our local time in Malibu was then almost 12:30 a.m., which meant for us it was early Wednesday morning.

"It's already Wednesday here," I said. "So if the war is going to start at 4:00 a.m. Thursday in Riyadh, that means it's going to start at 6:00 p.m. our time tonight, correct?

"Correct," Hart said.

"I thought you said we had until a week from this coming Friday," I said.

"Everyone thought that," Hart said. "But everyone was wrong."

Everyone was wrong? I had seventeen and a half hours instead of almost ten days? How was I going to successfully complete my mission in so little time?

"You're absolutely sure about this?" I said.

"Yes," Hart said.

"But before you were absolutely sure about it being a week from Friday," I said.

"Jack, that kind of talk is not going to help," Hart said.

"How could CENTCOM screw this up so bad?" I said. "Why should I believe them now?"

"Trust me, son," Hart said. "I've raked them over the coals about this. But I've checked all their current intel myself and I think they've got it right now. I'm sorry, but seventeen and a half hours is all you've got left."

A multitude of thoughts flooded my mind. Many of them centered on how CENTCOM could have made such a big mistake in the timing. But it really didn't matter just then, did it? I had no choice other than to go with their estimate. Because if I didn't, and I missed their deadline, all was lost.

The biggest immediate problem however was that the new deadline also wreaked havoc with my operational theory. I had been proceeding on the notion that the NASAD war games somehow held the answer to the Chinese insurmountable edge. I had been proceeding in that fashion mainly because of two things. One, much of what I'd learned about Dr. Nemo and the NASAD dark programmers - Carter Bowdoin's bet with the dark programmers, the dark programmers' massacre within the bunker, what Boole had said about his dead dark programmer friend Hugh's taunts, the nearly unquestionable linkage of Nemo's words 'I apologize for the enigmatic way in which I have contacted you' to the Enigma machine I had discovered in the bunker, and most of all, my belief that Dr. Nemo was a dark programmer himself - seemed to suggest that Dr. Nemo and the dark programmers had created the insurmountable edge. Two, the NASAD war games and the actual war with China had been scheduled to start at exactly the same moment - 6:00 p.m. local time a week from our next Friday night, which was 4:00 a.m. Riyadh time a week from Riyadh's next Saturday morning. But Hart's new information about the war's start date and time had just destroyed that timeline for me. Was I going to have to start all over? Come up with an entirely new theory in less than seventeen and a half hours?

But then an idea came to me.

My idea was a long shot, perhaps the longest of long shots.

To find out if that long shot had a fighting chance, I was going to have to contact Raj, the head of the NASAD Cyber Defense Hall team. I thought Kate might be able to do that, even at so late an hour. I needed to get back to her as fast as I could.

Hart said, "You still with us?"

Hart's voice shook me out of my reverie.

"Yes, sir," I said.

"Do you know how short seventeen and a half hours are?" Hart said.

"I assure you I appreciate that, sir," I said.

Jeff said, "We certainly do, sir."

Hart said, "What are you going to do about it?"

I said, "I guess we're just going to have to work faster than we thought."

Jeff said, "Yeah. Faster be good."

Hart said, "I meant what's your plan?"

I said, "You kinda threw me for a loop, sir. I'm going to need a little time to rethink things."

"Like how you're going to shut down those drone subs?" Hart said.

Not that again, I thought. Just then our van came to a curve in the road and the hills surrounding Kanan Dume momentarily flattened out. We were facing in a more southerly direction and I could see the lights of the Palos Verdes Peninsula in the distance. I rechecked the speedometer. Adelaide was continuing to maintain a reasonable speed.

"Yes," I said. "Like that."

"Don't lie to me, son," Hart said.

"Lie?" I said.

"Vandross told me you think the drone subs are bullshit," Hart said.

"I don't remember saying anything like that to him," I said.

"But you didn't deny it either when he asked you, did you?" Hart said.

I didn't say anything.

"If it's any consolation, Vandross didn't just come out and tell me what you were thinking," Hart said. "I had to force him to cough it up."

I still said nothing.

"As a matter of fact," Hart said, "the only reason I knew something was up was because I can read Vandross like a book."

I sighed.

"I think Vandross said something about that," I said.

"Well, don't worry about it," Hart said. "I'm off the drones too."

"You are, sir?" I said.

"I've been looking carefully at all the stuff you've been throwing Haley's way," Hart said. "Nuclear weapons and drone subs don't make sense anymore. The insurmountable edge has got to be something bigger and more all-encompassing."

"That's what I think," I said.

"Go with your gut, then," Hart said. "Especially since we're running out of time and we've got nothing else that's worth a rat's ass."

"You're quite the inspirational speaker, sir," I said.

Jeff said, "I dream my painting and I paint my dream."

"Van Gogh?" I said.

"Uh huh," Jeff said.

Hart said, "I know you two love that literary bullshit, but now's not the time. Haley actually has something of value to impart to you."

Haley said, "I do?"

"Very funny," Hart said. "Please give it to these knuckleheads before their attention begins to waver."

Jeff said, "I resemble that remark."

I said, "Curly? Three Stooges?"

"Yeah," Jeff said. "But some people think it mighta been Groucho who say it first."

"I could see that," I said.

Hart's face became more florid.

"Didn't I just say now was not the time!" Hart said.

The van had reached the point on Kanan Dume where there was a long, steep straightaway down to the Pacific Coast Highway. The lights of the shopping center on the west side of the highway and the stoplights at the intersection of Kanan and the PCH were visible ahead of us.

I said, "You did, sir."

Jeff said, "Sorry, General Hart, sir."

Hart said, "Thank you. Haley, proceed."

Haley said, "Gentlemen, given the time constraints we're now operating under, General Hart and I have determined finding Dr. Nemo is our best option."

Jeff said, "Pretty sure that be our determination for a long time."

"Agreed," Haley said. "Perhaps my choice of words left a little to be desired. In any event, we're still unsure of Dr. Nemo's whereabouts but we believe, thanks to the photos you sent us from the NASAD dark programmers' bunker, that we now know who he is and what he looks like. If our analysis is correct, Nemo may still be alive and not among the dead in the bunker."

I said, "You really believe you know what Nemo looks like?"

"Yes," Haley said.

"That's great work, Haley," I said.

"Thanks," Haley said. "But again, we couldn't have done it without the photos you sent us. So thanks to you as well."

"You're welcome," I said. "The only problem is I don't like the fact you used the word 'if' in relation to Nemo being alive."

Jeff said, "Yeah. That be on an emotional par with the inspirational speech General Hart just done give."

"Sorry," Haley said. "I'm just being honest."

"I accept your apology," I said. "Honesty is, after all, the best policy."

Hart looked like his head was going to explode.

Hart said, "Goddamnit!"

"Sir, take it easy," I said. "We don't want your blood pressure getting too high."

"Don't be telling me what to do!" Hart said.

We were about half a mile from the intersection of Kanan and the Pacific Coast Highway. Adelaide had crept up to fifty, which was only five miles over the speed limit, but it was still too fast for my comfort.

"Sorry, sir, I need you to excuse me for a moment," I said. I turned to Adelaide. "Adelaide, take it down a notch."

Adelaide frowned but brought our speed down to forty-five miles per hour once again.

"Okay, sir, I'm back," I said to Hart. "I'm happy not telling you what to do, but when you get a stroke don't say I didn't warn you." I paused. Hart didn't say anything. He closed his eyes and seemed to withdraw into his own world, a world that appeared to be consumed by deep breaths and counting inside his head. I knew he truly was afraid for his health, but I also knew he would never admit it. I thought about pushing him a little harder on the subject of taking better care of himself, but decided I'd probably gone as far as I could at that moment. I turned my attention back to Haley. "Haley, are you able to send us a picture of this person whom you believe might or might not be dead, and may or may or not be Dr. Nemo?"

"I can," Haley said.

"'Can' is akin to 'if'," I said. "They are not words I like to hear."

"What's wrong with 'can'?" Haley said.

Jeff said, "He mean if you were gonna send the photo, you just woulda sent it. But since you didn't, there gotta be a catch."

"Am I that transparent?" Haley said.

"When is a croquet mallet like a billy club?" Jeff said.

"You're saying I'm like the Cheshire Cat?" Haley said. "Boy, that is transparent."

Those last words must have penetrated the world of deep breathing and counting to which Hart had tried to escape as he suddenly looked further inflamed. To Hart's credit he did appear to attempt to overcome that inflammation by focusing even more strongly on his breathing and counting. Alas, that increased focus unfortunately didn't stop Hart from looking like he was going to leap through our phones' screens and strangle all three of us. I lowered my hand to a spot that couldn't be seen by my iPhone camera and surreptitiously signaled Jeff to be quiet.

Jeff said, "Who you shushing?"

I whispered, "Both of us. I don't want the old man to have a stroke."

"I never seen nobody shush himself before," Jeff said.

"Well, now you have," I said.

I leaned in close to the camera so that my face was the only thing Haley and Hart could see. I studied Hart's face for any signs of impending doom as I spoke. For the moment he seemed stable.

"What's the catch, Haley?" I said.

"It's not so much a catch as context," Haley said. "Since we're flying by the seats of our pants, and time is of the essence, I don't believe we'll have more than one shot at this and I don't want us to blow that shot. The picture I have fits the profile of Nemo, but pictures can be very powerful and, well, I don't want your opinion to be unduly influenced by the way he looks. Before I send you the picture I want to tell you the story, see if you buy it."

"You buy it?" I said.

"The story?" Haley said.

"Yeah," I said.

"I believe it's highly probable we've found our Nemo," Haley said. "But it doesn't really matter what I think. What matters is what you guys think. You're the ones on the ground."

"We're all ears," I said. "Oops, sorry, Haley hold on a sec."

The van was then very close to the Kanan Dume Road's intersection with the Pacific Coast Highway. Adelaide was again doing fifty miles an hour.

"Adelaide, slow down please," I said. "I'd prefer we don't make the turn onto the PCH up on two wheels. We can't risk flipping this thing, especially with the cargo we've got in the back."

Adelaide frowned once more, but gently tapped on the brakes.

"Okay Haley, go on," I said.

Haley said, "What's the cargo in the back?"

"You don't want to know," I said.

Hart, who still had his eyes closed but seemed to have calmed down considerably - I assumed due to his breathing and counting program - apparently had been paying close attention to what we had been saying despite his trancelike state.

Hart said, "Jack's got the Iglas. How else do you think he blew up that tunnel?"

"It wasn't really me who blew up the tunnel, sir," I said.

"'Indirectly' is what you said before," Hart said, still with his eyes closed. "Which is bullshit since I know your goddamn Bogota play when I see it."

"You don't mind we have the missiles, sir?" I said.

"We're way past that now," Hart said. "You gotta do what you gotta do."

"Thank you, sir," I said.

Hart said nothing in reply. He seemed to sink into himself again.

Haley and I exchanged a look.

"Should I continue?" Haley said.

I nodded.

"As you know," Haley said, "ever since you alerted us to the existence of Dr. Nemo, we've been building a profile based on what you told us. We believe Nemo is male, intelligent, a risk taker..."

Adelaide interrupted, "Why can't Nemo be a woman? Women are risk takers and intelligent."

"Yes, they can be," Haley said. "But we've carefully analyzed the recording of the call Dr. Lennon provided us with and the speech patterns are more consistent with a male speaker."

"You can do that even though the voice was disguised?" Adelaide said.

"Yes," Haley said. "We have sophisticated algorithms that are very reliable in that regard."

"Okay," Adelaide said. "Just so long as you're not being sexist."

"I can assure you, we're not being sexist," Haley said. "We believe Nemo is young..."

I said, "Most of the dark programmers were young."

"Most, but not all," Haley said. "Nemo is also probably a bit of an iconoclast. He revealed secrets to Dr. Lennon he was technically not allowed to reveal, and certainly did not follow proper channels in his reporting of his suspicions."

Jeff said, "Maybe he just paranoid like the colonel who be my schizophrenic roommate at Walter Reed."

I said, "Just because you're paranoid doesn't mean they aren't after you."

Hart, his eyes still closed, mumbled something but I couldn't make out what it was. He also must have put the phone down and braced it somehow as he was then rubbing his temples with both hands.

"What was that, sir?" I said.

Hart said, "Yossarian. 'Catch 22.'"

"Good one, sir," I said.

Hart groaned and jammed his fingers into his temples even harder.

We reached Kanan's intersection with the Pacific Coast Highway. There was a red light at the intersection. Adelaide didn't stop or slow down, but just drove through the light as she made a right turn into one of the PCH's northbound lanes. I checked around and behind us to see if there were any police cars. There weren't any. I was still worried, however, about how much trouble the Iglas and our other weapons could get us into if we were stopped for even the most minor of traffic violations.

"Adelaide, please don't drive through any more red lights," I said.

Adelaide said, "You can make a right turn on a red light."

"You still have to stop first," I said.

Haley said, "Adelaide, listen to Jack please. The three of you can't afford to be stopped."

Adelaide rolled her eyes and stomped on the gas. The van quickly accelerated. In a moment we would be going much too fast for our then present circumstances.

"Adelaide, don't accelerate beyond the speed limit," I said. "And when you get to the limit, keep it there."

Adelaide scowled, but eased off the gas pedal.

"Thank you," I said. I retuned my attention to Haley. "Sorry, Haley. Please go on."

Haley said, "Nemo is obviously skilled with codes and encryption or he wouldn't have been able to make a ciphertext we can't break. He is also not detached, like some scientists are, from the broader ramifications of his work. By that we mean he cares about how his work might affect his country. He has a patriotic streak."

A siren's caterwaul shrieked somewhere behind us. I turned my head to look in the side-view mirror. A California Highway Patrol car was closing in fast on us, its roof lights whirring, headlamps flashing, and side mounted red light flaring a brilliant piercing crimson.

Haley said, "That's not a siren, is it?"

I said, "I'm afraid it is, dear."

"Damn," Haley said.

I was surprised Hart hadn't said something about the siren too. I looked down at my iPhone screen and saw why. Hart was no longer rubbing his temples but instead had both hands squishing the sides of his head, including his ears. He also had his eyes closed and seemed to be gritting his teeth in pain.

I checked on the van's speedometer. Adelaide was going the speed limit. Had I missed the patrol car at the intersection when Adelaide blew through the red light? I was pretty sure I hadn't. There was a chance the patrolman wasn't after us, that he was racing towards another location, but that chance was so slim as to be nonexistent. The most likely explanation was that we had been spotted leaving the tunnel by one of the law enforcement first responders and they had called the van in.

Which would be bad.

Very bad.

Adelaide floored the accelerator.

"What are you doing?" I said to Adelaide.

"You want to explain to a cop why we have surface-to-surface missiles in the back?" Adelaide said.

"Pull over," I said.

Adelaide shook her head.

"We can outrun him," Adelaide said. "We're almost there."

"It's at least five miles to Kate's estate," I said. "Pull over."

Adelaide ignored me. The van continued to accelerate.

I leaned across Jeff, grabbed the ignition key, and turned off the engine. For good measure I reached over and shoved the transmission lever into neutral. The van instantly slowed down.

"What the hell!" Adelaide said.

Adelaide struggled with the sudden loss of power steering and power braking, but was able to pull off onto the right shoulder. The highway patrol car pulled in behind us and stopped. The patrol car's lights were so bright I couldn't see what the officer inside the car was doing. He or she stayed in their car, however.

I turned to Adelaide.

"Adelaide, I'm sorry," I said. "I know you feel strongly about honoring the Kazakh warriors, but now is probably a good time to clean the blood off your cheeks and forehead."

"Not happening," Adelaide said.

"It will just make things worse when that highway patrolman gets a good look at your face," I said.

"I honestly don't care," Adelaide said.

I could have kept arguing with her, but I knew that wouldn't get me anywhere. Wiping the Kazakh's blood off her face myself would have just caused a scene I'd rather the patrolman didn't witness. I was also fully cognizant of the fact that our current situation had much bigger potential problems associated with it than just trying to explain away the blood on Adelaide's face - the six Igla SSM's and the empty crate in the cargo area being the most obvious ones.

There was only one way out of those bigger potential problems.

I needed to snap Hart out of his painful reverie and get him to help us.

CHAPTER 101

I looked down at my cell phone screen. Hart, if anything, seemed worse than before. His eyes were squeezed more tightly shut, his teeth were more strongly gritted, and his hands had a more forceful vise-like grip on his head. I also thought I may have detected some barely audible moaning.

"General?" I said.

No response.

"General?" I said louder.

Still no response.

"General!" I yelled.

Hart's eyes snapped open.

"Goddamnit," Hart said through his gritted teeth. "Can't you see I'm in pain here?"

"I'm sorry, sir, but a serious situation has developed," I said. "Do you have anyone in the California Highway Patrol?"

"Now what?" Hart said.

"We just got pulled over," I said.

"How the hell did you manage that?" Hart said.

"I think we must have been spotted leaving the scene of the crime," I said.

"The tunnel?" Hart said.

"Yes, sir," I said. "It won't be good if they search the van."

"I know that," Hart said.

Hart stopped gritting his teeth and dropped his hands from the sides of his head. He appeared to take some deep breaths and to count to ten. I suppose the breathing and the counting worked wonders, because Hart's professional mien - a rock-hard, brutally focused, no-nonsense mien I considered to be the finest professional mien I had ever encountered - suddenly, one might even say miraculously, returned.

"Give me a minute and I'll get back to you," Hart said.

Hart's hand appeared gigantic in size for a moment as it approached his half of my iPhone screen and then that half went blank. Haley remained visible on her half.

Haley said, "What are you going to do?"

"The cop is still in the patrol car," I said. "As long as he or she stays there, I'm going to do nothing."

In the distance, I heard sirens approaching from in front of us and behind us, though they sounded like they were still far away. Either the highway patrol officer had called for backup, or the backup had already been on their way.

"Are those more sirens I hear?" Haley said.

"Yes," I said. "I believe we're about to be surrounded."

At the mention of the word 'surrounded', Jeff seemed to grow uncomfortable, as if the demons he fought hard to keep at bay were awakening in his mind. He leaned back against the seat, closed his eyes, and slowed his breathing. A pang of guilt ran through me as I wondered once again if I had done the right thing in asking Jeff to join me in Southern California.

"Jeff, you okay buddy?" I said.

"I'll be fine," Jeff said. "Just need a moment to relax."

"Alright," I said. "Anything changes you tell me."

Jeff said nothing. Haley gave me a questioning look.

"We're good," I said to her.

Haley nodded, then asked, "Is the van stolen?"

"Let's put it this way," I said. "It doesn't appear to be a rental."

"Maybe that's why they stopped you," Haley said.

"At this point, I don't think it really matters why," I said.

"Yes, you're probably right about that," Haley said. "Well, I suppose if you're just going to sit there for now, I might as well continue."

"I agree," I said. "No harm in using our time constructively while we wait for Hart to get back to us."

Haley leaned her head in towards her monitor and appeared to be looking closely at what she saw on the screen.

"Did Jeff fall completely asleep already?" Haley said.

"I believe so," I said.

"That was quick," Haley said. "Should I talk softly?"

"Don't worry," I said. "He's pretty hard to wake up."

"Okay," Haley said. "I want to build my case a little stronger before

I show you the photo of Nemo. Part of that case building is to provide you with more details of our process."

"Okay," I said.

"As you know, there were fifty-six people murdered in the NASAD bunker that housed the dark programming team," Haley said.

"Fifty-five dark programmers plus Rick Benavidez, the vice president of dark programming," I said.

"Correct," Haley said. "We have also confirmed the dead man in the photo you sent me was indeed Mr. Benavidez..."

Adelaide, who must have overheard our conversation, interrupted Haley.

"Mr. Benavidez was a patriot and a war hero," Adelaide said. "Death will be too good for whoever did this to him. We're going to avenge him."

"I like the way you think, Adelaide," Haley said. "Continuing then, including Mr. Benavidez, the total number of people that worked in the bunker on a daily basis, however, was fifty-nine. That's three more people than the fifty-six you found."

"Which means three of the dark programmers weren't there that day," I said, "and we've been hoping against hope that one of those three was Dr. Nemo."

"Romans 4:18," Haley said.

"That's where hoping against hope comes from?" I said.

"It does," Haley said.

"I didn't know that," I said.

"Now you do," Haley said. "In order to obtain Nemo's photo, we analyzed all the pictures you sent us of the dead dark programmers in the bunker. We compared those pictures to the fifty-eight dark programmers known to work there."

"I thought the dark programmers' identities were ultra top secret and were impossible to discover?" I said.

"They were," Haley said. "In fact, the NASAD computer systems have one of the best identity masking systems I've ever seen. All we were able to determine until you and Adelaide sent us the photos of the driver's licenses was that each dark programmer had a code name. Once we had the photo ID's, however, we hacked into the NASAD computers and ran software that used those ID's to see how the ID's were linked with the dark programmers' code names. After we determined how the code names were linked with the real people, we then reverse engineered the linkage to find the true names of the three dark programmers for whom you hadn't given us ID's. Those three programmers, of course, were the three programmers who weren't among the dead in the bunker. We never would have broken the NASAD system without your and Adelaide's assistance."

"Thank you," I said. "This 'we' that you're talking about who did the hacking, though. Is it you?"

"If I admitted that I'd have to kill you," Haley said.

The sirens I had heard approaching us earlier were now accompanied by flashing lights. Those sirens and lights materialized into four highway patrol cars that arrived nearly simultaneously at our location. Two of the highway patrol cars had approached from the south, which was to the rear of the van. Those two cars pulled in next to the first patrol car that had parked behind us. The two other patrol cars had come from the north, which was to the front of the van. Those two patrol cars pulled off the road at high speed, kicked up a lot of dust, then stopped about thirty yards away from the van's front end.

All the patrol cars, both front and back, were facing us. All of the cars also had their headlights on, so I couldn't see into any of them. The dust the patrol cars had kicked up floated in the light beams, the breeze causing the dust to spiral like tiny Oklahoma plains twisters.

Some of the dust made its way into the van's cabin and filled our nostrils with the smell of limestone and salt. I didn't know why none of the highway patrol officers appeared to be taking any action other than to watch us, but for the moment, it was fine with me. The longer the officers took, the longer Hart had to work on the solution I was waiting for him to provide.

Even though I'd turned off the van's ignition to make Adelaide pull over, I'd left the key in the position that allowed the van's lights to stay on. Since the lights were on, I realized that the officers were as equally blind as to what was going on inside the van as we were to what was happening inside the patrol cars. Not being able to see was likely to make the cops nervous. A nervous cop can be a trigger-happy cop.

"Turn off the headlights," I said to Adelaide.

"What difference does it make if they're on or not?" Adelaide said.

"I'll explain later," I said. "But for now, can you please just do as I say for once without arguing?"

Adelaide shut off the lights.

I returned my attention to Haley.

"Did you find the three missing dark programmers?" I said.

Haley said, "We found two. The first one was a thirty-one year old single woman. She lived in Pasadena. She had apparently stayed home from work yesterday since she was sick with the flu. It must have been a pretty bad case of the flu, since one of our MOM team members found her dead. The second one was a forty-two year old man, an ex-hippie who was on a Disney cruise in the Caribbean with his wife and three kids. He somehow found a way to fall overboard and drown. Obviously our enemy got to both of them before we did."

"Yes, it's obvious, and it's horrific too," I said. "It also seems to pretty much prove that our enemy was intent on killing all the dark programmers, not just Nemo. I suppose there is some good news, though, in all of this bad news."

"What's that?" Haley said.

"Neither the woman nor the man fits your profile of Nemo," I said.

"Correct," Haley said. "As far as the man is concerned, we also didn't think Nemo would go on vacation at a time like this."

"I would have if I were him," I said.

"I'm sure you would have," Haley said. "We don't believe the family of the man on the cruise ship has any reason to be under threat, but just to be careful, we helicoptered two FBI agents to the ship to watch over them."

"Did you dress the agents on the cruise ship as Peter Pan and Tinkerbell?" I said.

"That's a little over the top in the poor taste department even for you, don't you think?" Haley said.

"Sorry," I said.

"It is a funny idea though," Haley said.

"Thank you," I said. "Where's the third programmer?"

"We don't know," Haley said. "We have the third programmer's apartment in Northridge under surveillance as well as the residences of his known acquaintances and relatives. The third programmer hasn't been spotted yet, but he's an eighteen year old male who has been with NASAD five years."

"He started when he was thirteen years old?" I said.

"Yes, fresh out of graduate school, with Ph.D.'s in computer science, mathematics, and physics," Haley said. "His mathematics doctoral thesis was on the use of quantum mechanics in code-breaking."

"I don't know, Haley," I said. "You might be barking up the wrong tree."

"How so?" Haley said.

"He doesn't sound smart enough," I said.

Haley rolled her eyes.

More sirens wailed in the distance, all of them approaching rapidly. It sounded like there were perhaps two more vehicles coming from the north and two coming from the south. The sirens were accompanied by the 'thwacka thwacka' of helicopter rotors that were growing louder with each passing second. I again looked in my side-view mirror. A brilliant white searchlight pierced the night air a hundred feet above the earth. The light was about a quarter mile away but closing fast.

Haley said, "The same eighteen year old male worked with the dark programmers on NASAD's encryption software and computer systems security. He was also the most respected war-gamer of all the dark programmers. He led repeated trouncings of the defensive team at NASAD headquarters."

"I met the defensive programmers at the Cyber Defense Hall in NASAD headquarters," I said. "They're no slouches."

"No, they're not," Haley said. "Our hacking of the NASAD computers also allowed us to take a look at the dark programmers' email accounts. The man-child who led the dark programmers' assault team had been bragging in his emails there was no way the defensive team could stop his latest method of attack. That attack was to be unleashed in the war games planned for a week from Friday." Haley paused. "Jack, the fact that the war with China is going to start tonight instead of a week from Friday is a problem for us, isn't it? I mean, can we still hold on to your theory that the insurmountable edge lies within the NASAD dark programmer's war game software? Wasn't that theory based in large part on the fact that the date and start time of the war games and

China's commencement of combat action were one and the same?"

"I agree," I said. "That theory has come under attack. But I'm not ready to abandon it yet. Too much still points towards the theory being correct, especially if this man-child you've been describing turns out to be Nemo."

"Even if he does turn out to be Nemo, it still wouldn't change the fact that a week from Friday is not seventeen hours from now, and that the date and time the war games were scheduled to start is no longer the same date and time the actual war is scheduled to start," Haley said.

"I'm not so sure about that," I said.

"Come on Jack," Haley said. "Tonight is not next Friday!"

"If the man-child is Nemo, and he's as smart and tactically brilliant as your emails seem to imply, tonight absolutely could be," I said.

"You're not making any sense," Haley said.

"As soon as we get out of this highway patrol mess, I'm going to make a phone call," I said. "Depending on the results of that call, I'll know whether my current theory about the potential relationship between the NASAD war games and the Chinese insurmountable edge continues to hold water or not."

"Who are you going to call?" Haley said.

"Raj Divedi," I said.

"The director of the NASAD Cyber Defense Hall team?" Haley said.

"Yes," I said.

"How's Raj going to help us?" Haley said.

"I want to know more about the war game rules," I said. "Specifically, are sneak attacks allowed?"

Haley seemed to think this over for a moment.

"A sneak attack, huh?" Haley said. "Like tonight instead of a week from Friday night?"

"Yes," I said. "Like tonight instead of a week from Friday night."

"Hmm," Haley said. "I kinda like that idea. It actually fits pretty well with what we know about how Dr. Nemo thinks."

"That's why I thought of it," I said. "The sneak attack theory only holds up, however, if there's still no evidence that the insurmountable edge is already operational. Does that continue to be the case? All U.S. military systems are working normally?"

"It does," Haley said. "All U.S. military systems continue to function normally."

"Alright, that's good to know," I said. "So, do you know his real name?"

"Who?" Haley said.

"The man-child," I said. "Dr. Nemo."

"Billy Einstein," Haley said.

"No way," I said.

"Way," Haley said.

"And I suppose he's related to Albert?" I said.

"Not confirmed yet, but we believe Billy's grandfather was Albert's second cousin," Haley said.

Jeff stirred from his trance.

Jeff said, "Intelligence be a highly inherited trait."

I said, "You sure that's a politically correct statement?"

"No other way to explain all the dumb honkies in the world," Jeff said. He leaned back, closed his eyes again, then seemed to fall asleep almost instantly.

I said to Haley, "Sorry for the interruption. What else?"

Haley said, "Einstein was a close protégé of Paul Lennon."

"You're sure about that?" I said.

"Dead sure," Haley said.

The two pairs of sirened vehicles that had been approaching from both the north and the south were then less than a few hundred feet away. Now that they were close enough, I could see that all four were highway patrol cars. One car from each pair broke off and stopped broadside in the middle of the Pacific Coast Highway, blocking the northbound and southbound lanes. The other two cars screeched to a halt twenty yards away from us, their noses pointing in at the side of the van so that we were then closely surrounded by seven patrol cars.

As if responding to some silent cue, the seven highway patrol officers who had been behind the wheels of each of those surrounding patrol cars scrambled out of their vehicles. Their guns were drawn and they took cover behind their open driver side doors. The helicopter pulled up over the van and hovered no more than seventy feet above us. The downdrafts from the copter's rotors rocked the van and sent clouds of dust swirling violently around us.

Adelaide and I rolled up our windows. The dust clouds were so thick we could barely see the highway patrol cars. The clouds also meant that the officers couldn't see us once again, which negated my earlier decision to turn off the van's lights. There was a good chance the officers were about to get very jumpy. I was worried about them shooting first and asking questions later.

General Hart came back online, filling the other half of the cell phone's screen next to Haley.

Hart said, "All taken care of."

I said, "You're joking right?"

"No, no, everything's fine," Hart said.

I pointed my cell phone camera out through the windshield so it could take in the twister and the nightmarish light beams shooting at the van from front, side, and above. I pointed the camera back at me.

"I'll be right back," Hart said.

Hart's side of the screen went blank again. Adelaide turned in her seat and started to climb over the top of it, clearly intent on getting into the cargo area.

"Where are you going?" I said to Adelaide.

"This is ridiculous," Adelaide said. "We have plenty enough firepower to blow those assholes away. The chopper too."

"Good idea," I said.

That seemed to surprise her. She stopped climbing and looked at me.

"You serious?" Adelaide said.

"Sure, it just might work," I said. "Nothing wrong with killing a bunch of innocent American citizens. The highway patrolmen's wives and children will certainly be completely understanding when you explain to them why their husbands and fathers won't be coming home."

"Why would I have to do that?" Adelaide said.

"Because you're the one who's going to fire the missiles," I said. "I ain't doin' it and Jeff's asleep."

"Are you saying Jeff would fire the missiles if I woke him up?" Adelaide said.

"No," I said. "Jeff wouldn't do it even if he was awake."

Adelaide appeared to think this over for a moment, then turned around and sat heavily back down in her seat. She crossed her arms, and stared straight ahead.

"You wouldn't have let me do it anyway," Adelaide said.

"You wouldn't have done it anyway," I said. "Not if you thought about what you were really going to do. Which I'm sure you would have."

Adelaide said nothing.

"Unless of course you believe that being a good soldier means being a crazy, out of control, emotionally unstable lunatic," I said.

Adelaide sighed.

"That's not what I believe," Adelaide said. "I was just mad, okay?"

"Okay," I said.

The van continued to rock as the dust swirled and the helicopter engines thundered in our ears. I turned my attention back to my cell phone screen.

"Tell me more about Billy Einstein, AKA Dr. Nemo," I said to Haley.

Haley said, "You sure you want to do that now? I also saw your cell phone picture of what's going on outside the van when you showed Hart, you know."

"As long as Adelaide stays in her seat, things might turn out fine," I said.

Adelaide gave me a very mean look.

Haley said, "I'm not going to touch that one."

"Smart idea," I said. "What's this about Nemo being Lennon's protégé?"

"Billy Einstein's father was a special forces captain," Haley said. "He was killed in Iraq when Billy was ten years old. Despite Billy's academic prowess, he wanted to be special forces too. But Billy had already come to the attention of the CIA and the CIA told Milt Feynman about him. Everyone involved thought Billy had the exceptional talents needed for NASAD's national security and defense work, so they recruited him to NASAD. Billy at first didn't want to work for NASAD, but when he met Paul Lennon he changed his mind. Billy's emails suggest Lennon probably reminded Billy of his father and that Billy especially loved the fact that Lennon had been a special forces captain like his father had been. It also appears Paul Lennon and Billy had genuine affection for each other. When Lennon died, Billy went into a deep depression and almost left NASAD."

"But he stayed," I said.

"He stayed," Haley said.

"Do we know why?" I said.

"Our best guess in looking through his emails to his dark programmer friends is he probably thought his dad and Lennon would have wanted him to stay," Haley said.

"Makes sense," I said. "It sure would have been a lot easier on us if Kate had known about Billy Einstein. But it's not surprising she didn't. Mary Beth Lankowski, the head of NASAD's Human Resources Department, told me that the mentoring program that put Paul Lennon together with young geniuses like Billy Einstein had incredibly tight security surrounding it. Then again, one would think it was possible Paul could have mentioned some of his experiences with those kids to Kate."

"I don't think Paul Lennon would have said anything about Billy Einstein, or anything to do with the mentoring program in general, to Dr. Lennon," Haley said. "You didn't tell your wife any of the details of your missions did you?"

"No, I didn't," I said. "Mainly because I wasn't allowed to."

"Exactly," Haley said. "Now, I've got one last question to ask you before I send you the picture of Nemo."

"Just one?" I said.

"Yes," Haley said.

"Thank the Lord," I said.

Haley rolled her eyes again.

"My main concern at the moment is that his looks not influence your decision in any way," Haley said. "Before I send the photo then, I want you to tell me, after all you've heard, do we have the right guy or not?"

"Hard to imagine we'll ever find anyone better," I said.

"Okay," Haley said. "I'm sending the photo to you now."

Outside, the pitch of the helicopter engines changed, the slant of the beam from the copter's searchlight shifted - from nearly straight down to tilted more toward the ocean - and the dust cloud started to die down. A moment later, I could see the copter had moved a good distance away from us and was hovering above the other side of the highway. Though the dust cloud was dissipating, it still blocked my view of the highway patrol officers surrounding the van. The fact the helicopter had moved away from us, however, gave me hope that Hart had finally gotten his contact at the highway patrol to give the needed commands and that the officers would soon be pulling out.

But then the dust settled some more and the air was clear enough so that we could get a good view of the highway patrolmen and they of us.

Their guns were all pointed at the van.

They weren't pulling out.

One of the officers was holding a microphone whose cord led back inside his patrol car.

"Put your hands up where we can see them," the officer with the microphone said, his voice booming from a speaker mounted on his vehicle's roof. The officer looked older than the others, and was tall and lean with close-cropped black hair showing beneath his hat.

I pointed the cell phone camera towards the black-haired officer and his cohorts so Haley could gain an appreciation of our situation. I then propped the cell phone on the dash and pointed the camera at myself so that she could see me as I put my hands up over my head. Out of the corner of my eye I saw that Adelaide was still sulking, her arms crossed over her chest.

"Put your hands up, Adelaide," I said.

Adelaide looked at me, shook her head, and sneered.

"Coward," Adelaide said.

"Didn't we just talk about not being a crazy, out of control, emotional lunatic?" I said.

"Yeah, well this is different," Adelaide said.

"Different how?" I said.

"I'm not talking about launching any missile strikes against anybody am I?" Adelaide said.

I breathed in deeply and let it out through my nose. What had I done to deserve this? Somehow I had earned the privilege of experiencing all the pain of teenage angst and rebellion without the counterbalancing joys of early childhood parenting. I was at a loss as to what to do. I didn't want to provoke Adelaide as that might only make things worse. Letting Adelaide get herself killed, however, was not an option. Maybe Haley would know what to do.

"Haley, were you ever a teenager?" I said.

Haley said, "Let me guess. Adelaide is not raising her hands?"

"Good guess," I said. "I thought the officer making the request was rather polite, but Adelaide doesn't agree. She's refusing to comply."

Adelaide snorted.

"Who said they were polite?" Adelaide said.

Haley took a deep breath in and let it out through her nose in an almost exact replication of my own behavior a few moments before.

Haley said, "Adelaide, it doesn't do any of us any good if you get yourself killed."

"Surrender is not an option," Adelaide said.

"Where'd you get that from?" Haley said.

"Captain Sisko, 'Deep Space Nine,'" Adelaide said.

"'Star Trek'?" Haley said.

"You got a problem with that?" Adelaide said.

A loud gunshot sounded and a bullet pinged against the doorframe next to Adelaide's head. The bullet shattered the window glass, the shards raining down on Adelaide's lap. The patrolman who had fired the shot was a big, beefy guy in his twenties whose uniform seemed about two sizes too small for him. He looked like a rookie and his face was turning beet red in embarrassment. He lowered his weapon. The shot had clearly been fired in error, but that wouldn't have done any of us any good if it had found its mark.

The black-haired officer with the microphone shouted, "Hold your fire!"

Haley looked shocked.

"Was that a gunshot?" Haley said.

I said, "Yes."

"Adelaide, you listen to me," Haley said. "As a major in the United States Army I am ordering you to put your hands up. If you ever want a career in the Armed Forces you do as I say."

Adelaide said nothing but her hands went up.

"Are her hands up?" Haley asked me.

"Yes," I said. "Someday you're going to have to teach me how to do that."

Haley breathed a sigh of relief.

The black-haired patrolman with the microphone turned his attention back to us.

"You in the middle," he said through the microphone, "put your hands up where I can see them."

He meant Jeff. Jeff was still asleep. With all the attention I had been paying to Adelaide I had somehow forgotten Jeff needed to be tended to as well. I was afraid that if I touched Jeff he might startle and get himself shot. I gently lowered my right elbow, shifted my body against the door, and nudged the electric window switch. The window came down. I leaned my head out the window.

"He's asleep," I yelled.

The black-haired officer with the microphone seemed momentarily taken aback. Who could blame him? After all, how many men would sleep through a gunshot blowing out their window? The officer, however, appeared to quickly regain his composure.

"Wake him up!" the black-haired officer said.

"I don't think we really want to do that," I said. "How about if I come out there and explain?"

"Stay right where you are," the black-haired officer said.

Hart suddenly came back online, his face filling the other half of the screen next to Haley.

Hart said, "Sorry for the delay. We're good to go now."

"In what universe would that be in, sir?" I said.

"Give it a second, wiseass," Hart said.

The black-haired highway patrol officer looked like he was growing impatient. He raised the patrol car microphone as if to say something, but then abruptly lowered it. The officer leaned his head sideways to the left and put his ear close the to the microphone-speaker combination that was mounted on his shoulder. The combination was a device that was an entirely separate unit from the microphone he held in his hand. By the officer's reaction, it appeared someone was talking to him through the unit's shoulder speaker. The black-haired officer seemed to listen carefully for a moment, then reached to his side, pressed a button to activate his shoulder microphone, and looked as if he was responding to whoever had called him. There appeared to be some more back and forth between the black-haired officer and whoever was on the other end of the connection and the black-haired officer seemed to grow increasingly annoyed. But then the officer's expression suddenly changed. He smiled, and shook his head. He clicked off the communication and raised the patrol car's microphone to his lips.

"Lower your weapons," the black-haired officer said to his fellow highway patrolmen.

All the patrolmen looked questioningly at him.

"Don't make me say it again," the black-haired officer said.

The patrolmen lowered their weapons.

Adelaide snorted once more.

"Told you they'd back down," Adelaide said.

I didn't say anything. My cell phone made a small beep.

I looked at the phone.

Dr. Nemo's face was on the screen, staring up at me.

CHAPTER 102

I recognized the face. It was a handsome face, young, more boy than man, sunny and well scrubbed. There was only the slightest hint of a beard and the eyes were a luminous amber, almond shaped, and intelligent. The mischievous mouth was curled into a smile and full of bright white teeth. The cheekbones were high and the chin finely sculpted. The head was bigger than average size and surrounded by long, leonine, light brown hair that hung down to the man-child's shoulders.

Which was different than the last time I had seen that head.

The last time I had seen that head it had been covered with a big billed, blue Yankees baseball cap that had thrown its face into shadow, and its eyes were hidden behind dark sunglasses. The man-child the head belonged to had at that time been sitting by the shore of the lake at NASAD headquarters while the self-piloting sailboats were flying across its surface.

"I've seen this guy before," I said to Haley and Hart, both of whose faces were then sharing the screen with Dr. Nemo's face.

"Where?" Haley said.

"NASAD headquarters," I said. "Do you have a full length photo?"

"This one is full length," Haley said. "I'll just pull back on the zoom."

I stole a glance at Adelaide. I would have thought Adelaide would be curious to take a look at what was on my screen, but she seemed intent on scowling at the patrolmen assembled outside the van. I didn't wake Jeff, even though his input on what Haley was about to show me would surely have been valuable. It was always better to leave Jeff alone when his PTSD had ushered him into the realms of unconscious oblivion.

I looked back at my iPhone screen. Haley's zoom out had left the man-boy's body fully revealed. He was wearing a black Green Day t-shirt with a burning radio on it, blue jeans, and blue and orange Nike running shoes. He looked to be about six foot two and one hundred and eighty pounds. His body seemed strong and proportioned like an athlete. It was the same body I'd seen at the lake.

"Dr. Nemo wasn't wearing a Green Day t-shirt the day I saw him, but it's definitely him," I said.

"Green Day was playing in the background of the voicemail Nemo left Dr. Lennon," Haley said.

"I know," I said.

Hart said, "What's Green Day?"

"It's a band," I said.

"What kind of band?" Hart said.

"A punk rock band, sir," I said.

"What the hell is 'punk rock'?" Hart said.

"It's kind of hard to explain, sir," I said.

Haley said, "You think it could be a coincidence that Green Day is both on the shirt and in the voicemail?"

"Unlikely," I said.

"What was Nemo doing when you saw him?" Haley said.

"I thought he was watching some self-piloted sailboats racing on NASAD's lake," I said. "But I guess he was watching Dr. Lennon and me."

"So you could have taken him back then?" Haley said.

"I suppose," I said. "He attracted my attention for a moment, but my instincts about him weren't strong enough for me to really consider going after him."

"It sure would have been better if you did," Haley said.

Hart said, "Sounds to me like an obvious move. What the hell were you thinking, Jack?"

"I did my best, but I guess my best wasn't good enough," I said.

Haley said, "'Just Once', James Ingram?"

"Yes," I said.

Hart said, "Who's James Ingram?"

"A musician," I said.

"Is he in Green Day?" Hart said.

"No, sir," I said. "He's more of an R&B artist, sir."

"What the hell did you bring him up for then?" Hart said.

"I was just quoting him, sir," I said.

"Goddamnit!" Hart said.

"Sorry, sir," I said. "I also want to assure you, sir, that no one is sorrier than me that I didn't go after Nemo then. Be that as it may, Haley you were right not to show me the photo before you went over the profile.

Dr. Nemo looks exactly the way I would have thought he would look, so I easily could have been swayed by my first impression of his appearance alone. Which would have been bad, as there are probably a number of people that look like Dr. Nemo. I doubt there are a number of people who both look like him and also have the correct profile, however. Is the kid an athlete?"

"That's a hard call," Haley said. "When Billy Einstein was eight years old, he won MVP's in Pop Warner football and Little League baseball. But then he enrolled in college when he was nine, and that pretty much put a damper on his athletic career."

"He didn't try out for the varsity teams?" I said.

"I'm not going to dignify that with a response," Haley said.

Hart said, "No one with half a brain would either."

Ignoring Hart, I said, "What about Billy's mom and dad? Were they athletes?"

"Mom was an All American volleyball player at the University of Southern California," Haley said. "His dad was drafted by the Yankees out of high school, but decided to join the Army instead."

Which explained the Yankees cap, I thought to myself. Outside the van, the black-haired highway patrolman had gathered together the six other officers who had been in the cars surrounding the van and directed them to form a semicircle. The officers had all holstered their firearms. The black-haired patrolman appeared to talk to his fellow officers about something, but I couldn't hear what it was.

"I think I'll go with Billy Einstein being an athlete then," I said.

"Why do you care?" Haley said.

"Your profile is pretty solid as it is," I said, "but if Einstein's an athlete, it makes it even more solid for me."

"How?" Haley said.

"I'm not saying non-athletes don't take risks," I said. "But the kind of risks young Mr. Billy Einstein took on are at the far end of the spectrum. Exceptional athleticism tends to give a person more confidence in themselves. I'll bet in Billy's case it made him believe he could weather the increased risks he had to know he would face by contacting Dr. Lennon."

"I can buy that," Haley said.

Hart said, "I hate to admit it, but I think Jack is probably right."

I said, "Thank you, sir. I also like the kid's obvious brutality."

Haley said, "Obvious brutality? What are you talking about?"

"Look closely at the photo," I said. "It's right behind the eyes."

Haley and Hart both seemed to study the photo.

"Well?" I said.

Hart looked back up at me.

"It's there," Hart said.

Haley studied a moment longer, then looked back up as well.

"I see it now," Haley said. "I missed it completely before."

"That's because you've been working in bunkers too long," I said. "You're not out in the real world like I am, where I have to deal with it 24/7."

"Okay, macho man," Haley said. "But just remember it's because of what I do in my bunkers that you haven't had your sorry ass handed to you. Not yet, anyway."

A couple of the highway patrolmen seemed to be arguing with the black-haired officer. The patrolmen were pointing at the van and appeared to be demanding something unpleasant be done to us. It looked like the black-haired officer was keeping them under control, at least for the moment.

"No one loves you more than me, Haley," I said.

"I certainly hope that's the case," Haley said. She paused. "You're not saying the brutality could mean Einstein's the enemy are you?"

"Absolutely not," I said. "The athleticism and the brutality are just two more traits that might have given him the extra push needed to take the kind of courageous actions he's taken to date. Billy Einstein's our man. Or boy."

"You're sure?" Haley said. "Remember, we're running up on seventeen hours left before war breaks out. We can't afford to make a mistake."

"Billy Einstein is Dr. Nemo," I said. "Congratulations. You did it."

"Thanks," Haley said.

A text suddenly appeared across my screen, its banner partially obscuring the faces of Haley and Hart. The text was from Kate. It read, "Nemo's coming."

"Jesus goddamned Christ," I muttered under my breath.

"When?" I quickly texted back.

"4:00 a.m.," came Kate's response.

So soon? It couldn't be a coincidence could it? Wasn't it likely, given all that Nemo seemed to know about the insurmountable edge, that he would somehow be privy to the same information that Haley and Hart had just imparted to me - that the Chinese were to commence their war in less than seventeen hours and that we were running out of time to do anything about it? And if Nemo knew about that rapidly approaching deadline, wouldn't he also know it was now or never if he was going to succeed in revealing the secrets of the insurmountable edge to Kate - secrets for which Nemo had already risked life and limb to bring to light, secrets he surely believed represented America's best, if not only, hope to stop the war?

"Where?" I texted.

"Here," Kate's text said.

Haley said, "What are you doing? What's wrong?"

I shifted my focus on the iPhone screen from the texts to Haley's and Hart's faces. They both appeared to be keenly studying me. I almost told them that Dr. Nemo had just made contact with Kate and that he was on his way to see her, but stopped myself. I trusted Haley and Hart with my life, but...my instincts told me to keep my mouth shut. My gut told me that if Nemo was truly planning a visit to Kate's estate he was most likely watching the estate right at that moment. I had no idea how he could do that and still manage to escape detection, but I didn't think Nemo would make so bold a move as to meet Kate unless he had the estate under surveillance. If Haley or Hart took action on their own, no matter how well meaning, it might scare Nemo off.

I was pretty sure Haley would follow my wishes if I asked her not to do anything, but Hart was another matter. Hart might think he knew best, and without telling me, do something like send in reinforcements to the estate, or persuade Ray Carpenter to alter his security arrangements. Either of which probably wouldn't escape Nemo's notice if he was indeed actually watching. I couldn't risk anything interfering with my best, and perhaps last chance, to speak with Dr. Nemo.

"Wrong?" I said. "Nothing's wrong."

Hart said, "You're lying. I could tell you were reading a text. What's in it?"

"There's no text," I said. "My screen froze for a moment. I was just trying to clear it. Oops, there it goes again."

I wiped the texts off the screen just in case there was some sneaky way Haley had to take a screenshot of them.

"Bullshit," Hart said.

"Shh," I said. "Don't talk so loud. You'll wake Jeff up."

"One last time," Hart said. "What's in the text?"

"There's no text," I said.

Hart shook his head. He appeared to take a deep breath. Maybe he was even counting in his head again.

"Fine," Hart said. "You want to be that way, be that way. But you better know what the hell you're doing, Jack."

"When have I not?" I said.

"Let me count the ways," Hart said.

"Elizabeth Browning, sir?" I said.

"Yeah, Elizabeth Browning," Hart said. "Haley, are we done here?"

"Yes, sir," Haley said. "I still have to update Jack on a few issues, but you already know about them."

"Toodle-oo," Hart said.

He disappeared from my iPhone screen. Haley's and Dr. Nemo's faces expanded to fill the space where Hart's face had been.

I said, "Toodle-oo?"

Haley said, "I think that was meant for you. It means 'screw you' in French."

"No it doesn't," I said.

"The way Hart said it, it does," Haley said.

The black-haired highway patrol officer seemed to have finally quelled any rebellion among the other officers and their little meeting was breaking up. The other officers began walking back to their cars. The black-haired officer approached our van.

"Looks like we're going to have company," I said to Haley. "Hold on for a moment please."

"No problem," Haley said.

The black-haired officer sidled up to the van's passenger side door. He put his hands on the door's window frame, leaned his head in, and looked at Jeff.

"He really is asleep, isn't he?" the black-haired officer said quietly.

I nodded.

The black-haired officer extended his hand toward me. I scrunched around in my seat and shook it.

"I'm Sergeant Butler," the officer said. "Sorry for the inconvenience, General Wilder. Someone called in a van like this as being at the scene of a fire up in the hills, but clearly they were mistaken." Butler seemed to notice the Kazakh's blood on Adelaide's face and tipped his cap toward Adelaide. "Hello ma'am. It looks like you cut yourself. I have a first aid kit in my patrol car if you'd like some help cleaning up your wound."

Adelaide gave what at best could be called a half-smile to the officer.

"Thank you, Sergeant Butler, but we're almost home and I'd prefer to take care of it myself," Adelaide said.

"As you wish, ma'am," Butler said. He turned towards me and added, "I was in the 101st Airborne in Iraq. You and General Bradshaw are legends, sir. It's a pleasure to meet you both."

"The pleasure is all ours," I said.

"We'd be honored if you would allow us to escort you the rest of the way up the road," Butler said.

"It is we who would be honored," I said.

Butler stepped back and walked away. I turned to Adelaide.

"And you wanted to blow up that nice man," I said.

"I didn't know you were such a bootlicker," Adelaide said.

Adelaide leaned over Jeff's sleeping form and took a look at my cell phone screen. Apparently, her previous lack of interest in my proceedings with Haley and Hart had suddenly vanished with the wind.

"That Nemo?" Adelaide said.

"Could be," I said.

"He's cute," Adelaide said.

Haley said, "Did she say he was cute?"

"Yes," I said. "High praise indeed."

Outside the van, the highway patrolmen, all of whom had by then re-entered their vehicles, formed up their cars around the van. There were three cars in front, two in back, and two on either side. Officer Butler was in the car next to Adelaide. Butler leaned across his seat and gave Adelaide a wave of his hand. Adelaide pulled the van out onto the Pacific Coast Highway.

The highway patrol helicopter took a position directly over the van and the lead patrol cars also pulled out onto the highway. We, along with the copter and the patrol cars surrounding us, then all headed north together. The patrol cars that had been blocking off the highway left their positions and joined the rear of our procession. I felt like I was in a parade. It seemed like another opportunity to wave had arisen and I would have waved if there was anyone around to wave to.

Haley said, "It looks like you guys are on the move."

I turned my attention back to my iPhone.

"We are," I said. "We should be at Kate's estate within a few minutes. Now, what were the 'issues' Hart knows about but I don't?"

"We tracked down the donors for 'Doctors of Mercy'," Haley said.

"The 'charitable' organization that brought in the two planeloads of Afghans and Kazakhs?" I said.

"Yes, that organization," Haley said.

"Their name's a little misleading, isn't it?" I said.

"I suppose you'd prefer 'Doctors of Mercenaries'?" Haley said.

"I would, actually," I said.

"I'll run it by them," Haley said. "Maybe they'll consider a change. Continuing on then, the jets that unloaded the mercenaries were paid for under the terms of a sub-fund within 'Doctors of Mercy'. The sub-fund was specially directed to be used for the jet's operating expenses."

"Who was the source of the sub-fund?" I said.

"Not who," Haley said. "What. The sub-fund was a gift from a charitable trust domiciled in Qatar."

"Please don't tell me it's really terrorists who are behind everything after all," I said.

"You're afraid your buddy Agent Burnette might be right about something?" Haley said.

"Not just about something, but anything," I said. "Honestly, I couldn't live in a world where that was possible."

"That Qatar charitable trust has funded terrorism," Haley said. "But in this case, I'm pretty sure there's no terrorist aspect to the funding. The most likely explanation is that someone, or someones, used the charity to make it look like terrorists were involved."

"Phew," I said.

"'Phew' is right," Haley said.

"How did you figure all this out?" I said.

"I took a look at the trustee's books and records," Haley said.

"You mean you hacked into their books and records," I said.

"Must you be so crude?" Haley said.

"Always," I said.

Haley smiled.

"In any event," Haley said, "the money that was donated to the Qatar charity, and that ultimately wound up in the coffers of 'Doctors of Mercy', didn't come from the Qataris or any other country that supports terrorism. The funding actually came from a Florida corporation."

The convoy, consisting of our van and the highway patrol cars and helicopter, reached the small hill on the Pacific Coast Highway where my little Corolla friend had given his all the night before. I said a silent prayer for him.

"A U.S. company is behind this?" I said.

"Yes, and it's a very particular company," Haley said. "The Florida corporation is a division of NASAD."

"So we're supposed to believe NASAD is funding its own destruction?" I said. "That's too clever by half."

"You don't believe it then?" Haley said.

"No," I said. "And neither do you."

Haley smiled.

"The Cheshire Cat, again?" Haley said.

"In spades," I said.

"I don't think whoever set this whole thing up ever imagined we'd be able to reach beyond the Qatari trust and discover the NASAD connection," Haley said. "So while they did use NASAD's money, I don't believe they thought they'd get caught doing that."

"You're saying they used NASAD's money just to keep them from having to spend some of their own money?" I said.

"That," Haley said, "and perhaps they saw it as a kind of inside joke. I could see how the forces of evil would find it funny to hurt NASAD using NASAD's own money."

"I could see that too," I said. "However, as the great philosopher whose identity has been lost to history once said, 'He who laughs last...'"

"Laughs best," Haley said. "That 'he' better be us."

"It will be," I said. "There's another way to look at it though."

"What's that?" Haley said.

"It's fancy," I said.

"Fancy?" Haley said.

"In addition to being clever by half, everything our enemies have done so far is very, very fancy," I said. "They used top secret radar translocation technology to kill Milt Feynman and Paul Lennon. They went to great and complicated lengths to make the murders of the NASAD engineers look like accidents. The dark programmers were killed with carbon monoxide. They've imported mercenaries to our shores by disguising them as doctors. And it looks like the insurmountable edge is their idea of a very fancy way to take down the U.S. military by using our own software against us."

"You're right," Haley said. "It's almost like they're in love with their own brilliance. But, why didn't you mention Sammy and Lizzy? The stonings were a fancy - fancy in their hideousness - way to kill someone."

"I think about Sam and Lizzy all the time," I said. "I was about to mention them, but I felt like I was going to lose it if I did."

"Sorry," Haley said. "You okay?"

"For the moment, yes," I said. "So, there's still something you haven't told me, though."

"What's that?" Haley said.

Kate's compound was about half a mile ahead. A second helicopter - which I assumed belonged to the FBI - had joined the FBI helicopter that had been at the compound earlier. The two copters circled above the compound. The choppers' searchlights ignited the night sky, and I could just make out the sounds of their thundering engines filtering through the din of the highway patrol helicopter escorting us. The last bits of fog had blown inland and made the half moon visible. The moon seemed to balance itself on the ocean's horizon and its light broadcast a cone-like path across the surface of the sea that looked as if someone had laid a glittering pyramid flat atop the waves.

"How did the forces of evil get someone at NASAD to send money to the Qatari charity?" I said. "Especially to the sub-fund that was specifically earmarked to be used for 'Doctors of Mercy' planes to transport Afghan and Kazakh mercenaries into the U.S.?"

"The money wasn't sent by someone actually at NASAD," Haley said. "Control of the charitable giving at that NASAD Florida division was outsourced. The person it was outsourced to is Cynthia Upton."

"If I'm supposed to recognize that name, I don't," I said. "Who is she?"

"Again, not who, but what," Haley said. "Cynthia Upton is Carter Bowdoin's top lieutenant at Pennsylvania Avenue Partners."

"The noose tightens," I said.

"I wish we could just pick Bowdoin up and torture him," Haley said.

"That's always an option," I said. "But I still don't think we could flip a guy like that anytime soon, especially not in the next seventeen hours. We're better off with him running around free and hoping he makes a mistake that actually gives us something we can use."

"Like the identity of Dragon Man?" Haley said.

"I take it you're still drawing blanks on that topic?" I said.

"Unfortunately, yes," Haley said. "I do think we're getting closer to confirming the details of the deal Bowdoin and Dragon Man cut in Panama, however. And we're still sifting through Paul Lennon's military record to see if we can figure out why Dragon Man has such a stick up his ass about him."

"Stick up his ass?" I said.

"What?" Haley said. "Did I offend your sensitive little ears?"

"You kinda did," I said.

"Too bad," Haley said.

"I assume there's no progress on cracking Dr. Nemo's code either?" I said.

"There isn't," Haley said. "We also don't yet have a clear bead on anyone at NASAD who might have inserted the software altered with the dark programmers' war games weapon into the military's live operational systems."

"I'll be seeing Dr. Lennon very soon," I said. "Maybe she's made some headway on that issue. Anything else?"

"That's all I have at the moment," Haley said. "I'll keep you posted if anything changes, or if we get any results from our surveillance of Billy Einstein's apartment."

I was once again tempted to tell Haley about Kate's text regarding Dr. Nemo's potential upcoming visit, but 'need to know' caused me to hold my tongue.

"Au revoir," I said.

"Ciao," Haley said.

PART VI
NEMO

CHAPTER 103

Our convoy pulled even with the entrance to Freddy and Kate's estate. The highway patrol helicopter banked sharply right and flew off in an easterly direction over the foothills. Our highway patrol car escorts peeled away from us. Four of them headed south down the Pacific Coast Highway, while the other five headed north.

Adelaide drove the van up to the estate's gate. The gate was manned by a half-dozen FBI agents in body armor and carrying automatic weapons. Across the highway, four news vans with satellite dishes on their rooftops were parked on the shoulder. There were four news teams of two people each - a cameraman and a reporter making up each team - milling around outside the vans. An FBI agent was with the news teams, keeping them at bay.

The FBI agents at the gate opened it and waved us through. Security seemed to have doubled within the compound. Besides the second helicopter, there were more foot patrols with dogs and additional snipers on the tops of the houses. I had no idea how Dr. Nemo intended to get through all the added precautions, but I prayed he knew what he was doing.

Adelaide drove the van over the crushed gravel roadway that wound through the lawn to Kate's house. The grass was wet with precipitation from the fog. The palm trees fluttered softly, the wind rubbing the palms' fronds against each other. The sound of the rubbing made it seem as if someone was playing a musical washboard atop the palms' canopies. The salt smell of the ocean mixed with the scent of the flowering jasmines.

Adelaide pulled into the porte cochere in front of Kate's house. Agent Ray Carpenter was waiting there for us. Carpenter walked up to the van, leaned in through Adelaide's window. Carpenter appeared to notice the blood on Adelaide's face and seemed poised to say something about it. I signaled him from my seat on the other side of the passenger compartment with a finger to my mouth. Carpenter acknowledged my signal with a slight nod and said, "What happened to Bleckley's Crown Vic?"

"It melted," I said.

"Valley must be hot tonight," Carpenter said.

"That, and the fact it ran into an SSM it didn't like," I said.

"Let me guess," Carpenter said. "The guy who fired the SSM also ran into something he didn't like."

"Yeah," I said. "Adelaide."

Adelaide smiled.

"You want to tell Bleckley about his car, or do you want me to do it?" Carpenter said.

"I think it'd be more appropriate if you did it," I said.

"Somehow that's what I thought you'd say," Carpenter said. He leaned in farther, looked over Adelaide's shoulder into the van's cargo area. "The Iglas, huh? Nice."

"Probably better if you kept that to yourself," I said.

"My lips are sealed," Carpenter said.

"Is there someplace we can put the van where no one will mess with it?" I said.

"Dr. Lennon's garage okay?" Carpenter said. "I can lock the doors after we put it in."

"That'll do," I said. "Where's Dr. Lennon?"

"She's at the pool," Carpenter said. "Waiting for you."

"Seems a little late for a swim," I said.

"You'll get no argument from me on that," Carpenter said. "I've been trying to convince Dr. Lennon to go to a safe house ever since we left you at the crater site, but she just won't do it. At least she let us take her kids and the nanny, Elizabeth Wells, to one, and I finally got Margaret Lennon into one too. Burnette also took Freddy and his family to a safe house."

"I guess that'll have to do," I said.

"You're not upset I couldn't get Dr. Lennon to go too?" Carpenter said.

As Kate was waiting for Dr. Nemo, I knew there was no way Carpenter could have made that happen. 'Need to know' kept me from telling Carpenter that though.

"It would have been better if she'd gone," I said. "But in the short time I've known her, I've found Dr. Lennon to be pretty tough once she's made up her mind about something. I'm sure I couldn't have done any better. I assume you didn't let Burnette know which safe house you took

Dr. Lennon's kids and the nanny to?"

"I did not," Carpenter said. "I figure the less Burnette knows the better."

"Good," I said. "Let's keep it that way too, please."

"Will do," Carpenter said. "Oh, by the way, Manu and Mosi are off duty. Their mom lives in Carson and she's having a birthday party tonight."

"Noted," I said. "Anything else?"

"Not for now," Carpenter said.

"I guess I shouldn't keep Dr. Lennon waiting any longer," I said. "Would you mind helping Adelaide carry Jeff into bed while I hustle on over to the pool?"

Carpenter took a close look at Jeff's sleeping form.

"Why don't you just wake him up?" Carpenter said.

"Trust me," I said. "That wouldn't be a good idea."

"Let sleeping soldiers lie, huh?" Carpenter said.

"That's one way to put it," I said.

Together Carpenter and I unloaded Jeff from the van. Carpenter then grabbed Jeff under his shoulders while Adelaide grabbed his knees.

"You should probably try to get some sleep too, Adelaide," I said.

"I thought I'd join you and Kate at the pool," Adelaide said. "You know, get a few laps in."

"It's likely Kate will want to keep private whatever she has to say to me," I said.

"Look at you getting your panties all in a knot," Adelaide said.

"My panties aren't in a knot," I said.

"How come your face is turning red then?" Adelaide said.

A lesser man might have said that a person with blood all over their face hardly had a right to comment on the state of someone else's red face. I, being no such lesser man, or at least being so incredibly self-deluded that I believed I was not, made no such comment.

"My face isn't turning red either," I said.

"Whatever," Adelaide said. "Anyway, I was just busting your balls. I need some sleep. Besides, I wouldn't dream of interfering with you two lovebirds."

Adelaide raised her eyebrows and grinned in what could only be described as a lascivious manner.

I ignored her.

"Let's get this turkey into bed," Adelaide said to Carpenter.

Adelaide and Carpenter carried Jeff into Kate's house through its two huge front doors.

I made my way to Kate's pool, which was located at the northwest corner of her house. It was close to 1:15 a.m. by then. Dr. Nemo was supposedly due to arrive at 4:00 a.m., which meant he would show himself to Kate in just under three hours. Since we had a less than seventeen hours before war with China commenced, I tried as I walked towards the pool to come up with any kind of constructive, direct action I could take prior to Nemo's arrival that might help stop the war.

I focused on what I could do to either find Dragon Man or somehow bring to light the true nature of the insurmountable edge. I continued to believe that succeeding at one or both of those endeavors was my best chance to prevent the war. At that moment, my phone and Kate's computer were the only tools I had at my disposal to help me determine the true nature of the edge. There was little I could accomplish with those tools, however, in comparison to what Haley's team could achieve using all their technological resources. Thus, the only thing I even considered doing was leaving the estate and driving around for the next two hours and forty-five minutes trying to hunt down Dragon Man.

Which was obviously a pretty stupid idea for two reasons.

One, I had not even the faintest notion of where to begin such a hunt.

And two, if I left Kate's estate in service of that hunt, it was possible something could happen - from a flat tire to an ambush by another contingent of mercenaries - that might delay my return to the estate in time to meet Dr. Nemo.

I decided the best thing I could do was to spend those next two hours and forty-five minutes waiting for Nemo with Kate and try to recharge myself in anticipation of what could potentially be a hellish day to come.

I arrived at the pool. The area surrounding the pool had an un-obstructed view of the Pacific Ocean. The pool itself was about thirty yards long and ten yards wide. The pool was bordered by a deck made of large squares of grey slate tile, and the west side of the pool ended in an infinity horizon that made the pool's water appear to spill into the sea beyond.

A soft breeze coming in from the ocean blew across the surface of the pool and caused the water to ripple and make gentle lapping sounds that mingled with the roar of the surf. Children's float toys - a blow up sea horse, blue whale, and giant ducky - had been pushed by the breeze against the landward end of the pool and rocked back and forth against the pool's collar. Steam rose from a jacuzzi that also sat at that end of the pool.

At the north corner of the pool - the north corner being the corner furthest from the main house - lay a pool house. The pool house had been constructed in the same wood beam and glass style as the main house. The pool house's lights were on, though dimly, and, as the pool house's window shades were up, I could see that the house consisted of three rooms - a large living room, a kitchen, and a bedroom. A big, circular 24-hour nautical time clock mounted on one of the pool house's external beams showed the time to be 01:17 or 1:17 a.m.

The area surrounding the pool seemed to have been designed to be a place of calm, peaceful retreat. It was anything but calm and peaceful that night, however. FBI snipers patrolled the roof of the main house overlooking the pool, and the helicopters circling overhead were creating their own noise and light show. The copters' searchlights made sweeps across the main house, pool, and pool house every few minutes. The searchlights' beams vibrated unsteadily, mimicking the copters' own small, vibratory, up and down and side to side movements that the machines were making as they flew in broad paths through the sky.

Kate was at the pool lying on a wooden chaise lounge. The lounge chair was on the side of the pool closest to the main house. Its back was angled upright at forty-five degrees, and the chair's entire surface was covered with thick maize colored cushions. Kate's upper body was propped against the back of the lounge and she seemed to be focused intently on the pool house. I slowly made my way past a line of a dozen or so chaise lounges identical to the one upon which Kate lay, and sat down on the one next to her.

Kate was wearing a tight, aquamarine t-shirt that flattered her figure and short white shorts with one-inch cuffs that ended at her upper thigh. The loops of the shorts had a silver-buckled brown belt running through them and the belt elegantly accented the slimness of Kate's waist. Kate's tan arms and legs were set off nicely by the clothes, somehow making her arms and legs appear more shapely. Her feet seemed nearly naked, covered only by the barest of thinly strapped sandals. Her blond hair fell softly around her shoulders and her eyes and mouth seemed even more beautiful in the muted glow of the pool house lights. Her gold and diamond heart-shaped pendant hung from her neck, but she wore no other jewelry. She was wearing the same jasmine perfume she had been wearing when I met her the day before.

Kate didn't acknowledge me, just kept staring at the pool house, her look almost trancelike in its concentration. The air was cool and moist, and the night was dark outside the confines of the compound. I felt like the scene had the chance to be quite romantic if I could block out all the FBI activity. But, in truth, romance was not on my mind.

Seeing Kate in the midst of that dangerous war zone-like atmosphere had made me feel both anxious and afraid for her. Seemingly against my will, that anxiety and fear had then suddenly morphed into anger and frustration stemming from the fact Kate had exposed herself to potential peril despite my pleas that she go to a safe house.

Deep down I knew my feelings of anger and frustration were inappropriate and I tried to suppress them. After all, Kate was most likely waiting for Dr. Nemo to arrive, and it was up to her, not me, to decide whether or not she could risk her life in the service of so noble a cause. I'm ashamed to say I did a very poor job of tamping down my feelings, however, and my first words to Kate seemed to almost come out of my mouth of their own volition.

"Feel safe?" I said.

Kate did not turn to me, just kept looking straight ahead.

"Safe enough," Kate said.

"As safe as you felt when you were out at the drone submarine complex?" I said. "As safe as the dark programmers felt in their bunker in Burbank? As safe as your father and your husband felt flying in that Otter to Kodiak Island?"

Kate turned sharply to face me. Her eyes flashed angrily.

"You're being an asshole," Kate said.

I heard what she said, even as I found myself distracted by the delicate movements of her lips.

"I'm worried about you," I said.

"You don't think I realize how dangerous it is out here, Jack?" Kate said.

"I could have handled the meeting with Dr. Nemo by myself," I said. "You should have gone to a safe house."

"What makes you so certain Nemo would show if I wasn't here?" Kate said.

I, of course, knew instantly that Kate had made a very good point, and, upon hearing it, my anger and frustration immediately began to melt away. Normally, I would have been surprised by such a sudden sea change in my emotional state. But given the rather extreme lability of my emotions over those last few days - lability that was almost certainly due to, among other things, Jeff's pointing of the CheyTac at me, my participation in multiple gunfights, being Tasered and injected with elephant tranquilizer, dying, and racing through the burning tunnel on Kanan Dume that was probably as hot as any room in hell - I had already come to accept that, for me, there was a new normal. In fact, since I hadn't wanted to be angry and frustrated with Kate anyway, I took the sudden emotional shift as a welcome, if unexpected, gift.

"Sorry," I said. "You're probably right. I shouldn't be giving you such a hard time."

Kate didn't say anything. She turned back to face the pool house so that she appeared to me in profile. I enjoyed her profile, her elegant chin and nose - all of which, I somewhat guiltily noted, reminded me once again of my beloved Grace. My thoughts of Grace were short lived, however, as I suddenly realized that Kate was looking at the pool house in a way that made her appear as if she was expecting it to do something.

"Is that where Dr. Nemo said he would meet you?" I said. "At the pool house?"

"He didn't say where he would meet me," Kate said.

If Nemo hadn't told Kate where to meet him, then what the hell was she doing out here by the pool in the middle of the night? I was tempted to ask her that question, but, given the tenor of our communication up to that moment, I was afraid anything I might say along those lines could come out as too confrontational. So, instead of where, I shifted to when.

"Nemo just told you the time, then?" I said. "4:00 a.m., right?"

"Nemo didn't tell me the time either," Kate said.

"You *are* the person who sent me the texts that Nemo was coming, aren't you?" I said.

"Yep," Kate said.

"So, if Nemo didn't tell you," I said, "I suppose that means someone else did?"

"Nope," Kate said.

"Is this some kind of riddle?" I said.

Kate rolled her eyes, said nothing.

"Does rolling your eyes at me mean you think I'm stupid?" I said.

A small smile appeared at the corners of Kate's mouth. She turned to face me.

"The truth is," Kate said, "neither Nemo nor anyone else told me anything."

She shifted in her chair, bent down close to the pool deck, extended her arm under the chair, pulled out what looked like some kind of magazine, and handed it to me.

Once I had the 'magazine' in my hands, however, I realized it wasn't a magazine at all.

It was a Christmas catalogue.

The catalogue was titled 'Yuletide Favorites', had a picture of a snowman dressed like Santa Claus on the cover, and was about two hundred glossy pages long.

"Christmas in July?" I said.

"It's still June," Kate said.

"I was thinking about the Preston Sturges movie not the actual month," I said.

"Of course you were," Kate said. "An FBI agent brought it in with today's mail and put it on the kitchen table."

I knew it was standard operational procedure, given the current circumstances, for the FBI to open and inspect anything that would come to the estate. They would, of course, be looking for anything dangerous, and clearly had not considered the catalogue a security risk. Still, a Christmas catalogue in June? That would have raised my suspicions.

"I'm surprised they let this through," I said. "Did Carpenter throw Burnette's team a bone and let them be in charge of screening all mail and deliveries?"

"He did," Kate said.

"Sometimes Ray is too nice a guy," I said. "At least it's better than having Burnette handling actual physical security."

"Look at page 132," Kate said.

I flipped to the page. There was a very professional photograph of a sparkling pool and beautiful pool house, both of them bordered by shimmering palm trees on a bluff overhanging the Pacific Ocean. The sun was overhead, the sky was a brilliant cerulean blue, and the sun's rays spread across the ocean in the distance. A tan, extremely well proportioned, smiling, bikini clad, young woman with long dark hair stood by the pool. She had a tray of pool chemicals in one hand and a net on the end of a long aluminum pole in the other. The byline said, 'Get your pool ready for Christmas'. Under the byline was the name of a company - 'Ao Nang's Pool Service'. It was obviously an ad for a professional pool cleaning service.

There were two things about the photo that instantly caught my attention, however. One, there was a big, circular 24-hour nautical time clock mounted on the pool house in the ad that said the time was 04:00, despite the overhead sun. Two, I recognized the clock since I had just been looking at it. The pool house used in the Christmas catalogue's ad was Kate's actual pool house.

"Do you think the pool girl is Thai?" I said.

"You know Ao Nang?" Kate said.

"Yes," I said. "It's a beach resort in Thailand. I've been there, and it's quite beautiful."

"Paul and I went to Ao Nang too," Kate said. "It was one of the stops on our honeymoon. Paul and I kept our visit to Ao Nang a secret from everyone, so I don't see how anyone else even knows we went there."

One of the FBI helicopters made another flyby. The pool toys rocked, the palm trees rustled, and Kate's hair blew across her face. Kate brushed her hair back with her hand. I looked up at the roof of the main house. An FBI sniper had his eyes on Kate and me.

"I take it the girl in the ad is not your normal pool girl?" I said.

"She's not," Kate said. "And I've never heard of Ao Nang's Pool Service."

"Must be a nice Photoshop job then," I said. "So you think this was sent by someone who's been to your house before, knew Paul well enough so that they might have been told a family secret about your honeymoon, is clever enough to send a Christmas catalogue in June to catch your attention, and is desperate enough to risk trying to communicate the time of their arrival with the obvious time error on the clock - 04:00 being the middle of the night - when the photo was clearly taken in broad daylight?"

"That's quite a summary," Kate said.

"I try my best," I said.

"All that could fit Dr. Nemo, couldn't it?" Kate said.

"It could," I said. "It all could be a plant by someone trying to trick us into thinking it's from Nemo though."

"That's why I like the Ao Nang part," Kate said. "I don't see how our enemies could know about that trip."

"Even Freddy didn't know?" I said.

"No," Kate said.

"Do you have any reason to believe anyone on the estate other than Burnette's agent looked at this catalogue?" I said.

"No," Kate said. "And Burnette's agent looked pretty oblivious as to the true nature of the catalogue when he handed it to me."

"That's not hard to believe," I said, all the while thinking to myself that I certainly hoped the agent was truly as oblivious as Kate thought he was. Otherwise, sometime around 4:00 a.m., we might be paid an extremely unwelcome visit by Pigeyes himself. And if Pigeyes showed up I was pretty sure Nemo would hightail it out of here just as fast as his feet could carry him. Which would, of course, be disastrous. I added, "There's no date anywhere in the photo. What made you think Dr. Nemo was coming tonight rather than tomorrow or the next day?"

"I don't think that," Kate said. "I just figured he could come tonight, so I better not miss him."

"So if he doesn't come tonight," I said, "you plan on being out here Thursday and Friday morning as well?"

"If that's what it takes," Kate said.

"I admire your stick-to-itiveness," I said.

"Is that really a word?" Kate said.

"If it's not, it should be," I said. "In regard to your plans for the next two nights, however, I have some news for you."

"Is it good news?" Kate said.

"It's good news even if it's based on bad news," I said.

"Do you enjoy making my head spin?" Kate said.

"I enjoy looking at your head," I said.

Kate rolled her eyes again.

"Anyway, it's tonight or never," I said. "The Chinese intend to start their war at 6:00 p.m. today, instead of a week from Friday."

Kate looked shocked.

"Are you serious?" Kate said.

"Yes," I said.

"That's terrible news," Kate said.

"Not if we stop them," I said.

"But our chances are much worse since we have so much less time," Kate said.

"Correct," I said.

"You think Dr. Nemo knows about the change?" Kate said.

"I hope he does, because then the odds are much more likely he'll show up tonight," I said. "I'll have a better idea about that though if I can talk to Raj. Do you have Raj's number in your phone?"

"I do," Kate said.

"Will you call him, please?" I said.

"Right now?" Kate said.

"Yes," I said.

Kate took out her phone, looked up Raj's number, and dialed. While we were waiting for Raj to answer, I studied the Christmas catalogue's cover. There was no obvious stamp or electronic mail identifier on it.

"Raj isn't answering," Kate said. "I'll leave him a voicemail."

"Text him too, please," I said. "Tell him we need to know if the war game rules allow sneak attacks, and tell him it's urgent he gets back to you right away."

Kate left a voice message, typed in a text, and put her phone away.

"I think I see where you're headed," Kate said.

"You do?" I said.

"At least one of the reasons you believe that the Chinese insurmountable edge has something to do with NASAD's war games," Kate said, "is that the war games were scheduled to start at the same date and time we thought the Chinese war would commence. However, now that the actual war is starting earlier, you need an excuse for the war games to start at the newer, earlier date and time as well, correct?"

"Correct," I said.

"And if sneak attacks are allowed in NASAD's war games," Kate said, "such an attack could potentially bring those starting dates and times back into alignment?"

"Yes," I said. "That's my theory, anyway."

"What happens if sneak attacks aren't allowed?" Kate said.

"Then that theory doesn't work," I said.

"If it doesn't work," Kate said, "wouldn't that damage your overall theory that the insurmountable edge is related to the war games?"

"Yes," I said.

"Fatally damage?" Kate said.

"Probably," I said.

"What's your backup theory, then?" Kate said.

"Nothing else fits," I said.

"Does that mean you don't have a backup theory?" Kate said.

"Yes," I said.

"You're kidding, right?" Kate said.

"No," I said.

"Shit," Kate said.

"That's one way to put it," I said. "However, I'm sure if we had to, you and I could come up with some good alternate theories. I just don't think we should cross that bridge unless we come to it."

"So we just wait to see what Raj says?" Kate said.

"Or Nemo," I said.

"Oh, right," Kate said. "He would know too, wouldn't he?"

"I would certainly hope so," I said. I showed Kate the Christmas catalogue cover. "There's no stamp on this."

"I saw that," Kate said. "I figured Nemo couldn't risk mailing it because it would be too hard to make sure it was delivered on time."

"I agree," I said. "You think the catalogue was just dropped off in the mailbox and scooped up with today's regular mail delivery?"

"Yes," Kate said.

In the distance I heard barking coming from some of the patrol dogs. I turned in the direction of the sound and saw the beams of the two FBI agents' flashlights shining on the wall of Freddy's house. There was nothing in those beams other than the wall, however, and after a moment the dogs stopped barking and the agents pointed their flashlights at the ground and moved on.

"If that's the case, I guess it would argue that tonight really is the night Nemo plans to come," I said. "Otherwise it would have been dropped off tomorrow or the next day."

"I hadn't thought of that, but I can see your point," Kate said. "What I don't understand is how Nemo got it into the mailbox with all the security around here."

"Neither do I," I said. "I guess we'll just have to ask him when he shows."

Kate seemed to consider something.

"What if after all this time we've been referring to Dr. Nemo as a 'him,'" Kate said, "it turns out he's not?"

"You've circled back around to the possibility Nemo might be a 'her'?" I said.

"Couldn't the girl in the Ao Nang Pool Service ad be Nemo?" Kate said.

"It's possible," I said. "But the Christmas catalogue and the photo seem more like another coded Nemo message. I wouldn't think Dr. Nemo would put an actual picture of him or herself in it."

"I suppose that's true," Kate said.

"Plus I'm privy to information you don't have," I said.

"You're holding out on me?" Kate said.

"No," I said. "I just got here a few minutes ago and I haven't had time to tell you yet."

"Well, are you going to tell me now?" Kate said.

"Actually it's better if I show you," I said.

I put the Christmas catalogue down on my lounge chair and took out my cell phone. I brought Dr. Nemo's face up on the screen, and handed the phone to Kate. She appeared to study the photo.

"I don't think you'd be showing me this picture unless you believed it was Dr. Nemo," Kate said.

"That's exactly what I believe," I said.

"He's very young, isn't he?" Kate said.

"Eighteen," I said.

"What makes you think it's him?" Kate said.

I told Kate everything I knew about Haley's profiles of Dr. Nemo and Billy Einstein, and how the two seemed a perfect match.

"A relative of Albert Einstein, huh?" Kate said. "That certainly would explain why Nemo is so smart."

"It would," I said. "There's also one last thing I haven't mentioned... Billy Einstein was a protégé of Paul."

"He was?" Kate said.

I nodded.

"Let me see the picture again, please," Kate said.

Kate once more studied Billy/Nemo's photo. Her face got a faraway look, as if she was traveling back into the past.

"I don't recall ever seeing this person with Paul," Kate said.

"It might have been useful to us if you had," I said. "But given what Mary Beth said about the nature of Paul's top secret mentoring of NASAD's young geniuses, I suppose it's not surprising you don't."

"Speaking of those young geniuses, I've been afraid to bring it up, but please tell me no really young kids lost their lives in the bunker," Kate said.

"It didn't look like anyone was under eighteen," I said. "Maybe the recruitment program slowed down after Paul died or NASAD hasn't been able to find any kids who were qualified for the job."

"Thank the Lord for small favors," Kate said. "Eighteen is terrible too, but at least when I tell Mary Beth it won't make her feel worse than she already does. She sent me a text about an hour ago and she's heartbroken that she wasn't able to get you in touch with the NASAD vice president of dark programming. Mary Beth thinks if she had, you might have been able to save his life and also the lives of the dark programmers."

"Please tell her that just like you and I discussed, due to the security protocols your father and Vice President Benavidez installed, I don't think there was any way she could have gotten me through to Benavidez," I said. "And even if Mary Beth had gotten me through to him, there's no guarantee I could have saved anyone."

"That's what I did tell her," Kate said. "It didn't seem to help her much. Nevertheless, Mary Beth did get back to us with answers to the questions we asked her. She said she investigated the NASAD employees working on the teams that were supervised by each of the murdered drone sub engineers. She hasn't found anything that would appear to connect the team members to the dead engineers other than the fact that the team members worked for the engineers, and there is nothing suspicious about any of the employees that would suggest they were responsible for the murders. She also says she's had no luck with getting us any additional information on the young geniuses, the dark programmers, or anything to do with our Dr. Nemo anagrams like Omen Road, Ned Mor, or M Drone." Kate paused, then added, "But when we met with Mary Beth, didn't she mention that Paul sometimes brought the young geniuses here to the house?"

"She did," I said.

"Well then Dr. Nemo/Billy Einstein would be familiar with the estate's grounds, wouldn't he?" Kate said. "He might have even gone swimming in the pool."

"He easily could have," I said.

"If he did, it would explain how he was able to make the photo in the Christmas catalogue, wouldn't it?" Kate said.

"It would," I said.

"And if Dr. Nemo/Billy Einstein is familiar with the rest of the estate, isn't it possible he might know his way around well enough to slip by the massive security force that's been installed here?" Kate said.

"I certainly hope he does," I said. I paused. "I actually think he might have slipped by at least once already."

"You're talking about the cell phone I found under my pillow?" Kate said.

"I am," I said. "Also, even though you don't recognize Dr. Nemo/Billy Einstein, I do."

"You do?" Kate asked.

"I saw him," I said. "He was watching us when we were walking by the lake at NASAD yesterday morning. I thought there was something a little off about him, but my feeling wasn't strong enough to actually do anything about it."

"So we could have tried to approach him then?" Kate said.

"We could have," I said, "if I was some kind of god with supernatural mind reading powers."

"You aren't?" Kate said. "Because that's how I look at you."

"Thank you," I said.

Kate handed my cell phone back to me. She leaned back in her chair, closed her eyes, and crossed her legs. Her leg crossing caused her shorts to ride higher up her thighs, baring more skin than I thought I could handle. I don't know why, but it had taken me until then to realize her clothing might be a little inappropriate for the circumstances.

"I hope you don't mind me asking," I said. "But do you always dress like this when you're on a dangerous, top secret mission?"

"I don't know," Kate said. "This is my first dangerous, top secret mission. We'll have to see what I wear next time."

"Hopefully, you'll invite me along," I said.

"I wouldn't dream of doing otherwise," Kate said. "Actually, I'm dressed like this since I thought you'd be back much earlier. I had the cook make a nice dinner for us."

"I'm sorry I missed it," I said.

"Me too," Kate said. Kate's face suddenly transformed. She seemed upset. "Damnit, I must be more stressed out than you think I am."

"What is it?" I said.

"We were just talking about your insurmountable edge theory," Kate said. "I can't believe I didn't mention it."

"Mention what?" I said.

"I looked into the NASAD department that is responsible for updating the live, operational military software," Kate said. "It's awful news but..."

One of the FBI helicopters made a close pass overhead, drowning out Kate's voice. The rotor wash ruffled Kate's hair and agitated the pool's surface. The float toys rocked against the pool's edge. Kate grimaced, and again brushed her hair out of her face. Despite the grimace, something about the way her face looked with her hair completely pushed off it made her look more beautiful than ever. And also more like Grace.

"I didn't hear what you said," I said.

"I said it's awful, but there might be some good...," Kate said.

The FBI helicopter had made a quick U-turn over our heads and once again drowned out Kate's voice. Kate let the copter pass, then said, "I can't take much more of these flybys. That must be the hundredth one."

"How long you been out here?" I said.

"About fifteen minutes," Kate said. "I came out here a little while after I texted you that Nemo was coming." Kate slipped her legs over the side of the lounge chair and stood up. "Let's go in the pool house. It'll be quieter in there and I tell can you everything I learned about the process NASAD uses to update the military's live software systems once we're inside."

"You sure you want to leave your post?" I said.

"You're implying that would be some kind of dereliction of duty?" Kate said.

"Well...," I said.

Kate glanced up at the clock on the pool house.

"We've still got more than two hours until Nemo shows up," Kate said. "You don't really think we need to stay out here the whole time do you?"

"No," I said. "I'm just giving you a hard time because it's fun and I like doing it."

"Were you born a wiseass or did you develop into one over time?" Kate said.

"Ooh, that's a tough one," I said.

"I'll bet," Kate said.

We walked towards the pool house.

"I just thought of something," Kate said.

"Yes?" I said.

"Since we have so little time left before war is supposed to start, is there something we should be doing rather than just waiting for Dr. Nemo to show up?" Kate said.

"I was thinking about that too," I said. "There wasn't anything I could come up with, and trust me I'd do it if there was."

CHAPTER 104

Kate and I entered the pool house living room through the front door. The living room was about thirty by forty feet in size and decorated as expensively and tastefully as the main house. There were three large cream-colored leather sofas with big leather pillows. The sofas were arranged around a giant, dark mahogany entertainment center whose centerpiece was a fifteen foot flat screen television. The room's light was provided by dozens of small, soft spotlights recessed into the ceiling and the floor was made of four foot square, thick limestone slabs. To the right of the living room was a door that led to the bedroom.

The kitchen was a continuation of the living room and maybe half as large, but still big enough to feed an army. The kitchen was separated from the living room by a ten foot long teakwood dining table that had a dozen chairs. The chairs were made of chrome and had brown leather cushions. The kitchen itself had cabinets constructed of deep brown oak and a cherry wood floor. The island in the middle of the kitchen was topped with a slab of aquamarine marble. The refrigerator was a double-door, stainless steel Sub-Zero and the stove was a Viking with eight burners on it.

"I know we've important business to conduct," Kate said, "but if I don't eat I'm going to faint. Can I get you something too?"

"Sure," I said. "How about a nice bowl of clam chowder, followed by a Caesar salad with anchovies, prime rib medium well, and a baked potato with all the fixings?"

"You're making fun of the kitchen, right?" Kate said.

"Well, it is the biggest pool house kitchen I've ever seen," I said.

"It's probably the biggest pool house too," Kate said.

"True," I said.

"The whole place was built to entertain," Kate said. "But since I wasn't planning on having a party, and the cook is off duty now, I'm afraid you'll have to make do with what's in the cupboard."

"That's so disappointing," I said.

"You'll live," Kate said. "Go sit down on the couch and I'll be right back."

I sat down on the couch that was facing the television. I leaned my head back on one of the pillows. I hadn't planned on it, but leaning as I did, my eyes were put at an angle such that I was looking through one of the pool house windows at the snipers patrolling the roof of the main house. One of the snipers noticed I was looking at him. He stopped at the edge of the roof and gave me a thumbs up. I smiled and gave him the finger.

"I kinda like it in here," I yelled to Kate. "Except for the fact I feel like I'm in a fish bowl."

"I can fix that in a minute," Kate called from the kitchen.

There were a number of big coffee table books on the coffee table in front of me. There was one solely dedicated to cheetahs. I picked it up and thumbed through it, mainly because I was curious how someone could make an entire book only about cheetahs. The cheetahs apparently lived in the Okavango Delta in Botswana.

Kate returned from the kitchen with a tray of food and drinks and set it down on the coffee table. She noticed my reading material.

"I bought that book because I was curious how anyone could devote a whole book just to cheetahs," Kate said.

"I was just wondering the same thing," I said.

"Great minds think alike," Kate said. She pointed to some items on the tray. "We have Ritz crackers, smoked oysters, and olives."

The crackers were in a bowl, the oysters in a tin can that needed a key to open it, and the olives in an open jar. The tray also held some forks and napkins, along with two glasses filled with some indeterminate red liquid.

"Hmm," I said. "On second thought, maybe we should go out to eat."

"You know anything that's open at 2:00 a.m.?" Kate said.

"You're the one that lives around here," I said.

"That's exactly my point," Kate said. "And besides, even if there was somewhere for us to go, we'd never make it back in time for Nemo."

I lifted one of the glasses off the tray.

"What's this red stuff?" I said.

"Bloody Mary mix," Kate said.

"Vodka, huh?" I said. "Now we're talkin'."

"No vodka," Kate said. "They're virgin Bloody Mary's."

"You think we need to be sober when we meet with Nemo?" I said.

"I may be drunk, Miss," Kate said, "but in the morning I will be sober and you will still be ugly."

"Winston Churchill?" I said.

Kate nodded.

"Present company excluded, of course," I said.

"Of course," Kate said.

Kate lifted the other glass filled with Bloody Mary mix and clinked mine.

"To finally finding Nemo," Kate said.

"I wish there wasn't a movie by that name," I said.

"It is what it is," Kate said.

"It is," I said.

We drank our tomato juice. Two FBI SWAT agents with German shepherds walked by one of the pool house windows and looked in.

"Didn't you say you could do something about the fish bowl effect?" I said.

"Right," Kate said. "I did. Sorry."

Kate picked up an iPad off the coffee table, swiped it, and tapped the screen. Unseen motors whirred, and blinds rolled down from recessed channels in the ceiling. Within a few seconds, all the pool house windows were completely covered and we were shut off from the outside world.

"Better?" Kate said.

"Much," I said.

Kate sat down next to me on the couch. The scent of her jasmine perfume grew in intensity with her proximity. Kate was so close to me that her bare thigh was touching my leg. I wasn't sure if she realized her thigh was touching me or not, but if she did, I thought it would be rude of me to move my leg away. So I didn't.

Kate handed me the tin can with the oysters in it.

"Can you open this please?" Kate said.

I took the can, removed the key attached to its back, and used the key to peel open the can.

"You did that well," Kate said.

"Thank you," I said.

We ate some crackers, olives, and oysters and when we were done we wiped our mouths with the napkins.

"Well, that was a nice three minute interlude, but I suppose we need to get back to business," Kate said.

"As terrible as it is," I said.

"Yes, it is terrible," Kate said.

"Tell me," I said.

"The young man at NASAD responsible for updating the military's live operational software was Eric Beidermann," Kate said.

"Was?" I said.

"He's deceased," Kate said.

I took in a deep breath and let it out.

"How long?" I said.

"Twenty-four hours," Kate said.

"Don't tell me it was an accident?" I said.

"It was ruled one," Kate said. "But, as you and I know, it probably wasn't."

"What happened?" I said.

"He had a red Ferrari," Kate said. "He wrapped it around a tree."

"How old was Mr. Beidermann?" I said.

"Eighteen," Kate said.

"Can most eighteen year old NASAD employees afford a Ferrari?" I said.

"No," Kate said. "He lived in a small apartment in Oxnard and was driving a Prius up until about six months ago."

It may have been my imagination, but I felt Kate's bare thigh warming up against my leg. I did my best to ignore it.

"Where was he living yesterday?" I said.

"In a five thousand square foot mansion on an acre of land in a gated development in Calabasas," Kate said. "Eric bought it for six million dollars."

"What about the girl?" I said.

"How'd you know there was a girl?" Kate said.

"There's always a girl in these kinds of things," I said.

"Seventeen year old Czechoslovakian model," Kate said. "Quite beautiful. Long black hair, green eyes, petite, big breasts. She was in the Ferrari's passenger seat."

"Dead?" I said.

"Yes," Kate said. "It's all so sad."

"It's very sad," I said. "Hopefully, you and I can keep anyone else at

NASAD from suffering a similar fate."

"God, you don't know how much I wish for that," Kate said. "I'm sick to death about what's happened to so many of NASAD's finest people. I'm not sure I could handle it if anyone else was hurt or killed."

"That makes two of us," I said. "Do you have any idea where Eric got all the money?"

"I do," Kate said.

She took her iPhone out of the pocket of her shorts. She poked at it a few times and a video came up on the phone's screen. Two people were talking together in the video. One of them was a very young man and he was sitting at a cubicle in a sea of other cubicles in a large, open office space. The young man was scrawny, pimply faced, and greasy haired. I could see two big buildings through one of the windows behind him. I recognized the buildings as two of the office towers at NASAD's Westlake campus. I also recognized the man in the bespoke clothes standing next to, talking with, and giving a high five to the pimply faced young man. It was Carter Bowdoin.

"I assume that young guy that Carter Bowdoin is talking to is Eric Beidermann?" I said.

"Yes," Kate said. "When I heard about Eric's death, and learned about his newfound wealth, I instantly recalled what you told me yesterday about Carter Bowdoin. I asked NASAD's head of security, who I know to be discreet, to run our facial recognition software looking for any security camera recordings in which Carter and Eric Beidermann met together at NASAD headquarters over the last eight months. This video is what they found."

"Carter and Eric look pretty chummy," I said.

"Our head of security is also good friends with the local police," Kate said. "The police always give us a heads up if one of our employees is involved in anything that might be of concern to us."

"Wrapping one of their Ferraris around a tree would certainly qualify as a 'concern,'" I said.

"It would," Kate said. "The cops also know most of our work is top secret, so once they cleared Eric's and his girlfriend's deaths as an accident..."

I interrupted, "Though calling it an accident was probably a mistake, as we both just agreed."

"Correct," Kate said. "Anyway, once the police cleared the deaths they sent Eric's cell phone over to our head of security."

"What was on the cell phone?" I said.

"What makes you think we know what was on it?" Kate said.

"Cell phone passwords aren't as hard to crack as they're made out to be," I said. "I'm sure you've got someone at NASAD that could have opened up Eric's phone."

"You're right," Kate said. "And as long as you're such a smarty-pants, why don't you tell me what was on it?"

Kate had turned to me as she said this. Her breast grazed my arm and I got another heady dose of her perfume. Her thigh also seemed to continue to grow hotter against my leg. I had to pause for a moment to gather my thoughts, as, despite my best efforts at gentlemanly behavior, my blood was rushing everywhere except to my brain.

"I would say there would be a recent text or texts to Carter Bowdoin," I said. "Something like 'I need more money', or 'When am I getting that promotion?'"

Kate's cornflower blue eyes grew wide and she squeezed my arm.

"How did you do that?" Kate said.

The more important question was how was I going to remain professional unless I immediately got off that couch and took a cold shower?

"I don't know," I said. "Maybe it's because the kid was eighteen and Carter's a creep. Maybe it's because Carter seems to fancy himself some slick modern dude, but in the end, he's running a very old playbook."

"It is an old playbook, isn't it?" Kate said. "Our security chief also interrogated some of Beidermann's workmates. They told him Eric had bragged about working on some secret project for Bowdoin. I suppose all this goes to support your theory, doesn't it?"

"Yes," I said. "It's now much more likely than not that software containing the dark programmers' war game weapon was inserted into the live military systems. Carter Bowdoin and Mr. Beidermann are clearly the who, why, what, and when of the process that made that situation a reality, even if we don't yet know how Eric did it."

"There's another big part of the 'situation' we also don't know about," Kate said.

"You mean what the dark programmers' software is actually going to do that will justify the Chinese's belief it will provide them with an insurmountable edge?" I said.

Kate nodded.

"The best minds in the U.S. military are working on that right now," I said. "But I'm afraid the only way we're ever going to get the answer to that question is if Dr. Nemo shows up and gives it to us."

Kate checked the clock in the kitchen above the stove.

"Which means we won't know the answer for at least another two hours," Kate said. "I'm not sure I can wait that long. By the way, you do realize you ran off today from the crater site without ever telling me why you suspected Carter in the first place."

"I did, didn't I?" I said.

I then told Kate how I had suspected that Carter had been gambling with the dark programmers well before I had reached the crater. I also told her about Carter's trip to Panama, his presumed relation to Dragon Man, my theories regarding Dragon Man's connection to Chinese defense and engineering companies, the fact that Haley was looking into Dragon Man possibly being a princeling or princessling or one of their children or grandchildren, and about my belief that Carter had known in advance about the attempt on Kate's life at the drone sub complex.

"It's a disgusting scenario, but it makes sense," Kate said. "If the United States wins the war, Pennsylvania Avenue Partners owns a lot of companies that would participate in the rebuilding of the infrastructure in Saudi Arabia. If we lose, then the big Chinese engineering companies - all of which are owned by the relatives of politburo members - would handle the rebuilding. The contract would be in the billions, if not tens of billions, of dollars, and Carter gets a piece of it either way."

"That's how I see it," I said. "But don't forget, there's oil involved too. If the Chinese take over Saudi Arabia, that would be worth trillions to them."

"You think Carter would have a piece of the oil too?" Kate said.

"Why not?" I said.

"Yes," Kate said. "Why not." She paused. "I suppose it's possible, however, that Carter is just trying to buy up more of NASAD. Maybe he thinks that by damaging the company he can get a lower price."

"Carter and Dragon Man's project probably started sometime well before the murders of your father and husband," I said. "Which means it's been going on for at least three years. Can Carter purchase additional shares in NASAD for a low enough price so that his final profit is big enough to justify all that planning, effort, and expense?"

"Probably not," Kate said. "But isn't it a blatant case of treason, at least as far as Carter is concerned?"

"It is," I said. I paused. "I guess it's possible even Carter Bowdoin might draw the line at treason."

"Or not," Kate said.

"I can go with 'or not,'" I said.

Kate took both of my hands in hers and looked directly into my eyes.

"Do you really believe Carter had my father and Paul killed?" Kate said.

"I do," I said.

Kate sighed.

"I know I acted impulsively at the crater today," Kate said, "but now I really mean it. I want Carter Bowdoin dead."

"If I were you, I'd feel exactly the same way," I said.

"I'm sure you think it's too dangerous for me to try to kill him myself," Kate said, "not to mention, that I'd have no idea how to even begin to go about doing it."

"I wouldn't expect you would," I said.

"I'd like to propose a compromise, however," Kate said.

"A compromise?" I said.

"I want to be there when you do it," Kate said. "Promise me you'll make that happen?"

I took a deep breath and let it out. I stared into Kate's eyes. I had expected to see a pleading there but there wasn't any pleading at all. It was more like a demand. Kate's eyes had a hard look, as hard a look as any I'd seen in my life.

"I promise," I said.

"Thank you," Kate said.

She squeezed my hands, then suddenly seemed to notice something about my right hand. She bent forward and looked closely at it.

"You're wounded," Kate said. "You didn't have this when you said goodbye yesterday afternoon. What happened?"

"I'm not sure," I said.

"What the hell does that mean?" Kate said.

"I've been busy," I said. "Could've been a lot of things."

"Tell me," Kate said.

I told her about the assassins at Professor Lennon's house and our run-in with the Kazakhs at the tunnel on Kanan Dume. I'm not sure why I did it - maybe I was showing off - but I threw 'need to know' out the window, and told her about the six Iglas as well.

"You've got surface-to-surface missiles in my garage?" Kate said.

"Yeah," I said. "I hope that's okay."

"In a strange way, it's actually kind of sexy," Kate said.

She looked over at the kitchen clock again.

"We've still got about two hours until Dr. Nemo shows up," Kate said. "What do you want to do?"

"I don't know," I said. "Maybe watch TV?"

"I'm too nervous for that," Kate said. "I need to do something relaxing. Do you know how to dance?"

"Dance?" I said, my voice suddenly hoarse.

"What?" Kate said. "You're acting like you've never heard the word."

"I know how to dance," I said, barely able to speak. "Would you like to dance?"

"I thought you'd never ask," Kate said. "Jazz okay?"

"Sure," I said.

Kate picked up the iPad again. After a swipe and a few pokes the room lights dimmed and Grover Washington, Jr. began to play over unseen speakers. They were very good speakers.

"'Let It Flow' from the 'Winelight' album?" I said.

"I'm impressed," Kate said. "You're very much a man of the world, aren't you?"

"Let's not go too far," I said.

Kate smiled. She stood up, took my hand, and led me to the center of the living room. She then placed my hands on the small of her back, put her arms around my neck, and rested her head on my shoulder. We started to dance. The heightened scent of Kate's perfume alone would have been enough to kill me, but I also had to contend with the fact her breasts were pressed up against my chest and her hair was caressing my cheek.

"You're a good dancer," Kate said softly.

The music kept playing. We kept dancing. 'Let It Flow' moved right into 'In the Name of Love'.

"Other than Adelaide," Kate said, "I didn't see any other women at the ranch."

"It might be a stretch to call Adelaide a woman," I said. "But no, there aren't any."

"No one since your wife died?" Kate said.

"No one long term," I said.

"Me either," Kate said.

"You're saying there's been no one long term since Paul died?" I said.

"No one at all," Kate said.

"That's a long time," I said.

Kate gently shifted her head so that her mouth was closer to my neck. I felt her warm breath on my skin. We kept dancing.

"I tried but nothing was right," Kate said.

"I understand that feeling," I said.

"This may sound stupid...," Kate said.

"Nothing you could say would sound stupid," I said.

"Thank you," Kate said. "The truth is, I had pretty much lost hope that there would ever be anyone that could ever feel right again."

"I know that feeling too," I said.

"But I don't feel that way now," Kate said.

"Because you have hope?" I said.

"I do," Kate said.

"Because this feels right?" I said.

"It does," Kate said. "What about you?"

"I only wish I had words to describe just how right," I said.

Grover Washington, Jr. started playing 'Take Me There'. I slightly lowered my head so that my lips were barely touching Kate's ear. She moaned softly.

"Why do things work this way?" Kate said.

"I don't know," I said.

"Maybe it's fate," Kate said.

"I'd like to think so," I said.

Kate lifted her face to mine. We kissed. Our lips and mouths were full of heat and seemed to have known each other forever. The kiss went on and on. Minutes passed. We danced with our bodies even more closely pressed against each other. Finally, we came up for air.

"I want to do more," Kate said.

"More?" I said.

"You know what I mean," Kate said.

"Right now?" I said.

"Yes," Kate said.

"We don't have much time," I said. "Nemo will be here soon."

"Then we'll hurry," Kate said.

"I don't like to hurry," I said. "Do you?"

"No," Kate said. "But the alternative is worse."

"Yes," I said. "It would be, wouldn't it?"

Kate hesitated for a moment.

"I feel awkward undressing in front of you," Kate said.

"Should we turn off the lights?" I said.

"No, no," Kate said. "That won't help."

"What should we do then?" I said.

"Do it for me," Kate said.

"You want me to undress you?" I said.

"Yes," Kate said. "Start with my shirt."

"Do you have a defibrillator close by?" I said.

"You're being silly," Kate said.

"I'm serious," I said. "You know I just died yesterday morning. I'm feeling like I might do it again."

"Stop it," Kate said. "Take off my shirt."

'Take Me There' rolled smoothly into 'Just the Two of Us'. While Kate kept dancing, I used both my hands to gently grab the bottom of her t-shirt on either side of her waist. I rolled the t-shirt up her belly, chest, and then over her arms and head. When I was done I was staring at her breasts inside a sheer black lace bra. Her breasts were large and looked as firm as they had felt when they had been pressed against me.

"Jesus," I said.

"Get rid of the t-shirt and take off my bra," Kate said. "The snaps are in the back."

I looked down at my hands. I had been so enthralled, I hadn't realized I was still holding the t-shirt. I let the t-shirt fall to the ground and moved closer to Kate. I reached around to her back to undo her snaps. Kate's breasts rubbed against my chest as she danced.

"How do you expect me to concentrate while you're doing that?" I said.

Kate laughed.

"Just do it," she said.

I undid the last snap and moved the straps down off her arms. Kate's nipples were big, erect, and such a light color they were almost pink. I dropped the bra, then unbuttoned and unzipped her shorts. They fell down around her ankles to the floor. Under her shorts Kate had been wearing a sheer, black lace thong. I grabbed its straps on either side of her hips and pulled it down her legs. The tops of her thighs were shapely and toned and the triangle of hair above the gap between them was golden. I kneeled down and lifted each foot, one after the other, so that she was free of the shorts and thong, then slipped off her sandals. I stood back up. Kate kept dancing. The only thing she was then wearing was the diamond and gold pendant around her neck.

"What are you waiting for?" Kate said.

"I like watching you," I said.

"Take off your clothes while you watch," Kate said.

"I feel awkward undressing in front of you," I said.

Kate giggled. She stepped in close to me, quickly undid the buttons on my shirt, then slid my shirt off my body.

"Umm," Kate said. "You have a nice chest."

"Thank you," I said.

Kate kneeled down. She took off my shoes and socks, then reached up and undid my pants button and unzipped my zipper. She pulled my pants down my legs, then helped me step out of them. I was left standing only in my boxers. Suffice it to say, my boxers were not lying flat against my pelvis.

"Looks like someone's been doing a little more than just watching me," Kate said.

"Some things are out of my control," I said.

"I'm shocked," Kate said.

"No, you're not," I said.

Kate laughed and slid my boxers down to my ankles. I stepped out of them. Kate stood and kissed me again. Our naked bodies pressed closely together. The heat between them was nearly unbearable. My senses were so heightened, Kate's perfume nearly overwhelmed me.

"Shall we retire to the bedroom?" I said.

"You first," Kate said.

"You first," I said. "I want to watch you walk."

"I'm self-conscious about my ass," Kate said.

"It's a beautiful ass," I said.

"I'm sure you think so," Kate said. "But, please, you first."

"I have a better idea," I said.

"You do?" Kate said.

"I do," I said.

Before she could say another word, I kissed her, and as I did, I lifted her into my arms. I kept kissing her as I carried her into the bedroom.

CHAPTER 105

Kate and I were lying naked under the sheets of the four poster bed in the pool house's bedroom. The sheets were great - they must have been some kind of 1200 thread count Egyptian cotton or something. Kate had just awakened, having been asleep for a little over an hour.

"Let's do it again," Kate said.

"It's 3:45," I said. "Nemo will be here in fifteen minutes."

"You've been watching the clock?" Kate said.

"Someone had to," I said.

Kate put her hand between my thighs and slid it up between them, not stopping until she got all the way to the top.

"Looks like my new friend isn't worried about the time," Kate said.

"Yeah, well, your new 'friend' doesn't have much of a brain," I said.

Kate giggled, then rolled over, straddled my hips, and lowered herself down onto her new friend.

"Don't worry," Kate said. "We'll be quick."

They were. It was two minutes later, at 3:47, when Kate said, "Shower?"

"As long as I can watch you," I said.

"Did you say 'watch' or 'wash'?" Kate said.

"Actually both would work," I said.

Kate laughed and jumped out of the bed. I watched her run to the bathroom, paying special attention to her ass. Her ass looked as good running as I had predicted it would. By the time I joined Kate in the bathroom, she already had hot water running in the shower. We carefully washed each other, making sure we were each squeaky clean.

By 3:55 a.m. we were both fully clothed and back in our chaise lounges by the pool. There was as yet no sign of Dr. Nemo/Billy Einstein.

The pool toys were still rocking against the side of the pool. Out at sea, the lights of the Coast Guard cutter were rolling up and down with the waves. The two FBI helicopters continued to circle and illumine the night sky. The FBI dog patrols remained on duty.

I could sense the FBI snipers on the roof behind me, but I didn't look up at them. Boys will be boys, and I was sure their juvenile minds had conjured up all sorts of lewd scenarios regarding Kate's and my behavior over the last few hours. Acknowledging the snipers in any way would have only given them the opportunity to bombard me with snarky smiles and obscene gestures, an opportunity I took great pleasure in denying them.

"I'm starting to have doubts Nemo can get through all this security," Kate said.

"Starting?" I said.

"I assume by the tone of your voice that means you've had them all along, Mr. Genius?" Kate said.

"Big doubts, unfortunately," I said. "But I've been hoping Dr. Nemo knows something we don't."

"You mean like something Dr. Nemo, AKA Billy Einstein, might have learned from my husband Paul if Nemo actually visited here while Paul was still alive?" Kate said.

"Correct," I said. "Whatever Nemo's going to do, his options seem pretty limited, though. That's a damn tough swim past the Coast Guard. Nemo certainly isn't going to just drive through the front gate. And no matter how brave Nemo is, I doubt he'd attempt to parachute in."

"The snipers would cut him to ribbons if he did," Kate said.

"They would," I said. "But they'd also cut him to ribbons if they spotted him, no matter what method of approach he chose."

"Maybe we should have told the snipers on the roof of my house Nemo was coming?" Kate said.

"You've changed your mind about who we can trust?" I said. "If you have, we can still tell the rooftop snipers. We could also tell every other FBI agent patrolling your estate that Nemo is coming."

"No, no," Kate said. "We can't do that."

"Yes we can," I said. "We can do whatever we want."

"No," Kate said. "I still don't trust anyone here other than Agent Carpenter."

"Neither do I," I said.

Out of the corner of my eye I suddenly detected movement coming from the direction of the main house. I turned my head. There was a figure rapidly approaching us. The light was dim, and the figure was still far away from Kate and me, but I was pretty sure that its doughy shape and discombobulated walking style meant it could only be one person...

Freddy.

"Kate!" Freddy yelled. "What are you still doing here?"

"Freddy?" Kate said.

"Who else do you think it would be?" Freddy said.

Freddy, breathless, hustled up to us, stopped, and stood between our chaises. He was wearing a rumpled blue suit but no tie, and his right front shirttail hung sloppily over his belt. He wiped away the sweat from his brow with his jacket sleeve. That gesture was annoying enough on its own, but I instantly worried Freddy's presence might produce an extremely bad complication. I considered it highly probable Dr. Nemo would run away if he saw Freddy. I was pondering how to get rid of Freddy - short of grabbing him by the scruff of the neck and hauling him away - when the chances for that extremely bad complication grew frighteningly higher.

Because another figure had just exited the main house.

The figure was momentarily illuminated by the searchlights of one of the FBI choppers as it passed overhead. I could see that the figure was actually a porcine man in full black SWAT regalia, the black pants too short for his legs, the end of the black jacket's sleeves riding up his naked forearms, and the helmet too small for his large head. His legs looked like they were about to give out from carrying his chunky body toward us and I could hear his labored breathing. A Heckler and Koch machine gun was strapped over the man's shoulder, his right hand on it such that it pointed directly at Freddy, Kate, and me - though by his body language the man clearly did not intend to shoot us anytime soon. He was simply lazy and rude, and unfit to be carrying a firearm.

I didn't need to see the man's face to know it was Special Agent Burnette.

I was in a horrible situation. It might have been possible to quickly get rid of Freddy alone, but both Freddy and Burnette together? That seemed an incredibly desperate long shot. To make matters worse, the clock on the pool house said it was then exactly 04:00 a.m. The time of the hoped for rendezvous with Dr. Nemo had arrived.

I knew what I needed to do at that moment was to swiftly come up with a plan to deal with Freddy and Burnette.

But I also realized whatever plan I came up with needed to start with a proper analysis of what the two men's presence by the pool meant in terms of Nemo's potential visit.

Did Freddy and/or Burnette know that Nemo planned to meet Kate?

Because if either or both of them knew, it was likely there would soon be a throng of FBI reinforcements encircling the pool area. An expectation of FBI reinforcements would demand an entirely different plan than one that did not contemplate reinforcements. Developing a plan to deal with FBI reinforcements would of course be an especially daunting challenge...

I was getting ahead of myself, however.

First things first.

Did the men know Nemo was coming?

I began by considering Freddy.

From what I could see, Freddy seemed focused on Kate. Since Freddy was a fairly transparent guy who wore his thoughts and feelings on his sleeve, I was pretty sure I would have seen Freddy make at least a few furtive glances in search of Nemo. I had not seen him make even the slightest glance away from Kate, however. I felt it therefore highly likely that Freddy knew nothing of Nemo's impending visit.

On to Burnette.

I had a hard time believing Burnette would have shown up at the pool alone if he knew Nemo was coming. Wasn't it more likely he would have come with his entire twelve man FBI agent entourage? Or that any additional reinforcements he had summoned up beyond the members of his entourage would have already arrived on the scene?

The answer to those two questions seemed a resounding yes.

Which meant my rapid fire analysis - an analysis that of course could have been completely wrong - had concluded that neither Freddy nor Burnette knew that Nemo was planning on meeting Kate.

With that conclusion in hand, I focused on how to get rid of Freddy and Burnette. It seemed a lot harder task to get rid of Burnette so I considered what might be done about him first. Working as quickly as I could, I came up with four options.

Option one. Kill Burnette right then and there.

Unfortunately, for obvious reasons, that wasn't a viable option.

Option two. Advise Burnette about Nemo's impending visit and tell Burnette the best thing he could do was scram. Which could have worked if Burnette had been a reasonable man and a friend of my current mission.

But Burnette was completely unreasonable, and an enemy, not a friend, so option two was out.

Option three. Shame Burnette for having let Freddy leave his safe house and return to the near war zone-like atmosphere of the estate, then try to get Burnette to talk Freddy into going back to the safe house.

Which wasn't a bad idea except for the fact that I could see no other reason for Freddy to have returned to the estate other than to try to convince Kate to go back to the safe house with him. If I was correct, Freddy's actions were certainly impressive in their level of loving concern for his sister, but the odds of Kate actually going back with him were pretty much zero. Burnette talking Freddy into leaving the estate without Kate, and doing so within a time frame that didn't cause Nemo to bolt, therefore seemed an unlikely proposition.

Option four. Let Kate handle everything and pray Kate could convince Freddy there was no way she was leaving the estate, and that it would be best if he and Burnette got on their way as quickly as possible.

Not a great option, but at the moment it seemed my only option. The option did, however, if successful, have the benefit of getting rid of both Freddy and Burnette in one fell swoop. Which, of course, relieved me of the burden of having to consider any options that focused only on getting rid of Freddy.

I could only hope that Dr. Nemo/Billy Einstein would stick around until option four played itself out, if, indeed, Dr. Nemo wasn't already long gone after seeing Freddy and Burnette come on the scene.

Freddy said, "What's wrong with you, Kate? Don't you realize how dangerous it is here?"

"I thought you were at a safe house, Freddy," Kate said.

Burnette lumbered up next to Freddy. Burnette's entire body was heaving and his Heckler and Koch was pointed at Kate. I reached up and gently pushed the gun's barrel away. Burnette looked down at my hand, then at me, and sneered. I smiled.

Freddy said, "I was at a safe house until I heard you hadn't gone to one too, Kate. Agent Burnette was at the safe house with me, but I ditched him to come get you." Freddy gave Burnette a dirty look. "I guess he figured out where I was headed and decided to chase me down."

Which pretty much confirmed for me that Burnette and Freddy were not there for Nemo.

I was surprised that Burnette had so far kept his mouth shut. What had gotten into the man?

Before I could ponder that question further, however, my mind was overtaken by an image of what might have happened had the chasing down to which Freddy had just alluded continued beyond its current terminus at the pool house.

I saw Freddy's and Burnette's fat rolls bouncing to and fro.

I saw the two men's chests heaving as they gasped for breath.

I saw their chubby legs taking short, choppy steps, until finally those steps shortened and stopped altogether as the both of them keeled over and fell to the ground.

I saw Freddy and Burnette lying on the ground with their faces turning blue and their tongues hanging out of the corners of their mouth.

I suppose that image could have kept playing itself out all the way to its natural conclusion, wherein Freddy and Burnette lay dead on the poolside tiles, but just then I heard Kate responding to Freddy, and I was brought back to the real world.

"It was sweet of you to think of protecting me, Freddy," Kate said.

"I know," Freddy said. He grabbed Kate's arm. "Come on, let's go."

Kate yanked her arm out of Freddy's grasp.

"Your sweetness however does not equate to me going to the safe house with you," Kate said. "I'm staying here."

"Didn't they tell you the terrorists have surface-to-surface missiles?" Freddy said. "They're probably aimed at us right now!"

Burnette said, "Dr. Lennon, what your brother Freddy said is true. The terrorists do have surface-to-surface missiles and it truly would be best if you went to the safe house with us." Then, turning to Freddy, Burnette added, "Freddy, leaving the safe house was a very bad idea. Not only have I had a devil of a time catching up to you, but I can't guarantee your safety if you stay here. We need to go back immediately."

I couldn't believe my ears. Had Burnette really just said that? 'Go back immediately'?

"That sounds like a great idea," I said.

"No one asked your opinion, asshole," Burnette said.

Freddy said, "I'm not leaving without Kate, Agent Burnette."

I noticed movement off in the distance. It hadn't been much, just a slight rustle in the bushes that lined the estate's northern wall about fifty yards from us. The area between the pool house and the northern wall consisted of fairly steeply sloped land. The slope ran down away from the pool house, and there was a ravine at the bottom of the slope. The area had been left to pretty much return to its natural brushy habitat and there were no paths running through it. That brushy landscape would have been as close to ideal as any for someone coming from outside the borders of the estate's property to approach the pool house.

While the area could be viewed by the rooftop snipers and FBI foot patrols, I didn't see any FBI foot patrols moving through the area nor were any of the snipers looking in the direction of rustling I had seen. I knew the rustling wasn't due to the wind since the movement had been confined to just a small section of the shrubbery and the shrubbery surrounding that small section was completely still. I peered intently at that small section, but was unable to see whatever had made the movement. My hunch, of course, was it had been Dr. Nemo/Billy Einstein.

Burnette said, "Dr. Lennon you should come with Freddy and me."

Kate said, "With all due respect, Agent Burnette, your record in regard to my safety hasn't been quite up to snuff."

I said, "You can say that again."

Burnette said, "Why don't you mind your own business, shit for brains?"

"Sticks and stones may break my bones, but words will never harm me," I said.

More movement again caught my eye. This time it wasn't coming from anywhere near the estate's northern wall, but rather from out at sea. In the moonlight, I discerned a line of dark pelicans flying toward us. The pelicans were about a half mile north of us, a hundred yards offshore, and about ten feet above the waves. The pelicans reminded me of the pelicans I had seen from the beach the day before. There was something not quite right about the birds, but I couldn't put my finger on what it was.

Freddy interrupted my thoughts.

"Jack, please this is serious," Freddy said. "Tell Kate she has to come to the safe house with us."

I looked up at Freddy, though in my mind I was still seeing the pelicans. Freddy's face was pleading. There was no anger in it, just concern. But Freddy also seemed strangely distant and far away from me, like I was looking at him through the wrong end of a telescope. Time slowed down, as it had for me many times over the last two days. Freddy spoke again and I saw every movement of his lips, cheeks, tongue, and eyes in ultra-slow motion, as if his face was encased in thick molasses. I couldn't make out his words as they sounded like they were coming off a recording where someone had reduced the playback to one tenth of normal speed.

I turned back to face the pelicans and realized what was wrong.

The pelicans' flight had none of the graceful, soaring peaks and falling valleys that I had seen on the beach before. Their flight line was straight, perfectly flat, and level. No living thing on earth moved like that. It clearly wasn't possible that the dark forms flying towards us could be pelicans. At that moment the forms were only four hundred yards away from the estate. They broke formation, accelerated rapidly, and headed directly for us.

I snapped out of my reverie and got to my feet.

"Kate, Freddy, get into the main house now," I said. "Take cover behind whatever you can find and don't move until I come for you."

Burnette glared.

"I'll give the orders around here," Burnette said.

Kate stood up.

"Shut up Burnette," Kate said. "Jack what is it?"

"No time Kate," I said. "Please. Go now."

Whatever it was, the look on my face, the sound of my voice, the way my body moved as I pointed at the entrance to the house, *something* told Kate to run. She grabbed Freddy's arm and pulled him with her. Freddy went, too startled to resist. As Freddy and Kate moved away from me, it seemed to be as if a primitive tableau was playing out before me, an older sister fleeing with her younger brother, protecting him from the forces of evil.

Burnette was frozen in place, seemingly torn between chewing me out and running after Freddy and Kate.

"Go," I said to him. "Take care of them."

Burnette's eyes narrowed for a moment. He appeared as if he was about to say something - something confrontational and nasty no doubt - but then seemed to think better of it, and quickly ran after Kate and Freddy. I would have gone with Burnette, but there was one more person I was deathly concerned about, and I believed, at least at that moment, that Freddy and Kate would be safe enough in the house without me.

"Billy!" I yelled at the northern wall. "Take cover!"

I turned back to the sky and was instantly consumed by the fear that my exhortation to Nemo/Billy may have been too late to do him any good.

The drones were upon us.

CHAPTER 106

The first drone cleared the top of the estate's seaside cliffs. It was a stealth drone, powered by small jet engines, and its black wings were flat and wide and perhaps thirty feet from tip to tip. A multi-colored flame of orange, red, and yellow suddenly appeared beneath the drone's belly, the flame accompanied by a seething hiss of deadly intent. I knew the shape and color of the flame and the distinctive sound of the hiss could only mean one thing - the drone had launched a Hellfire missile.

I followed the Hellfire's line of flight. It was headed for one of the two FBI helicopters that were circling in the sky above the estate. The helicopter wasn't going to stand a chance. The Hellfire struck home and the chopper exploded in an ear-splitting thunderclap, a fireball of white hot phosphor streaming tendrils of blazing fuel. The concussion from the blast jolted me. I barely kept on my feet. The cool ocean air suddenly became so hot that I felt like I had been thrown into a superheated oven. For the second time that night, the acrid smell of combat burned my nostrils.

I turned to where I had last seen Kate, Freddy, and Burnette running towards the nearest door into the main house. They were lying on the ground about twenty yards from the door and struggling to get up. The blast's concussive force had apparently knocked them down.

Three more black stealth drones crested over the cliff's edge and came right for us. Bullets sprayed from machine guns mounted under their wings, the bullets' tracers appearing like lightning streaks against the black of the sky. I sprinted after Kate and watched helplessly as dozens of rounds tore into Burnette and Freddy. Burnette's bulletproof vest seemed to offer no protection at all, and Freddy's suit coat was cut to ribbons as the two men fell, having barely just risen to their feet. Kate dove back down to the ground at the sound of the first bullets. Miraculously - at least it seemed so then - the bullets missed her by a wide margin as she lay curled in a fetal position.

The three drones banked to the right, then peeled off like fighter planes in a dogfight as they honed in on the FBI snipers on the rooftops of Freddy's and Kate's houses. The snipers fired at the onrushing mechanical birds, but their shots only bounced off the drones' fuselages, the snipers' rifles useless in the face of so lethal an assault. The drones' machine guns fired long sustained bursts and the snipers fell, their bodies shredded.

A dozen or more new stealth drones suddenly came into view as they cleared the cliff. The drones circled the estate, letting loose barrages of rapid machine gunfire. They were hunting down the FBI foot patrols, none of whom would have any hope for escape.

I checked on the last spot I believed Dr. Nemo/Billy Einstein to have been. There was no sign of him. The drones, however, were not firing at the spot and none of them were heading towards it. Was it possible the drones' pilots didn't know Nemo was here?

Staying low, I continued to run towards Kate. Above me, the remaining FBI helicopter raced through the night sky, coming directly at us, making what the pilots must have believed was a last-ditch attempt to protect Kate and Freddy. Somewhere in the back of their minds, the chopper pilots had to be cognizant of the fact that their attempt was most likely desperate and doomed - already doomed by half since Freddy was already dead, though the pilots had no way of knowing that - but they were making it anyway. I admired the pilots' valor. The chopper, however, never got within fifty yards of us. Another Hellfire missile whistled out of the darkness and the helicopter detonated in a caterwauling starburst of molten steel and blinding light. Another concussion wave hit me. I felt like someone had slammed me with a giant steel fist. The searing heat that followed singed the hair on my arm.

I kept moving.

Burnette's body lay in my path to Kate. I bent down over Burnette, pulled his Heckler and Koch MP5 submachine gun from under his body, and draped its strap over my shoulder. Normal protocol would have demanded I check Burnette's neck for a carotid pulse, but there was no neck left to check.

Kate uncurled herself from her fetal position and crawled along the ground toward Freddy. She reached out a hand, grabbed Freddy's shoulder, turned him face up, covered him with her body, and put her lips to his ear.

I joined Kate. Freddy's body was torn, his limbs barely attached to his torso. It looked like nearly every quart of blood that had once coursed through his arteries had drained into a puddle at his side. Despite my unwavering attention on the deadly chaos going on all around us, I found myself feeling sad for Freddy. It wasn't only because he was Milt Feynman's son and Kate's brother, but because I had believed by then that Freddy probably wasn't an evil son of a bitch like Carter and Dragon Man - he had just been dumb and naive. If Milt hadn't been murdered, things might have turned out much differently for Freddy.

"Kate, we've got to get out of here," I said.

Kate was focused only on Freddy. She didn't acknowledge me in any way.

"Kate, we've got to go," I said.

All she said was, "Freddy, talk to me. Talk to me."

The three drones had circled back and appeared to have taken a bead on Kate and me. My only choices were to lift Kate off the ground and make a run for the house or cover her with my body. I didn't think we could make the house in time, so I laid on top of her, the three of us - Freddy, Kate, and I - then sandwiched together. Kate kept asking Freddy to talk to her. It was as if she couldn't see the bloody mass of ragged blood vessels, ripped muscles, torn skin, and leaking fluids right in front of her eyes.

The three drones flew directly over us, but for some reason did not fire. I watched as they banked hard left and up, disappearing into the night sky. Had there been another more urgent target? Or had their pilots simply miscalculated their attack angle? I had no way of knowing, but I had to assume they would soon be back. I needed to get Kate to safety as fast as possible. The question was where did safety lie amid the battlefield that then surrounded us? It was a question for which at that moment, I had no good answer.

Kate must have been stirred by the sound of the drones' jet engines, as she suddenly tried to raise herself on her hands and knees, seemingly not knowing I was on top of her. She struggled, wrenched her head around, and faced me. She appeared to realize only then that I was there. Her eyes had the glassy stare, and her skin the grey pallor, of someone in the incipient stages of shock. When she spoke her voice was hoarse.

"Get off me, Jack," Kate said.

"I'm trying to keep you alive," I said.

"I have to help Freddy," Kate said.

"He's dead, Kate," I said.

"You don't know that," Kate said. "Now get off me."

She continued to struggle. I wrapped my arms around her, held her tight. Kate clawed at my face, elbowed me in the ribs, head butted me under my chin, and then, summoning almost superhuman strength, she twisted and rolled free from me. She was instantly on all fours, her face over Freddy's face. I reached for her again, trying to pull her down flat to the ground where she would be less of a target. She lashed out with her fist and hit me with a ferocious uppercut to the jaw. It stunned me. Kate repositioned herself over Freddy, placed her mouth over Freddy's mouth, and blew air into him. But the air did not reach his lungs, only bubbled up through the bloody pond that was his neck. After four breaths, Kate shifted her position, interlaced her hands, placed her palms on whatever was left of Freddy's breastbone, and started chest compressions.

I had seen behavior like Kate's before on killing fields the world over. Warriors form close relationships with the members of their combat teams, and no matter how highly trained those warriors are, they may at times try to revive a dead comrade, sometimes for hours, no matter how dangerous or hopeless such an attempt might be. In many instances, one had no choice but to let the activity burn itself out. The struggle that might ensue between the desperate, would-be resuscitator and the team members trying to pull him or her off the dead comrade could easily injure both the resuscitator and the team members. I thought Kate's attempt to resuscitate Freddy represented a similar situation to the ones I had seen on the killing fields. But I didn't have hours, let alone minutes, for Kate to become cognizant of the reality of her brother's fate. I was going to have to get Kate away from the open, unprotected area surrounding the pool and into some form of shelter if she was to have any chance of surviving the night.

Suddenly, there was a deafening boom behind me. I turned to see the ocean lit as if by the sun. A pillar of fire rose from its surface to the dome of dark night above. The waves were illumined for hundreds of yards in every direction.

I knew the Coast Guard cutter was gone.

I scanned the sky for the three drones that had killed Burnette and Freddy and had only seconds before seemed poised to let loose with a barrage upon Kate and me. I couldn't be sure it was the same ones, but I spotted three drones above an area that appeared to coincide with the location of the estate's main gate. The tracers from the drones' machine guns showed the guns were raining their rounds down upon the area, their firing both massive and relentless. If the FBI agents at the gate were not already dead, they soon would be. Any news crews that dared to venture across the highway to get a closer look at the action would almost certainly be killed as well.

I decided my best option to save Kate's life was to get her into the main house. I knew the house would, at best, provide only a temporary haven - it would not withstand a missile attack or the collective machine gunfire of two or three drones. But I needed a place where I could think, if only for a short time, and, against all odds, perhaps come up with a plan that would get us off the estate and safely away from the drones.

I began to reach for Kate, intent on doing whatever I had to do in order to haul her into the house. I quickly pulled my hand back, however, when I sensed a danger potentially more acute than the drones.

There was movement in a doorway leading from the main house to the pool.

I positioned myself between Kate and whatever might be coming our way. I whipped Burnette's Heckler and Koch MP5 from my shoulder, clicked off its safety, and raised and aimed it, ready to fire at the spot from which the movement had come.

"First rule," a voice from the darkness said. "You don't aim no gun at a man unless you intending to kill him."

"You're one to talk," I said.

It was Jeff. He was wearing only his Shoemaker t-shirt, a pair of white boxers illustrated with a picture of Ron Turcotte, and his shoes. Turcotte was clothed in Penny Chenery's blue and white checked jockey silks and sitting astride the chestnut Secretariat. One of the Kazakhs' AK-12's was slung over Jeff's shoulder. Adelaide, who still hadn't washed the Kazakh's blood from her face, quickly joined him. Adelaide wore black ninja pajamas, had sandals on her feet, and also had an AK-12 on her shoulder.

Jeff and Adelaide looked up at the sky, watching the drones as they went about their business above and around Freddy's house, circling and diving, looping and rolling, noisily spitting out thousands of deadly rounds. The FBI agents on the ground were returning fire, but the sounds of their weapons were quickly growing less and less frequent.

It was a massacre and there wasn't anything we could do about it.

"Drones over Malibu," Jeff said. "Bet there more than a few Pakistanis who would find that highly ironic."

Jeff gestured with his head towards Kate.

"She don't know Freddy's dead do she?" he said softly.

I nodded.

Adelaide said, "How can Kate not know he's dead?"

I said, "It's complicated."

Jeff said, "Complicated be right. No time for explaining now." He noticed the bleeding scratch on my face. "Kate do that?"

I nodded again.

"Not like it ain't anything we never seen before," Jeff said.

"Or won't see again," I said.

Adelaide noticed Burnette's body lying on the pool tiles.

"That that asshole FBI agent?" Adelaide said.

"Special Agent in Charge Burnette to you," I said. I gestured with my chin towards the estate's northern fence. "I think Nemo is out there."

Jeff looked at the spot to which I had gestured, then up at the sky.

"Drones know Nemo here?" Jeff said.

"Probably not," I said. "None of them have been anywhere close to where I think he is."

Jeff moved his gaze back to the fence and appeared to study the heavy brush that covered the area between it and us.

"How'd Nemo get onto the estate?" Jeff said.

"I don't know," I said. "But, whatever method he used, it must be one only he knows about. Otherwise there's no way he would've gotten by all the security."

"You think maybe he's got some kind of secret passageway?" Jeff said.

"That's as good a guess as any," I said.

"If it good enough to get him in," Jeff said, "it good enough to get him out. Kate too."

"Good point," I said.

"Secret passageway also be having the advantage of being a lot better than your first plan," Jeff said.

"My first plan?" I said.

"Look like you was gonna drag Kate into the house," Jeff said.

"That was only temporary," I said. "I needed a place to think."

"Temporary be right," Jeff said. "Those drones slice you up in there whenever they want."

"I know that," I said.

"'Course I suppose we could call Haley and ask for air support," Jeff said.

"I don't mean to insult you," I said, "but that idea is probably even worse than my idea about dragging Kate into the house."

"Yeah, you right," Jeff said. "That kind of stuff only do any good if it worked out before we need it."

"It does," I said. "There's probably a whole host of legal issues preventing such a thing from happening as well."

"Like those laws forbiddin' military action on U.S. soil?" Jeff said.

"Yes," I said.

"I can see that," Jeff said. "So, what we waiting for? We got a plan. Let's be executing it."

"The secret passageway?" I said.

Jeff nodded.

I was in full agreement with Jeff. Nemo's 'secret passageway' was probably our best option for escape, especially since at that moment I didn't have any better ideas.

We had two problems though.

One, we needed to quickly find out if the presumed passageway actually existed.

Two, if Nemo/Billy could indeed help us, we needed to get him to trust us enough to provide that help.

The best thing would have been if Kate herself could have asked Nemo for his help, but she was lost in her own world as she attempted to revive Freddy. It would only have wasted valuable time if I had attempted to distract her enough to try to get her to understand what I needed her to do.

I turned toward the spot where I believed Nemo was hiding.

"Billy!" I shouted at the darkness. "I know you don't know me from Adam, but I also know you've seen Dr. Lennon and me together. I've got to get her out of here as soon as possible. Do you know a way out?"

There was no response.

I waited another moment, then shouted again. "Billy, if Dr. Lennon stays where we are now, they're going to kill her. If I take her into the house, she's probably just as dead. You showed incredible courage in contacting her about the horrific things going on at NASAD. Don't let your actions go to waste."

Forty yards away, the high brush near the estate's northern fence rustled once more. I cursed under my breath, certain Dr. Nemo/Billy Einstein was going to make a run for it. But a second later, I realized I was wrong. The outline of a head appeared above the thick foliage. It was too dark to clearly discern the head's facial features, but when the person to whom that face belonged spoke, I was - despite the constant gunfire and roar of the drones all around us - just able to make out what he was saying.

"There's a tunnel," the voice yelled.

CHAPTER 107

A tunnel.

Wouldn't a tunnel explain how Nemo had gotten onto the estate? Wouldn't a tunnel also be our ticket out of here?

"Where does the tunnel go?" I yelled back.

"To the other side of the highway," the voice said. "Into the foothills."

"Can we all fit in it?" I said.

"Yes," the voice said.

"Good," I said. "Get back down. We'll come to you and you'll show us the way."

"Do you need me to help carry Mr. Feynman?" the voice said. "It looks like he might be hurt pretty bad."

Obviously Billy couldn't tell from where he was just how bad.

"We'll manage," I said. "Stay out of sight. We need you healthy."

The head ducked back down.

"He's right about carrying Freddy," I said to Adelaide and Jeff. "We're going to have to take Freddy with us. Kate won't leave without him."

Adelaide said, "But Freddy's dead."

Neither Jeff nor I said anything, just looked at her.

"Why are you looking at me like that?" Adelaide said.

Again Jeff and I said nothing. Something seemed to click in Adelaide's head.

"Okay, fine, I get it," Adelaide said. "The fact Kate won't leave without Freddy is the complicated thing you guys said we don't have time to discuss right now."

"Correct," I said. I turned to Jeff. "You and Adelaide carry Freddy and I'll help with the resuscitation."

"Resucita...?" Adelaide began, but quickly stopped herself. "Sorry, I'll keep my mouth shut."

Jeff said, "Sound like a plan to me."

"You don't have to be rude," Adelaide said.

"I weren't talking about you keeping your mouth shut," Jeff said. "I be talking about us carrying Freddy."

I knelt down next to Kate.

"Kate, we have to get Freddy to a hospital," I said. "Adelaide and Jeff will carry him. While we're moving, you keep giving him mouth to mouth, and I'll do the chest compressions. Is that okay with you?"

Kate looked at me, then up at the soaring drones firing their machine guns at the FBI foot patrols. Kate appeared for a moment as if she was confused by what she was seeing, as if somehow she had forgotten about the drones' presence. That moment quickly passed, however, and Kate seemed to come to grips with the gravity of our situation, even if she had not yet faced the fact Freddy was dead.

"Yes," Kate said. "You're right. We need to get Freddy to a hospital."

Adelaide backed up in between Freddy's legs and grabbed his ankles. She hoisted his ankles up so that they were resting on her hips and she was facing away from him. Jeff, facing Freddy, grabbed Freddy's shoulders and lifted them off the ground. Freddy's body then lay flat and face up between Jeff and Adelaide. Kate took my hands and placed them on Freddy's chest.

"Thirty compressions a minute, okay?" Kate said.

"Got it," I said and started the compressions.

Kate blew a breath into Freddy's mouth, lifted her head up, and said, "Everyone please be as gentle as you can," then resumed breathing for him.

With Adelaide leading the way, the four of us set off towards Dr. Nemo's position. The light from the flaming wreckages of the downed FBI helicopters danced in the palm fronds, reflecting back at us with a strange, eerie beauty. The drones continued to circle in the sky and rain down machine gunfire on the corner of the estate opposite to us. The drones appeared preoccupied with their task even though I no longer heard any return fire. Though the drones had not come back for us yet, I had little doubt it was only a matter of minutes, if not seconds, before they did.

The fact that Dr. Nemo had been hiding in a spot about forty yards from us also put him about fifteen yards above the bottom of the ravine that ran parallel to the northern fence line. We wanted to get to him as soon as possible, but it was going to be a tough go. The hillside between him and us was steep and covered by dense growths of California sagebrush, buckbrush, deerweed, chapparal broom, saltbush, and other native vegetation. Some of the plants were as much as five feet tall and just as wide.

After about two minutes - but which felt much longer - of shoving our way between gaps in the brush we reached the spot where I thought I had seen Nemo. He came out from under a big California sagebrush plant and joined us. He had a black hoodie pulled over his head, but I recognized the handsome, angular face from Haley's photograph. Nemo's jeans, socks, and running shoes were also black. Adelaide, Jeff, and I all took a close look at him, but Kate never took her eyes off of Freddy.

"Dr. Nemo, I presume?" I said.

"Yes, sir," Billy Einstein said.

"May I call you Billy?" I said.

"Yes, sir," Billy said.

"I'd shake your hand, Billy, but as you can see I'm somewhat preoccupied at the moment," I said, continuing the chest compressions.

Kate, surprisingly, must have been paying attention to our conversation.

"Go ahead and shake his hand Jack," Kate said. "I'll take over everything from here. You stay close to Billy and keep him safe."

"You sure about that?" I said.

"I'm sure," Kate said.

"Okay," I said. I stopped my compressions, stepped away from Freddy's body, and shook Nemo's/Billy's hand. "Billy, I'm certain you know that was Dr. Lennon who just spoke, and also the person we are working on is Mr. Freddy Feynman, but I'd like to introduce you to..."

"I've been studying your history ever since I saw you at NASAD, General Wilder," Billy interrupted. "And I know who your comrades are, sir. That's General Jeffrey Bradshaw, and the young woman is Adelaide Monroe."

Adelaide and Jeff gave Billy a quick nod.

"Well done," I said. "Can you show us the way out of here?"

"Yes, sir," Billy said. "We have to go down into the ravine. About a hundred and fifty yards up the hill is a drainage pipe. The entrance to the pipe has a false front that makes it looks like a person would never fit into the pipe, but when you push the front aside, you can see there is actually plenty of room. The pipe goes under the Pacific Coast Highway and exits on the highway's other side. I used the pipe to get onto the estate without being noticed."

"Paul Lennon showed the pipe to you?" I said.

"Yes, sir," Billy said.

"Lead the way," I said.

Billy appeared to have become distracted and didn't immediately do as I had requested. I assumed the reason for his distraction was, that even though Billy had been intermittently looking over in Freddy's direction, he seemed to have just noticed how shot up Freddy's body was, and he was most likely wondering why Kate was bothering to try to resuscitate Freddy. When Billy finally looked away from Freddy, it was Adelaide who caught his eye. Adelaide gestured her chin towards Kate, then signaled Billy by shaking her head and mouthing a silent 'Shhh'. He nodded in reply and returned his attention to me.

"Follow me," Billy said.

Billy led us down towards the bottom of the ravine. I stayed close to Billy. Adelaide, Jeff, and Kate, along with the lifeless Freddy, were right behind us. The ravine wended its way west to the ocean, but to the east it went up the hill towards the tunnel that was Billy's secret passageway. As east was where we needed to go, that's the direction Billy turned when we reached the ravine's bottom. The fence that ran along the northern boundary of Freddy and Kate's estate was then high above our heads to our left, and the rest of the war zone-like estate was above us to our right.

The ravine's bottom was a dry, narrow creek bed. It was lined on both sides by sharply sloping, brush-covered hillside, and moved in a zigzag, switchback pattern up the steep climb to the highway. The surface of the creek bed was strewn with dead branches, fallen leaves, and stones that ranged in size from small pebbles to medium-sized boulders. Most of the branches and stones were loose, which made the footing very unstable.

Our goal, of course, was to get to the tunnel as quickly as we could. If sprinting up the hill had been a viable option, that is what we would have done. But rapid movement was impossible due to the branches and stones, the steep, narrow, switchback nature of the creek bed, and the dense, encroaching brush. I estimated it would take us at least five to six minutes to get to the tunnel.

Adelaide and Jeff must have been tiring from carrying Freddy's body up the hill, but neither of them said anything. Behind us, the night sky continued to be lit up by the burning carcasses of the FBI helicopters and the Coast Guard cutter. The cutter's burning fuel had spread over the surface of the sea and the flames danced across the waves. The air remained alive with the harsh clatter of machine gunfire. For whatever reason, the drones still seemed to be paying us no heed.

"Billy, I hate to say this, but there's a good chance one or all of us won't survive the night," I said. "Operationally, it would be a good idea to give me the password to the file you sent Dr. Lennon."

"I'm sorry sir, but it's not that simple," Billy said. "There's a number of steps we have to follow and more than one password."

"Okay," I said. "What's the first step?"

"Does Dr. Lennon still have a copy of the file I sent her on her phone?" Billy said.

"You don't have a copy with you?" I said.

"No, sir," Billy said. "I thought it safer if I didn't have a copy in my immediate possession in case I was caught."

Billy's decision to keep the file out of his immediate possession seemed a reasonable one. I wasn't too worried about his decision at that moment either, as between Kate, Haley, and myself, there were already multiple copies of the file, one of which was on my phone.

"I don't think now would be a good time to ask Dr. Lennon for her phone, since as I'm sure you've already noticed, she's a bit preoccupied," I said. "I've got a copy of the file on my phone, though. Let's use it instead."

"Sorry, sir," Billy said. "It has to be Dr. Lennon's phone. The file transfer can only be accomplished after Dr. Lennon uses her fingerprint on her own phone."

"You're saying we can't use any other file or any other phone?" I said.

"That's correct, sir," Billy said. "Dr. Lennon's phone is the only phone that can initialize the file in such a manner that it can be used."

I stumbled on a loose boulder and grabbed the branch of a small scrub oak to keep from falling. I gave a quick look around after I'd regained my balance. The drones continued to fire at everyone but us. It seemed like only a matter of time, however, until we would become the focus of their attention. I didn't want to interrupt Kate from what she was doing with Freddy's body, but, with so few hours left before China was set to begin its war, the sooner I got Nemo's/Billy's file decoded and up and running the better.

"I'll go ask Dr. Lennon for her phone," I said.

I turned away from Billy in order to ask Kate for her phone, but Billy grabbed my arm and pulled me towards him.

"Sorry, sir, but we might as well wait until we get to my car before you do that," Billy said.

"Why is that?" I said.

"I have a special patch cord in the car," Billy said. "After the file on Dr. Lennon's phone has been initialized, we need the patch cord to effectuate the transfer of Dr. Lennon's file to my phone. After the transfer, I can process the file so that it can be used to deactivate the war games software all of us in the dark programming division helped produce."

"It can't be done wirelessly?" I said.

"As you know, sir, anything wireless can be hacked," Billy said. "A physical connection is the only safe way to go."

"How far away is the car?" I said.

"About five miles north of here," Billy said. "I hid it in the brush in the hills and walked to the estate."

Billy had walked a long way but I didn't believe we would have to walk back to his car. Once we got through the tunnel to the other side of the Pacific Coast Highway, I could call someone to arrange transportation to the car and we could travel as soon as it was safe to do so.

Of course, *when* it would be safe to travel was a big question mark. As I was then preoccupied with getting us into the tunnel, I really couldn't afford to give that question much thought at that moment. However, I didn't think the drone attack could go on forever without some kind of intervention from forces friendly to our side. Maybe Haley and Hart would find some sneaky way to get around the laws preventing military action on U.S. soil? Maybe the FBI had some kind of arrangement with the Air Force? In any event, it seemed likely to me the drone threat would be resolved with plenty of time left for us to get to Billy's car, use his patch cord to deactivate the insurmountable edge, and derail China's war plans.

"I assume you left the patch cord in your car since, like the file, you didn't want it in your immediate possession if you were caught?" I said.

"Correct, sir," Billy said. "I also felt that if Dr. Lennon and I made it back to my car without being apprehended, it would be as good a confirmation as any that we could safely use the file together and not have it fall into the wrong hands."

I smiled.

"There was a little more to it than that, wasn't there?" I said.

"Sir?" Billy said.

"If Dr. Lennon was with you at the time the file was activated it would provide a certain amount of cover for your actions," I said. "It would help mitigate the concerns you touched on in your voicemail to her about violating your security oath."

"Yes, sir, that was definitely a component of my decision making," Billy said. "Another component of course was the fact I knew you were working with Dr. Lennon. I felt confident she had found someone in the military who would know what to do with the file."

A dog howled in the distance, then suddenly went quiet. There was another loud explosion and I thought it possible that the gas tank of one of the FBI's vehicles had ignited. Three drones flew over our position and kept on going.

"I definitely know what to do with it," I said. "As soon as we get it decoded, I'll send it to a genius woman military officer who is hiding out in a NORAD bunker right now. The Chinese won't stand a chance once it's in her hands."

"That's good news, sir," Billy said.

We slowed down for a moment as our path suddenly became much more difficult to navigate. The brush lining the creek bed was tightly encroaching from both sides, leaving a gap that was at most two feet wide. The bed had also gotten very steep so that it was almost like we were climbing a set of stairs. When we got through that section both Billy and I were breathing very hard. We stopped for a moment and waited as Kate continued to administer cardiopulmonary resuscitation while Adelaide and Jeff carried Freddy's body through the section. We moved on after everyone had cleared the section.

"What happens after the transfer of the file to your phone?" I said.

"I will activate a multilayered security system that requires the simultaneous use of my phone, my fingerprints, and an Enigma app," Billy said.

"There's actually an app that mimics an Enigma machine?" I said.

"There is, sir," Billy said.

Will wonders never cease?

CHAPTER 108

All of us kept marching, shoving aside any brush that blocked our way and stepping carefully between the stones of the creek bed. The flames from the burning FBI choppers and Coast Guard cutter continued to light up the night sky. The breeze coming in from the ocean had stiffened and the air was full of the smell of burning fuel. There was a continuous cacophony of machine gun bursts from the drones.

"How does the Enigma app work?" I said to Billy.

"Once I unlock the file on my phone with two of my fingerprints," Billy said, "I then use another fingerprint to generate the key for the Enigma app. The Enigma app will then use the key to decode the file and we can use the file."

"You originally coded the file with the Enigma app?" I said.

"Yes, sir," Billy said. "I modified the app itself so that it has ten to the fourteenth times the number of combinations that an Enigma machine has."

"That's ten to the fourteenth times ten quadrillion, right?" I said.

"It is," Billy said. "But don't ask the name of the number as I haven't got a clue."

"Damn," I said. "I was beginning to think you knew everything."

Billy laughed.

"I definitely don't, sir," Billy said. "Ten to the fourteenth times ten quadrillion combinations are so many combinations that there's no computer in existence that can crack the code. Not yet anyway."

"I'm sure you're right about that," I said. "My team has the best decryption specialists on earth and they have access to as many supercomputers as they need. They haven't even come close to cracking your code."

We passed the the halfway point of our journey up towards the Pacific Coast Highway. The top of the ravine and the entrance to Billy's secret passageway were then about seventy-five yards away from us. I checked on Adelaide and Jeff. They both appeared to be struggling a bit under the weight of Freddy's body. Adelaide tripped on something on the creek bed floor but quickly regained her balance. Kate was still compressing Freddy's chest and intermittently blowing air into his mouth.

"So Billy, you need your fingerprints from three different fingers in order to completely unlock the code?" I said.

"Yes, sir," Billy said.

"Which fingers are they?" I said.

Billy appeared momentarily taken aback, but then his expression changed to one of understanding.

"In case I don't survive you intend to harvest them, sir?" Billy said.

"You put it more bluntly than I would have," I said, "but, yes."

"Right index followed by the right thumb unlocks the file," Billy said. "Left little finger is the password for the Enigma app."

I smiled.

"I guess the fastest thing for me to do would be to just cut off both your hands then," I said.

"If you say so, sir," Billy said, smiling in return. "If I'm dead I won't need them anyway."

A cell phone rang inside of Freddy's jacket. Adelaide and Jeff maintained their steady forward progress with Freddy's body, but Kate momentarily stopped blowing air into Freddy's mouth. Kate, her hand moving slowly, as if under some automatic, unconscious control, reached into Freddy's jacket breast pocket and took out the ringing phone. Kate looked at the phone, appearing both confused and worried, as if wondering how she was going to get Freddy to take the call.

"Hello," Kate said, answering the phone. "Hello. Who is this?"

She listened for a moment, pulled the phone from her ear, studied it, then put it back against her ear. She seemed frustrated.

"Say something," Kate said into the phone. "If there is someone there, say something."

Kate grimaced, then ended the call and slid Freddy's phone into her pocket. I was curious as to who was calling Freddy at 4:15 in the morning. I didn't think it was a good question to ask Kate just then, however, and decided to talk with her about it later.

I checked the sky. The drones still appeared to have no interest in us.

"So once the file is unlocked, what happens?" I said to Billy.

"Your team will need to send the file to every military device currently running NASAD's software," Billy said. "The file's software coding will deactivate the war game weapon immediately upon receipt."

"You do realize the software containing the dark programmer's war game weapon has probably already been inserted into every military device currently in service?" I said.

"I'm sorry, sir," Billy said. "I never thought in a million years that could happen."

"I understand that," I said. "But you agree that it has probably happened at this point?"

"Yes, sir," Billy said. "It's probably happened. I've been thinking that way ever since I learned two weeks ago that Carter Bowdoin had become friendly with Eric Beidermann."

"The man at NASAD responsible for updating the live software systems?" I said.

"Yes, sir," Billy said. "Eric is dead now."

"He is," I said. "News must travel very fast within NASAD."

"Almost as fast as the speed of light, sir," Billy said.

As fast as the speed of light...

I suddenly had an idea about how whoever was controlling the drones knew that Nemo/Billy might be at Kate's estate that night.

"Billy, did you call Eric Beidermann to confirm your suspicions about the software with your war games weapon getting into the live military computer systems?" I said.

"I did, sir," Billy said. "Eric wouldn't outright admit that he'd uploaded the weaponized software into the live systems, but I could tell from the way he hemmed and hawed that he had."

"Did you identify yourself to him?" I said.

"I had to, sir, otherwise he wouldn't have spoken to me," Billy said. "I told him I was a dark programmer, and I gave him my name."

Our progress was slowed again as our path along the creek bed once more became very steep, and almost completely blocked by the encroachment of thick deerweed and tall buckbrush. I checked on Adelaide and Jeff. Carrying Freddy's body through the narrow gap in the brush seemed especially difficult for them but they were making steady progress. Somehow Kate had remained at Freddy's side and was continuing her efforts at resuscitation. Below us the flames from the cutter continued to reach over a hundred feet into the sky. Another dog howled.

"What day did you call Eric?" I said.

"Last Friday," Billy said.

"The same day you called Dr. Lennon and left her a voicemail, correct?" I said.

"Yes," Billy said. "But I used a burner phone to call both Eric and Dr. Lennon. I threw it away right after I spoke to Dr. Lennon. Did I do something wrong?"

"Let's not go there right now," I said. "Why did you contact Dr. Lennon instead of asking the NASAD vice president of dark programming for help with your concerns?"

I purposely hadn't used the vice president's real name, Rick Benavidez. Again, I doubted Billy, or any of the dark programmers, would have known Mr. Benavidez by anything other than a code name, and that wasn't the moment to get into a discussion with Billy regarding the vice president's true identity.

"Well, sir, the vice president was a great man, but he was also a very cautious and precise man," Billy said. "He would have wanted me to be able to fully verify all my suspicions before he took any action. There was no way I could do that in the time I felt I had left, so I looked for another way to deal with the problem."

"That was a pretty gutsy call on your part," I said. "But I also think it was the right decision. Did any of the other dark programmers also suspect that the war games software might have been weaponized for use against our own military?"

"I wasn't aware of anyone else," Billy said. "But I didn't share my thoughts with anyone else either."

"Was that because you didn't know who you could trust?" I said.

"Yes, sir," Billy said. "Everyone seemed obsessed with the amount of money we might win on the bet against the defensive team. It was the only thing they seemed concerned about."

"That's not surprising," I said. "Now, you weren't in the bunker when the other dark programmers were killed..."

"That was horrible, sir," Billy said.

"It was," I said. "But if you weren't there, where were you?"

"Since Friday, I've been staying in a hotel up in Oxnard," Billy said. "I wanted to be close to Dr. Lennon in case she tried to get in touch with me."

"I assume you also didn't want to be found by anyone who might be looking for you?" I said. "You probably paid cash for the room, only used burners for other calls, that kind of thing?"

"I did," Billy said. "I was trying to be careful in case somehow I had come under suspicion after calling Eric. No one knew where I was."

I stepped awkwardly on a loose boulder. I stayed upright despite badly twisting my ankle. My ankle throbbed with a dull pain, but I didn't think it was sprained. It wouldn't have mattered if it had been though. We had to keep pressing forward.

"Did you drive your own car to the motel?" I said.

"Yes, but I only paid cash for gas," Billy said.

"Which was smart," I said. "But the problem is the car itself."

"It is?" Billy said.

"I think so," I said. "Here's what probably happened. There are some very bad people out there who have figured out a way for the Chinese to use your war games weapon to attack the U.S. military. Those people have access to extremely sophisticated technology - including surveillance technology - and they were monitoring Eric's calls. When you identified yourself to Eric, those bad people became very worried that you might be able to disrupt China's war plans by interfering with the ability of the Chinese military to use your and the dark programmers' war games software. Those people then started listening in on your burner phone and heard you talking to Dr. Lennon. They've been after you and Dr. Lennon ever since. I think they found you by tracking down your car."

"But how could they do that?" Billy said. "I threw the burner away."

"Where did you call Eric and Dr. Lennon from?" I said.

"From my apartment," Billy said.

Three drones banked sharply over our heads. Their jet engines made a thunderous roar and their machine guns spit fire at a target somewhere near the center of the estate. Tracer bullets rose up from the ground, I assumed from the rifle of one the FBI agents. The bullets had no effect on the drones that I could discern, but I nonetheless appreciated the valiant effort of the agent.

"In Northridge?" I said.

"Yes, sir," Billy said.

"Like I said, you're up against people with very sophisticated technology," I said. "They probably hacked into every surveillance camera surrounding your apartment and started looking for your car. Most businesses and a lot of homes have those cameras. I'll bet there are dozens of cameras between your apartment and your motel in Oxnard that are good enough to read your license plate. There's a good chance they even used satellites to look for your car. The only things that have probably kept you alive up until now are, one, that it must have been a brutal process to find and then hack into those privately owned surveillance cameras, and two, that even if they did use a satellite, they would have had to search thousands of square miles."

Billy tripped on a branch in the creek bed. The branch was brittle and it broke with a loud snap from the force of his forward movement. I caught Billy's arm before he fell.

"Thank you, sir," Billy said.

"You're welcome," I said. "My guess is that the people looking for you would have gone after you as soon as they found you, however. Given the fact we're under assault at this very moment, that says to me they didn't find your car until tonight when you left it up the road and headed here."

"I didn't think of any of that," Billy said.

"Next time you'll do better," I said. "By the way, how did you get from Oxnard to NASAD without being detected the day you saw Dr. Lennon and me at the lake?"

"I took the bus and walked," Billy said. "I figured that was the safest thing to do. I got back to Oxnard the same way."

"Low tech, but a good move," I said. "Now, one more thing. If even a small part of you believes that anything that happened to the dark programmers in the bunker is your fault, it's not. I'm convinced Bowdoin and his cohorts, in order to cover their tracks, intended to kill not just you, but all the dark programmers."

"I hate to put it this way, but that makes me feel better," Billy said.

"Good," I said. "Not that it really matters, but I've also got a hunch that Bowdoin and his cohorts, since they couldn't find your car, were probably hoping against hope that you'd slipped by them somehow and were in the bunker when they killed everyone else."

"That would have made their lives easier, I suppose," Billy said.

I was momentarily taken aback. Billy's response was not what I had expected.

"You've got a cold-blooded streak in you, don't you?" I said.

"I hope so, sir," Billy said.

I laughed.

"Billy, you're my kind of guy," I said.

We had about fifty yards to go to get to the top of the ravine. The climb was still steep and Billy and I were breathing heavily. The brush behind us obscured Adelaide, Jeff, Kate, and Freddy, but I could hear labored breathing coming from their direction as well.

I checked the sky again. It was lit up even brighter than before by the raging flames consuming the FBI choppers and the Coast Guard cutter. The drones, however, were still ignoring us. Which seemed incomprehensible to me. I thought we would have been by far their most important target. Had something gone haywire with whatever battle plan they were executing? Whatever was going on with them, our best option - and as far as I could see, our only option - continued to be to get to Nemo's secret passageway before the drones began hunting us anew.

"Let's get back to Beidermann," I said to Billy. "After you heard about the relationship between Carter Bowdoin and Eric Beidermann, you programmed your deactivation file and decided to contact Dr. Lennon, correct?"

"Yes, sir," Billy said. "It took longer than I thought to program the file. Also, it took a while for me to work up a plan to approach Dr. Lennon that I didn't think would put her in danger."

I thought to myself, 'Well you can see how well that plan worked'. But, of course, I didn't share that thought with Billy.

"Why did you choose Dr. Lennon as your contact?" I said.

"I knew her husband, Paul Lennon, very well and would have trusted him with my life," Billy said. "During all my time at NASAD, I have never known Dr. Lennon to be anything other than an honorable, upfront person. She also, as you know, has a very powerful position within the company. Dr. Lennon was the only person I felt I could approach that I could trust to both understand my situation and keep me safe. I thought if I could to explain to her what had happened, she might have the power to clear the way for me to run the file. I couldn't risk running the file without such clearance, since the software code in the file could be viewed as extremely dangerous and disruptive. If the military didn't know why I had developed the code, my intentions could have been taken the wrong way, and I might have been considered a threat."

"Which could be bad," I said.

"I didn't want to be executed, sir," Billy said.

The brush thinned out and our path through the creek bed widened again. We began to make better progress up the hill towards the passageway. Two dogs barked somewhere far away from us. More tracer bullets rose up from a location that seemed to be close to the center of the estate. I followed the bullets' skyward phosphorescent paths but could not see any sign of their target. The breeze gained in force, and the smell from the fumes of the burning choppers and cutter became stronger and more pungent.

"That's understandable," I said. "I assume the reason you decided you had to come to the estate to see Kate today was because the war with China will commence at 6:00 p.m. tonight?"

"Well sir, I wasn't aware of the actual date or time that the war with China would start," Billy said. "However, since tonight at 6:00 p.m. is exactly when the war game software the dark programmers and I designed was going to launch its attack and begin the NASAD war games, I thought there was a high likelihood that the Chinese's real war could commence at the same time. I felt if I was going to do anything about stopping the war, it was pretty much now or never."

"That's also understandable," I said. "Is your software completely inactive until it launches its attack? All systems would appear to be functioning normally to the defensive team in the NASAD Cyber Defense Hall?"

"Yes, sir," Billy said.

"And as the NASAD war games are actually scheduled to begin a week from Friday, by programming your war game software to turn on tonight, you were essentially programming a sneak attack, correct?" I said.

"Correct, sir," Billy said.

"Are sneak attacks allowed under the NASAD war game rules?" I said.

"I've never seen anything that says you can have a sneak attack," Billy said. "But, then again, I've also never seen anything that says you can't."

"Just like you've never seen anything about whether you can or can't alter the copy of NASAD'S software you were given to study for the war games, and then substitute that altered copy for the version of the software the programmers in the Cyber Defense Hall expected to be defending during the war games?" I said.

"Exactly like that, sir," Billy said.

I smiled.

"I like the way you think, Billy," I said.

"Thank you, sir," Billy said.

"For my own peace of mind, will you also please confirm that my thinking about what you were up to has been correct, that that is what you planned to do?" I said.

"Sir?" Billy said.

"You were going to substitute the altered copy?" I said.

"Yes, sir," Billy said.

"Thank you, I said. "So, what portion of the U.S. military computer systems did your war game software target? And whatever you do, please don't tell me it has anything to do with the drone subs."

"Drone subs, sir?" Billy said.

"Your code name," I said. "Dr. Nemo. Like in 'Twenty Thousand Leagues Under the Sea."

"Wasn't Nemo a captain, sir?" Billy said.

"Yes, he was," I said.

"My code name isn't spelled the same way," Billy said. "It's Nimo with an 'I.'"

"With an 'I'?" I said. "Not an 'E'?"

"Yes, sir," Billy said.

A chill ran down my spine as something started to click in the back of my mind in regard to that 'I.' Whatever that something was, it was just out of reach, and before I could explore it any further, another wave of drones appeared, again seemingly from out of nowhere. I assumed the drones must have swooped low along the hillside to the east, where despite the light of the moon, they would have been nearly impossible to see. There were six of them and they were headed right for us. There was a malevolent elegance to their flight, as they soared wingtip to wingtip at the perfectly calculated altitude for the job they had at hand. Below their wings the drones carried not rockets, or machine guns, but something far worse.

That something far worse was canisters.

I'd been briefed on those canisters and knew what they most likely contained. The canisters were made in Russia and I certainly never expected to see the canisters mounted on NASAD drones that had been made in America. American drones were never meant to carry such canisters. The U.S. military would never countenance the use of what was in those canisters on any battlefield anywhere, or at any time.

The canisters and their contents would not be used by the U.S. even if our troops were facing the most dire consequences. As to how the canisters came to be mounted on the drones, I had no clue. But our enemy had already proven their ability to obtain Russian-made Iglas, and if they could get Iglas, then it wasn't a stretch for me to assume they could obtain the canisters as well.

Adelaide and Billy stared at the drones, frozen in their tracks like deer caught in the headlights. Both of them must have had no idea about what was going to happen next, let alone what to do when it did.

Jeff and I had stopped too. But only long enough to identify the threat.

And that took less than a second.

The two of us turned away from the sky and looked at each other, almost as if our moves had been choreographed. Jeff, like I, knew what was coming at us, knew the canisters below the drones' wings were filled with gas, gas from which there was no escape.

Jeff, like I, knew the situation was hopeless.

Jeff, like I, knew that we were still going to give it a try.

"Sorry," I said to Billy.

I scooped him off the ground, laid him across my back, his chest on my shoulders, his left side facing up, and then, after hooking my left arm under his left knee, grabbed his left forearm with my left hand in a classic fireman's carry. Jeff dropped Freddy, shoved Adelaide aside, grabbed Kate, and had Kate over his shoulder in the same position I was using for Billy before Kate had time to protest or respond in any way.

The entrance to Billy's secret passageway was still thirty yards away. I ran as fast as I could up the ravine. Jeff, carrying Kate, was in close pursuit. Adelaide, apparently realizing that Jeff and my actions meant something was seriously amiss, had also dropped Freddy, and was running fast behind Jeff without having needed either Jeff or me to tell her to do so.

I had taken at most five steps when I heard the drones' canisters start to hiss. I had taken at most another three steps when the drones passed within a few feet of the top of my head, the fast moving air from their screaming jets whipping through my hair, the air warm and smelling of burning aviation fuel. The canisters' gas was odorless and colorless, but I could feel its oiliness seeping into my eyes, nose, and mouth, and through my skin. Half a step later, the muscles in my legs became weak, then flaccid, and I tumbled onto the ground, using my final remaining bit of strength to roll and break Billy's and my fall. The last thing I felt before I lost all muscular control was Billy's motionless body rolling away from me as I wound up on my back staring at the moon and stars above.

CHAPTER 109

I expected to pass out, but did not. I expected not to be able to breathe, but I could. The muscles of my thorax were useless, but my diaphragm, apparently unaffected by the nerve gas, worked my lungs like a bellows, sucking air in, and forcing it out. My eyes could move in all directions, though not well.

My brain was even less well.

The gas had addled my brain far beyond even the befuddled mess that had been created by the stress and strain of those past two days. My mind presented me a with a vision of a largemouth bass that had just been torn from its aquatic home and dropped onshore by some pitiless fisherman. I watched as the bass flopped about in its final death throes, its gills gasping for oxygen.

I rotated my eyes to the left. Freddy's body, which we had left behind in order to make our mad dash up to the entrance of Nimo/Billy's secret passageway, was nowhere to be seen. Adelaide, Billy, Jeff, and Kate were sprawled out not far from me on the ravine floor. I knew all four of them were alive because I could see their abdomens minutely rising and falling with each breath driven by the muscles of their diaphragms. I tried to call out to them, but could not.

I shifted my gaze upwards to the moon and the stars. The six drones that had gassed us were making a synchronized, sweeping circle and passing over a wide swath of the estate to the south. They continued to empty their canisters. My mind, acting under the sway of its own quixotic impulses, dispensed with its dying bass image and flooded me with absurdly out of place stream of consciousness visions from my memory banks -

Crop dusters I had seen spraying wheat fields in Midwest America...

Ancient single-engine Cessnas rigged for mosquito abatement I had watched gliding over impoverished towns in Kenya, Tanzania, and Ethiopia...

And giant DC-10's I had witnessed dousing forest fires in Siberia.

I tired to ignore the visions as best I could and focus my thoughts on what was happening out on the estate. Any FBI agents left standing after the initial drone machine gun assault would soon be immobilized by the gas and flat on their backs just like me. Unfortunately for me, my brain, again beating to its own quixotic drum, ran with that image of the agents, and, abandoning the crop dusters, Cessnas, and DC-10's just as it had abandoned the bass, morphed my inner being into a grey-jacketed potato bug trapped on its back. That imaginary bug was unable to turn over no matter how hard it tried.

Somehow I shoved that vision aside, and just as I did, I became aware that something around me had suddenly changed. For a moment, I couldn't figure out what it was. Then it came to me. It was the sound. The gunfire on both sides - drones and FBI agents alike - had completely stopped. All I could hear were the waves, the wind rustling through the palms, and the distant, intermittent explosions coming from the funeral-like pyres of the helicopters' and Coast Guard cutter's remains. I knew then that all resistance was gone, the battle over, every FBI agent was either dead or paralyzed or would be soon.

In the relative silence, thoughts came to me quickly, most of them questioning. Why had the drone assault been conducted in the way it had? The drones never seemed to even try to kill Adelaide, Billy, Jeff, Kate, or me. It had to have been a conscious decision, didn't it? The drones' targeting capabilities were too precise, their optics too good, for the drone pilots not to know exactly what they were doing.

There could only be one explanation.

They wanted us alive.

Someone or something was coming for us.

CHAPTER 110

I shut out the sounds of the wind, waves, and distant explosions and listened for whatever was coming next. I didn't just listen but looked as well, trying not to be distracted by the shadows of the burning helicopters' pyres, shadows that danced on the hillside brush and wall of Kate's estate. My mind, increasingly dazed and confused by the psychotropic effects of the nerve gas, began to see those shadows as demon warriors from some depraved underworld. The demons' arms were long and jagged and they shook at me with terrible menace. The demons' legs hopped to and fro, and the demons' mouths opened in vicious snarls.

I did my best to keep the demons at bay while I focused on the sky. I felt whatever was coming for us would most likely be coming by air, if only because that's what I would have done. The unpredictability of the ocean currents, tide, and force of the waves would make a sea landing difficult, and maneuvering Adelaide, Billy, Jeff, Kate, and me down the side of the bluff to the beach and into any waiting vessel would be too slow and too cumbersome. The enemy might have considered using ground vehicles, but such vehicles would have almost certainly been ruled out as they would be far too risky to use. The enemy would have foreseen that the drone attack would quickly generate a massive response from reinforcements within the sheriff's department, highway patrol, and FBI, and that multiple roadblocks would soon be in place on the Pacific Coast Highway. Getting by one roadblock might be viewed as a reasonable gamble, but getting by more than one would surely have been perceived as quite perilous, and most likely doomed to failure.

Time passed. It could have been seconds. It could have been minutes. I didn't know. I saw the drones head back to sea and heard the whine of their engines drop in pitch and then finally disappear entirely.

I tried to come up with a plan. But what options did I have? I couldn't even spit at anyone who came for me. The most I would probably be able to manage was an evil eye.

My iPhone started ringing. It rang and rang and rang until it finally stopped. The call couldn't have been from Adelaide, Jeff, or Kate, which left the next two most likely suspects as Hart and Haley. Sorry Hart and Haley, but unless my giving the enemy the evil eye worked, I was sure I was soon to be captured or killed and you two were going to be on your own.

I kept scanning the portion of the sky I could see with my still immoveable head, but saw nothing but the night and the stars.

Then I heard a new sound.

A machine-made sound.

I couldn't see what was making the sound, but it was a sound I had heard many times before. Sometimes while I was being transported within the machine that produced it, sometimes as I waited for the machine to arrive, and sometimes as I waved goodbye at the machine as it left me in the middle of nowhere.

I turned my eyes in the sound's direction.

I waited and waited.

And then what I knew was coming appeared in my field of vision.

A Black Hawk helicopter was racing across the sky towards me.

That particular Black Hawk was unlike any Black Hawk I had ever seen, however.

It was a stealth Black Hawk.

But stealth or no stealth it was still a Black Hawk, and for a moment I thought, 'oh good, an old friend, we're going to make it'.

Those thoughts though were just the mushy fruits born from the orchards of my nerve gas addled brain. Any wild fantasies I held about the Black Hawk transporting a rescue team were quickly dispelled when I saw what appeared to be a whole new fleet of drones accompanying the helicopter. The drones were circling about three hundred feet above their stealth Black Hawk mother ship, protecting it just as destroyers provide security at sea for their leviathan aircraft carrier patriarchs.

The sounds of the Black Hawk's engines increased in volume until they became a thunderous roar, their pitch growing higher with each passing second. The moon was suddenly blacked out as the chopper's huge, dark fuselage, almost as wide as it was long, passed only fifty feet above my head. The earth vibrated in deep harmonic waves, waves that rolled through my body and made my bones shake. Massive cyclonic winds generated by the Black Hawk's rotors buffeted me, pushing the air so violently around my face it made it hard to breathe. The winds also dried whatever moisture was still left in my eyes and my eyes felt like someone had taken sandpaper to them.

A moment later, the din of the Black Hawk's engines began to soften and then cut out entirely.

The stealth Black Hawk had landed.

CHAPTER 111

The sea breeze that was ruffling my hair pushed the smoky smell of the Black Hawk's burned fuel into my nostrils where it mixed with the already resident tang of exploded gunpowder. I estimated from how far away the Black Hawk's engines had sounded when they had cut out that the helicopter's pilots must have found a landing spot close to the edge of the ravine. I checked on Adelaide, Billy, Jeff, and Kate. They had not moved, but their abdomens' continued rising and falling let me know they were still alive.

I thought about what I could have done differently. Should I have anticipated that a stealth Black Hawk, along with drones armed with Hellfire missiles and nerve gas, would be used in an assault on Freddy and Kate's compound? It would have been the first time such machines were used in an attack on American soil, but still...

Perhaps I had been too focused on what I already knew, that the enemy had surface-to-surface missiles, and had been too comfortable with the fact that Carpenter - with Hart and Haley's assistance - seemed to have been well prepared to stop any attack on Kate's estate by the Iglas. Jeff was pretty good at anticipating weird and theoretically unanticipatable things like Hellfires and nerve gas, but Jeff had never said word 'Boo' about the possibility our future might involve us confronting those kinds of lethal weapons.

I tried to take some consolation in that fact, but could not.

Maybe I should have forcibly kidnapped Kate and taken her to a safe house myself? That idea did not survive even brief additional reflection, however. Kate and I had been waiting for Dr. Nemo/Billy Einstein - or as I newly understood it, Dr. Nimo/Billy Einstein - to show up at the pool house. If Nimo was coming, we had to be there. There was too much at risk if Kate and I had left the estate and missed meeting with him.

I blamed no one but myself for what had happened to us, but wasn't it really Nimo/Billy who was at the root of all our problems? All the important shots in this mission had ultimately been called by an eighteen year old - a well meaning eighteen year old genius who was doing his best - but an eighteen year old nonetheless. There was no way he was experienced enough to understand all the potential pitfalls in his plan. Because of that lack of understanding - and my failure to adequately anticipate and prepare for what had befallen us - we were all probably going to die.

And it wasn't going to be an easy death.

The drones could have killed us at any moment, and the most likely reason we weren't already dead was because our enemy wanted to know what we knew about the Chinese insurmountable edge. Our enemy probably wanted to determine if their war plans had been compromised, and if so, what if any actions they needed to take. Wasn't torture the method they would use to get whatever we knew about the edge out of us?

I heard feet running along the ground and moving rapidly towards me. I estimated there were about eight feet in all. Which most likely meant four mercenary commandos were coming for us. Jeff would probably be hearing and thinking the same thing. Maybe Adelaide would be too.

Hopefully, Kate was still so worried about Freddy, that even if she sensed the mercenary commandos' approach, her awareness of them remained on the periphery of her consciousness, and thus she might not yet be feeling any fear. But Kate would be undoubtedly overwhelmed by fear when they took her. Maybe it was just the workings of the gas on my mind, but somehow my imagined momentary respite for Kate soothed me, though admittedly the extent of that soothing was nearly infinitesimal.

Because of his youth and inexperience, I figured terror was the only thing Nimo/Billy - despite his obvious courage - would be feeling. Thinking that made me even angrier I had let Billy and Kate down.

I tried to will my anger and adrenaline, and whatever other hormones and chemicals were circulating in my body, to overcome the effects of the nerve gas.

It didn't work.

The commandos got closer and closer, so close I could hear the sound of their breathing. The ends of their shoelaces clicked against their boots and the cloth of their pants made thrumming sounds as each leg rubbed against the other. All four - my predicted number had been correct - ran right by me in single file as if I did not exist. They were all tall and sinewy, dressed from head to toe in black: t-shirts, cargo pants, boots, and gloves - the gloves presumably to protect them from stray bits of gas on our bodies as they picked us up. The men also wore gas masks and had standard Army issue black Colt .45 pistols in holsters at their sides. The skin of their faces visible at the sides of the gas masks was weathered and almond brown. Their long hair was black, as were their beards, which were also long.

Which said to me that the men were almost surely Afghans. Afghans, who - thanks to Haley's photos of the men that had gotten off the Doctors of Mercy flight, my discovery of the notched boots at the stoning site, and last but not least, Bobby's and Timmy's apparently spot on descriptions of the men who, along with Dragon Man, had stoned Sam and Lizzy to death - I'd felt certain I was going to encounter at some point.

I had no way of knowing whether these Afghans were the same Afghans who had played baseball with Sam and Lizzy's heads. But I thought it very likely that the Colt .45's in the Afghans' holsters had been given to them by the same U.S. special forces soldiers who had taught either them or their commando compatriots how to play America's favorite pastime.

Within a few seconds, the Afghans were moving back the way they had come, only this time they went in two pairs. Each pair had a motionless body strung between them, one Afghan held the arms and one held the legs. The bodies were those of Billy and Kate.

I was sure the Afghans would be back for Adelaide, Jeff, and me. Two more trips, the last one only needing one pair of Afghans for the odd man, or girl, out. Who would they leave for last? I had no idea. All I could do was wait and watch the aerial ballet above as the drones circled in and out of the moonlight. At least, I thought, Adelaide, Billy, Jeff, Kate, and I would all be together in the stealth Black Hawk. If we were together, there was a chance Jeff and I could free all of us if the Afghans or their bosses made a mistake.

The Afghans returned. Two of them wordlessly lifted me from off the floor of the ravine. The pain in my hip and shoulder joints was excruciating and became more so as they started jogging away with me. All I could see of the Afghans was the gas mask clad face of the one holding my shoulders - the face swung up and down against the background of the sky and stars above. The eyes behind the mask's two large clear plastic oval eyepieces looked more alien than human. My gas addled brain took that image and ran with it. It flooded me with visions of myself as some hapless human abductee being carried off towards a waiting phalanx of alien doctors. The doctors were standing in front of a bank of ugly looking medical devices and were clearly enjoying the prospect of using those devices to perform excruciatingly painful invasive medical exams on me.

Suddenly, a distinct 'pfft pfft' sound cut through the air and my brain's imaginary visions of the alien doctors instantly disappeared. The eyepieces of the mask of the Afghan holding my shoulders filled with bright crimson blood and spicules of pale, white skull bone. The four Afghan hands gripping me went limp and I was dropped from a height of about three feet. My head and back cracked on the rocks lining the bottom of the ravine. The two Afghans crumpled and their bodies fell next to me.

Another 'pfft pfft' murmured through the air followed by the thump, thump, thump of three bodies hitting the ground behind me. There was also a smacking sound which I assumed was a skull hitting stone. I guessed two of the bodies hitting the ground were Afghans. The third body and the skull probably belonged to either Adelaide or Jeff, but I didn't know which of them the Afghans had been carrying so I couldn't be sure.

A new set of footsteps closed in on me. The footsteps sounded quicker and more agile than the Afghans' footsteps had sounded. A form sidled up to me and blotted out the sky. The form, clad as it was in all black - pants, jacket, bulletproof vest, gas mask, boots, and gloves - looked exactly like the first four Afghans I had seen. My heart fell - I had hoped from the sound of the footsteps that someone other than an Afghan had come for me. I found myself momentarily wondering why this Afghan had killed his companions. But then I noticed the Afghan was carrying an M14 and had a Kevlar helmet atop his head, and I realized the eyes looking at me from behind the gas mask's plastic eyepieces belonged to Ray Carpenter.

Carpenter knelt down over me and studied my face. I moved my eyes from side to side.

"Your eyes are moving," Carpenter said. "I'll take that to mean you're not dead. Sorry I didn't make it here sooner. I got within a hundred yards of you, but had to go back and get my gas gear when I saw the canisters."

I moved my eyes again, this time in the direction of Adelaide and Jeff.

"Yeah, Jeff and Adelaide are okay too," Carpenter said. "I can see them breathing. It looks like they dropped Adelaide on her head, so she's probably going to have a bad headache. She's young though, so I think she'll handle it just fine."

I moved my eyes toward and away from the Black Hawk three times in rapid succession.

"I'm trying to figure out the same thing," Carpenter said. "But I just don't see how I can keep that Black Hawk from lifting off without potentially hurting Dr. Lennon and that young kid they took inside. I know you and Jeff would know what to do, but you guys are as useful to me right now as two sacks of potatoes." Carpenter paused. "Is the kid Dr. Nemo?"

I knew Carpenter was still spelling Nemo with and 'E' instead of an 'I', but there was nothing I could do to correct him at that moment. That said, Carpenter's assessment of the identity of the 'young kid' was otherwise perfectly accurate. I moved my eyes up and down, signaling what I hoped Carpenter would see as a 'Yes'.

"You could have told me he was coming," Carpenter said.

I shrugged as best as I could with my eyes.

"Yeah, I get it," Carpenter said. "'Need to know', right?"

The Black Hawk's engines roared loudly and the rotors whined.

"Aw, shit," Carpenter said. "They're moving out."

The cyclone wind buffeted me again and I knew the chopper had become airborne.

"These assholes have always been one step ahead of us," Carpenter said. "They must know what's coming for them even now."

'What's coming for them?' I thought to myself. I gave Carpenter the best questioning look with my eyes that I could muster.

"Hold on," Carpenter said. "I'll show you."

Carpenter supported my head and lifted my chest off the ground as the Black Hawk roared over us, quickly gathered speed, and, staying low, headed inland towards the seaside hills. Carpenter then put a knee against my spine to keep me upright and gently turned my head to face north.

"I got Hart to call in the cavalry, but I'm afraid it's going to be a case of too little, too late," Carpenter said.

Carpenter pointed into the sky. I saw tiny specks of orange light flare over the sea about twenty miles north of us. I recognized the flares. They were the signature firings of fighter jet afterburners.

"F/A-18 Super Hornets coming down from Point Mugu," Carpenter said. "Don't ask me how Hart got them to help us out, because I don't know. All I know is that he did. Oh, and by the way, Hart is sending antidotes for the gas. Sorry I didn't have the foresight to have some on hand at the estate."

I signaled with my eyes as best I could that I understood, then shifted my gaze back to the sky. None of the dozens of drones overhead had accompanied the Black Hawk when it left. What the drones did do, however, was to stop their circling and line up to face the incoming F/A-18's.

The drone pilots were probably thinking they could put up a good fight, but what they should have done was run.

It is one thing to play video games in the safety of some dark bunker somewhere.

It is quite another to take on real Navy flyboys.

And so, while the drones waited in their line - perhaps trying to look menacing, or maybe waiting to get the F/A-18's in range of their weapons - the Navy jets banked up into the sky, dove, rolled, and...

Unleashed hell.

The F/A-18s' Vulcan cannons and air-to-air missiles destroyed the entire drone fleet in seconds and the drones exploded into tiny pin-wheeling flaming fragments that lit up the sky like it was the Fourth of July. The drones hadn't even managed to get off a single one of their Hellfire missiles.

The Navy jets banked sharply inland and took off in the direction the stealth Black Hawk had taken. But unless the Navy pilots had a visual - which I highly doubted since the pilots had been far away from the estate when the Black Hawk had departed, and the night was also still quite dark despite the moonlight - it was unlikely the pilots were going to be able to find the helicopter. Stealth technology works.

I realized then my only hope to find Kate and Billy was if Hart and Haley had been watching and were tracking the helicopter. I knew, however, that that was a long shot. Our enemies were sophisticated and they had the advantage of planning out their attack on the estate well in advance. I had little doubt that the people behind the attack were also covering their tracks by using powerful technology to block the sensor and imaging systems of our satellites. After all, hadn't our enemies had access to similar technology in the form of the NASAD tools that could fool radar into mislocating any object the radar was attempting to track? And hadn't our enemies used that radar to falsify the true positioning of Milt Feynman and Paul Lennon's Otter as it fell into the Alaskan seas and took the two men to their watery graves?

Deep down inside I knew the Black Hawk, and Billy and Kate along with it, was gone.

Hopelessly.

Gone.

CHAPTER 112

At 4:45 a.m., about twenty minutes after the Black Hawk had disappeared into the night sky, a U.S. Navy helicopter from Point Mugu Naval Air Station dropped off the nerve gas antidote. Ray Carpenter injected the antidote into Adelaide, Jeff, and me as we lay in the ravine. Carpenter, knowing the antidote could take at least ninety minutes to be fully effective, and also knowing there was little he could do for us in the meantime, left us where we lay and went looking for any other survivors on the estate.

At 5:00 a.m. firemen arrived. Using hoses attached to red and yellow pumper trucks, they began to subdue the smoldering ruins of the FBI choppers that had fallen to earth. Coast Guard boats circled the sea below the cliffs, the guardsmen looking for survivors of the attack on the cutter. The roaring sound of the boats' engines rose and fell as the boats rolled in between sea swells, the engines' sounds occasionally disappearing entirely when a large wave broke on shore.

A team of hazmat techs - a team whose members were controlled by Ray Carpenter, and a team that also most assuredly did not include any of the hazmat techs who had been at the site of the bunker where the NASAD dark programmers had been murdered - reported to the estate at about 5:00 a.m. as well. The team carried Adelaide's, Jeff's, and my still immobile bodies to the pool area and laid us out next to each other on chaise lounges. Adelaide was on my right, and Jeff on my left. The hazmat techs burned our clothes, thoroughly decontaminated us, and dressed us in blue jeans, t-shirts, and combat boots. Modesty had not been an issue since the hazmat techs had placed Adelaide, Jeff, and me behind our own individual screens during the process.

A half hour after the hazmat team had laid us out at the pool, the sun began to peek over the coastal mountains to the east of Freddy and Kate's estate. The cool early morning sea breeze stiffened and dissipated the smell of charred metal and burnt helicopter fuel. Adelaide and Jeff seemed to be breathing fine, but neither of them yet had any significant control over other parts of their bodies. I, however, had recovered well enough to talk and use my phone.

I took my phone out of my pocket and noticed that it had indeed been Hart who had called me while I had been immobile from the gas. After Hart's success with getting an assist from the Navy flyboys, I had begun to think he might also be able to rustle up a few special forces professionals to assist Adelaide, Jeff, and me as we went forward with our mission. I was also worried sick about Billy and Kate, and hoping against hope Haley and Hart had been able to find some trace of the Black Hawk.

I immediately dialed Haley and Hart and the two of them appeared in side by side half screens on my iPhone. Haley was sitting in front of the computer banks at NORAD. Her eyes sparkled, her smiled glowed, and her hair had a beautiful sheen to it. Hart looked grumpy and appeared to be at a forward command station in the Arabian desert. The time difference made it late afternoon at Hart's location. He was dressed in desert camouflage and standing outside a large tent. Behind him, Army officers intermittently entered and left the tent.

"Good day, General," I said into the phone. "Carpenter told me it was you who got the Navy to take out the drones. Good work, sir. However, wasn't that against the law?"

"I have my ways," Hart said.

"Of course you do," I said. "Does that mean Jeff, Adelaide, and I can get some help out here? Some Rangers or Seals, maybe a battalion of Marines?"

"Sure, why not?" Hart said. "And while I'm at it, maybe I'll tell Homeland, the CIA, the DIA, and every goddamned intelligence agency in the country what we're up to. Hell, maybe I could even ask for congressional approval too."

"I see your point, sir," I said.

"You do, huh?" Hart said.

"Yes, sir," I said. "You're implying such action would create a bureaucratic nightmare that would not only not do any good, but also thwart us at every turn and guarantee the failure of our mission. Especially since we have so little time left."

"That is exactly what I'm implying," Hart said. "Maybe next time you'll think before making any more ridiculous requests."

"I will, sir," I said. "However, just to confirm, sir, that help from the Navy flyboys was a one time thing, correct?"

"Yes, it was a one time thing," Hart said. He held up his right index finger and thumb to his cell phone's camera and squeezed his fingers together until only a tiny gap remained between them. "And it came this close to being a no-time thing!"

"But didn't you just say you had your ways?" I said.

"Aargh!" Hart said.

"Sorry, sir," I said. "I suppose that after everything that happened to their agents out here, you're probably having a hard time keeping the FBI out of your hair as well?"

"Damn right I am," Hart said.

"Well if anyone can manage us through these difficulties, it's you, sir," I said. "Carpenter also told me about forty-five minutes ago that neither you, nor the Navy pilots, have found any trace of the Black Hawk. Anything change since then?"

Haley said, "I'll answer that. No, nothing has changed. We're conducting the search with everything we've got, but still can't find a trace. Whoever did this was able to crash our satellite signal. The crashing occurred just after we saw someone crawl out of the bushes in the ravine. Carpenter filled Hart and me in on everything that happened at the estate. From what Carpenter said, that 'someone' in the bushes was Dr. Nemo."

"I can confirm it was Nemo," I said. I was of course thinking 'Nimo,' not 'Nemo.' However, since neither Haley nor Hart yet knew about the change in spelling, I didn't want to distract them from the current topic of our conversation by updating them with that information at that moment. "But signal crashing is not supposed to happen to you guys."

Hart said, "And you're not supposed to be lying flat on your back while Kate Lennon and Dr. Nemo/Billy Einstein are kidnapped and taken God knows where."

"Touché, sir," I said. "Don't worry though. I'm going to fix that just as soon as I can walk. Also, sir, I apologize for not taking your call. The same gas that made it impossible for me to stop Kate's and Nimo's kidnapping also kept me from answering my phone. What did you call about?"

"I'm so pissed off I don't even remember," Hart said.

"I'll be here when you do, sir," I said.

"I can't tell you how happy that makes me feel," Hart said. "Now, Mr. Genius, you just said you would fix the problem as soon as you could walk. Does that mean you have a plan and that all the searching Haley, I, and everyone else are doing is in vain?"

I said, "I do have a plan, sir."

"I'm all ears," Hart said.

"Adelaide, Jeff, and I have a van," I said. "We're going to get into it and start looking for the Black Hawk. We find the Black Hawk, we find Kate and Billy."

"You know the range of a Black Hawk, son?" Hart said.

"Three hundred and seventeen miles, sir," I said.

"Assuming the Black Hawk didn't refuel, how many square miles would you have to cover to adequately search for it?" Hart said.

"Probably a lot, sir," I said.

"That's a stupid ass answer and you know it," Hart said.

It was a stupid ass answer, but it was the first answer my nerve gas addled brain had come up with. Hart's insult, however, pushed me to force my way through all that addling and do the calculation. The area inside a circle is π times the radius squared. Assuming the Black Hawk could have gone in any direction, but most likely did not go out to sea, that would mean I was looking at about half the area inside a circle whose radius was three hundred and seventeen miles. That came out to over one hundred and fifty thousand square miles.

"It's about one hundred and fifty thousand square miles, sir," I said.

"And you actually believe you can cover all that area in that beat up van of yours and find Kate before they kill her and Billy Einstein?" Hart said.

"You make an excellent point, sir," I said.

Jeff stirred next to me.

"Who you talking to?" Jeff said.

I covered my phone's camera and microphone with my hand and looked over at Jeff. He hadn't moved from the last position I'd seen him in. I assumed Jeff could speak but do nothing else. I snuck a quick peek at Adelaide as well. Adelaide hadn't moved either. She appeared to be just staring up at the sky.

"Haley and Hart," I said to Jeff.

"Ask Hart why the hell he took so long to get those Super Hornets here," Jeff said.

"Hart's already pissed off enough as it is," I said.

Haley's muffled voice said, "Jack? Jack are you there? We can't hear or see you."

I ignored Haley for the moment.

Jeff said, "Don't care if Hart pissed off. He almost got us killed."

"Fine," I said. "You want to ask him, ask him yourself."

Keeping the screen and microphone covered, I extended my phone to him.

"You crazy?" Jeff said. "Get that thing away from me."

"Oh," I said. "It's okay for me to get yelled at, but not you?"

"I be more sensitive than you," Jeff said.

"Right," I said.

I pulled the phone back in and uncovered the screen and microphone.

"Sorry," I said to Haley and Hart. "Lost transmission there for a moment. I'm back now, though."

Hart growled, "Lucky us."

"Thank you, sir," I said. "Now, Haley, before I forget, I'd like to extend you my congratulations."

"What for?" Haley said.

"I've been able to confirm, without qualification or equivocation, that Billy Einstein and Dr. Nimo are one and the same," I said.

"Was there ever a doubt?" Haley said.

"Not on your end, I'm sure," I said. "I do have one question for you, however. Are you spelling Nemo with an 'I' or and 'E'?"

Hart said, "Sweet Jesus. Have you completely lost your mind? What the hell difference does that make?"

"Maybe none," I said. "It's just that Billy Einstein told me it was with an 'I'."

Haley raised her eyebrows.

"Which makes it Nimo instead of Nemo?" Haley said.

"Yes," I said.

"Nimo wasn't the captain of the 'Nautilus'," Haley said.

"No, he wasn't," I said.

"Doesn't that pretty much do away with the 'Twenty Thousand

Leagues Under the Sea' angle?" Haley said. "And wouldn't that also make your hunch about the drone subs being a red herring much more likely to be correct?"

"I believe it would," I said. "Especially when we add in the fact Dr. Nimo/Billy seemed to have no idea what I was talking about when I mentioned the drone subs."

Hart shook his head, then grumbled, "I hate to say it, but even though I've been on board with the idea that the drone subs aren't the source of the insurmountable edge for a while, you got there a lot faster than I did, Jack. And I agree with Haley's assessment that it looks pretty certain it will turn out you were right all along."

"Thank you, sir," I said. "Don't worry, I won't say 'I told you so.'"

"You just did, asshole," Hart said.

"Force of habit, sir," I said. "Anyway, getting back to that crashed satellite signal. I assume neither of you know who crashed it?"

Haley said, "Whoever did it used top secret NASAD technology. I don't think it would be a stretch to believe whoever did it is also the same entity that commandeered NASAD's top secret radar mislocating technology to falsify the true position of Feynman and Lennon's Otter when it was flying over the Gulf of Alaska."

"That's what I was thinking," I said.

"In any event, whoever it was, they only crashed the signal for about an hour," Haley said. "And we're pretty sure we've found a way to keep them from doing it again."

"An hour was plenty enough time in this situation, though," I said.

"You mean for the Black Hawk to get away?" Haley said.

"I do," I said.

"It definitely turned out that way," Haley said. "I guess we could even go so far as to say that since the satellite that was crashed is a NASAD product, and our enemy seems to be intimately aware of how many of NASAD's systems function, our enemy knew it would take us at least an hour to fix the satellite."

"And that they could rely on that hour in planning the Black Hawk's getaway," I said. "What about Dr. Lennon's cell phone? Did you ping it to try to find her location?"

"There was no need to try," Haley said. "Ray Carpenter found two cell phones on the ground underneath where the Black Hawk landed. One was Dr. Lennon's and the other had a cell phone cover illustrated with a repeating 'E = mc^2' motif. If the one with the cover doesn't belong to Dr. Nimo/Billy Einstein, I'll eat my hat."

"You don't have a hat," I said.

"Then I'll eat yours," Haley said.

"I don't have one either," I said.

Hart said, "Are both of you insane? Cut this shit out."

"Yes, sir," I said. "So Haley, I assume you believe the bad guys in the Black Hawk must have thrown both phones out the chopper's door after they took off?"

"Affirmative," Haley said.

"Are the phones still working?" I said.

"They're not," Haley said. "Carpenter told me that both phones were shattered beyond repair."

"We better hope that Carpenter doesn't know much about phones," I said.

"Why?" Haley said.

I told Haley and Hart about Billy's special patch cord, his Enigma machine app, the fingerprint passwords, how Billy's and Kate's phones needed to be working in order to activate the file Billy had sent Kate so that the file could be used to disable the insurmountable edge, and the fact that Billy had programmed the war game software to launch at 6:00 p.m. local time tonight, a launch that was, in effect, a NASAD war game sneak attack. I also told Haley she needed to start searching for Billy's car which he had hidden in the foothills about five miles north of Kate's estate, since Billy had stowed his special patch cord in the car.

Hart said, "So we know how Einstein planned to use his file in order to disable the insurmountable edge, but we still don't know exactly how the edge works?"

"Correct, sir," I said.

"Why the hell didn't you ask him?" Hart said.

"I was about to," I said, "but then we got gassed."

Hart said nothing.

"I do think the information I got that Nimo/Billy's war game software was going to initiate its NASAD war game sneak attack at 6:00 p.m.

tonight was especially valuable though, sir," I said. "It allows us to proceed with a high degree of confidence that the Chinese insurmountable edge and the dark programmers and Nimo/Billy's war game software are one and the same."

"Haley told me that you and she had pretty much committed to that assumption anyway," Hart said.

"That's true," I said.

Haley said, "Yes, that is true. But I, for one, feel much better now about what we're doing in terms of our search for the insurmountable edge. I also think it's interesting there's such a thing as an Enigma machine app. I certainly didn't know one existed."

"I didn't either," I said.

Hart grumbled, "That's wonderful. You both learned something new today. The question is what are we going to do next?"

Haley said, "I think the first thing we have to do is try to fix both Billy Einstein's and Dr. Lennon's phones. I'll ask Carpenter to send them over as fast as possible." She paused, seemingly thinking about something. "You know, both Billy and Dr. Lennon would have to have been fingerprinted for their security clearances. If we can get a copy of their fingerprints, maybe we can reverse engineer the passwords."

"I keep forgetting how smart you are," I said.

"No you don't," Haley said.

"You're right," I said. "I don't."

"You wouldn't happen to know which of Billy's three fingers he used for the prints, do you?" Haley said.

"As a matter of fact, I do," I said.

I told her which ones.

"Excellent work," Haley said.

Hart said, "You know why Jack has that information, don't you, Haley?"

"Sir?" Haley said.

"He needed to know which ones to cut off in case Einstein was killed and he couldn't get the body to us," Hart said.

"Sir!" I said. "What you must think of me!"

"Shut the hell up," Hart said. "Now listen to me. We've only got a little more than twelve hours until war commences and, as all of us know, once it does, Kate's and Einstein's lives won't be worth a hill of beans. Getting Einstein back alive is also our best chance of figuring out what the Chinese insurmountable edge is. Haley and I are working on getting a bead on the Black Hawk's location, which should lead us to Kate and Einstein's location as well. Seeing how it must be clear to even your dumbass brain that you aren't going to do any good running around in your van trying to search 150,000 square miles, I'm ordering you, Jeff, and Adelaide to get some food into yourselves and whatever rest you can. You're sure as hell going to need every last bit of energy you can rustle up once we find Kate and Einstein and give you the 'go' order to retrieve the two of them."

"*If* you find them, sir," I said.

"What kind of shit for brains attitude is that?" Hart said.

"Sorry, sir," I said. "It must be the nerve gas."

"You turning into a whiner on me?" Hart said.

"No, sir," I said.

"You better not be," Hart said. "Now go do as I said."

"Yes, sir," I said.

CHAPTER 113

As much as I wanted to immediately start looking for the Black Hawk and thereby find Kate and Billy Einstein - and may God forgive me, but at that moment, despite how important finding Billy was to stopping the war with China, my fevered mind was much more worried about finding Kate - I knew Hart was correct. Driving the Kazakhs' van around California trying to search 150,000 square miles would most likely accomplish little other than waste time and energy. Haley and Hart had the world's most sophisticated equipment at their fingertips with which to look for the Black Hawk. They had drones, satellites, spy planes, and probably more than a few devices whose cutting edge technology was known only to MOM's wizards. If anybody could find the Black Hawk, and Kate and Billy along with it, it was MOM. As soon as Hart and Haley found Kate and Billy, they would tell me, and I would go, and go hard.

Thus, despite being buffeted by nearly constant waves of intense emotion - impatience, fear, longing, and frustration being chief among them - I did exactly as Hart had instructed me to do. Once Adelaide, Jeff, and I had fully recovered - which took about half an hour after I had gotten off the phone with Haley and Hart - we all piled into the Kazakhs' van.

The van had somehow miraculously survived the night's activities with its cargo of automatic weapons and Igla surface-to-surface missiles intact. With Adelaide driving, we traveled down the Pacific Coast Highway in search of a diner. Adelaide no longer had the Kazakh's blood on her face, I assumed because the hazmat techs had washed it off when they decontaminated us. It was 6:30 a.m. when we found a diner in the Point Dume Plaza.

Point Dume Plaza is a big shopping center on a bluff overlooking the sea, but with no view of the sea. The diner's front door was tinted glass framed in wood and there were large eastern facing plate glass windows on either side of the door. The diner was nearly empty when Adelaide, Jeff, and I walked in, and the sun, then just barely peeking out above the coastal mountains, shown brightly through the diner's windows.

We sat down at one of the diner's blue leather banquettes. The banquette was next to a window and the sunlight, which had made our tabletop warm to the touch, also began to warm us as well. White paper place mats with scalloped edges, stainless steel place settings, coffee mugs, salt and pepper shakers, a sugar jar with a metal top with a hinged opening, a yellow plastic bottle of mustard, a red plastic bottle of ketchup, and a green capped clear plastic bear-shaped bottle filled to the brim with maple syrup were all arrayed on the table. Everything very civilized and calm.

Which created quite a contrast to Adelaide, Jeff, and me.

All three of us had puffy, glazed eyes, and hair that was matted and still smelling of the chemicals that the hazmat team had poured on us. Adelaide also had a bruise on the side of her arm and a big welt on the back of her head. Both injuries were courtesy of the fall she had taken when the Afghans had dropped her after they had been killed by Ray Carpenter. Jeff had a large cut on his cheek. He had gotten it when his body had quickly succumbed to the paralytic effects of the nerve gas - much more quickly than mine had - and he had tumbled face first onto a rock. My body was scrunched and twisted due to the pain in my left knee and shoulder. Both joints had been injured - to be precise, my left knee had actually been further injured - when I fell awkwardly while trying to keep Billy from getting hurt in the milliseconds just after our exposure to the nerve gas.

An exceptionally cheery, well-tanned, blond haired waitress, wearing a light blue uniform with a white apron and sneakers with no socks, came up to take our order. Her tan nicely complemented her blue eyes and the light shade of the blue uniform nicely complemented her tan. She held a pot of coffee and poured us each a cup. I caught her checking out Jeff. She appeared to like what she saw. I knew the only reason she had focused on him was because if she looked at me, the sun would have been in her eyes.

The waitress said, "Either you three have been partying nonstop for a week, or you're on the run from a holdup gone bad. If I had to choose, I would say holdup gone bad."

Adelaide growled, "Mind your own business."

The waitress was unfazed.

"It looks like you have a pretty big bump on your head," the waitress said. "We have a first aid kit if you need it."

"What part of 'mind your own business' don't you understand, lady?" Adelaide said.

"You remind me of my kid sister," the waitress said. "She's in the California women's prison at Chowchilla."

"Do I look like I care?" Adelaide said.

I smiled at the waitress.

"You'll have to excuse her," I said. "She's playing a pit bull in her school play and she's worried that if she doesn't stay in character she might lose her edge."

The waitress said, "I get it. I'm an actress too."

Adelaide said, "Why am I not surprised?"

The waitress left and returned about ten minutes later with our food. We had all ordered the same thing - pancakes, scrambled eggs, bacon, and orange juice - though Adelaide, who loves bacon, had ordered more bacon than Jeff and I had. Three more orders to be exact.

As the waitress laid the plates on the table, she did a very good imitation of a snarling dog and barked at Adelaide. Adelaide reached out to grab the waitress's hair, but I blocked her arm with my own before she could do any damage. The waitress backpedaled to safety.

"Down, Adelaide, down," I said.

"Should I get her a bone?" the waitress said to me.

Adelaide said, "Yeah, go ahead and get me a bone. The first thing I'll do with it is shove it up your ass."

The waitress wagged her finger at Adelaide.

"Bad doggy," the waitress said, and laughing, she left our table.

I said, "Adelaide, why are you being so mean?"

"I don't like her type," Adelaide said.

"What type is that?" I said.

"Ditzy blonds," Adelaide said. "They give women a bad name."

Jeff said, "You a feminist now?"

"What?" Adelaide said. "I'm a feminist since I don't want women to get a bad name?"

Adelaide and Jeff continued to bicker. I suddenly felt very hungry.

Ignoring Adelaide and Jeff, I grabbed the little bear and poured syrup over my pancakes. I cut a wedge of pancakes with my fork, popped the wedge in my mouth, and chewed. While I was chewing, my phone rang. It was Haley, her gorgeous face once again adorning my screen.

"I hope you're calling me to tell me you already found the Black Hawk?" I said.

"I wish," Haley said.

I took the salt shaker and salted my eggs, stabbed the eggs with a fork, and piled them into my mouth.

"Do I really have to watch you eat?" Haley said.

"I'm hungry," I said, my mouth still full of eggs.

"Could you at least point the camera away from your face?" Haley said.

"If I did, I wouldn't be able to see you," I said. "Which would make me sad."

"We certainly don't want you sad," Haley said.

"Thank you," I said. "Why did you call?"

"We got a break, and suddenly a lot more pieces of the puzzle have come together," Haley said. "However, before I tell you the good news, I have some bad news too."

"What's the bad news?" I said.

"Up until about ten minutes ago, our teams watching Carter Bowdoin had him and Bryce Wellington in their rooms at the Peninsula Hotel in Beverly Hills," Haley said. "But they're not there now, and we don't know where they are."

"So Carter slipped through your surveillance and probably managed to take Wellington with him?" I said.

"Looks that way," Haley said.

"Any idea how he did it?" I said.

"No, but we're working our asses off trying to find them again," Haley said. "Once we do, you'll be the first to know."

"Thanks," I said. "What's the good news?"

"Take a look at this picture," Haley said.

Haley disappeared from the screen. Jeff and Adelaide, despite their bickering, must have been paying attention to Haley's and my conversation. They both instantly stopped what they were doing, and leaned in to take a peek at the photograph that took Haley's place on my iPhone screen.

The photograph was of two young men who looked to be about nineteen years old. They both wore blue jeans, white running shoes, and navy blue hoodies imprinted with the Yale logo and the words 'Yale University' in white letters. Each man had an arm around the other's shoulder. The hand of each man's arm not around a shoulder held an open Budweiser beer. By the glazed look in the men's eyes and their sloppy smiles, it appeared that the beers weren't their first. Or second. Or third. My best guess was that they were on their sixth.

Behind the two young men was a big football stadium with grass-covered walls above its entrance tunnels. White, wispy clouds floated through the sky above the stadium. The sky itself was the flat aquamarine of autumn. A lot of equally young-looking people wearing Yale and Harvard hoodies were milling about between the two young men and the stadium. I made the daring deduction that these people were Harvard and Yale students. The Yalies outnumbered the Harvardians by about two to one.

I recognized one of the two young men with the sloppy smiles and beer cans. It was Carter Bowdoin. The guy Carter had his arm around was a little Asian dude. The Asian dude had an arrogant sneer on his face that was only slightly attenuated by his beery haziness. It was the kind of face most people would like to punch.

The photo disappeared. Haley came back. This time she took up only half of the screen. Hart had joined her on the other half. He was still in the Arabian desert.

"So what do you think?" Haley said.

"Looks like Harvard is playing Yale at Yale," I said. "Day game."

Haley frowned.

"Is that all you see?" Haley said.

"No, that's not all I see," I said. "It's just that what I see is making me sick to my stomach."

Jeff said, "That make two of us."

Hart spit. I couldn't see where the spit landed. I hoped it was somewhere on the desert sand and not on his own foot.

"Make it three," Hart said.

Adelaide said, "Four. I may be young but I know what I'm lookin' at."

Haley said, "It's five. I almost threw up the first time I saw the photo too."

I said, "Five it is then. However, assumptions are one thing and proof is another. Have you got anything else to support that Carter Bowdoin's Yale chum is one and the same with our own present-day little Chinese dude, AKA Dragon Man?"

"You of course remember the photo I showed you taken at the 'Save the Whales' charity event in Beverly Hills?" Haley said. "The one where Carter Bowdoin was standing next to an expensively clothed man – a man you and I decided was our Chinese Dragon Man?"

"I remember," I said. "Carter and Dragon Man appeared to be surveying a line of NASAD engineers waiting to get into the event. The engineers didn't know it at the time, but standing in that line was their death warrant."

"Correct," Haley said. "What we are focused on at this moment about the charity event photo, however, is what we were able to see of Dragon Man's face. The photo only showed a very small portion of the back of Dragon Man's jaw and ear, so it was not enough to identify him, but what we were able to extract was sufficient to compare to a computer-aged face of the Asian student with Carter at the Yale football game."

"And...?"

"It was an exact match," Haley said. "The Asian student at Yale and Carter's Chinese friend at the charity event/Dragon Man are the same person."

"That's very good work on your part," I said.

"Thank you," Haley said.

"Please, though, whatever you say next, don't say that Bowdoin and his Yale buddy AKA Dragon Man were roommates," I said.

Haley shrugged.

"Sorry," Haley said. "But, yes, they were."

Jeff said, "We shoulda checked this shit out a long time ago."

Hart said, "Don't beat yourself up boys. We only came across the photo of Carter's Chinese friend at the charity event yesterday."

I said, "Haley, what's the roommate's name?"

"Liu Jingping," Haley said. "Goes by 'Kenny'."

"How do you get 'Kenny' from 'Jinping'?" I said.

"Hell if I know," Haley said. "However, like I said, a lot more pieces have fallen into place as well. Look at this..."

A picture of a Chinese man in his sixties wearing a green and red military uniform and a high peaked red and green hat with a large black brim replaced Haley and Hart on the screen. The man had cold black eyes, and his dark, almond face was clean shaven. His lips were thick, his nose flat, and his large round nostrils formed two dark holes that seemed to burrow straight into his skull. Short, razor-cropped, black hair spread from beneath the edges of the peaked hat and there was a wide swath of skin around his abnormally small ears. The tunic of his collar was tight around his thick neck and the muscles of his shoulders and arms bulged beneath the muslin cloth. The man's narrow, upturned mouth and slightly closed, heavy, lidded eyes made him look like he thought he was cunning. He probably was, because pinned to his chest were dozens of multicolored medals, and the insignias on his shoulder epaulets, collar, and hat said he was a very high-ranking general in the Chinese Army.

Haley and Hart came back on screen.

"Don't tell me Kenny's a princeling," I said.

Jeff said, "Stop saying that 'don't tell me' shit. It ain't working out for us at all."

"Sorry," I said.

Haley said, "Son of a princeling. The picture is of General Liu Jiabao, Kenny's father. Kenny's grandfather was Liu Li, a hero of the Cultural Revolution. Kenny is the seventh son of seven sons."

"I thought the Chinese were only allowed one child," I said.

"The elite classes work under a different set of rules," Haley said.

"Of course they do," I said. "What does Kenny do for a living?"

"Kenny is the managing partner of the Golden Dragon Fund," Haley said. "Golden Dragon is a private equity fund based in Beijing."

Jeff and I looked at each other.

"Same as it ever was," I said.

"Look that way," Jeff said.

Adelaide said, "Talking Heads?"

"How'd you know that?" I said.

"'Remain in Light's' a classic, dude," Adelaide said.

Jeff said, "Kenny got a large automobile, beautiful house, and beautiful wife?"

Haley said, "Many large automobiles, many houses, and three very beautiful wives. Wives are in Shanghai, Beijing, and Macao."

"Busy little asshole," Jeff said.

I said, "Let me tell you about the very rich. They are different from you and me."

Adelaide said, "F. Scott Fitzgerald."

Jeff said, "Dang. You on a roll, girl." Then to Haley, he added, "One of the cars a Ferrari?"

Haley smiled.

"Yes," Haley said. "Ferrari, Rolls, Lamborghini, '57 Chevy."

Jeff poured some more syrup on a piece of bacon, shoved the bacon in his mouth, and chewed.

"He drives a '57 Chevy around China?" Jeff said, his mouth full.

Haley nodded.

"Damn," Jeff said. "He doesn't happen to have any eagle, panther, or tiger statues outside any of them houses does he?"

"As a matter of fact he's got all three," Haley said. "And a leopard statue too."

Jeff turned to me.

"What'd I tell you?" Jeff said.

"I don't remember you saying anything about a leopard," I said.

"That's low, even for you," Jeff said.

"It was pretty low," I said.

Hart spit again.

"Let's get back on track, please," Hart said.

I shoveled some more eggs into my mouth and took a sip of coffee.

"We can do that," I said. "Haley, tell me about how Kenny's Golden Dragon Fund is the biggest stakeholder in whatever the hell the Chinese equivalent of Halliburton is."

"You're ruining all my suspense," Haley said.

"I'm sure there's at least one thing you've got that will be a surprise," I said.

Haley looked uncomfortable. She bit her lower lip and appeared to fidget slightly.

"Well...," Haley said.

I gave her a questioning look.

She gestured with her chin to something off-screen. I followed where her chin was pointing and found myself looking at Jeff. He was looking down at his plate and carving his stack of pancakes into little triangular wedges. I looked back at the screen, gave Haley another questioning look, and mouthed, "Jeff?"

Haley nodded.

I thought about her response for a moment. I was highly doubtful there was anything she knew about Jeff that I didn't already know. And yet something was on her mind, something she probably thought could hurt Jeff. Whatever it was, it wasn't worth the risk if it was something that could destabilize Jeff's fragile PTSD self.

"Later," I mouthed.

Haley nodded. She then continued on as if we had never had our little interlude. "There are actually a number of such Halliburton equivalents. The one that is most likely in play here, however, is the Chairman Mao Industrial Reconstruction Legacy Corporation. The major shareholders of the corporation are the Golden Dragon Fund and Sun Chunxian's mother. Sun Chunxain is the politburo member in line to become the next vice premier and secretary of the Central Committee. Sun's ascension, by the way, could happen any day now since the current vice premier is quite ill and is rumored to be resigning soon."

"So what you're saying," I said, "is that Kenny's Golden Dragon fund, the Chairman Mao Industrial Reconstruction Legacy Corporation, and the next vice premier of China are pretty much one big happy family?"

Since I had finished my pancakes, I reached across the table, forked one of Jeff's pancake wedges, and put the wedge in my mouth. Jeff gave me a dirty look.

"Yes," Haley said. "But it's not just a big family, it's an enormous family. Both Chairman Mao Industrial Reconstruction Legacy Corporation's and Golden Dragon Fund's boards of directors are made up entirely of close relatives of standing committee members of the politburo of the Chinese Communist Party. For completeness sake, I should also add that the largest shareholders in the Golden Dragon Fund are Kenny Liu's parents."

"They must be very proud of their little boy," I said.

"I bet they are," Haley said.

"Does the Chairman Mao Industrial Reconstruction Legacy Corporation focus their business on any particular area?" I said, mumbling a bit since my mouth was full of Jeff's pancakes.

"They do," Haley said. "They specialize in oil services. They drill wells, put out well fires, build the roads to and from the oil fields, and construct oil field employee housing, power lines, and pipelines. They have over ten thousand people working in Iraq right at this moment."

"If Saudi Arabia gets trashed in a war, how many people do you estimate Chairman Mao will need to supply to rebuild it?" I said.

"At least eighty thousand," Haley said.

"The contract already inked and signed?" I said.

"We believe so," Haley said.

Adelaide reached across the table, and in a replay of my move, snared one of Jeff's pancake wedges. Jeff tried to spear the back of her hand with his fork but missed and put holes in the table instead. I didn't think Jeff would miss unless he wanted to, at least I hoped that was the case.

Adelaide, chewing on Jeff's pancakes, said, "So, United States wins the war, the contract is worthless. Serves them right."

Jeff said, "Golden Dragon Fund win no matter who win."

"What are you talking about?" Adelaide said. "U.S. isn't going to hire those Chairman Mao assholes."

Jeff poured syrup on his last piece of bacon and popped the bacon into his mouth.

"That's right," Jeff said. "They ain't. U.S. and the Saudis gonna hire whatever engineering firm be owned by Carter Bowdoin's Pennsylvania Avenue Partners."

Haley said, "Jeff is correct. Brown Robinson, Ltd., one of Halliburton's biggest competitors, was recently acquired by Pennsylvania Avenue Partners. Brown Robinson was awarded the contract this week for the post-war rebuilding of Saudi Arabia."

Jeff wiped some syrup from his lips with a napkin.

"That's because it's the low bid," Jeff said. "Which doesn't matter, since the bid goes out the window once work commences. They gonna charge whatever they gonna charge. Get paid for it too."

Adelaide said, "Fine. Whatever. But Jeff said Golden Dragon wins no matter what. If Pennsylvania Avenue Partners gets the contract, how is that a win for Golden Dragon?"

Haley said, "Adelaide you're correct that Golden Dragon wouldn't normally make a penny if China loses. But Golden Dragon and Pennsylvania Avenue Partners are partners."

"Partners? A U.S. military contracting company and Chinese military contracting company are partners?" Adelaide said.

"Yes," Haley said.

"That's the most screwed up thing I ever heard," Adelaide said. "We allow this kind of shit?"

"No, it's not allowed," Haley said. "But that didn't stop Kenny Liu and Carter Bowdoin from forming such a partnership. And, thanks to your uncle, General Wilder, we knew where to look to get the proof that they'd done it."

Jeff said, "Proof, huh? That surprise me they be stupid enough to leave proof lying around."

"What's the saying, Jeff?" Haley said. "There's no honor among thieves?"

"The two old Yalie roommates didn't trust each other, huh?" Jeff said.

"Apparently not," Haley said. "The proof we found is in the form of a document that was locked away in the safe deposit box of a Panamanian Bank. The document is signed by both Kenny and Carter - they even went so far as to have it notarized - and it outlines how the profits from any rebuilding work in Saudi Arabia will be split equally between their companies no matter who does the actual rebuilding work. The document also goes into great detail about the mechanisms they will use to transfer the money between the funds without detection."

Haley's words were pretty much just a confirmation of what I had suspected Carter and Kenny had been up to, but for some reason hearing them just then as they came out of her mouth had made me furious. Maybe it was the unadulterated evil of the two men. Maybe it was because it made me think about the massive waste of human life Carter and Kenny had caused - and if war broke out, were about to continue to cause - in the service of their greed. Maybe because in my mind's eye I suddenly saw Carter and Kenny torturing Kate and Billy.

Whatever had caused my fury, however, was also causing my heart to race and my breathing to become shallow and rapid. I felt faint.

Adelaide said, "How'd you get into a safe deposit box of a Panamanian bank?"

Hart cleared his throat.

"That information is above your pay grade, little lady," Hart said.

"I don't get paid squat," Adelaide said.

"Exactly," Hart said.

The waitress returned with a fresh pot of coffee. This time she didn't do any dog imitations. Which was too bad, since I thought she did a pretty good job last time. She kept a wary distance from Adelaide, filled our cups, and left.

I left my cup on the table, as another cup of coffee was the last thing I needed in my then current state. I bent forward, rested my chin on the table, and tried to take some deep breaths to calm myself. Some of the coffee's steam wafted over my face. The steam slowly transformed into a vision of Freddy's mutilated body lying next to the pool. I still didn't think Freddy had been mixed up in Carter and Kenny's foul plans. There was only one way to find out, however. I took a deep breath and shoved aside the vision of Freddy as best I could.

"Freddy Feynman wasn't on the documents memorializing the deal between Pennsylvania Avenue Partners and Golden Dragon, was he?" I said.

Haley shook her head.

"No," Haley said. "I haven't seen any evidence Mr. Feynman was aware of the documents either."

"The deal that Freddy Feynman made between NASAD and Pennsylvania Avenue Partners was above board?" I said, almost gasping for breath.

"You don't look so hot," Haley said.

"I think I might be having a reaction to the antidote," I said.

Hart said, "That's not another one of your bullshit answers is it, son? If you're not going to be able to finish this mission off, tell me now. I don't have any idea what I'll do if you can't, but at least it will give me some time to try to come up with something."

"Hazmat guys said it might take up to five hours for us to be completely free of any potential side effects from the gas and the antidote," I said. "That would be about oh-nine-thirty, so I've still got a little under three hours to go."

"You aren't a hundred percent by then, I need to hear about it," Hart said.

"You will, sir," I said. "So Haley, again, please, what about Freddy and the NASAD-Pennsylvania Avenue Partners' deal?"

"That deal was unquestionably above board," Haley said. "The documents outlining the financial arrangements between NASAD and Pennsylvania were all signed in the United States and witnessed by dozens of lawyers on each side. There was no need for them to be hidden away in a Panamanian safe deposit box."

I nodded. I guess my relief must have shown on my face. Jeff leaned across the table, put his head between my head and my cell phone, and looked directly into the phone's camera.

"Jack happy Freddy stupid, but not evil," Jeff said. "Still a sentimental fool, ain't he?"

Haley smiled.

"Yes," Haley said.

I gently pushed Jeff back in his seat.

"Did you find a personal connection between Kenny Liu and Captain Paul Lennon?" I said.

"We did," Haley said. "It was actually fairly easy to establish once we found out who Kenny was."

Haley and Hart again disappeared from my iPhone screen. A map came up in their place. The map showed the border area between southern China and northern Myanmar. Adelaide and Jeff leaned in closer and all three of us watched as the picture zoomed into a spot that appeared to be about half a mile inside the border on the Myanmar side.

The area was a heavily forested, dark green jungle. The ground was shielded from view by the jungle canopy. The picture continued to zoom and an unnatural clearing in the jungle took shape. In the center of the clearing was a charred and mangled shape that looked like the remains of an airplane crash. I assumed the unnatural look to the clearing had to have been caused by the explosion that most likely followed the crash.

"The area you are looking at is in the Northern Shan State of

Myanmar," Haley said off-screen. "The vehicle whose remains you see was a Predator drone with highly advanced technology, including stealth and laser aiming capabilities. It was being used by the CIA in a clandestine effort to assist Myanmarese rebels in the area. When the drone crashed, its auto-destruct mechanism failed to deploy properly. A team was sent to recover whatever it could and then destroy everything else in order to keep the technology from falling into unfriendly hands. As I am sure you noticed from the graphic I showed you, the site was only approximately seven hundred yards from the Chinese border."

The graphic vanished and Haley and Hart returned.

Jeff said, "Why are you beating around the bush Haley darlin'? No need to say 'unfriendly' when you be meaning Chinese."

Haley smiled.

"You're right, General," Haley said. "The powers that be did not want the technology to fall into Chinese hands."

I said, "Captain Paul Lennon led the recovery team?"

"He did," Haley said. "The Chinese had also become aware of the drone and sent in their own team."

Jeff looked up at me.

"The distinction between the past, present, and future be only a stubbornly persistent illusion," Jeff said.

"T. S. Eliot?" I said.

"Nope," Jeff said. "Tommy say something similar in 'Burnt Norton' - 'Time present and time past are both perhaps present in time future and time future contained in time past. If all time is eternally present all time is unredeemable' - but not that."

Adelaide said, "Who's Tommy?"

"Girl, we gotta work on your education," Jeff said. "Tommy be T. S.'s first name."

I said, "If it's not T. S., then there's only one other person it can be. Can I get a second chance?"

Hart whistled loudly. We looked up to see the fingers of both his hands in his mouth.

"Can we please stick to the point?" Hart said.

"This is the point," I said. Then to Jeff, I added, "Gonna go with Albert."

Adelaide said, "Einstein?"

"You're full of surprises, aren't you," Jeff said. "Billy Einstein's distant cousin, Albert, be correct. Everything come full circle."

Adelaide smiled. But then her face quickly dropped.

"I'm confused," Adelaide said.

"Why are you confused?" Jeff said.

"I don't understand how Albert Einstein is the point," Adelaide said.

Hart said, "You aren't the only one, little lady."

I said, "What Jeff is saying, Adelaide, is that Carter's friend Kenny Liu is trapped in time."

Jeff nodded.

"Kenny hell-bent on revenging the past, only he lives in the present," Jeff said. "That's why he's screwing up the future."

Adelaide appeared to consider this. I sneaked a peek at Hart. He looked pissed.

"Jesus!" Hart said.

I said, "Haley, who did Kenny Liu know on the Chinese patrol?"

The waitress arrived with more coffee. She emitted a soft bark at Adelaide. Adelaide appeared to be still thinking over Jeff's statement about Kenny being trapped in time, and seemed not to even notice. The waitress leaned over and poured the coffee, getting closer to me than she had before. She smelled of fresh lavender soap.

"Can I get you anything else?" the waitress said.

"Not now," I said. "Thank you."

The waitress left. We turned our attention back to Haley.

"The Chinese team was led by Liu Zhengsheng," Haley said.

Jeff and I looked at each other.

"Same last name as Kenny," Jeff said.

"How much you want to bet it's not his cousin?" I said.

"What?" Jeff said. "All the sudden I look like a sucker to you?"

"Sorry," I said.

Hart whistled again. We turned back to the screen. Haley was waiting patiently.

"Liu Zhengsheng was Kenny's oldest brother," Haley said. "He was a colonel in the Chinese special forces. When Liu Zhengsheng's team arrived on the scene, there was a firefight between Lennon's and Liu's men. Liu's team took heavy casualties and Liu was killed by Captain

Lennon. Liu's team withdrew. Paul Lennon's team took what they needed from the drone, destroyed the rest, and returned home. Paul Lennon was awarded the Silver Star for his efforts, which must have been the medal that was missing from the box you found in Sarah Lennon's home."

Jeff said, "If I were Kenny, and Paul Lennon killed my brother, I'd be pissed."

I said, "Pissed enough to order the killing of Lennon's whole family?"

"Yeah," Jeff said. "Might even put on a dragon mask while I was doing it."

"I take it that means you are now absolutely, positively convinced Dragon Man and Kenny Liu are one and the same?" I said.

"We already decided Dragon Man and Carter's friend at the 'Save the Whales' charity event be one and the same," Jeff said. "Now we know Carter's friend has a name and it be Kenny Liu. So yeah, I'm convinced."

"Me too," I said. "However, there is one more question I would like to ask Haley before we consider this a completely closed matter."

Haley said, "What's the question, Jack?"

"We know that both Kenny Liu and Dragon Man seem to be inordinately fond of yellow socks," I said. "Do we also know if Kenny has any special love for Chinese emperors?"

"Glad you brought that up," Haley said. "Take a look at this. I believe it nicely links together the yellow socks Kenny was wearing at the charity event, what Bobby and Timmy told you about Dragon Man's yellow socks, and what Bobby and Timmy said about Dragon Man's mask with five claws."

Hart and Haley again vanished and another picture took their place. This one was of the tomb of Emperor Qin Shi Huang, who was the first emperor of China. The tomb is east of the Chinese town of Xi'an and contains a vast terra cotta army of warriors, chariots, and horses. The terra cotta army was built to protect Qin in the afterlife. In the picture on my screen, the tomb was brightly lit and decorated for a party. There were hundreds of men and women dressed in black tie formal wear milling about the terra cotta soldiers. In the center of the tomb was a huge golden throne. Kenny/Liu Jingping was sitting on the throne. He was wearing the bead veiled, mortar-board-like crown and flowing, ornate yellow robes of a Chinese emperor.

Jeff said, "Looks like Kenny throwing himself a royal party."

I suddenly felt much more lightheaded. It seemed like the walls of the diner were closing in on me. A moment later I passed out.

CHAPTER 114

When I finally began to arise from my unconscious state, I found myself on my back and staring at a bright, blue, cloudless sky. The sound of pounding surf filled my ears, I could feel fine grains of sand between my fingers and against the back of my head, and my nose was filled with the smell of salt and seaweed. It was very warm and sweat was trickling down the sides of my forehead. I swatted a sand flea that had alighted on my arm and made the audaciously bold deduction that I was on a beach somewhere.

I propped myself up on my elbows to have a look around.

I confirmed I was indeed on a beach.

I was also about thirty yards above the point where the tide's current waterline ended. Adelaide and Jeff were building a sand castle right at the edge of the water, using the wet sand to construct moats, towers, and walls.

Manu and Mosi were helping Adelaide and Jeff with the sand castle. The two Samoan twins were dressed in light blue suits that were too small for their giant bodies, along with white dress shirts and royal blue ties. They were both barefoot, their black oxford lace-up shoes and black socks piled on the sand at a spot where the waves couldn't reach them.

I assumed Jeff and Adelaide had carried me to the beach after I had passed out. I supposed they'd decided that as long as we couldn't take any action to rescue Kate and Billy until the stealth Black Hawk helicopter was found, we could wait at a beach just as well as in the diner. I also deduced that the fact we were all still on that beach meant that the helicopter, along with Kate and Billy, was still missing. I was pretty sure that if the Black Hawk had already been found, Adelaide and Jeff would have thrown my unconscious body into the van and the three of us would currently be on our way to the helicopter's location. I had no idea how Manu and Mosi had found us, but I was sure I would soon find out.

Farther away from shore, the sun's rays had flattened into wafer-thin panes of bright light on a glassy ocean surface, the breezes that would likely rise later in the day then nonexistent. Surfers sat waiting for waves big enough to ride. A five pelican synchronized flight team flew just above the surfers' heads, the pelicans rising and falling in a sine wave.

I heard the faint sound of cars moving behind me and turned to look. Separated from me by a vast expanse of white sand beach, and an equally vast asphalt-covered parking lot, lay a very busy Pacific Coast Highway. The Kazakhs' van and the Maybach were parked next to each other in the row of the lot that was closest to the sand.

A father and son were standing in the sand just beyond the parking lot and flying a kite. Seagulls squawked and stalked in big groups as they looked for food near the seemingly infinite number of blue trash cans that lined the beach. To my left, high bluffs cut the beach off from access to all points south. A nearby sign said the name of the beach was 'Zuma'. I remembered Zuma Beach wasn't far from the diner. Jeff and Adelaide had not transported me any great distance.

The sun was well above the foothills east of the highway. By its height, I estimated the time to be about 11:30 a.m. I took out my cell phone. It was 11:40 a.m. Close enough. But not good news. The Chinese were set to commence their war at 6:00 p.m. local time. A lot of time had gone by since I passed out in the diner, so much time that there were then less than six and a half hours to stop the war.

We also had less than six and a half hours to find Billy and Kate. If we didn't find them within that six and a half hour window, the two of them were probably as good as dead. That was because I believed Billy and Kate's captors had taken the two of them to find out if Billy and Kate had revealed anything to anyone that might compromise the insurmountable edge's effectiveness. If in six and a half hours the war went off without a hitch, the captors would have no further use for Billy and Kate, and they would be killed.

My eyes were suddenly attracted to movement in the parking lot. A small white Honda SUV was pulling into the lot. The SUV's doors opened and two blond-haired kids, a boy, who looked to be about five years old, and a girl, who looked to be about four, got out. The boy was dressed in blue swimming trunks and the girl in a red two piece bathing suit. Both children wore flip flops and each of them carried their own green, red, and white beach ball that was almost as big as they were. A blond petite woman in a black bikini - who I assumed was the kids' mother as she closely resembled them - exited the driver's door. She carried an overlarge blue canvas beach bag.

The kids started dribbling the beach balls on the asphalt, which was then hot enough to send heat waves off its surface. The heat waves were a few feet high and made the kids slightly blurry. The kids' altered shapes slowly changed in my mind's eye to Paul Lennon's murdered children, Sam and Lizzy. Sam and Lizzy stared at me for a moment and then spoke. They spoke not in little kids' voices but in Billy Einstein's and Kate's voices, and what they said was, 'Why didn't you come for us?'

I knew there was no way I could have saved Sam and Lizzy from their horrible deaths as I hadn't even been aware they were in trouble. I also knew there was nothing I could do for Billy and Kate until Haley and Hart found the Black Hawk. Despite what I knew, I still became overwhelmed with grief and guilt. I felt like my entire being was about to dissolve into a quivering gelatinous mass.

I needed to do something to distract myself from the visions and voices and that awful feeling of impending dissolution. I turned away from the kids and tried to focus my eyes on the surfers at sea. I couldn't focus at all, however - everything was just a distorted mass of color and odd shapes. I went into a full blown panic. The only thing I could hear was Nimo/Billy's and Kate's voices saying over and over, 'Why didn't you come for us?'

Then another voice intruded.

"Man, you look really messed up," the voice said.

I tried to find the source of the voice, but could not.

"I right in front of your face, bozo," the voice said.

Still, all I could see was a seething, psychedelic blur.

Hands grabbed my shoulders and shook me. Then one of the hands lifted off my left shoulder and I felt a sharp slap across my cheek.

My eyes finally began to focus.

Jeff's face appeared in front of me. His nose was inches from mine.

"I starting to think we two peas in a pod," Jeff said.

I didn't say anything. I took some deep breaths. My panic began to subside.

"I know what you're hoping your problem is," Jeff said. "Taser, elephant tranquilizer, dying for seven minutes, nerve gas. But that ain't it."

"Bullshit," I said.

"Ain't no bullshit," Jeff said. "You got full blown PTSD."

"It's a stress reaction," I said. "You said so yourself."

"It's a stress reaction only if it goes away," Jeff said.

"It'll go away," I said.

"Okay with me if it doesn't," Jeff said. "I could always use some help looking for IED's under my bed."

"Funny," I said.

"Matter of fact," Jeff said, "I'm kinda looking forward to seeing what it's like having two lunatics running around the ranch."

"That's a delightful idea," I said.

"Of course, then we couldn't let Adelaide go off and join the Army," Jeff said. "We'll be needing her to keep us straight."

"God forbid," I said.

I took some more deep breaths. I began to feel almost normal again.

"Have I been out since I fainted in the diner?" I said.

Jeff nodded.

"We could have stayed there until you returned to the land of the living," Jeff said. "But I figured it was only a matter of time before Adelaide tear that sweet little waitress's head off."

"What are Manu and Mosi doing here?" I said.

"They got back from their momma's birthday party this morning," Jeff said. "When they heard what happened to Kate, they begged Carpenter to tell them where we were. Say they wanna help us."

"Help us, huh?" I said. "That's an idea that might be more trouble than it's worth."

"I say we cross that bridge when we come to it," Jeff said.

"Fine," I said. "Whatever you want. No word on Kate and Billy or the Black Hawk?"

"Nope," Jeff said.

"Don't like sitting around," I said. "Maybe we should start looking on our own."

"Haley and Hart on it," Jeff said. "We just gotta be patient."

"You sure they'll tell us as soon as they know something?" I said.

"No question about that," Jeff said.

Jeff sat down next to me. We both watched as the boy and the girl with the beach balls, accompanied by their mother, walked down to the ocean. Thankfully, the two children had become themselves once again, and no longer resembled Sam and Lizzy. Once the kids and their mom got to the ocean's edge, the kids began to play a game. The children would wait until a small wave had crawled up the sand and begin to recede. They then threw the beach balls into the gentle current flowing back to sea and waited. When the next wave caught the balls and brought them back in close to shore, the children snatched the balls out of the water. They threw the balls into the water and retrieved them over and over again. Each time it appeared to seem new to them.

As I watched the children play, I began to go over in my mind what I'd learned over the previous few hours. I thought about Billy's/Nimo's and Kate's phones, Billy's and Kate's fingerprints, Billy's patch cord and Enigma machine app, and the insurmountable edge. While Jeff had overheard my conversation with Haley and Hart about those aforementioned subjects, I realized I hadn't reviewed any of it them with him. Reviewing things with Jeff was usually a good idea.

"As long as we're just sitting here waiting for Haley and Hart to call and tell us where the Black Hawk is," I said, "maybe we should go over what we know. Get a plan ready for when they do find it."

"Sound good to me," Jeff said.

"So what do you think?" I said.

"Think we gotta lot of things working against us right now, maybe too many things," Jeff said. "Billy's and Kate's phones be broke. Even if Haley fixes them, we're relying on converting a copy of Billy's and Kate's fingerprints into some crazy ass passwords to make it all work."

"Fingerprints change over time too," I said. "Assuming Haley finds the copies of Billy's and Kate's prints that were used to get their security clearances, the fingerprints still might be older than the ones they used as passwords for their phones."

"All that digitizing and everything those phones do might mean even the slightest change could produce the wrong password," Jeff said.

"That's what I'm afraid of," I said. "We should probably try to come at this from a completely different angle."

"I agree," Jeff said. "Let's be giving it some cogitation."

We both were silent as we thought things over.

After a couple of minutes had gone by, I said, "You have any ideas?"

"Nothing good," Jeff said.

"I have one," I said. "Don't know how good it is, because it still relies on Haley and Hart finding the Black Hawk in order to use it."

"Can't be worrying about finding the Black Hawk," Jeff said. "That's out of our control. All we can do is be prepared for when it is found."

"That's almost profound," I said. "Kinda Buddha-like."

"Not surprising," Jeff said. "Buddha done stole a lot of his shit from me."

"Didn't know that," I said.

"Lot of things you don't know," Jeff said. "What you got?"

"Assuming Haley and Hart find the Black Hawk, and that Billy and Kate are being held captive in close proximity to it, we go in and free the two of them," I said. "We then ask Billy what part of the military's computer software the insurmountable edge targets. We tell Haley what Billy says, then maybe she can disable the edge, phone or no phone."

"It a start, but didn't Billy say that file he put on Kate's phone is the thing that deactivates the insurmountable edge?" Jeff said. "I bet Haley needs that deactivation sequence in Billy's file. Otherwise, how is she gonna get the insurmountable edge out of every computer the U.S. military has?"

"Good point," I said. "If you're right, and if Billy's and Kate's phones really are completely shot, we'd probably need Billy to recreate the deactivation sequence."

"Billy would have to work fast, too," Jeff said. "Only time he have is whatever time left between after we find him and when war commencing."

A particularly large wave rolled in from the ocean. The wave took out the seaward wall of Adelaide, Manu, and Mosi's castle. The three of them scrambled to rebuild the wall. The wave also threw the two children's beach balls higher onto the beach and the kids chased after them.

"That might be hard to do, even if Billy is as big a genius as everyone says he is," I said.

"Billy also gotta be a living genius," Jeff said. "You and me both know there's a good chance he's already dead. Kate too."

"I know," I said.

Jeff turned to face me. He looked into my eyes for what seemed like a long time before speaking.

"You know there's a reason you aren't supposed to get attached to someone while you're on a mission," Jeff said. "Can cloud your thinking. Lead you to make mistakes."

"I understand," I said.

"Not that you made any yet," Jeff said.

"Not so sure about that," I said.

"If you did, they small," Jeff said. "And I be forgiving you for them."

"That's nice of you," I said.

"What you went through with Grace was as hard as it gets," Jeff said. "I've always been praying you find someone new."

"Thanks," I said.

"You're welcome," Jeff said. He paused, then added, "Damn. You know what? Speaking of mistakes makes me remember something I've been thinking about for a while. I should have mentioned it before."

"What's that?" I said.

"Billy's eighteen," Jeff said.

I smiled.

"We're in sync, my friend," I said. "As always."

"That means you agree Einstein's a genius, but maybe he's lacking in experience?" Jeff said.

"Yes," I said.

"And such lack of experience means it's possible he might not have thought of everything?" Jeff said. "Like maybe Dr. Nimo/Billy screw up somehow and his insurmountable edge got a flaw?"

"Other than the grammar," I said, "that's exactly how I'd put it."

"Question is, what'd he screw up?" Jeff said.

"I have no idea," I said.

"Well, I counting on you to figure it out," Jeff said.

"Me?" I said. "What about you?"

"You do better under pressure, so we best be putting it all on you," Jeff said.

"Nice try," I said.

"Okay, I'll help you," Jeff said.

"Thank you," I said. "I guess even though we just did a lot of cogitating, we better do some more?"

"Yep," Jeff said. "Now's a good time too. Especially considering we've got a little more than six hours to stop a war."

We quietly watched what was transpiring on the beach in front of us. The kids continued to play with their beach balls in the waves. Adelaide, Manu, and Mosi had fully rebuilt the seaward wall of their sand castle and added a keep. Jeff seemed to be thinking hard. I thought hard too, but the brutal truth was I didn't have enough knowledge about the details of what Nimo/Billy had done, let alone enough technical expertise and training, to even begin to come up with any mistake that he might have made. Of course, Jeff didn't have that knowledge or expertise either. Jeff broke our silence after a few minutes.

"You got anything?" Jeff said.

"Not yet," I said.

"Me neither," Jeff said. "Well, seeing how we're getting nowhere at the moment, I think it's a good time to bring up another important subject. It's a subject you yourself might one day come to appreciate."

"What's that?" I said.

"There's nothing worse than trying to make a crazy person feel like they crazier than they is," Jeff said.

"Did I do that?" I said.

"You and Haley both," Jeff said. "I saw you signaling her not to tell me something."

"It's true," I said. "I did."

"What was it?" Jeff said.

"I don't know," I said. "I never found out."

"You telling the truth?" Jeff said.

"I am," I said.

"Well, let's be finding out then," Jeff said.

"You want me to call her right now?" I said.

"Unless you got a better way," Jeff said.

I called Haley using FaceTime. She appeared on my screen after the first ring.

"Sorry, guys," Haley said. "I haven't found the stealth Black Hawk yet. We did, however, find Dr. Nimo/Billy's car in the area about five miles from Dr. Lennon's estate, right where he said it would be. There wasn't anything of any value in the car except Billy's special patch cord.

The patch cord isn't going to be of any use to us though unless we can get Billy's and Dr. Lennon's cell phones working, which I highly doubt we will."

"Haley, we ain't calling about the Black Hawk or the patch cord," Jeff said. "We calling about the surprise."

"Surprise?" Haley said.

"Yeah," Jeff said. "The surprise you didn't wanna tell me about in the diner."

Haley shifted her gaze, and though the screen was small, I got the distinct impression she was looking to me for guidance.

"Don't be looking at Jack," Jeff said. "I'm the one doing the talking."

I said, "It's okay."

Haley said, "How can you okay it? You don't know what it is either."

The look on Haley's face made me start to second-guess myself about letting Jeff see what she had. Because Haley's look told me whatever she had, it was bad. There was a risk that if I changed my mind and told Haley not to show Jeff her surprise, I might wound Jeff's already weak self-esteem. But there was also a risk that if I gave Haley the go ahead, whatever she showed Jeff might release Jeff's menagerie of PTSD demons. No matter what my final decision turned out to be, I needed to make it quickly. The longer I took to decide, the more Jeff could read my hesitation as doubting him, which would be almost as bad as telling Haley not to show him whatever she had.

I went with my first instinct.

"It's fine," I said. "Please show Jeff what you've got."

"You sure you want to see this, Jeff?" Haley said.

Jeff said, "I'm sure."

"Okay," Haley said. "What I'm about to tell you grew out of our discovery of the link between the Golden Dragon Fund, Pennsylvania Avenue Partners, and NASAD. Because of that link, we decided to conduct further investigations into Golden Dragon's other business interests. We found..."

Jeff interrupted.

"I'm hearing, but I'm not seeing," Jeff said.

"Excuse me?" Haley said.

"You said you weren't sure I wanted to see this," Jeff said. "But you ain't showing me nothing."

"The visual won't add anything to what I have to say," Haley said.

"Were you goin' to show it to Jack in the diner?" Jeff said.

Haley hesitated.

"What's that hesitatin', Haley?" Jeff said. "You ain't thinking of lying to me, are you?"

Haley sighed. "Yes, I was going to show it to Jack."

"So you can show it to me," Jeff said.

Haley turned ever so slightly away from the camera and seemed to do some work on her computer.

"Stop that," Jeff said.

"Stop what?" Haley said.

"You look like you're photoshopping or something," Jeff said. "Just show me the damn visual, Haley."

Haley sighed. She disappeared from view and two photographs filled the screen. The photos were of a site I had visited two and a half years before, and what the photos showed was bad.

Very bad.

Because what had happened at that site two years ago was what had propelled Jeff into the hell of PTSD.

I stole a glance at Jeff. His face revealed nothing but a seemingly quiet calm. If his mind was in turmoil, he certainly wasn't showing it.

I looked at the first photo again. Images of what had occurred at the site back then began to flood my own consciousness. I thought for a moment it was me who was going to have a nervous breakdown, not Jeff. The moment passed, however.

The site depicted in Haley's first photo was located in the searing desert badlands of Sudan. At the time the photo was taken, the sun was high in a cloudless, pale blue sky and the earth was parched, flat, and cracked. A few acacia trees with thin trunks and wide, leafy canopies dotted the landscape at distant intervals from each other. Interspersed at random places between and under the acacias were over a hundred misshapen sack-like forms lying on the ground. Someone who had not been at the site at that time may have had a hard time identifying the forms from the photo alone. Since I'd been there, however, and seen the forms with my own two eyes, I knew exactly what the forms were. They were the bodies of dead mercenaries, their countries of origin foreign and hostile to the United States.

Haley's second photograph was a close up of a huge granite boulder that lay at the center of the site. The boulder's surface was pockmarked by thousands of rough-edged, tiny stone craters and covered by crisscrosses of thick hemp rope that spread like a spiderweb in all directions. On the very top of the boulder, lashed beneath those crisscrosses, was my good friend, General Jeffrey Bradshaw.

Jeff's face had been beaten and his eyes and lips were puffy and dark purple. Blood leaked from his nostrils and out of his ears. His arms and legs were splayed wide and his abdomen had been filleted open. Jeff's intestines spilled out of the wound, hanging on both sides of his body.

Seven more sack-like shapes were piled below Jeff at the base of the boulder. But those sack-like shapes were not more dead mercenaries. They were the bodies of U.S. special forces soldiers, all of them in uniform, and all of them headless.

Jeff and the seven dead special forces soldiers represented all the members of the team that General Bryce Wellington - in the Army then, but of late with Carter Bowdoin's Pennsylvania Avenue Partners - had requested Jeff lead on an emergency rescue mission. The mission had been launched due to a report that a U.S. Army transport plane had crashed at the site and that its surviving personnel were in grave danger of being killed or captured by roving bands of Sudanese Islamic jihadists. The mission's goal was to extract those personnel, but it was later determined that neither the plane, nor the Army personnel, ever actually existed. The official story was that Bryce Wellington, due to inexperience, had been tricked into sending Jeff's team after a fictional plane.

Jeff's team had parachuted into the site, but once there, had quickly lost contact with their mission handlers. The handlers couldn't know it at the time, but the reason they had lost contact was not only that Jeff and his team were fighting for their lives after having been ambushed by well over two hundred mercernaries, but also, as Jeff later told me, Jeff believed his team's communications had been blocked by sophisticated jamming equipment. Most of the mercenaries, as the photo showed, were killed in the assault.

As the hours without contact from Jeff's team continued to mount, the mission handlers became increasingly concerned about the status of Jeff and his men. After twelve hours had gone by without any communication from Jeff's team, a second team was assembled to look for Jeff and his men. The second team's commanders were uncomfortable, however, about sending their troops in without better information on what had befallen Jeff's unit.

During that time, I was in a hospital bed recuperating from knee surgery but was carefully monitoring the situation. When I heard of the second team's delay, I became both worried about Jeff and his men, and furious about the delay. I told the second team's commanders to go to hell and left the hospital against the vigorous protests of my doctors. I immediately went to the Sudan, where alone and unaccompanied by any other soldiers, I searched for Jeff and his team.

I found Jeff and his men approximately 36 hours after they had initially landed at the site. When I found Jeff, he was in the exact same position atop the boulder as he was in Haley's photograph.

In fact, everything in Haley's photograph looked exactly the same as it had when I found Jeff and his team at the site.

Everything, except for one thing, that is.

Haley's photograph also depicted a group of a dozen men standing in front of the boulder, none of whom were there when I had arrived at the site.

The man in the center of the group was a very dark skinned Chinese man with fine jet black hair, thin lips, and eyes like black marbles. The others were a motley crew of ethnic types from different republics within Central Asia. All twelve of the men wore battle fatigues, had AK-47's slung over their shoulders, extra ammo mags on their belts, and floppy combat hats on their heads to protect against the desert sun. The two men on the far right looked familiar but their faces were too obscured by war paint, beards, and the combat hats to be sure. All the men had their arms around each other and were smiling for the camera. It was clear Jeff was their trophy. He could just as well have been some downed elephant or water buffalo.

The photograph itself seemed to have been printed on high gloss paper. The colors were very bright and sharp and the image's definition very high. There was a caption in Chinese characters and also in English above Jeff and the men. The caption read, "When America's Finest are what you are after..." At the bottom of the photograph were more Chinese characters in big block form that I guessed was some kind of name. Below the big block Chinese characters were what appeared to be contact phone numbers and an email address.

Jeff looked at the two photos without expression. If he was falling to pieces beneath that countenance, there was no way anyone would ever know. The one thing I did know, however, was that Jeff was not just looking, but reading as well. Jeff can read, write, and speak Chinese. I cannot.

Finally he said, "Very original."

"What's it say?" I said.

"'Heise De Shui,'" Jeff said. "Means Blackwater in Chinese."

"I guess they didn't get the memo Blackwater changed their name to Xe and then to Academi," I said. "And then to...hell, it doesn't matter."

Haley came back on the screen.

I said, "Chinese Blackwater does pretty much the same thing the U.S. company formerly known as Blackwater does?"

"Yes," Haley said. "Heise De Shui is a Chinese company that provides contract military services."

"Owned by Kenny Liu's Golden Dragon Fund, no doubt," I said.

"Yes, it is," Haley said.

Just as Haley said that, I noticed that the current near the children had shifted and formed a riptide. The kids' beach balls had gone out, gotten caught in the rip, and were not returning.

Jeff said, "It's a good ad. Very flattering. It get them much business?"

Haley was taken aback.

"Uh...," Haley said. "We're not sure."

"It should have," Jeff said. "You know if Emperor Kenny the Dragon Man ever takes a personal interest in any of Heise's contractual duties?"

"Yes, Kenny does," Haley said. "Heise De Shui is intermittently called upon by the Chinese government to put down uprisings of ethnic minorities that often occur in China's northeastern provinces. We assume Heise De Shui is used so that the government can claim that actions taken against the minorities are nongovernmental in nature. Kenny Liu has occasionally accompanied the Heise De Shui contractors on the missions."

"I assume 'put down uprisings' is a polite way to say massacre the natives?" Jeff said.

"It is," Haley said.

"Emperor Kenny do any shooting?" Jeff said.

"No," Haley said. "Apparently he likes to watch."

"How about his bud, Carter Bowdoin?" Jeff said. "He ever go with Kenny on those missions?"

"We haven't completely verified it yet," Haley said, "but, yes, we think Carter Bowdoin did go at least once, maybe twice."

Jeff nodded.

I said, "Carter going along on a field trip with Heise De Shui to northern China seems like it would need authorization from someone much higher in the food chain than even Kenny 'Dragon Man' Liu. You have any idea who that someone might be?"

"Not yet," Haley said. "But you'll be the first to know if we figure it out. By the way, Jack, did you recognize the two men on the right side of the photo? They're two of the Kazakhs you came across in the desert at the rest stop two days ago."

"I thought they looked familiar," I said.

The kids' beach balls, still caught in the riptide, were drifting farther out to sea. Their mother appeared to tell the children to stay put, then went into the ocean after the balls.

"The man in the center is Liu Dejiang," Haley said. "He is one of Kenny's older brothers, the second son of the seven sons, to be exact."

Jeff said, "Dejiang still alive?"

"I don't know," Haley said.

"No matter," Jeff said very quietly. "Kenny'll do."

"What was that, Jeff?" Haley said.

"Nothing," Jeff said.

Unlike Haley, I'd heard exactly what Jeff had said. I knew what Jeff meant too. He didn't need to take out his revenge directly on Liu Dejiang. He'd be sure whatever he did to Kenny - once he found him - would more than make up for all the things Kenny's older brother Deijang had done to Jeff and Jeff's team.

As for me, I took heart in Jeff's reaction. I figured it meant he was dealing quite well with any horrors Haley's photograph might have caused to be dredged out of his unconscious.

Haley said, "There are two more items you both need to know."

"And they are?" I said.

"The first one is we did some digging after we learned of Heise De Shui's connection to the Kazakh mercenaries," Haley said. "As you know, MOM can gain has access to, among other things, every video camera in every airport in the world. Using our facial recognition software, we ran the photos of the passports that customs had of the mercenaries who got off the Doctors of Mercy flights in Dallas and Oklahoma City against the video recordings of those worldwide airport cameras."

"What'd you find?" I said.

"Three of the Kazakhs on the Doctors of Mercy flights had previously been in the United States," Haley said. "They came separately and on different dates, but each of them arrived shortly before, and left shortly after, one of the 'accidental' deaths of a NASAD drone sub engineer."

"Pretty talented guys," I said. "Any of them among the Kazakhs we already killed?"

"Sadly, no," Haley said.

"Hopefully I'll come across the three of them soon and put the kibosh on any of their future travel plans," I said. "I assume you don't have anything yet on whether or not Heise De Shui mercenaries were involved in the deaths of Milt Feynman, Paul Lennon, and the other nine engineers?"

"No," Haley said. "But we're working on the assumption that they were involved. We're studying flight logs out of Kazakhstan and the entry and video records at U.S. airports to see if we can prove Heise De Shui mercenaries were in the U.S. around the time of the deaths. If they were here, I'm sure it won't be long before we identify them."

"Identify them and track them down, yes?" I said.

"Yes," Haley said. "And do some kiboshing as well."

"Good," I said. "What's the second item you mentioned?"

"We found records of a wire transfer two and a half years ago from Heise De Shui to Uruguayan bank accounts in Bryce Wellington's name," Haley said. "The wire was for ten million dollars and occurred the day after Wellington requested Jeff's team go on the emergency rescue mission in the Sudan."

"Looks like we have another strange coincidence on our hands," I said.

Jeff said, "Ain't no coincidence."

"I was being facetious," I said.

"'Facetious' too big a word for you," Jeff said.

Haley said, "The account also already had over twenty million dollars in it at the time of the Heise De Shui transfer."

I said, "Let me guess. Wellington hit the Uruguayan lottery?"

Jeff said, "Pennsylvania Avenue Partners lottery more like it."

Haley said, "Jeff is correct. The first twenty million was wired in one lump sum by a Dutch subsidiary of PAP that is based in Curacao. General Wellington received it almost three years ago."

I said, "That's around the time that Milt Feynman and Paul Lennon's Otter was blown up over the Gulf of Alaska."

Haley said, "Yes. It is also around the time that Bryce Wellington's godson, the now deceased Colonel Riley Whitelock, was the NASAD military liaison."

Jeff said, "Looks like stealing top secret GPS mislocating and radar evading technology a mighty lucrative gig for Bryce and Riley."

"It was for Bryce anyway," Haley said. "We haven't been able to find any record of Riley receiving even a cent."

I said, "Bryce ripped off his own godson, huh?"

"Looks that way," Haley said.

Jeff said, "What's worse? Ripping Riley off, or having him killed?"

I said, "Good point."

Haley said, "One more thing. I finally found out who got Burnette assigned to the investigation of Whitelock's death."

"Was it Carter Bowdoin?" I said.

"It was," Haley said.

"What a surprise," I said.

On the beach, the kids' mom had retrieved the beach balls from the riptide. She moved the kids to a place that was away from the rip and also closer to Jeff and me. The kids had resumed the game.

A cell phone began to ring. The ring seemed familiar and I tracked its sound to the mom's beach bag, which lay on the sand above the tide line. The kids' mom went to the bag and took it out. I heard the ringing better when it was out of the bag. It was the same ringtone that I had heard on Freddy's phone earlier that morning, shortly before the drones came in with the nerve gas.

I realized then that I had been an idiot for the bazillionth time in the last few days.

"Oh shit," I said.

"What?" Haley said.

"I think we can find Kate," I said.

"How?" Haley said.

"We can track her cell phone," I said.

"But I've got Kate's cell phone," Haley said. "Don't you remember Carpenter found hers and Billy Einstein's on the ground beneath where the Black Hawk had landed? I told you I was going to ask Ray to send them both over to me."

"I'm sorry," I said. "I didn't mean Kate's cell phone. I think she's got another one."

"Kate has two cell phones?" Haley said.

"Last night her brother Freddy got a call just before we were hit with the nerve gas," I said. "I thought it was odd he was getting a call at 4:00 a.m., but that's not what's important. The important thing is that Kate answered the call for him since Freddy was already dead. She took the phone out of Freddy's jacket pocket."

"You're losing me Jack," Haley said.

Jeff said, "I sorry to admit it, but you're losing me too."

I said, "Kate asked who it was that was calling, but no one ever answered her. It made her really annoyed, and when she finally hung up, she put Freddy's phone in her pocket."

Haley said, "In her own pocket? Not in Freddy's?"

"Yes," I said.

Jeff said, "Now I be getting it."

Haley said, "Me too. The bad guys found Kate's and Billy Einstein's phones and threw them out of the Black Hawk, but since they didn't throw Freddy's phone out, it means they probably didn't find it."

I said, "Which means there's a chance Kate still has it."

Haley seemed to think this over.

"I'll bet the reason the bad guys didn't find it is because they didn't even stop to consider that Kate would have a second one," Haley said. "You have to admit the mercenaries have been making a lot of mistakes ever since they met up with you in the desert, Jack."

"I agree," I said. "I'd be dead by now if they hadn't."

"It wouldn't be just you, either," Haley said. "Adelaide, Jeff, Kate, and Paul Lennon's sister, the professor, would be dead too."

"That's probably true," I said. "But let's not start underestimating these guys. All the mercenaries we've come across are reasonably well-trained, just nowhere near as well-trained as our own special forces soldiers are."

"No one's going to start underestimating anybody," Haley said. "So, let's hope you're right, and that Kate is still alive and was smart enough to turn off the ringer."

"If Kate's not alive I'm going to kill myself," I said.

Haley again looked taken aback.

"That sounds a bit extreme, Jack," Haley said.

Jeff said, "Yeah. Don't be saying stuff like that."

I said, "Why not? If Kate's dead, I deserve to die."

Haley seemed to study my face through the screen.

Haley said, "You look like you're serious."

I had never felt more serious about anything in my life. In retrospect, my feelings were probably due to my stress reaction, but killing myself truly seemed at that moment like what I would do if Kate was dead.

"I am serious," I said.

"I can see you feeling that way if Kate is dead, but that's a pretty big 'if', isn't it?" Haley said.

"I don't know," I said. "Right now I'd say it's about fifty-fifty."

"How'd you come up with those odds?" Haley said, then held up her hand. "Wait. Forget I asked. Now's not the time to be arguing about something like this. Just promise me that before you kill yourself, you'll call me."

"Why?" I said. "You think you can talk me out of it?"

"Yes," Haley said. "I do."

Jeff said, "If she don't, you better be calling me next. Anybody can talk you out of anything, it's me."

I said, "Call you? You'll probably be there when I do it."

"Really?" Jeff said.

"Really," I said.

"Good," Jeff said. "Haley, we got nothing to worry about. I won't let him do it. Besides, it won't happen anyway. He's just talking crazy due to his stress reaction."

Haley said, "Yeah, Hart warned me about that."

I said, "Hart told you about my stress reaction?"

"It's no big deal, Jack," Haley said. "People in our line of work get them from time to time."

"It is a big deal if everyone's talking about me behind my back," I said.

Jeff said, "We're talking to your face, dude."

I don't know how it happened, but I suddenly broke free of my suicidal thoughts and realized how insane I must have sounded to Haley and Jeff. I didn't say anything for a moment, just looked back and forth between the two of them, trying to think of a way to get out of the little mess I had created for myself. I decided the best thing to do was to just change the subject and proceed as if I'd never said anything odd or untoward, and was, in fact, functioning perfectly rationally.

"Haley, I'm surprised you would doubt Kate in the slightest," I said. "There's no question she's smart enough to turn off the ringer."

Haley and Jeff looked at each other as if to say 'Where'd that come from?' As I continued to be committed to appearing to be perfectly rational, I, of course, ignored them.

"What we really have to hope for, is that Kate wasn't tied up when she woke up from the nerve gas, and that no one called Freddy before Kate was able to deal with the ringer," I said.

Haley and Jeff exchanged another look. After a moment they both shrugged, which I took to mean they had decided to go with wherever I was taking all of us.

Jeff said, "That's probably not too much to hope for."

"You don't think so?" I said.

"Nope," Jeff said. "But doesn't matter what I think. Haley gonna ping Freddy's phone and we gonna get an answer lickety-split."

CHAPTER 115

Haley went silent for a moment while she pinged Freddy's phone. Jeff and I watched the kids play with their beach balls in the surf as we waited for Haley to tell us what, if anything, the ping had produced. The children's game was the same as it had been since they had started playing it. The children threw the beach balls into the outgoing tide and snatched the beach balls up when the incoming waves brought them back in again.

Haley's voice came back on the line about two minutes after her initial ping.

"We might have caught a break," Haley said. "I've found Freddy's phone."

"Where is it?" I said.

"Somewhere in the middle of Topanga Canyon," Haley said.

"That's only about twenty miles from us, isn't it?" I said.

"It is," Haley said. "Hold on while I retask the satellites and also get some surveillance drones out that way."

I actually knew Topanga Canyon pretty well. I had spent a week in the canyon as a teenager with a friend whose family had a house there. I remembered Topanga as a place that had a strange vibe to it and that the vibe permeated everything. The vibe wasn't as intense as the Hells of Beppu, the rocks of Socotra, or Stonehenge, but it was undeniably there.

I also knew Topanga as a place that attracted the kinky and the odd, the loners and the outliers. Actors, artists, hippies, and musicians lived there side by side, isolated from the surrounding Los Angeles suburbs by Topanga's high mountain ridges. Topanga Canyon Boulevard, a slow moving road with dozens of hairpin turns, is the canyon's only entrance and egress. The Chumash and Tongva tribes had once made Topanga their home, but they had vanished into the mists of time. Gone too was Elysian Fields. Elysian Fields might have been worth a visit. It had been a nudist colony.

Haley said, "Looks like Freddy's phone is in a house on some kind of large ranch-like compound."

"Can you show us what you're seeing?" I said.

"Here it comes," Haley said.

Jeff and I peered closely at my iPhone's screen as it filled with a satellite image. The image centered on what Haley had called a ranch-like compound. I was able to see that the compound was situated in one of the many smaller canyons that shoot off from the main canyon of Topanga. Those smaller canyons varied in width from narrow to wide, but all of them meandered in whatever way the streams that had created them had flowed in eons past. The canyon the ranch-like compound was in was wider than most, and it snaked its way east into the surrounding mountainsides.

The satellite image zoomed in. I could then make out what appeared to be a public road traversing the western border of the compound. The public road connected to Topanga Canyon Boulevard. The distance from the boulevard to the compound looked to be about three miles. The satellite image grew larger and larger and I could see that the compound consisted of an approximately one hundred acre site that was surrounded by what looked to be barbed wire strung between wooden fence posts. There was a roughly rectangular clearing in the middle of the site but most of the site was covered by scrub brush that was intermittently dotted by trees.

Five buildings on the compound that looked like they could be houses came into view. The buildings sat at the edge of the rectangular clearing. The clearing itself was maybe three hundred and fifty yards long, two hundred yards wide, and about fifteen acres in size. A dry creek bed ran down the edge of the property that was opposite and across from the house-like buildings. A series of trails transected the eastern portion of the site, most of the trails petering off into deep brush.

"Haley, are those five buildings houses?" I said.

"They are," Haley said. "Freddy's phone is pinging in the largest of them."

Jeff leaned closer to my iPhone screen. He seemed to take particular interest in one segment of the satellite image.

Jeff said, "What are those four little things moving around the edges of that clearing?"

I said, "Looks like they're keeping a pretty regular spacing."

"I bet they're sentries," Jeff said.

"Can you zoom in on them, Haley?" I said.

"Sorry, we're at the limits of this satellite," Haley said. "I'll have another one available in fifteen minutes. It will have infrared capabilities as well."

"Will the infrared be powerful enough to enable you to look inside the houses?" I said.

"It's very good infrared, Jack," Haley said. "If there's a mouse in one of those buildings it will spot it."

I peered more closely at the image on the screen. There was something I was hoping would be there and I looked hard for it. I didn't find it.

"Unfortunately," I said, "there's something I don't see."

"What's that?" Haley said.

"A Black Hawk," I said.

Jeff closely studied the screen as well.

"Don't see one either," Jeff said.

Haley said, "You think maybe they moved it?"

I said, "Either that, or they've hidden it somehow, or we've got the wrong spot."

"You really think we've got the wrong spot?" Haley said.

"Probably not," I said. "But I'd feel better if the Black Hawk was there."

"I'd feel better if it was there too," Haley said. "But you still have to pay a visit to the compound since Freddy's phone is there, don't you?"

"I don't see how we have any other choice," I said. "It looks like there's a fire road high above the northern edge of the compound that might be a good place to do some reconnaissance. You think you can direct us there?"

"I can," Haley said. "But Jack..."

"Yes?" I said.

"I can't get you any military reinforcements, you know that right?" Haley said.

"I do," I said. "Those have been the rules of engagement from the moment I started this mission. U.S. soldiers can't take action on U.S. soil. It's already been risky enough for MOM just having Jeff and me involved. I suppose we could get hold of Ray Carpenter and see if he can help, though."

"Unfortunately there's a problem with that as well," Haley said.

"I knew you guys might need some assistance, so I already broached adding Carpenter to your team with Hart. Hart, however, categorically ruled it out. He said not only could it blow Carpenter's cover with MOM, but, if Carpenter got hurt, the FBI, especially after what happened to Burnette, would conduct a thorough investigation into Carpenter's death. An FBI investigation like that could potentially reveal MOM's involvement in this mission and thus put all our operations in jeopardy. Hart won't risk it."

"That's understandable," I said.

"You want me to reach out to the LAPD or the L.A. County Sheriff?" Haley said.

"I don't think that would work for us," I said. "They'd have jurisdiction, which would mean they'd be in control. I can't see them acting fast enough considering our deadline issues."

Jeff said, "Yeah. If Kate and Billy in one of those houses, it's gonna be a hostage situation. SWAT team is going to want to bring in a negotiator. Negotiator happy to wait things out. We ain't gonna wait."

Haley said, "So I guess you're on your own then. You going to bring Adelaide with you?"

I said, "She's a good shot. We can use the extra gun."

"Adelaide's really that good?" Haley said.

Jeff said, "She's good."

I looked at Jeff.

"Why are you looking at me like that?" Jeff said.

"She's good is very high praise from you," I said. "I'm actually kinda shocked you said that."

Haley said, "You're not the only one who's shocked."

Jeff said, "Adelaide worked hard. Work paid off. She deserves the praise."

I said, "When you get a moment it might be nice of you to tell Adelaide what you think."

"Thinking it one thing," Jeff said. "Telling her another. Don't want nothing going to her head."

Haley said, "Adelaide would love to hear a compliment from you, Jeff. I say you just tell her."

"I'll consider it," Jeff said. "But considering it is as far as I'm willing to go right now."

I gave Jeff my 'come on you're being ridiculous' look. He just stared back at me, however.

I said, "Haley, it appears Jeff's mind is closed on that subject for the time being. And as our 6:00 p.m. deadline is fast approaching, Jeff and I better get on our way. The two of us will start working on a plan for what we'll do when we get to Topanga Canyon. The plan will, of course, be subject to modification depending on whether or not you get any useful additional info from that satellite with the better infrared capabilities that you're waiting on to pass over the compound."

"Sounds good to me," Haley said. "The drones will also be in position soon. We'll use them to track anyone or anything that might leave the compound."

"Including the Black Hawk, please," I said.

"If the Black Hawk is there, we won't lose it again," Haley said. "Now that it's daylight, we'll be able to keep a visual on it. Its stealthiness in regard to radar won't matter."

"Excellent," I said. "It will probably take us at least forty-five minutes to get to the compound, so I feel much better now that you've got eyes on it."

"I'll get back to you as soon as I have any more information," Haley said.

She clicked off.

"Let's gather up Adelaide and get out of here," I said to Jeff.

"I know I just said Adelaide a good shot and all," Jeff said. "But you sure bringing her along is a good idea?"

"I've been sort of drawing up a combat plan in my head ever since I saw how the compound is situated in that canyon," I said. "We're going to need Adelaide to pull the plan off. I'm pretty sure we'll be able to find a shooting perch for her that's relatively safe."

"Plan involve getting the best sight lines from the canyon walls?" Jeff said.

"It does," I said.

"Plan assume most of those mercenaries who aren't patrolling the property are probably resting in those four little buildings that look like houses?" Jeff said.

"Yes," I said.

"Plan contemplate using those six Iglas we got in the back of our van to do some vaporizing of the buildings and their presumed occupants?" Jeff said.

"Absolutely," I said.

"I think we're thinking of the same plan," Jeff said.

"Why wouldn't we be?" I said.

Jeff and I joined Adelaide, Manu, and Mosi where they were working on their sand castle.

"Adelaide, get your shoes and socks on," I said. "We've got to go."

"They found Kate and Dr. Nimo?" Adelaide said.

"We think so," I said. "Come on. Time's a wasting."

Adelaide put on her shoes and socks. Manu and Mosi hurriedly put on theirs as well.

"Where you two think you're going?" I said.

Manu said, "We're coming with you."

"No you're not," I said. "This is way too dangerous."

Mosi said, "Dr. Lennon is our responsibility."

Manu said, "We cannot rest until Dr. Lennon is brought back to safety."

I said, "It could easily be argued that in this instance Dr. Lennon's safety is much more my responsibility than yours. She did, after all, invite me down here from my ranch specifically for that purpose. I do welcome your help, but Adelaide, Jeff, and I can probably do almost as well on our own."

Mosi said, "It is a point of honor."

"I'm all for honor," I said, "but there's a good chance, in this case, honor will get you killed."

Manu said, "It is Faaaloalo."

"Faaaloalo?" I said.

Jeff said, "That's the Samoan code of honor. Samoans would rather die than violate Faaaloalo."

Mosi said, "General Bradshaw is correct. We would rather die."

I said, "Is he now? And just how did you know that, General Bradshaw?"

"You be better off asking what I don't know, rather than how I know what I do know," Jeff said.

"Truer words were never spoken," I said. "Manu and Mosi, I'm sorry but..."

Manu interrupted, "It is not just that we would rather die, but our family would kill us due to the shame we will have brought upon them if we did not kill ourselves."

"Kill you?" I said.

Manu and Mosi solemnly nodded. I looked over at Jeff, my resident Faaaloalo expert. Jeff nodded too.

Adelaide, who appeared to have been paying close attention to the conversation, said, "Manu and Mosi are tough, Uncle Jack. Fearless too. I saw what they did on the jump tower."

Jeff said, "I second that."

I said, "Well, this definitely complicates things."

I pondered the situation. The competing scenarios I was coming up with made my head spin. If Kate died during our assault on the Topanga compound and I had forced Manu and Mosi to stay behind, then Manu and Mosi would apparently either kill themselves or be killed by their relatives. If Kate survived the assault and Manu and Mosi were with me, but were themselves killed in battle, then Manu and Mosi would be just as dead as in my first scenario. If Kate survived and Manu and Mosi weren't with me, then the twins would be alive, but what would it mean for Faaaloalo? And what would it mean to Manu and Mosi if Kate died and they had come with me into battle and survived? Of course, the best possible outcome from the twins' point of view was they helped Adelaide, Jeff, and me rescue Kate and all of us made it out alive. But what were the odds of that...

I didn't get a chance to calculate those odds just then, however, because my thoughts were suddenly disrupted by the sound of incredibly loud music coming from the direction of the parking lot. The song being played was 'I Only Have Eyes for You' by the Flamingos and that particular version of the song had a big bass line that rattled my body. I turned to look where the song was coming from and saw a black 1962 Buick Electra convertible lowrider pulling into the parking lot. The car was so low it was only six inches off the ground. There was a surfboard sticking out of the back seat, and an ancient male Latino surfer with long black hair was driving and grooving to the beat. On the seat next to him was a very young, very pretty, bikini-clad Latina.

The Buick parked next to the Maybach and the Latino surfer shut down the music. I did not, however, use the relative silence to resume calculating the odds of the outcome I had just identified as the best one for the twins. That was because the sight of the Maybach made me start to rethink not just my views regarding Manu's and Mosi's participation in the upcoming assault on the Topanga compound, but my views regarding the assault itself.

My rethinking was brought on by the fact that I began to envisage just how useful the Maybach might be at the compound. The use I had in mind related to the Maybach's excellent high security qualities, qualities that made the car almost tank-like.

My rethinking also created a conundrum, however. That was because the rejiggered assault plan for the Topanga compound then percolating in my brain demanded one of the twins drive the Maybach. I had no illusions though that the brothers would allow themselves to be separated, so that meant they would both be along for what could easily turn out to be a death ride. Could I risk the twins' lives in order to gain the use of the Maybach?

I looked at Manu and Mosi, then back at the Maybach, then back at Manu and Mosi.

They looked so innocent.

And so eager.

And seemingly so committed to Faaaloalo.

But they also looked like...

Men.

And aren't men allowed to choose their own fate?

Hell, they were already much older, and perhaps wiser, than most young men who throughout the ages had enlisted to serve their countries in time of war.

And make no mistake about it, this was a war.

A war that, if we succeeded in defusing the Chinese's insurmountable edge in time, we could stop before it even started.

Manu's and Mosi's actions could wind up saving hundreds of thousands of American soldiers' lives.

Still, there was no way the brothers could appreciate how truly dangerous coming along with Adelaide, Jeff, and me was surely going to be.

I went back and forth in my mind between 'yes', the twins could come, and 'no', they could not. In the end, however, I suppose it was hubris that got the better of me. I convinced myself I could - on top of everything else I would need to do at the compound - protect the two brothers from serious harm. Protect them as long as they followed my instructions to a 'T', that is.

"Manu and Mosi," I said, "you both understand it is very likely you will die today if you accompany us on the next phase of our mission?"

Manu said, "Yes, sir."

Mosi said, "We understand perfectly, sir."

"And you are absolutely sure you want to risk your lives for the life of Dr. Lennon?" I said.

"We do, sir," the twins said simultaneously.

"And at all times you'll do exactly what I tell you to do, without argument or hesitation?" I said.

"We will, sir!" the twins said in unison.

"Okay, Manu and Mosi," I said. "I hope I don't regret this, but Faaaloalo it is. You're good to go."

The twins smiled from ear to ear. The five of us set off for the Zuma Beach parking lot where the Maybach and the Kazakhs' van awaited us.

PART VII

TOPANGA

CHAPTER 116

It was nearly 12:45 p.m. when Adelaide, Jeff, and I took off in the van for Topanga Canyon with Manu and Mosi in the Maybach in close pursuit. We were following the directions Haley had downloaded to my iPhone that would take us to the fire road above the compound where we planned to conduct our reconnaissance. Time was precious, but we needed to stop before we got to the compound to pick up some binoculars and cell phone headsets. The binoculars would enhance our surveillance and the headsets would allow all of us to be able to communicate hands free without being overheard. The closest place on our route to buy those items was an electronics store in Woodland Hills.

The fastest way from Zuma Beach to Woodland Hills was Kanan Dume Road, but that wasn't an option for us since the tunnel on Kanan was closed due to our escapades the previous evening. We took Malibu Canyon Road instead, racing along its torturous curves through a lush countryside covered by coastal sagebrush and oak, walnut, and willow trees. 'Racing' might be an overstatement, however. I made Adelaide stay close to the speed limit to be sure we avoided any further potentially unpleasant encounters with the law.

I was running out of the Woodland Hills electronics store with the binoculars and headsets when Haley called again on FaceTime.

I answered the call.

"What's up?" I said.

"We've learned more information about the Topanga compound," Haley said. "I'm also going to put the compound up on your screen."

I stared at my iPhone screen as I simultaneously snatched open the van's passenger door and jumped into the seat next to Jeff. Jeff leaned in to look at the screen with me. I gestured to Adelaide. She started up the van, and pulled out of the electronics store's lot. Followed by Manu and Mosi in the Maybach, we resumed our journey to the compound.

Haley was streaming a live, close-up video of the Topanga compound. It became clear that the compound's five house-like buildings which I had seen earlier were, indeed, houses. The camera panned across the houses. None of the houses bore any resemblance to any other, and between them they covered a broad range of architectural styles.

"The compound's houses were built in the 1960's by the scion of a wealthy Chicago real estate family," Haley said. "The scion was a drug addict and his family exiled him to Topanga, where he lived out his days in a drug stupor and ultimately died of an overdose. The scion ran the compound like a kind of commune before his death. I'm going to focus more closely on the main house now."

A sprawling, dilapidated, ranch-style house filled the screen. It looked to be about five thousand square feet, and while its warped and weathered wood siding appeared to have been painted green long ago, the siding was then returning to its bare, naked state. The house's front door was also made of wood and its top half was constructed of glass panes intersected by thin wood strips. A few large, rotting, spoked wagon wheels lay in the front yard, probably dumped there to give the place a rustic feel. Potted plants hung from under the roof's eaves, but all of the plants had withered and died due to neglect. Two wind chimes also hung from under the roof. The chimes appeared to be of a type that most likely would have had at least twelve chimes when they were new, but they then had only five chimes left between them. Two black Suburban sport utility vehicles were on either side of the house's front door. The Suburbans were parked broadside to the house, one behind the other.

Haley shifted the satellite's camera view, and she panned across the four small houses to the south of the main ranch house. They looked like little mini-mansions. There was one Spanish, one Cape Cod, one English country home, and a miniature Italian palazzo. The mini-mansions were all in the same state of disrepair as the main ranch house. They were also tiny in comparison to the ranch house - none of them looked like they could be more than four hundred square feet in size. Each of the small houses had a nondescript white van parked in front of it.

"Who had the wacky taste in architecture, the scion or the commune members?" I said.

"Hard to say," Haley said. "They certainly are architectural monstrosities though."

"They kind of look like tiny mini-mansions don't they?" I said.

"They do," Haley said.

"You think they were used as guest homes?" I said.

"Then and now," Haley said.

"'Now' as in there are guests inside them at this very moment?" I said.

"Yes," Haley said. "Lots of guests too."

Our caravan had just left the Topanga Canyon Boulevard business district that was close to the 101 Freeway and was passing through the residential flats of Woodland Hills north of the Santa Monica Mountains. One-story homes lined the boulevard, most of them looking as if they had been built in the 1950's. Aspen, eucalyptus, and oak trees grew in the homes' yards.

"If you had a lot of guests you'd need a lot of vans too, I suppose," I said.

"You're talking about the four white vans parked outside the mini-mansions?" Haley said.

"I am," I said. "Do you know who the guests are?"

"I think I can make a good guess," Haley said.

Haley zoomed out and trained the camera on the clearing surrounding the mini-mansions.

Jeff said, "There are those four little things we saw before. Only now they're big."

Four Afghans were patrolling the perimeter of the clearing.

I said, "So, you're saying the mini-mansions' guests are Afghan mercenaries, Haley?"

"Yes," Haley said. "Probably Kazakhs too. Infrared suggests there are somewhere around forty to forty-five people spread out between the ranch house and the mini-mansions. But it's going to take us a little while to analyze all the data. I'll be able to do better in about twenty minutes when a satellite with even more sophisticated infrared sensors passes over the compound."

"I thought you said the last satellite could find a mouse if you wanted it to," I said.

"It didn't turn out to be as good as I thought it would be," Haley said. "The one coming is definitely more sophisticated."

I noticed two sets of what looked like broken down goalposts about twenty yards in from both ends of the clearing.

"Are those goalposts?" I said.

"Yes," Haley said. "The clearing was used as a polo field."

"If the scion and his friends truly were druggies, those games must have been pretty dangerous," I said.

"I pity the poor horses," Haley said.

"So do I," I said. "Is Freddy's phone still pinging in the ranch house?"

"Yes," Haley said.

"So that probably means Kate and Billy are in the ranch house?" I said.

"I would think so," Haley said.

"Which also probably means that if Carter Bowdoin, Kenny 'Dragon Man' Liu, and Bryce Wellington are at the site, they're probably in the ranch house as well," I said.

"Why do you say that?" Haley said.

"If I were them I'd want to be somewhere close to Kate and Billy where I could watch over them," I said. "Plus there's ego involved."

"Ego?" Haley said.

"Carter, Kenny, and Bryce all fancy themselves men of a certain class, don't they?" I said. "The ranch house is huge compared to the mini-mansions. I don't think those guys would be caught dead in a mini-mansion."

"I'm not sure how scientific that is," Haley said, "but I can see your point."

The camera panned back to the ranch house. I noticed a small cinder block building to the north of the house I hadn't seen before.

"What's in the cinder block building?" I said.

"Nothing living," Haley said. "It used to be a recording studio."

"The scion was a musician?" I said.

"Wannabe," Haley said. "But it never went any further than that since he couldn't sing or play a musical instrument."

"Probably wouldn't have had enough time to practice anyway, what with the drugs and all," I said. "You haven't shown me the Black Hawk yet. I assume you still haven't found it."

"Not yet," Haley said.

The van and the Maybach continued along Topanga Canyon Boulevard and passed out of the Woodland Hills flats. We then climbed south into the Santa Monica mountains, mountains whose peaks bordered Topanga Canyon itself. The houses along the boulevard began to thin out and soon there was nothing but steep dirt embankments covered with scrub brush on either side of us.

"It seems like it would be a pretty big risk for Carter and Kenny to take over that entire compound without some kind of legal right to it," I said. "Did you find anything along those lines?"

"Yes," Haley said. "Even though the scion is dead, the compound has remained in the possession of his wealthy Chicago relatives. It's a minuscule portion of the family's wealth, but their property management company occasionally leases the compound to anyone who can afford it. The current lessee is a corporation registered in New Zealand. The corporation's name is Marshall Johnson, Ltd. No one named Marshall Johnson exists, however, and the corporation operates no discernible business."

"Too bad you're not a betting woman," I said.

"Why is that?" Haley said.

Jeff said, "Because he wants to bet that Marshall Johnson is a front for Carter or Dragon Man."

The satellite photos disappeared from the screen. They were replaced by Haley's beautiful face. She was smiling broadly.

"I wouldn't take that bet even if I was a betting woman," Haley said.

Jeff turned to Adelaide.

"Hey, Adelaide, wanna make a bet?" Jeff said.

"You think I'm a moron?" Adelaide said. "I've heard every word you said."

"You wanna make the bet or not?" Jeff said.

Adelaide took her eyes off the road, gave Jeff a hard look.

I said, "Adelaide, please. Keep your eyes on the road."

"Like I told you before, my peripheral vision is great," Adelaide said. "I can see fine."

"Okay," I said. "But when you roll the van and the Iglas explode and we're all being burned up in the ensuing fireball, don't say I didn't tell you so."

"Don't worry," Adelaide said. "I won't." She again focused a hard look on Jeff. "As for you Mr. Big Mouth, I don't want to make a bet about that Carter Bowdoin/Dragon Man 'front' shit. But I do have another one if you're interested."

"What that be?" Jeff said.

Quick as a snake, Adelaide reached out with her right arm and put Jeff in a headlock. She kept her left hand on the steering wheel.

"That I can goddamn kill you and drive at the same time," Adelaide said.

Jeff started cackling. Haley rolled her eyes.

"I think I better be going," Haley said. "I'll check back in with you when you get to the compound."

I said, "You mean *if* we get to the compound."

CHAPTER 117

Fifteen minutes later, just after 1:45 p.m., we parked the van and the Maybach on a dirt fire road that traversed a mountain ridge near the northern border of the Topanga compound. The top of the ridge was about fifty feet above where we had parked. The compound, which was on the other side of the ridge, was about two hundred and fifty yards below the ridge top. The mountain ridge blocked any view of the fire road from the compound, so it was impossible for the mercenaries to see us. The fire road, after winding its way down off the ridge, ultimately met up with the paved public street that ran along the compound's western border. That western border was also the compound's front edge. We had gone nowhere near that side of the compound on our way up to our current position.

Jeff and I had come up with a battle plan after getting off our call with Haley. We knew the plan could change if Haley came up with additional information for us, but we felt we had to start somewhere.

The first part of the plan was to unload the AK's, MP-443 Grach semi-automatic pistols, and the Iglas from the van. Adelaide, Jeff, Manu, and Mosi did the unloading while I hiked up the mountainside to an outcropping of large boulders that lay at the top of the ridge. The boulders were all at least ten feet tall and there was dense, high grass growing around them.

I hid in the grass and, using the binoculars I had purchased from the electronics store, scanned the compound. The sight angles from my position weren't quite good enough to see everything I needed to see, so I decided I was going to have to move down the slope and get closer to the compound. I hooked up my also recently purchased headset to my cell phone and called Jeff to tell him what I planned to do.

Jeff answered on the first ring.

"Look up at the top of the ridge," I said.

He did. I waved at him.

"What are you doing waving at me?" Jeff said.

"I wanted to make sure you could see me," I said.

"You don't need to wave for me to see you," Jeff said. "What the hell is wrong with you?"

"That's kind of like the pot calling the kettle black, isn't it?" I said.

"What you want?" Jeff said. "Can't you see I'm unloading the Iglas?"

"I need to move closer to the compound to get a better look," I said. "While I'm doing that, I think all of you should carry the Iglas to where I am right now. Please bring me an AK and some extra ammo mags too. You can hide everything behind the boulders and then wait there for me to get back. Adelaide can keep her Grach pistol, but you might as well give our Grachs to Manu and Mosi. You can show Manu and Mosi how to use them while you're waiting."

"Manual labor be outside scope of your white man responsibilities, huh?" Jeff said.

"Correct," I said. "And I have a white man's burden too."

"I bet it a mighty heavy burden," Jeff said.

"If you only knew," I said.

"Go do what you gotta do, massah," Jeff said. "Me and the other slaves be doing our best to hold down the plantation until you gets back."

We hung up. I scrambled down the mountainside, staying low and hiding under the brush in order to avoid being spotted by any of the mercenaries in the compound below. After five minutes of scrambling, I found a suitable place from which to observe the compound. I laid down flat, nestling into the brush and dirt.

The sun was high in the sky and the air was still and warm. Sweat collected on my upper back beneath my t-shirt. Oaks and sycamores dotted the mountainside surrounding me and their scent mingled with the smell of drying brush. Black crows cawed, clicked, and cooed in the trees' branches. Cottontail rabbits, lizards, quail, and squirrels darted to and fro, making brittle scratching noises as their feet plowed through the dried layer of oak leaves that covered most of the ground. A red-tailed hawk circled silently, riding the thermals directly overhead.

Two hundred yards below me was the compound.

I lifted the binoculars to my face and focused on the rectangular clearing surrounding the compound's living quarters. There were still four sentries patrolling the perimeter of the polo field. They looked like the same Afghan sentries we had seen on Haley's satellite feed, but I couldn't be sure. The Afghans had Russian AS Val silenced rifles slung over their shoulders and bullet-laden magazines in bandoliers criss-crossing their chests. The Afghans kept a constant distance between each other as they walked. None of the perimeter's four sides ever had more than one sentry on it at any time.

I studied the compound. I noticed that some of the trails I had seen earlier on the satellite feed ended in wooden staircases with railed platforms atop them. What those platforms were for, I had no idea. The ranch house and the mini-mansions looked just as I had seen them.

Something was out of place, however.

The something was in a grove of lushly leaved eucalyptus trees that lay just beyond the compound's buildings.

And the something had a shape that had not been made by nature.

I zoomed in with the binoculars.

The something was the stealth Black Hawk.

The Black Hawk was parked in a small clearing in the eucalyptus grove. Camouflage netting covered the top of the helicopter and massive amounts of leaves, small tree limbs, and other deciduous debris lay on top of the netting. The camouflage, coupled with the thick rainforest-like canopy created by the eucalyptus trees, had made the Black Hawk invisible to Haley's satellites.

I pointed my cell phone's camera at the helicopter. My cell phone has a military grade camera that is much more powerful than those found in an off the shelf iPhone. I zoomed in tightly on the Black Hawk, snapped a photo, and texted the photo to both Haley and Jeff.

Jeff and I had already decided that if we found the Black Hawk, we needed to disable it. We couldn't risk the helicopter being used by our enemy to escape the compound, especially if they had Kate and Nimo in tow.

We had considered two options for disabling the Black Hawk. The first option had been to sneak up to the Black Hawk and render it incapable of flight while causing as little damage as we could to the expensive machine, perhaps by simply smashing its instrument panel. Taking the helicopter out of action by sneaking up to it seemed a risky proposition, however, since the Black Hawk was then being well guarded.

Jeff's and my second option had been to blow up the Black Hawk with an Igla SSM. Given the absolute necessity of preventing the Black

Hawk from taking off, and the current state of the security around it, that second option was probably what we were going to have to use.

I knew Jeff would keep a sharp eye on the helicopter once he received my text about its location. If anything transpired that made Jeff feel the Black Hawk had to be blown up sooner rather than later - such as the beginnings of any activity looking like the aforementioned enemy escape attempt - then blow it up he would.

Movement on the opposite side of the polo field caught my eye. Through my binoculars I saw a black Suburban exiting what was probably the driveway that connected the compound to the public street along its western border. I couldn't see the street or tell how long the driveway was because the driveway was lined on both sides by dense eucalyptus groves.

The Suburban drove across the polo field and rolled to a stop behind one of the other two Suburbans that were parked in front of the ranch house. Two Afghans exited from the newly arrived Suburban, one from the driver's door, the other from the front seat passenger door. The Afghans then opened the SUV's rear hatch and removed trays of food. It was very fancy food. They carried the trays inside the ranch house.

Haley called using FaceTime. I spoke with her through my headset.

"That photo you sent me the Black Hawk?" Haley said.

"Yes," I said.

"Nice camouflage job," Haley said. "No wonder we didn't spot it before."

"Impossible to see from the air," I said. "Now I have to figure out what to do with it."

"What do you think you're going to do?" Haley said.

"Blow it up," I said.

"You're going to make a lot of people at the Defense Department very unhappy if you do," Haley said.

"You got a better idea?" I said

"Couldn't you just disable it?" Haley said.

"If we had time I might be able to figure out a way to sneak past those sentries with the Vals and dig my way through all the debris on top of the chopper without being noticed," I said. "But we don't have time."

"Bad guys have the same problem don't they?" Haley said.

"What do you mean?" I said.

"Seems to me they would need at least fifteen minutes to clear away all that crap once they decided to take off," Haley said. "That should leave you plenty of time to stop them."

"Kate and Nimo/Billy could easily be killed in any attempt to, as you put it, 'stop them,'" I said. "There's also a chance the bad guys get Kate and Billy into the Black Hawk and take off. I know you said you wouldn't lose track of the Black Hawk again, but grabbing Kate and Billy is going to be a hell of a lot easier down here on the compound than up in the sky."

"It's a two hundred million dollar machine, Jack," Haley said.

"And soon it will be a two hundred million dollar pile of molten junk," I said. "Now, can we please focus on something constructive? Like telling me the latest intel you've gleaned from your infrared sensors?"

"You want to start with the ranch house?" Haley said.

"That's as good a place as any," I said.

I shifted my binoculars to the ranch house.

"The satellite we just accessed had much better infrared capabilities than the previous one," Haley said. "We think there are currently nine people in the house. The seven people that were there just before the two Afghans that just arrived in the Suburban have had very consistent movement patterns. The five people in the living room..."

"Hold on," I said. "How do you know they're in the living room?"

The red-tailed hawk that I'd seen circling the compound earlier appeared to spot something in the trees on the south side of the polo field. The hawk dove towards the trees but was met by two blackbirds who quickly drove him back up into the sky.

"I downloaded the architectural plans from the county recorder's office," Haley said.

"Of course you did," I said. "Go on."

"The five people in the living room have pretty much stayed there, getting up only to go to the kitchen or the bathroom," Haley said. "The two Afghans that just got out of the Suburban are now in the kitchen along with the two individuals that were previously roaming the house."

"The two were roaming as in patrolling?" I said.

"It certainly appeared that way to me," Haley said.

"Which means those two are probably mercs whose job is to guard the ranch house," I said.

"I concur," Haley said.

"If any of the four mercs in the kitchen change their location, please advise me as soon as you can," I said. "For now, however, please give me whatever you've got on the five people in the living room."

"Three of them are very close together and the other two are parallel to the three, but a few feet away," Haley said. "The two people that are parallel to the other three are also about eight feet from each other. My best guess is that the three people that are close together are sitting side by side on a couch, and the other two people are sitting in chairs facing the three on the couch."

"How many of the five people in the living room have only moved to go to the kitchen or the bathroom?" I said.

"Actually, only the two in the chairs have moved from their seats," Haley said. "The three on the couch haven't moved at all. What's interesting is that the person in the middle of the three on the couch appears awake, but the two people flanking that person are either asleep or unconscious."

I knew that the most sophisticated satellite infrared sensors available - which were clearly the ones that Haley then had access to - could not only track all the occupants' positions, but could also report on whether the person being scanned was most likely conscious or asleep/unconscious. The conscious ones registered higher heat readings as they were more active.

"Here's what I think," I said. "Our previous analysis was correct - Carter Bowdoin, Kenny 'Dragon Man' Liu, and Bryce Wellington are definitely in the ranch house. They're all awake and make up three of the five people in the living room. Carter and Kenny are sitting in chairs facing the couch. The three on the couch are Kate, Billy, and Wellington, with Wellington being the one in the middle. Kate and Billy are asleep or unconscious."

"Whoa, whoa, whoa," Haley said. "We aren't sure who's in the room, let alone where they're sitting."

"I'm sure that at least three of the people in the living room are Bowdoin, Liu, and Wellington," I said.

"Absolutely sure?" Haley said.

"Come on Haley," I said. "Even forgetting for the moment those boys' wouldn't let themselves be caught dead in a mini-mansion, what other explanation is there for the fact the two Afghans who just got out of the Suburban were carrying a tray of finger sandwiches, a half dozen bottles of Krug champagne, and a box of what looked to be Cuban cigars?"

"I didn't see that," Haley said.

"That's because you're not out here with me in nature-ville sweating your ass off while a bunch of bugs make mincemeat out of your face," I said.

"I'm really missing something, aren't I?" Haley said.

"You are," I said.

"Oops, hold on a second," Haley said. "It looks like two of the four mercs in the kitchen are heading back towards the front door."

"Requisitioning more supplies from the Suburban?" I said.

"That could easily be what they're up to," Haley said. "I would, however, like to point out that your assumption those supplies are for Bowdoin, Liu, and Wellington may be defective."

"How so?" I said.

"Well, did you even consider the fact that a lot of people like the kind of stuff the Afghans just toted in?" Haley said.

"Yeah, and a lot of people fly around in stealth Black Hawks, have their own Afghan and Kazakh mercenary army, and are in possession of Freddy Feynman's cell phone," I said.

"Technically they don't have possession of Feynman's cell phone," Haley said. "Since it's still on, we believe Dr. Lennon still has it."

The two Afghans I had seen take the trays of food out of the Suburban exited the front door and headed back towards the Suburban.

"You know," I said, "you're being quite nit-picky."

"I'm always nit-picky," Haley said.

"True," I said. "But this is way beyond your normal."

"I'm worried," Haley said.

"You should be," I said. "Our whole plan depends on the mental acuity of two hallucinatory generals with PTSD, the sniping talents of a teenage girl, and the combat driving skills of a pair of giant Samoan twins."

"Manu and Mosi have combat training?" Haley said.

"No," I said. "They're going to be learning on the job."

"Jesus, Jack," Haley said.

"Chill, Haley," I said. "Anything goes wrong, it's on my head, not yours."

"You know I don't give a damn about blame," Haley said.

"I know," I said. "You just want things to turn out well."

"I most certainly do," Haley said. "Back to the people in the living room. I'll grant you the sleeping and/or unconscious ones are most likely Dr. Lennon and Billy Einstein. But why do you think it's Bryce Wellington between them?"

"Because I think he's probably guarding Kate and Billy since it's kind of a menial task," I said. "It's something Carter Bowdoin and Kenny Liu would order him to do."

"Which, by the process of elimination, means Carter and Kenny are the ones moving around?" Haley said.

"Yes, Sherlock," I said.

"Would that make you Watson?" Haley said.

"Moriarty more like it," I said.

Haley suddenly looked down and away from the camera.

"Damn," Haley said.

"What is it?" I said.

"Kate's cell phone just got a text," Haley said.

"I thought Kate's cell phone was out of commission?" I said.

"The cell phone itself is," Haley said. "But we've hacked Kate's phone number and we're monitoring her calls, emails, and texts."

"Shoot, why didn't I think of that?" I said.

"Because you have me," Haley said.

"Still, I should have thought of that," I said.

"You want to beat yourself up or hear the text?" Haley said.

"Text please," I said.

"It's from Raj Divedi, the guy in charge of NASAD's cyber defense war game team," Haley said. "Raj says, 'Sorry for taking so long to respond. My phone ran out of battery. The war games have of course been cancelled due to the tragedy that occurred yesterday at the NASAD site in the north San Fernando Valley. War game sneak attacks, however, have never been specifically addressed and as such would not be prohibited. It is an interesting idea, though. Why do you ask?'"

Haley looked up from the text and back at me.

"Jack, when you first told me about your theory about NASAD war game sneak attacks you said you were going to call Raj about them," Haley said. "You had Kate do it instead?"

"Yes," I said. "Kate had Raj's number in her phone. It was easier for her to do it. She both texted Raj and left him a voicemail."

"What do you think?" Haley said.

"I think Raj needs to keep his phone battery charged," I said.

"I'll be sure to tell him," Haley said.

The two Afghans unloaded some more trays of food from the back of the Suburban. Those trays held what appeared to be about forty deli sandwiches, along with some bottles of ketchup and mustard. I assumed the sandwiches represented the lunch for Carter and Kenny's mercenary army.

"The other thing I think is that Raj's text just further confirms what Dr. Nimo/Billy told me about his NASAD war game sneak attack," I said.

"I agree," Haley said. "It also makes me even more comfortable that our theory that Dr. Nimo/Billy's war game software and the Chinese insurmountable edge are one and the same is correct. I was worried that might not be the case when we found out that the Chinese had moved up the date and time for starting their war, since the start date no longer matched the date of the commencement of the NASAD war games. But now that we know Billy's sneak attack was allowed, or at least not expressly prohibited, and that his sneak attack effectively changed the NASAD war games start date and time so it exactly matches the date and time the Chinese are set to begin their war tonight, I feel much better we're still on the right track. The timing of the sneak attack explains why the military's systems are continuing to function normally too. The insurmountable edge in all likelihood won't be activated until 6:00 p.m. tonight."

"For all we know," I said, "the Chinese might have built their entire war plan around the start date and time that Billy programmed into his war game sneak attack."

"That could easily be the case," Haley said. "So we'll use Raj's message to give us absolute confidence we can continue on this track and don't have to invent any new theories?"

"I'm not sure 'absolute' is the right word," I said. "But the current theory is still the best one we've got and I don't think we have any choice other than to go with it."

"You're referring to the fact that we have only a little less than four hours left until the Chinese war starts and it would be pretty tough to come up with a new theory at this late date?" Haley said.

I shifted the binoculars to the four guest houses.

"I am," I said. "What's going on in the mini-mansions?"

Haley said, "There's eight people in the Spanish, seven each in both the English country home and the Cape Cod, and five in the Italian palazzo."

"People, huh?" I said. "I thought we already agreed they were mercenaries?"

"I'm being cautious," Haley said. "I mean, it's possible that Bowdoin, Liu, and Wellington are just having a party for a bunch of their closest friends."

I rolled my eyes.

"Fine," Haley said. "I'll grant you they're mercenaries."

"What are the mercs in the mini-mansions doing right now?" I said.

"Most of them appear to be napping," Haley said. "Two to three in each house are also gathered in the living room watching television."

The infrared sensors of the satellite Haley was using could also pick up electronic signatures of television sets.

"It doesn't look to me like any of the mini-mansions are over four hundred square feet?" I said.

"They're not," Haley said.

"It also looks like they're pretty shoddily constructed," I said. "Any of the plans you downloaded suggest serious reinforcing of any kind?"

"Are you asking me because you're wondering if anyone inside any of the mini-mansions could survive an Igla surface-to-surface missile attack?" Haley said.

"I might be," I said.

"Well, you don't have to wonder," Haley said. "You hit the mini-mansions with your Iglas, there is absolutely no way anyone inside is coming out alive."

I used the binoculars to check on the four Afghans with the Russian AS Vals and bandoliers who were patrolling the perimeter of the polo field. They continued to all walk at the same speed and keep a constant distance between one another.

"I've still got the same four mercs on the perimeter," I said. "Anybody else patrolling I haven't seen yet?"

"I believe there are two more sentries," Haley said. "I've got two active heat signatures close to the driveway leading into the compound from the main road. The signatures are about fifty yards from the edge of the polo field."

I focused my binoculars on the spot where the driveway entered the clearing that held the polo field. The two groves of tall eucalyptus trees surrounding the driveway continued to make it impossible for me to see anything that might be on the driveway more than a few yards from the polo field.

"How far is it from the polo field to the public street that goes in front of the compound?" I said.

"About five hundred yards," Haley said. "There's an eight foot high stone wall guarding the compound along the street and there's a gate cut in the wall."

"If I were the mercs patrolling the driveway, I'd be down by the street guarding the gate," I said.

"Probably worried about being seen from the street," Haley said. "They must figure whoever comes up from the gate will be funneled into them by the road."

"To each his own," I said.

I again focused the binoculars on the main ranch house. The two Afghans were carrying their trays of deli sandwiches in through the house's front door. Other than that there was no movement anywhere near the outside of the house and nothing had changed since I last looked at it.

"Okay, then," I said. "By my count, we have four mercenaries in the ranch house, twenty-seven in the mini-mansion guest houses, and six patrolling the compound. That makes thirty-seven. Fifty-nine originally came in on the two 'Doctors of Mercy' flights. We killed three at the rest stop, four at the drone sub site, four at the professor's house, and seven up at the tunnel on Kanan Dume. Ray Carpenter killed four at Kate's estate. That's a total of twenty-two dead. Twenty-two from fifty-nine is thirty-seven. It appears that everyone is present and accounted for."

"Thirty-seven is what I have as well," Haley said.

"Doesn't seem like a fair fight," I said.

"Not for the mercenaries, it doesn't," Haley said. "Do you want a fair fight?"

"Never," I said.

"Military Strategy 101?" Haley said.

"Military strategy since 20,000 B.C.," I said.

"Soldiers way back then didn't want a fair fight either, huh?" Haley said.

"No soldier who ever lived wants a fair fight," I said.

"Makes complete sense to me," Haley said. "By the way, I just got some more information on Marshall Johnson, Ltd., the lessee of the compound you see before you."

"Who's the ultimate beneficial owner, Pennsylvania Avenue Partners or the Golden Dragon Fund?" I said.

"Neither," Haley said. "It's Colonel Liu Zhengsheng."

"Kenny 'Dragon Man' Liu's dead brother?" I said. "The one Paul Lennon killed in Myanmar?"

"One and the same," Haley said. "Of course, Marshall Johnson winds its way up through highly opaque private holding companies in the Cayman Islands, Mauritius, and Singapore before it gets to Zhengsheng."

"I guess Kenny's brother must have owned it when he died and Kenny must have kept the company around so he could use it in his vengeance plans," I said. "Kind of a symbolic tribute to his dead brother Zhengsheng."

"From what I know of the Dragon Man, he's certainly sick and twisted enough to do a thing like that," Haley said.

"If I have time, I'll ask Kenny how he got that way," I said.

"Sick and twisted?" Haley said.

"Yes," I said. "His challenge will be to answer me while I strangle him to death."

"Isn't strangling too easy a way for him to go?" Haley said.

"Yeah, you're probably right about that," I said. "I'll have to think of something better. Well, I suppose it's time to rally the troops."

"Good luck, Jack," Haley said.

"Thank you," I said. "I'm gonna need it."

CHAPTER 118

I climbed back up the mountain ridge. Adelaide, Jeff, Manu, and Mosi were waiting for me behind the boulders at the top of the ridge. Jeff, an Igla SSM at his side, was peering through the dense, high grass growing around the boulders and keeping an eye on the compound through a set of our newly acquired binoculars. Adelaide and Jeff had AK-12's over their shoulders and extra ammo magazines in their pockets. Each of the Samoans had a Grach MP-443 semi-automatic pistol tucked into his waistband. Jeff had left the AK and ammo magazines he brought for me next to a boulder. I slung the AK over my shoulder and stuffed the magazines into my pockets.

"Nice guns, Manu and Mosi," I said.

"Thank you, sir," Mosi said.

"Don't be drawing them unless I tell you to, okay?" I said. "I'm sure Jeff has you pretty well trained by now, but due to your lack of experience you're probably just as likely to shoot yourselves as a bad guy."

Manu said, "We understand, sir. General Bradshaw says we are only to use the Grachs as a last resort."

"General Bradshaw is right," I said. "But even then, not until I say so."

Manu and Mosi said in unison, "Yes, sir, General Wilder."

I turned to Jeff.

"No one moving for the Black Hawk?" I said.

"Nope," Jeff said. "I make heap big fire if they does."

"That how the Chumash and the Tongvas would have said it?" I said.

"Would if a racist honky be putting words in their mouth," Jeff said.

"What does that make you then?" I said.

"A racist person of color," Jeff said. "Chumash and Tongva be forgiving me since right now I'm channeling their warrior spirit."

"I'm sure that warrior spirit will come in very helpful," I said. "Alright everyone, it's time to go over the plan. Manu and Mosi, if you're going to back out, I need to know now."

"We are not interested in backing out," Manu said.

"Mosi, you agree with your brother?" I said.

"We are ready to die for Faaaloalo," Mosi said.

"Hopefully it won't come to that," I said. "Here's what we're going to do. Haley's infrared confirms there are nine people in the ranch house. We believe it's highly likely that four of them are mercenaries and the other five are Dr. Lennon, Dr. Nimo/Billy Einstein, Carter Bowdoin, Bryce Wellington, and Kenny 'Dragon Man' Liu. Our goal is to get Billy and Kate out alive, which is complicated by the fact they're probably unconscious at the moment and also heavily guarded. As we are seriously outnumbered, we will rely on surprise..."

Jeff said, "And the Iglas."

"And the Iglas," I said. "The Iglas are a great leveler - no pun intended - and should move the combat odds strongly in our favor. Manu and Mosi will drive the Maybach and take Adelaide as close as possible to the base of the mountain ridge at the southern edge of the compound. The best place to drop her off is at that point right there, directly across the canyon from us." I pointed at the spot I was referring to in order to make sure everyone understood exactly where they were supposed to go. "Once all of you are there, Adelaide will exit the Maybach and climb the mountain ridge on that side of the compound until she gets to that large boulder about two hundred yards above the compound's polo field. Do you see that boulder, Adelaide?"

Adelaide nodded.

"That boulder will be where you'll shoot from," I said. "Move under the brush on your way to it and make sure you can't be detected by anyone on the compound while you're moving." I turned to Manu and Mosi. "Manu and Mosi, after you drop off Adelaide, take the Maybach to a spot somewhere on the street near the front entrance of the compound where you can't be seen from the driveway, and wait for me there." I paused. "Jeff, I still think we have to disable the Black Hawk, otherwise we risk the bad guys getting away and probably taking Kate and Billy with them. If that happens, not only is our entire mission ruined, but Kate and Billy will most likely wind up dead."

"I agree," Jeff said.

"With the Black Hawk being as well guarded as it is, I believe our only option for disabling it is to blow it up," I said.

"Seems a shame to waste such a nice machine, though," Jeff said.

"That's pretty much how Haley feels too," I said.

Adelaide said, "Bigger shame if those assholes get away and wind up killing Kate and Billy."

"Correct," I said. "So, getting back to the plan. Once Adelaide is in position at the boulder, we'll use the first Igla to take out the Black Hawk. After the Black Hawk is blown, Jeff and I will use four more of the Iglas to destroy the four mini-mansion guest houses. Haley has also confirmed by infrared that those mini-mansions hold twenty-seven of the mercenaries. Most of the twenty-seven mercenaries are napping and the ones who aren't are watching television. It is unlikely any of those mercenaries will survive an Igla attack, but we have to be ready if they do."

"Any of them stagger out alive, I'll be happy to finish them off," Adelaide said.

"Happy or unhappy, that's part of the plan and what I'm counting on you to do," I said. "Jeff and I will back you up."

"I don't need any backup," Adelaide said.

"Interesting you should say that," I said. "Jeff, what was it you were telling Haley a while ago?"

Jeff gave me a dirty look.

"Now, now, behave yourself," I said.

Jeff spit.

"Fine," Jeff said. "Adelaide, I am very impressed with your shooting. You've become one of the best shooters I've ever seen."

Adelaide looked at me.

"Is this some kind of joke?" Adelaide said.

"No joke," I said. "He pretty much told Haley the same thing."

Adelaide looked stunned.

"Jeff, that's the nicest thing you've ever said to me," Adelaide said.

"Yeah, well don't be getting all emotional on us," Jeff said. "We got work to do."

Adelaide, ignoring Jeff's admonishment, stepped up close to Jeff and hugged him.

"What you doing, girl?" Jeff said.

"Giving you what you deserve," Adelaide said.

Surprisingly Jeff let her hug linger. Manu and Mosi both smiled as they watched the embrace.

Finally, Jeff said, "Okay. That's enough of that."

He stepped out of Adelaide's grip.

I said, "Thank you both for that very touching interlude. Alright, then. Once we've cleared the twenty-seven mercenaries in the mini-mansions, and the six mercenaries patrolling the grounds of the compound, there should be only four mercenaries left inside the ranch house. Manu and Mosi, using the Maybach - which will double as a tank for our purposes - will deliver me to the ranch house. Then, with Jeff and Adelaide covering me, I will enter the house and commence to free Kate and Billy."

"Plan sounds foolproof to me," Jeff said.

Manu and Mosi nodded their heads.

I said, "Why are you two nodding your heads?"

Manu and Mosi looked at each other. Some kind of unspoken communication passed between them.

Manu said, "Uh...because we like the plan?"

"So it sounds foolproof to you?" I said.

Manu and Mosi looked at each other again. More unspoken communication.

Mosi said, "It's not?"

Jeff said, "Nothing's foolproof. Million things could go wrong."

Manu said, "But you said..."

"Doesn't matter what I say," Jeff said. "Use your head."

Manu and Mosi didn't say anything.

I said, "I'd go into more detail if we had time, Manu and Mosi, but, to put it as simply as possible, there's only five of us - arguably only three of whom have any idea what they're doing - and there are thirty-seven of them."

"Oh," Manu and Mosi said simultaneously.

"But don't worry boys," I said. "The plan, while not foolproof, is as good as we can make it. And if something goes wrong, we'll just adapt."

Jeff said, "We good at adapting."

"One last thing," I said. "We need to get inside the ranch house and complete our rescue within twenty minutes of the Igla SSM's being launched. Twenty minutes is the maximum window of time we estimate we'll have before members of the Los Angeles Fire Department arrive to put out the fires the Iglas will surely ignite."

"Already enough collateral damage on this mission," Jeff said. "Don't want no dead firefighters."

"No we don't," I said. "Okay, time for a com check."

Manu and Mosi gave me blank stares.

"Headsets, men," I said. "Put them on and dial in as we discussed."

Everyone put on their headsets and dialed into one of MOM's encrypted conference call lines. I listened as a recorded woman's voice announced we had all joined the conference. It was a decidedly low-tech communication solution, but I felt it would suffice.

"Everyone hear me okay?" I whispered into my microphone.

Adelaide and Jeff both softly said, "Yes."

Manu and Mosi said nothing. Instead, both of them gave me a thumbs up.

"Manu and Mosi, the point of a com check is to be sure we can all hear each other," I said. "I won't be able to hear a thumbs up when you take your assigned positions."

"Sorry," Manu said.

"Sorry," Mosi said.

"That's better," I said. "Adelaide, Manu, and Mosi, on your way please."

Jeff and I watched as the three of them carefully picked their way down the steep hillside, got into the Maybach, and drove away.

Jeff and I put our cell phones on mute.

"Should take Adelaide about seven to eight minutes to get to the base of the mountain ridge and then probably another fifteen minutes to get into position atop the boulder," I said. "Shall we get ourselves and the Iglas ready in the meantime?"

"Yes, we shall," Jeff said.

There was a narrow crack between two of the outcropping's two largest boulders. I wedged my feet and hands into the crack and climbed about three quarters of the way to the top. We had all six Iglas with us. Jeff handed them to me one by one, and I shoved them onto the top surface of the boulder. We both then scrambled up the crack and lay flat next to the missiles, our AK's still on our shoulders. We peered through our binoculars over the edge of the boulder and down at the compound below.

Jeff said, "They're still just ignoring the Black Hawk. Four patrolling the perimeter continuing to patrol. Can't see the two sentries supposed to be down near the front gate. Ranch house itself quiet as a mouse. If Haley right those mercs in mini-mansions are napping, it's gonna be a much longer nap than they expected when they put their heads down on their pillows."

"An eternity longer," I said. "We good to go, then?"

"Oh my goodness, yes," Jeff said. "The stuff dreams are made of. We're gonna run the picket fence at them."

"Shirley Temple in 'Poor Little Rich Girl', Humphrey Bogart in 'The Maltese Falcon', and Dennis Hopper in 'Hoosiers'?" I said.

"An homage," Jeff said.

"Shirley, Humphrey, and Dennis all lived in Topanga?" I said.

"Uh huh," Jeff said. "But they're all dead now."

The red-tailed hawk dipped its right wing, raised its left, and began a clockwise circle that took it closer to the ground. A slight breeze fluttered through the oak leaves. A jackrabbit scampered through the brush.

"I just thought of something," I said.

"What is it?" Jeff said.

"It's something I should have thought of before and I'm annoyed I didn't," I said. "Actually it's more of a question than a thought. The question being, why did those boys stick around?"

"Kenny, Carter, and Bryce?" Jeff said.

"Uh huh," I said.

"They probably think it's too hard to get out of the country if they've got Kate and Billy with them," Jeff said.

"Maybe," I said.

"That 'maybe' sounds likes you got a better idea," Jeff said.

"I think if Kenny, Carter, and Bryce wanted to leave, they could probably have found a way to take Kate and Billy with them," I said. "And, given what we know of their plans regarding the insurmountable edge, they also most likely believe they've taken care of everything they need to take care of in order to be sure those plans can now go off without a hitch. They have Kate and Billy, they killed all the dark programmers, and they killed that Eric Beidermann kid, the one who uploaded the software containing the dark programmers' war game weapon into the live military computer systems. So anyone who knew or knows anything that might be able to stop them is either dead or in Kenny's, Carter's, and Bryce's control. My guess, then, as to why they're sticking around is that Kenny the Dragon Man has unfinished business and there's no way he's going to leave the country until it's finished."

Jeff pulled the binoculars from his face and looked at me. Overhead, the red-tailed hawk rode a thermal, spiraling higher into the sky.

"Kate and Paul Lennon's kids?" Jeff said.

I nodded.

"Probably Lennon's sister, Margaret, too," I said. "Must annoy the hell out of Kenny he was able to kill Paul Lennon's parents, Sam, Lizzy, and Sarah, but that Kate's kids and the Professor have somehow escaped execution."

"Kids and the Professor all in a safe house, though," Jeff said.

"Burnette might have found out where they are," I said.

"But it was Ray Carpenter who arranged everything," Jeff said.

"I'm sure Carpenter wouldn't have told Burnette where he stashed the kids and Margaret Lennon, but I don't see how Carpenter could have gotten everyone to safe houses without help," I said. "That would mean there are most likely other people in the FBI besides Carpenter who also know where the kids and Margaret are. One of those people could have told Burnette."

"Burnette, God rest his soul, be stupid," Jeff said. "But even stupid as he be, Burnette at least be knowing it none of Carter's business where Kate's kids and Margaret is once they in a safe house. He tell Carter that kind of information, then we gotta believe maybe Burnette was evil too."

"I don't think Burnette was evil," I said. "But I can envision a scenario where maybe Carter Bowdoin convinced Freddy they couldn't trust Ray Carpenter. Maybe Carter told Freddy they needed to know where Kate's kids and the Professor were to be sure they were safe. Freddy had a good heart. He'd worry about his niece and nephew, and maybe even about their Aunt Margaret as well. Freddy and Carter then could have gone to Burnette together and told Burnette what they thought about Carpenter and that they felt it was best if Burnette made sure the kids and Margaret were being properly taken care of."

"Carter and Freddy tell Burnette they don't trust Carpenter, Burnette eat that up," Jeff said. "Burnette pull rank and move the kids and the Professor." Jeff paused. "But if they moved, wouldn't Carpenter know and tell us?"

"I'm not sure Carpenter would have known," I said. "Burnette could easily have told his FBI cohorts to leave Carpenter out of the loop."

"Okay, I guess I'm able to buy that," Jeff said. He paused again, seemingly thinking about something. "Then again, I don't know. I understand Freddy might worry about the kids, and maybe even Margaret, but when we saw Freddy at that crater, he seemed like he had plenty of issues with trusting Carter."

"Freddy, God bless his soul, seem like a particularly strong-minded individual to you?" I said.

"I see your point," Jeff said. "Freddy could have been talked into any-thing, even something against his better judgment. Better call Carpenter. Tell him if the kids and Professor Margaret are still in the first safe houses he put them in, he better move all of them now. If the kids and Professor have already moved from the first houses, he better move them again. And whatever Carpenter does, he has to do it without anyone else in FBI knowing a damn thing about it."

"That's exactly what I'll tell Carpenter," I said. "I'll tell Vandross what's going on too. That way, if Carpenter needs help with any of the moves, he can call Vandross and get Vandross to assist him. Still, it's only a short term solution, isn't it?"

"Yeah," Jeff said. "Professor and the kids can't be living in safe houses forever."

"No, they can't," I said. "Which is why we gotta kill Kenny."

"Killing Kenny only way they can live normal lives," Jeff said. "We was going to kill Kenny anyway, though. Carter and Bryce too."

"Yes we were," I said. "I just wanted to highlight that we are killing all three of them not just for vengeance, but also as part of our higher calling."

"Our higher calling being protecting the living," Jeff said.

"Yes," I said.

"I agree," Jeff said. "Us killing Kenny, Carter, and Bryce protects the living and avenges the murders of Sam and Lizzy, Sarah Lennon, Milt Feynman, Paul Lennon, Paul Lennon's parents, and all those dead NASAD employees and FBI agents too."

"Killing Kenny, Carter, and Bryce also avenges what was done to you and your team by Kenny's mercenary company Heise De Shui in the Sudan," I said. "All of which - protecting the living and avenging the dead - is why we can't afford to screw this thing up."

Jeff looked closely into my eyes.

"You're just saying all this because you think the pressure is gonna keep me focused," Jeff said. "You're afraid I'm not focused, I'm gonna mess up."

"You're one paranoid asshole," I said.

"Swear to me you weren't thinking like that," Jeff said.

"I swear," I said. "It was for both of us. The pressure keeps me focused too."

"Fine," Jeff said. "And just in case you were afraid I was going to mess up, you can rest assured I'm not gonna do that."

"Good," I said. "Because on top of everything else, we have to stop a war."

"Yes, we do," Jeff said. "Now, go make those calls to Carpenter and Vandross."

"Mind if I text?" I said.

"Texting good," Jeff said.

I took out my iPhone and texted Ray Carpenter and Vandross about Professor Margaret and Kate's kids. I felt comfortable that would keep them safe until we took care of Kenny 'Dragon Man' Liu.

Manu's voice crackled in my earpiece.

"This is Manu," Manu said. "I am rechecking my com. Ten four."

Because we were all conferenced in, Jeff had also heard what Manu had said.

"You tell him he need to do another com check?" Jeff said.

"No," I said.

"What the hell is he doing that for then?" Jeff said. "And what's with the ten four shit? Manu gonna be talking a bunch of extraneous crap, it gonna be hard to concentrate on what we need to do."

"Manu and I had a conversation about that exact same topic a couple of days ago," I said. "Thought I made him understand he shouldn't use language like that."

"Clearly he ain't teachable," Jeff said. Jeff paused a moment, then added, "Both twins could be dead soon. Suppose it might not hurt if you humor him."

I nodded and un-muted my microphone.

"Roger that, Manu," I said into my headset.

"Who is Roger?" Manu said.

Jeff said, "Then again, maybe humoring him not such a good idea."

I said, "Manu, don't worry about Roger. Where are you?"

"We are approaching the drop off point," Manu said. "Ten four."

"You're staying well away from the compound's entrance, correct?" I said.

"Yes," Manu said. "Ten four."

"How long until you drop Adelaide off?" I said.

"Two minutes," Manu said. "Ten four."

Adelaide's voice loudly joined the conference.

"What the hell is wrong with you, Manu?" Adelaide said. "Stop saying ten four!"

"Okay," Manu said. "Ten four."

There was the sound of scuffling.

"Hey," Manu said. "Get your hands out of my eyes, Adelaide. I can't see."

Jeff and I looked at each other.

"Better not to listen," Jeff said.

I nodded. We both removed our headsets and, using our binoculars, watched the guards below come to their respective corners of the perimeter. They made sharp right angle turns, passed each other - appearing to make small nods of acknowledgment as they did so - and continued on their way.

"They're disciplined," Jeff said.

"Shame it's all going to waste," I said.

"They should have chosen a different profession," Jeff said.

"Like plumbing?" I said.

"Or mailman," Jeff said.

"What about movie usher?" I said.

"Movie usher good," Jeff said. "They got some nice theatres in Almaty."

"I know," I said. "I once saw a movie called 'Mongol' in Kabul."

"How was it?" Jeff said.

"Not bad," I said.

"So, what we saying then," Jeff said, "is if those mercs were movie ushers instead of mercs, they could be watching 'Mongol' right now instead of dying for Carter Bowdoin, Dragon Man, and Bryce?"

"Um-hmm," I said. "And day would become night and night would become day."

"Stevie Wonder?" Jeff said.

"Sort of," I said.

The red-tailed hawk let out a high-pitched scream like a steam whistle, spread out its wings, and began a slow controlled dive with its talons outstretched. The hawk floated down, until he finally disappeared into the brush. A few moments later he rose with a jackrabbit clutched in between his legs and flew quietly away.

"Hawk knows what's he doing," Jeff said.

"He does," I said.

The muffled crackle of Manu's voice came again from Jeff's and my headsets' earphones. We put our headsets back on.

"Sorry, Manu," I said. "Did you say something?"

"We just dropped off Adelaide," Manu said. "Ten four."

"Is she proceeding to her assigned location?" I said.

"Yes," Manu said. "Ten four."

Adelaide said, "De oppresso liber."

Mosi said, "Are we supposed to understand what she just said?"

I said, "It means to liberate the oppressed."

Jeff said, "Which is what we about to do."

Manu said, "Ten four."

CHAPTER 119

Jeff and I kept our binoculars trained on the compound while we waited for Adelaide to get into position on the opposite side of the canyon. The sentries continued in their tight pattern around the perimeter of the clearing and no one entered or exited the main ranch house or the mini-mansions. I ran our plan for rescuing Kate and Dr. Nimo/Billy over in my mind. It seemed like a reasonably good plan, but the more I thought about it, the more I realized it had one pretty glaring hole.

I covered my headset microphone and said to Jeff, "Let's put our phones on mute. I don't want everyone listening in to what we're going to talk about."

Jeff nodded and we both muted our phones

"I'm worried the plan is missing a piece," I said.

"We only came up with it twenty minutes ago," Jeff said. "Probably missing a whole lot of pieces."

"This one's pretty big," I said.

"What is it?" Jeff said.

"Well, first off, whatever plan Carter, Kenny, and Bryce have been using to guide their actions, that plan most likely didn't include us showing up here, correct?" I said.

"That's the most likely case, yes," Jeff said.

"And whatever their plan is, we're about to subject it to a whole world of hurt in the next few minutes," I said.

"We better be doing that," Jeff said.

"What I'm worried about," I said, "is that, since Carter, Kenny, and Bryce are so arrogant, and also seem to be lacking in experience in these matters, their response to our attack might be a bit desperate and perhaps even unpredictable."

"So you're saying it might be good if we give some consideration to predicting it?" Jeff said.

"I am," I said.

"What's your prediction?" Jeff said.

"Even without the LAPD or L.A. County Sheriff getting involved, this thing is likely going to turn into a hostage situation once I get in the ranch house," I said.

Jeff seemed to think about this.

"You're right," Jeff said. "I was assuming you would just be blowing those assholes away, then grabbing Kate and Billy."

"Me too," I said. "But if they set up so I can't do that..."

"We shoulda considered this before," Jeff said. "We just out of practice, or are we getting stupid in our old age?"

"I'd say both," I said.

"Both sound right," Jeff said.

A lizard scurried along the boulder in front of our faces. The lizard stopped for a moment, and using that short, jerky, rapid movement that lizards use, turned his head to face us. He flicked out his tongue at us, blinked a few times, flicked out his tongue again, then hastily scurried away and disappeared down the crack between the boulders.

"Is that lizard making fun of us?" I said.

"Definitely seem that way to me," Jeff said.

"Do you think he thinks we're stupid and out of practice too?" I said.

"I think everybody does," Jeff said. "So, how you see it going down if Carter, Kenny, and Bryce have guns pointing at Kate's and Billy's heads or bombs taped to their chests?"

"Well, since Carter, Kenny, and Bryce will be the ones with the hostages, I'd say everything is going to depend, initially at least, on how they've analyzed their new situation," I said.

"'New' meaning that we're in their faces now?" Jeff said.

"Correct," I said. "I think that once they see that we've eliminated their contingent of mercenary guards and blown up the Black Hawk, they'll realize pretty quickly that their perfectly laid plans have been shot to hell. The only thing they'll be focusing on is escaping. Carter, Kenny, and Bryce will also know a whole bunch of cops and firemen could be showing up at any moment and they aren't going to want to deal with the cops and fireman any more than we're going to want to. Which means what Carter, Kenny, and Bryce are going to want is not only to get out of here, but to get out of here as soon as possible. They're not going to risk a prolonged hostage standoff."

"Carter, Kenny, and Bryce aren't stupid," Jeff said. "They're going to figure out it isn't just enough to escape the compound. They'll know they gonna be the subject of a massive manhunt after everyone sees what they done here. Which mean they're gonna know if they wanna avoid being locked up for the rest of their lives, they also gotta get out of the country fast as they can."

"Agreed," I said. "Which means they'll most likely insist on taking Kate and Billy with them to ensure safe passage. They're also going to need a plane."

Jeff smiled.

"I see where you're going with this," Jeff said.

"You do, huh?" I said.

"Kinshasa," Jeff said.

"Give the man a prize," I said. "We do exactly what we did in Kinshasa. We tell the bad guys they can take hostages on the condition I go with them, then we get them a plane..."

"Then we take it all away," Jeff said.

"God willing," I said. "So, we need to come up with a place they'll believe it will be both safe for them to fly to and also one I'd agree to go to as well."

"Can't be China," Jeff said. "They ain't gonna buy you be stupid enough to trust you ever be coming back home from China if you fly there with them."

A mercenary exited the front door of the mini-mansion that looked like an English country home. The mercenary, who appeared to be a Kazakh, stood outside the front door for a moment as he stretched his arms above his head and did a few squats. He then went back inside.

"How about Costa Rica?" I said.

"Costa Rica?" Jeff said.

"Yeah," I said. "Costa Rica is neutral and they set up some kind of special economic zone with China a while ago. Costa Ricans wouldn't want to mess up their relationships with us or the Chinese."

"Might work," Jeff said. "Let's see if Haley can set it up. She gotta make it look real though, just like she did in Kinshasa."

"By real, I presume you're speaking of getting everyone diplomatic passports for Costa Rica?" I said.

"Uh huh," Jeff said. "Like I said, Carter, Kenny, and Bryce aren't idiots...strike that, Bryce definitely is an idiot. At least one of the other two though, probably Carter, gonna wanna make sure the whole thing is real and ask to see the passports before they get on the plane."

"I think you're right about that," I said.

I put the conference line on hold, unmuted my iPhone, and called Haley on FaceTime. Jeff looked at my phone's screen with me as Haley answered. Haley still looked as beautiful as ever despite the fact she was going on her third day without sleep.

"What comes to mind when I say the word 'Kinshasa'?" I said.

"You think you might be looking at a hostage situation?" Haley said.

"Yes," I said. "If there is one, the plan will be to convince Bowdoin, Liu, and Wellington to go with Dr. Lennon, Dr. Nimo/Billy Einstein, and me to a neutral site, and that once we all arrive at the neutral site, the three of them will be allowed to go free in exchange for letting me have Dr. Lennon and Billy."

"Jack, I remember what we did in Kinshasa, okay?" Haley said. "You want to use Switzerland as the neutral country again?"

"Jeff and I were thinking Costa Rica," I said. "It's closer to us than Switzerland."

Haley seemed to think this over.

"Costa Rica should work," Haley said. "I better set up some diplomatic passports like the ones we used in Kinshasa right now. Before they agree to go with you, Bowdoin, Liu, and Wellington will probably want to check up on how they're going to get into Costa Rica."

"That's exactly what we were thinking," I said. "We'll need a plane too, of course."

"Okay with you if we let them use their own?" Haley said.

"They have a plane close by?" I said.

"Pennsylvania Avenue Partners has a long-range business jet on the tarmac at Van Nuys Airport," Haley said. "The airport is only about forty-five minutes from your location."

"Really?" I said. "They've got a jet just sitting there? No flight plans have been filed?"

"No flight plans," Haley said. "The jet has been there for over a week. Bowdoin and Wellington flew in on it and I guess it's just hanging around until they decide to go somewhere else."

One of the Afghan sentries patrolling the perimeter of the polo field stopped and removed a canteen from where it had been hooked to his pants belt. He unscrewed the canteen's cap, took a few sips of whatever liquid the canteen contained, put the cap back on, and rehooked the canteen to his belt. Apparently cognizant of the fact his stopping had put him out of position in terms of the spacing he and his comrades had been maintaining while patrolling, the sentry quickly hustled back into position.

"Can the PAP jet reach Costa Rica without refueling?" I said.

"Yes," Haley said. "It might even be able to fly nonstop to Asia if they wanted."

"Hmm," I said. "Let's let them use it then, shall we? Maybe I'll negotiate that jet being our ride back as well."

"To make it more believable there *will* be a ride back?" Haley said.

"That's the idea," I said. "There's still a chance I can avoid a hostage situation, so we may not need the passports or the jet. In regard to the passports, however, it would be better to have them available sooner rather than later."

"Did I or did I not say I'd set them up right now?" Haley said.

"You did," I said.

"Bye," Haley said.

She hung up. I reconnected to the conference line and muted my phone.

"I feel better now that Haley is on board with Kinshasa," I said to Jeff.

"Me too," Jeff said. "I got no doubt Haley will hold up her end. We still got one more problem though."

"What is it?" I said.

"Carter, Kenny, and Bryce most likely gonna figure out pretty quick they only need one hostage to force us to let 'em go," Jeff said.

"You're saying they're going to kill Kate or Billy?" I said.

"There's a chance of that, yeah," Jeff said.

"Why?" I said. "Two hostages are still better than one. Plus they have to know killing either of them is going to seriously piss us off."

"Normally, that would be true," Jeff said. "But this ain't a normal situation."

"What hostage situation is normal?" I said.

"None," Jeff said. "What I should have said is that this situation is completely whacked out. Emperor Kenny seems like one unstable shit-for-brains to me."

"Okay," I said. "I can see your point. If he only needs one hostage, Kenny might kill Kate or Billy for sport alone."

"Uh huh," Jeff said.

Two Kazakh mercenaries exited the Italian palazzo mini-mansion. They sat down on some lounge chairs on the palazzo's porch and they each lit up a cigarette. One of them seemed to notice the red-tailed hawk circling over the compound. He pointed his cigarette in the hawk's direction and appeared to say something to his comrade, who then looked up into the sky. The comrade mimed a pistol with his right hand and shot at the hawk. The first Kazakh gave the comrade a big thumbs up and took another drag on his cigarette.

"Those Kazakhs seem easily amused," Jeff said.

"They do," I said. "So which one? Kate or Billy?"

"Could be either one," Jeff said. "I'm thinking the only reason both of them are still alive is that Carter, Kenny, and Bryce didn't get outta Kate or Billy what they wanna know yet."

"That being what Kate or Billy might have told us about the insurmountable edge that could allow us to stop their evil plans?" I said.

"Yeah," Jeff said. "Insurmountable edge software has likely been installed at least two weeks now in the active military computer systems, so all Carter, Kenny, and Bryce got to do is hope they get to six o'clock tonight without us figuring out a way to make sure Billy's program doesn't start working."

"So, their biggest worry concerning you and me has to be that we might find out something that could thwart the edge," I said. "That being the case, Carter, Kenny, and Bryce have to kill Billy."

"I agree," Jeff said. "Billy much more likely to know something that can help us than Kate would."

"So their most likely course of action is to kill Billy and save Kate as a hostage?" I said.

Jeff nodded.

"As much as we know Kenny love to see Kate dead to be satisfying his sicko personal vendetta, we don't have to worry about him killing her now because then he loses his ticket out of here," Jeff said. "Carter, Kenny, and Bryce gotta also know they're all dead if they kill Billy and *then* kill Kate, since if they do that, you'll blow away them three assholes faster than they can say Jack Robinson."

"They kill Kate, that's exactly what would happen," I said.

"Except you can't do it," Jeff said.

"Why not?" I said.

"Because even though we don't think torture gonna work to get them to tell us what the insurmountable edge is, we have to give it a shot," Jeff said.

"A long shot being better than no shot since the stakes are so high?" I said.

"Couldn't have said it better myself," Jeff said. "However, the way I see it, our best chance of stopping the edge is still a living Billy. So what we really gotta do is keep that nut job Kenny from killing Billy no matter how cute Kenny think such an action might be."

The two Kazakhs sitting on the porch of the Italian palazzo each mimed a few more pistol shots in the hawk's direction. They guffawed together, stood up, stubbed out their cigarettes, slapped each other on the back, and headed back inside the mini-mansion.

"Not that we care," Jeff said, "but it does appear those mercs' last moments on this earth gonna be happy ones."

"'Not that we care' is the operative phrase," I said. "Do you have any suggestions on how to stop Kenny?"

"I do," Jeff said.

"Pray tell," I said.

"Moment you walk in that room, you put the barrel of that AK-12 in Emperor Kenny the Dragon Man's ugly face," Jeff said, pointing to the rifle hanging from my shoulder. "Then you make it crystal clear if he hurts anybody, you're gonna splatter his brains all over the floor."

I stared at Jeff for a moment.

"Really?" I said. "That's your suggestion?"

"You don't like it?" Jeff said.

"I like it," I said. "It's also the first thing I would have thought of the moment I walked in the room and I saw it was a hostage situation."

"Must be a good idea if both of us came up with it," Jeff said.

"That's one way to look at it," I said. "The other way to look at it would be to admit our options are pretty goddamn limited."

"They are," Jeff said. "But there's also a bright side."

"What's that?" I said.

"We've done all our calculating and forecasting before you're actually in the room with those clowns," Jeff said. "Now you can be acting without hesitation, and I feel more comfortable about your safety."

"Thank you," I said. "Your concern is appreciated."

"You're welcome," Jeff said.

A dozen quail flushed from the brush just below the boulder Jeff and I were perched on. Jeff and I both instantly focused our binoculars on the sentries patrolling the compound. They didn't seem to have noticed the sound. I had just taken the binoculars away from my eyes when another flash of movement suddenly caught my attention. The movement had come from a spot in the brush on the mountain slope on the opposite side of the canyon. The spot was about thirty yards from the boulder we had chosen for Adelaide to shoot from.

I zoomed my binoculars in on the spot.

The movement I had seen had come from Adelaide. She was wriggling along the ground under the brush with her AK. Clearly she hadn't been careful enough in choosing her cover, because the brush she was trying to hide under was much too sparse. If I could see her, that meant it was also possible for the sentries to see her as well.

I looked over at Jeff. He appeared to be watching Adelaide too. He put down his binoculars, turned to me, and shook his head. We both unmuted our phones.

"Adelaide, stop moving," I said into my headset.

"What's wrong?" Adelaide said, still moving.

"I can see you," I said.

"That's because you know where I am," Adelaide said.

"No," I said. "I knew where you were going, but not how you were going to get there. Stop moving. Now."

"Fine," Adelaide said.

She stopped moving.

"What do you want me to do?" Adelaide said.

"Backtrack about twenty yards," I said. "The brush is much thicker there. Then continue a bit higher up where the brush also appears to be thicker until you get to the boulder."

"You know how hard it is to crawl through this stuff?" Adelaide said.

"Do you know how easy it will be for the sentries to kill you if they see you?" I said.

"Shit," Adelaide said.

She backed up. I waited until she disappeared into the brush and then checked on the sentries again. They still seemed unaware of Adelaide's or Jeff's and my presence.

"It looks like Adelaide will be in position in about five minutes," I said to Jeff. "Let's prepare the Iglas."

We activated all six Iglas and laid them side by side on the boulder's surface. We knew how we were going to use at least five of the missiles - one Igla for the Black Hawk and one for each for the compound's four mini-mansions. That would leave one Igla left for the unexpected. Plan for the unexpected was rule number twenty-one in the Wilder combat manual.

Adelaide's voice came through my headset just after we had activated the last Igla.

"I'm in position," Adelaide said.

I focused my binoculars on the boulder we had chosen for her on the other side of the canyon.

"I can't see you," I said.

"Isn't that the idea?" Adelaide said.

"Yes," I said, "it is. You have a bead on the southernmost perimeter guard?"

"I'm locked in," Adelaide said.

"No second thoughts?" I said.

"No second thoughts," Adelaide said.

"Most people killing someone for the first time have second thoughts," I said.

"I just killed the Kazakhs last night," Adelaide said.

"That was with a car," I said. "This is with a gun."

"You want me to have second thoughts?" Adelaide said.

"No," I said.

"Then shut up," Adelaide said.

"I'll honor your request as it pertains to you, but I still have to talk to Manu," I said. "Manu, you still there?"

"Ten four," Manu said.

Adelaide said, "Manu, I told you to cut that ten four shit out."

"Roger that," Manu said.

"That goes for Roger as well," Adelaide said.

"Ten four," Manu said.

"Screw this," Adelaide said. "I'm acquiring a new target."

"The windows are bulletproof," Manu said. "I'm rolling them up now. Ten four."

Jeff and I shared a look.

"She can't see the Maybach, can she?" Jeff said.

"No," I said. "The Maybach is down on the street. The trees are in the way."

"Good," Jeff said.

Adelaide said, "Who says I'm going to stay where I am? All I gotta do is climb down off of this mountain…"

I said, "That's enough, Adelaide. You too, Manu and Mosi. I don't want to hear another word from any of you other than a simple yes or no. And Manu, no matter what happens, you stay where you are until I get there. You got that?"

There was no response.

"Manu, did you hear me?" I said.

"I thought I wasn't supposed to talk?" Manu said.

A crow flew very close to Jeff's and my heads, so close we could feel the whoosh of its wings. Two screeching blackbirds followed quickly in the crow's wake, the blackbirds apparently intent on driving the crow from their territory. The blackbirds dive bombed the crow, ducking in for sharp pecks, retreating, then ducking in again.

"I didn't say that," I said. "I said you can only say yes or no."

"Yes," Manu said.

"Yes what?" I said.

"Yes, yes," Manu said.

Jeff said, "I think he mean he'll stay where he is until you get there."

"Is that what you meant, Manu?" I said.

"Yes," Manu said.

"Good," I said. "Adelaide, as soon as the first missile hits, you will take out the southernmost guard, then move clockwise around the perimeter, taking out each of the other guards in turn. Please confirm."

"I know the plan," Adelaide said.

"Yes or no, please," I said.

"What does 'I know the plan' sound like to you?" Adelaide said.

"Yes or no?" I said.

"This is unbelievable," Adelaide said. "Your fire teams put up with this crap?"

"The members of my fire teams did whatever I told them to or they stayed home," I said. "You want to go home?"

"You're kidding, right?" Adelaide said.

"No," I said. "You can start walking right now. When we're done maybe we'll pick you up."

"Jesus," Adelaide said. "Yes, okay. I confirm. And by the way, ten four."

Manu said, "Why can she say that and I can't?"

Jeff said, "Shut up, Manu."

I said, "That was very well put, Jeff. You'd make a good general."

"I am a general," Jeff said.

"Indeed you are," I said. "Continuing to review the plan, then. Adelaide, Jeff, and I will pick off any perimeter guards you miss..."

Adelaide interrupted, "I won't miss."

I ignored her.

"If the guards along the main driveway start heading to the ranch house, take them down too," I said. "Your third level targets are anyone trying to leave the ranch house. Just be sure they don't have Kate or Dr. Nimo/Billy with them. Jeff will assist you if needed in taking care of any activity coming from the mini-mansions."

"Got it," Adelaide said.

"At any time during our attack, if anybody has any questions or problems, make sure I hear about them immediately," I said. "The party starts in about thirty seconds."

I turned to Jeff.

"You ready?" I said.

Jeff nodded.

"Chopper first, then mini-mansions one east and two east," Jeff said.

"One west and two west for me," I said. "Oh, and don't hit the ranch house."

"I won't if you won't," Jeff said.

Jeff raised the first Igla surface-to-surface missile to his shoulder and took aim at the Black Hawk beneath its camouflage cover.

I sighted in on the westernmost mini-mansion, which also happened to be the Italian palazzo.

"Damn," I said. "I just thought of something."

"What?" Jeff said.

"What if these houses are designated historical monuments, you know, like landmarks?" I said. "We could get in a lot of trouble if they are."

"These pieces of shit ain't no landmarks," Jeff said. "In fact, I bet we gonna get a medal from 'Good Housekeeping' for cleaning up this hellhole."

"You're probably right," I said. "On the count of three. One...Two... Three."

We both fired our first missiles.

CHAPTER 120

The Iglas tracked dead on target.

The Black Hawk exploded in a ball of flame and dark smoke rose to the sky.

The Italian palazzo mini-mansion evaporated into thin air.

Jeff and I dropped our empty missile launchers and picked up two more Iglas, our reloading process taking no more than two seconds for each of us. The sentry on the southernmost portion of the polo field's perimeter started to turn his face in the direction of the Black Hawk's burning shell, but what, if anything, he saw of the helicopter, no one will ever know. Before the sentry's turn was completed, his head snapped back and he crumpled to the ground.

Adelaide's sniping lessons had paid off.

Jeff and I fired our second missiles.

I watched mine track, even as I was releasing the launcher and taking my AK-12 from my shoulder. My missile struck home and mini-mansion two west - the Cape Cod - was no more. A millisecond later, Jeff's target, mini-mansion one east - the English country home - dissolved in a blast of fire.

The three sentries left standing on the clearing stared at the flaming wreckage of the Black Hawk and then shifted their stares to the burning hulks of the three destroyed mini-mansions. Their training seemed to take over then, however, and they began to turn their heads in an apparent search for the source of the missiles that had hit the three homes.

The northernmost sentry seemed to spot Jeff and me and rapidly raised his rifle toward us. Before he could get his eye behind the rifle's scope, the back of his head blew off and he fell to the ground like a sack of potatoes.

Adelaide had made another fine shot.

By then I had my eye squarely behind the scope of my own AK and was tracking the easternmost sentry. The sentry moved his head to face in Jeff's and my direction, then toward Adelaide, then back to Jeff and me, as if he wasn't sure if he should take out the Igla fire team that was blowing up the mini-mansions or the sniper who was killing his friends.

I put a bullet in his forehead so he wouldn't have to think about it any longer.

I moved the barrel of my AK towards the fourth sentry, the one on the western perimeter. The sentry's head snapped back before I had acquired it in my sights, however, his knees giving way as he fell backwards without having fired a shot.

Chalk up another kill for Adelaide.

Jeff let fly with his third missile. Mini-mansion two east - the Spanish style villa - vaporized in a thunderous roar of white smoke and red flame.

I let my AK fall to my side and dangle on its shoulder strap. I lifted my binoculars to my face and scanned the compound. No one had made it out of any of the mini-mansions alive. The four white vans that had been parked outside the mini-mansions had been vaporized along with the homes. The two mercenary guards who had been hidden behind the trees that lined the compound's driveway that came up from the public street were just then running onto the polo field and headed for the ranch house. Both of them looked like Kazakhs and the house was still a good three hundred yards from their location. I assumed the occupants of the ranch house were by then fully cognizant of the destruction Adelaide, Jeff, and I had caused and had told the two Kazakh guards to get back to the house as quickly as possible. The guards were moving without the benefit of cover, however, and that was not a good idea.

The front door of the ranch house opened. Two Afghans stuck their heads slightly out of either side of the door's frame, apparently to follow the progress of their Kazakh compatriots across the polo field. Both Afghans looked to be armed with AK-12's. AK's or no AK's, the behavior of the two Afghans in the doorway seemed very questionable to me - indeed, as questionable as the behavior of the two Kazakh guards running across the polo field - since I would never have exposed even the smallest part of my head to my enemy.

"Great shooting Adelaide," I said into my headset. "You see the two mercenaries who just exited the compound's driveway that leads from the street and are now running onto the polo field?"

"Yes," Adelaide said.

"You take them and I'll take the Afghans peeking out of the ranch house door."

"Got it," Adelaide said.

I raised my AK and I sighted in on the Afghan on the left side of the ranch house's front doorframe. Before I could fire, I heard a soft 'pfft', and the Afghan's head exploded in a spray of blood and bone. I sighted on the Afghan to the right of the doorframe, but again, before I could fire, I heard a soft 'pfft', and watched as the head of the Afghan on the right shattered into tiny pieces.

The closeness of the 'pfft' sound had given me a pretty good idea of what had just happened. I lowered my rifle and turned to look at Jeff.

He was blowing the smoke away from the barrel end of his silenced AK.

"Ahhhh," Jeff said.

"Well done," I said.

"Thanks," Jeff said. "Feel good too."

Jeff and I both turned to look at the two Kazakhs running towards the ranch house across the clearing. Adelaide must have been waiting to get as good an angle as possible before firing, because it wasn't until the mercenaries were twenty-five yards from the house's front door that the sides of their heads were blown off. The loose limbed, nearly head-less bodies ran on a few steps, then crumpled to the ground in formless heaps. Fountains of bright red blood flowed from the dark holes between the Kazakhs' shoulders. The blood fountains soaked the Kazakhs' shirts and pooled onto the earth.

"Two more nice shots, Adelaide," I said into my headset.

"Thank you," Adelaide said.

I turned to Jeff.

"What were those two guys thinking?" I said.

"I think someone else be doing their thinking," Jeff said.

"You think Wellington ordered them to hightail it back to the ranch house?" I said.

"Yeah," Jeff said. "Bryce clearly in a panic."

"I'll buy it," I said. "I say we keep Bryce panicking too. You want to do the honors on the Suburbans?"

Jeff used his AK to shoot out two tires on each of the three Suburbans. The tires he chose were the front and back tires on the sides of the vehicles that faced us. The vehicles were all left listing to that side.

I scanned the compound again with my binoculars. Flames were rising fifty feet into the sky from the sites of the mini-mansions and the shell that had once been the Black Hawk.

"Time for me to meet up with Manu and Mosi's tank brigade and commence our ground assault on the ranch house," I said to Jeff. "You okay with holding down the fort with Adelaide?"

"I'm good with that," Jeff said.

"You'll keep that last Igla fired up in case we need it?" I said.

"That's the plan," Jeff said.

"Adelaide, you kill anyone that leaves the house as long as it's not Kate or Dr. Nimo/Billy Einstein, okay?" I said into my headset.

"My pleasure," Adelaide said.

"Manu and Mosi, stay where you are until I get there," I said.

Manu said, "Adelaide has been saying words other than yes or no."

"I realize that," I said.

"Does that mean we can too?" Manu said.

Adelaide said, "If you do, you better be sure to keep those bullet-proof windows rolled up nice and tight."

CHAPTER 121

I left Jeff behind on the boulder at the top of the ridge and raced down the mountainside towards where the Kazakhs' van was parked on the fire road. My feet alternately slipped and gained purchase on the loose sandstone. Lizards darted out of my way, a covey of quail flushed from the brush, and two crows cawed at me. By the time I got to the van, my left knee was throbbing, my lungs burning, and my heart racing. I yanked open the van's driver door and climbed in. The van's engine started on the first crank. I slammed the transmission into gear, floored the gas pedal, and took off down the road, the engine whining, the van fishtailing as its tires rattled, thumped, and kicked up a cloud of dust and small rocks.

It was then about 3:12 p.m., nearly three minutes after we had initiated our attack on the dead scion's Topanga compound. We probably had at most twenty more minutes until the first units of the Los Angeles fire and police departments arrived on the scene. I focused on the road in front of me, taking each of its hairpin turns on two wheels, cutting it as close to the edge of the fire road and the steep canyon drop beyond as I dared. Sweat stung my eyes, built up between my palms and the steering wheel, and pooled on the back of my shirt. My lungs started to burn a little less, but my heart continued to race and my skin seemed to have caught on fire from the excess energy produced by my nervous system going into hyperdrive.

The skirmishes of the last few days had produced their own visceral responses, but they had all been reactive to sudden and unexpected events. What I felt at that moment was an excitement of a different nature. I was carrying out a battle plan far more complicated than the one we had executed at the tunnel on Kanan Dume Road, and it was a plan that required precision, skill, and timing, all while under great risk. I had to be incredibly vigilant in order to be prepared to make the quick adjustments that could mean the difference between life and death as I pursued the plan's ultimate objective of freeing Kate and Billy.

I was in a place I had not been in for more than two years.

I liked being there.

I reached the end of the fire road where it joined with the paved public street that led to the compound's entrance. The van's tires, front then rear, slammed into the street's raised asphalt berm, sending two sharp jolts up my body. I kept the gas pedal floored. The ride smoothed once I was fully on the pavement and the tires began to hum. The engine wailed in my ears and the outside air rushed in a loud whoosh over the van's metal exterior.

Fifteen seconds after leaving the fire road I spotted the Maybach parked on the street about two hundred yards in front of me. It was about thirty feet south of the compound's main gate, a location that could not be seen from the compound's driveway. Ten feet to the right of the Maybach lay the eight-foot-high wall of stacked fieldstone slabs that guarded the compound's western border. Oaks towered both inside and outside the fieldstone wall and blocked out nearly all the sunlight. Across the road from where the Maybach was parked was a dry creek bed bordered on either side by oaks and sycamores. Boulders and a carpet of brittle, dry oak leaves littered the bottom of the creek bed.

"Manu," I said into my headset, "You should be able to see me coming up on you now. Unlock the doors."

"Ten four," Manu said.

I quickly closed the distance between the Maybach and me. When I was twenty feet away from the Maybach, I slammed on the brakes and skidded to a halt, my maneuver leaving me directly across the street from the Maybach. I killed the van's engine, peered through the front and side windows looking for any un-friendlies. I saw no mercenaries either in the trees, atop the wall, or running down the compound's driveway toward me. I did, however, see a lizard in standard lizard vertical climbing position scurrying up the slick bark of a lone aspen tree, his movements defying gravity in a way I always had trouble believing was possible.

So far so good.

"Manu, have you seen anyone moving towards you since we last spoke?" I said into the headset.

"No," Manu said. "Ten four."

"Good," I said. "I'm coming in."

I grabbed my AK-12, checked one last time for any potential threats, then grasped the van's door handle, shoved the door open, and jumped to the ground. Crouching low, I dashed across the street, grabbed the Maybach's rear door handle with my left hand, pulled the door open, quickly leapt into the Maybach's back seat, and slammed the door shut behind me.

"Okay, Jeff, I'm in the Maybach," I said into my headset. "What's happening out there?"

"Not a creature be stirring, not even a mouse," Jeff said.

"Choppers in the air? Sounds of approaching sirens?" I said.

"Nada," Jeff said.

"We're ready to enter the compound, then," I said. "I'm getting Haley back on the line."

I texted Haley. She joined the conference call a moment later.

"I've got your diplomatic clearances in Costa Rica," Haley said. "All systems go for your ground war?"

"Yes, once I find out from you what the status is within the ranch house," I said.

"Everything is the same in the ranch house except for two things," Haley said. "The first change I'm sure you know about - two of the original four mercs that were in the ranch house are now dead and lying inside the house's front door. The second change is that the two mercs of the original four who are still alive have left the kitchen and taken up positions that would be consistent with guarding the entrances to the living room."

"The five people who were sitting in the living room and facing each other haven't moved?" I said.

"They have not," Haley said.

A squirrel ran along the top of the compound's fieldstone wall. The squirrel stopped, got up on its back feet, looked around, ran along the wall a few more feet, then jumped off the backside of the wall and disappeared.

"We have to assume they know we're coming for them," I said. "The question is what are they going to try to do about it?"

"You're about to find out, aren't you?" Haley said.

"We are," I said.

"I know you're working against the clock to get out of there before the authorities arrive, but we really should go over something before you get started," Haley said.

"What is it?" I said.

"The NASAD software running the U.S. military's computer systems has tens of thousands of discrete sections of code and each of those code sections has its own special function," Haley said. "We're now working with computer algorithms that compare Dr. Nimo's/Billy Einstein's psychological profile against the portions of the NASAD software code that all of us at MOM believe may be most vulnerable to an alteration that would produce the so-called insurmountable edge. We've decided our best bet is the edge is in the integration code. I'm telling you all this because there's a good chance Billy is unconscious and you might be able to rouse him only long enough for a few questions, maybe even just one question. If you think you're only going to get one question, ask him if the edge is in the integration code. The safest thing, in fact, would be for you to phrase the question as simply as possible. Make it a Yes/No question, one Billy could answer with a nod. Just say, 'Billy, yes or no, did you mess with the integration code?' If he gives us a yes, we can focus our search to that one narrow area and we might have a shot at defeating Billy's software weapon without any further help from him."

"We're still certain Billy's software weapon hasn't turned on yet?" I said. "All military computer systems are still functioning normally?"

"There's no sign the weapon has turned on," Haley said. "Everything is definitely functioning normally."

"What does the integration code do?" I said.

"It allows all the hardware systems to work together," Haley said. "If you want to fire a missile from a fighter jet, for example, the GPS from the satellites has to integrate with the jet's avionics, which in turn need to coordinate with the missile's aiming systems."

"So if Billy found a way to screw up the ability for each of those kinds of systems to work together, he would screw up everything?" I said.

"He would," Haley said. "And, screwing up the ability of the systems to work together would definitely qualify as an insurmountable edge if we can't find a way to undo what Billy did."

"Okay," I said. "If I can only ask Billy one question, I'll ask him that.

I hope I can have a nice, long conversation with him, though."

"If Billy's dead you also know what to do, right?" Haley said.

"You were able to fix his phone?" I said.

"I'm still skeptical, but my team feels they're getting close," Haley said.

"Don't worry, I know we need Billy's fingerprints," I said. "If for some reason we don't recover his entire body, you'll at least get his hands."

"Good," Haley said.

"One last thing," I said. "I'm going to need you to stay on the line until we get Kate and Billy safely away from here. The next part of the plan is likely to be the most dangerous part, and I may need your assistance on an instantaneous basis."

"I wouldn't have it any other way," Haley said.

"Thank you," I said. "Manu, please start the car and head for the gate. Adelaide, any un-friendlies poke their heads out of the ranch house, take them down as long as you have a clean shot that won't risk hitting anyone else inside."

"I'm already on it," Adelaide said.

Manu started the Maybach's engine, put the car in gear, pulled out onto the street, and drove slowly towards the compound's front gate.

"I don't think we have to worry about taking any fire until we're on the portion of the polo field near the ranch house," I said to Manu. "If we do take some fire, however, just keep moving and do exactly as I tell you."

"Ten four," Manu said.

Adelaide said, "Goddamnit!"

I said, "What's wrong, Adelaide?"

"I can't stay on this call," Adelaide said.

I said, "Why not?"

"Because I can't take this ten four shit for another second!" Adelaide screamed.

"You'll be fine, Adelaide," I said. "Just ignore him."

"I can't!" Adelaide said.

Manu said, "Adelaide please don't scream so loud. It hurts my ears. Ten four."

"Aarghhhh!" Adelaide said.

Manu guided the Maybach off the street and onto the short dirt driveway that led to the compound's gate. The gate was closed and lay in a gap about fifteen feet wide between the ends of the compound's fieldstone wall. Manu stopped a few feet in front of the gate. Groves of tall, thick oaks guarded both sides of the gap on the inner and outer sides of the wall. A slight breeze ruffled the oaks' leaves, making them softly chatter, and a half dozen crows abruptly took flight from the oaks' branches.

The gate consisted of two swinging doors, the doors constructed of horizontally oriented pine slats that had been nailed to a frame of pine two-by-fours. The pine was weathered to the point of decrepitude. Each of the doors rested on a set of three pairs of rusty hinges that had been screwed into two posts on either side of the driveway. Some of the bolts had fallen out of the hinges' bolt holes, leaving dark, empty cavities where the bolts should have been. Both doors sagged where they met in the middle of the gate's opening, and they were linked together by a padlocked chain strung around the vertical inner two-by-fours of their frames. The chain and padlock were an interesting idea, but given the state of the gate's wood and hinges, they weren't going to do much good against what I had in mind, which was to bust the gate down by driving right through it.

"Adelaide, Haley, and Jeff," I said into my headset, "still no evidence of any human activity between the front gate and the ranch house?"

"No," they all said.

I leaned forward against the Maybach's front seat ready to tell Manu to go ahead and punch through the gate, but stopped myself when I noticed Manu's physical condition. Actually both the twins' physical condition. Little beads of sweat had appeared on the sides of their giant foreheads and the beads were beginning to trickle down next to their sideburns. The twins' breathing was shallow and fast. Manu clutched and unclutched the steering wheel. Mosi wiped his forehead with his forearm.

I leaned farther forward, put my head between the two giant Samoans, and patted each one on the shoulder.

"Everything's going to be okay boys," I said. "We got two of the best shooters in the world in Adelaide and Jeff providing cover. You got me in the back seat. We have a level five security Maybach with two-inch thick Lexan windows and the optional Improvised Explosive Device

Protective Bottom Plate. We're safe in here. Nothing can get to us."

Manu turned his head to the right, and Mosi turned his head to the left, so that they were both facing me. Their lips trembled slightly.

"I'm telling you boys, you'll be fine," I said. "Just be sure not to get out of the car, okay?"

The twins appeared to think about this. They looked at each other for a moment, seemingly again sharing some kind of private thought transfer no one outside their twin world would ever be privy to. They both nodded at me. It didn't appear to be a confident nod, but one that seemed to say the twins were both doing their best to buck up and be true to Faaaloalo.

I found their behavior quite brave.

Bravery was always a good thing in my book.

"Excellent," I said. "Eyes forward."

Manu and Mosi turned to face out the front window. I sat back against my seat, double-checked my AK to be sure there was a round in the chamber and that the safety was off, then put the gun in ready position across my chest.

"Drive," I said.

"Drive?" Manu said.

"Yes," I said.

"Through the gate?" Manu said.

"Yes, through the gate," I said. "And as I believe it will be helpful to do so with as much speed as possible, floor it please."

CHAPTER 122

The Maybach's 5.5 litre, 550 horsepower V12 biturbo engine roared to life with a throaty low-pitched burble as Manu floored the gas pedal. The rear tires spun, the rubber treads letting loose with a whining friction moan as they searched for, then found purchase in, the dirt of the driveway. We shot forward and the Maybach's nose smashed into the gate. The gate's two hanging panels exploded into a cloud of rotted wood and flying pieces of rusted metal. The Maybach was not slowed in the slightest by the impact and we rapidly gained momentum as we sped along the driveway toward the compound's clearing. In under three seconds we were going over forty miles an hour and the oaks lining the driveway quickly gave way to dozens of towering eucalyptus trees, their trunks whizzing by in a blur. The driveway's incline had as of yet prevented me from seeing the ranch house, but once we crested the incline we would have full view of the house and the clearing that held the polo field.

Haley said, "You're about three hundred yards from the edge of the clearing."

I said, "We should be there in about ten seconds. Any change inside the ranch house?"

"No," Haley said. "You're good to go."

"8,7,6,5...I can see the tops of the goalposts," I said.

"Oh shit!" Haley said.

"Oh shit, what?" I said.

"Stop the car!" Haley said.

I had worked with Haley long enough to know that when she said stop, she meant stop. To do otherwise was to risk life and limb. Manu had either not heard her command or did not understand its importance, however, and we kept barreling forward.

"Manu, did you hear Haley?" I said.

He didn't answer.

I leaned forward and put my mouth close to his ear.

"Manu, stop the car," I said.

Manu shuddered as if I had frightened him. He turned his head to me, a wild, uncomprehending look in his eyes.

"Everything is going to be fine," I said. "Just stop the car."

"N...n...n...now?" Manu said.

"Right now," I said.

Manu slammed on the brakes. The Maybach skidded along the driveway out past the last of the eucalyptus trees and onto the front edge of the clearing. It came to a stop about twenty yards from the first set of goalposts, which also put us about three hundred and fifty yards from the ranch house.

"Good job, Manu," I said. "Now just hold tight."

Manu nodded, his whole body shaking.

"What's going on Haley?" I said.

"I've got a new heat signature," Haley said.

"Where is it?" I said.

"It's coming from what's labeled on the ranch house floor plans as a billiard room," Haley said.

"A billiard room?" I said.

"That's what it says," Haley said.

"What do you think the heat signature is from?" I said.

"I don't know," Haley said. "But it's very big and it's very hot."

"How big is the room itself?" I said.

"Big," Haley said. "At least twenty by twenty feet."

"So it's big enough to hold a vehicle?" I said.

"Yes," Haley said. "At least one, maybe two."

"The heat signature could be coming from an engine then, yes?" I said.

"Yes," Haley said.

"Can I see the exterior of the room from where I am?" I said.

"You should be able to," Haley said. "It's at the far right end of the house. It's fronted by what look like French doors."

I lifted my binoculars and scanned the ranch house and the surrounding area. The sites where the mini-mansions had been were about forty yards south of the house and they were ablaze with dancing red and yellow flames that extended fifty feet into the air. The crackle and pop created by the burning of the mini-mansions' structural remnants came softly through the Maybach's windows, and faint smells of wood smoke and burning gasoline filtered in through the Maybach's ventilation system. More flames rose from a spot farther south of the mini-mansions' site where the remains of the Black Hawk were smoldering. A few eucalyptus trees were also ablaze surrounding that spot. The three black Suburbans were still in front of the house, listing to the side on which Jeff had blown out their tires.

I scanned back to the right side of the ranch house. The wall there was faced with eight identical ten foot high French doors made of glass and wood crosshatches. The doors were all side by side, creating a span of about twenty-five feet. The doors were also staggered, each door slightly behind the door to its left, and all the doors seemed to be on some kind of track. It appeared the system had been designed so that the doors would open from one end like an accordion. I couldn't see through the doors' glass because curtains had been hung on the doors' interior sides that fully covered the glass. A three step high staircase made of well-weathered two-by-fours ran the length of the base of the doorway.

The height and width of the doors confirmed it was a big room. It could easily contain one or more vehicles.

"Damnit," Haley said.

"What is it now?" I said.

"We've got movement," Haley said.

"Where?" I said.

"The living room," Haley said. "The people we've been assuming are mercenaries are leaving the room."

"Where are they headed?" I said.

"To the billiard room," Haley said.

"The mercs have a sudden urge to play billiards?" I said.

"I didn't say that," Haley said.

"I know," I said. "Anyone else on the move?"

"No," Haley said. "The other five in the living room are maintaining their positions."

"Jeff you hearing all this?" I said.

Jeff's voice came through my headset, "I is."

"What do you think is going on?" I said.

"I think anyone who can get their hands on a stealth Black Hawk, probably is also able to get their hands on another device equally antithetical to the goals of this here mission," Jeff said.

"That's what I'm afraid of," I said. "Haley are the mercs in the billiard room yet?"

"Yes," Haley said.

"What are they doing?" I said.

"They appear to be moving on either side of some large object," Haley said.

"Can you give me an approximate size of the object?" I said.

"I'd estimate it at about fifteen feet long and ten feet wide," Haley said.

"Big billiard table," I said.

"I don't think it's a billiard table," Haley said.

"Neither do I," I said. "Is the object off to one side of the room or in the center of the room?"

"I would place it pretty close to the side of the room," Haley said.

"Means there's enough space for another one of whatever it is," I said.

"Agreed," Haley said. "If you care, the object is also to the right side of the room from your point of view."

"I do care," I said. "If it leaves the room, I'll know which side I can expect it to come at me from."

Manu and Mosi shared a look. It was not a look of calm and equanimity.

"Don't worry boys," I said to them. "Whatever they have we can handle. We're just trying to figure out what it is we're going to have to handle."

Manu and Mosi made slight nods. They also quivered a little. I had never seen two three hundred and fifty pound Samoans quiver in tandem before. It seemed like something that would usually only happen in dreams. I lost my focus for a moment as I pondered that notion. Losing focus was not a good thing to do at a time like that. I pinched myself and I refocused.

"What are the mercs doing now?" I said to Haley.

"They're still standing on either side of the object," Haley said. "Wait...one merc appears to be climbing."

"Climbing where?" I said.

"On top of the object," Haley said.

"Jeff, you thinking what I'm thinking?" I said.

"If you're thinking he's climbing on top of a Humvee, yeah," Jeff said.

Mosi and Manu quivered again. I continued to keep my focus, however.

"That's what I was thinking," I said.

Haley said, "Hold on...he's climbing back down now and...huh."

"'Huh' what?" I said.

"The original heat signature is growing hotter," Haley said. "If our guess is right, and the heat signature actually is coming from an engine, that would mean the engine is revving up. Also the merc who just climbed back down appears to be returning to the living room and the other merc is walking towards the French doors."

"Looks like they're getting ready to come at us," I said.

"But there's only one guy left in the room," Haley said. "What kind of damage can one guy by himself do with a Humvee?"

"Not much," I said. "But I got a hunch that's not what we're looking at."

"What are we looking at?" Haley said.

"I think the one guy left in the room is just there to open the doors," I said. "I think the other guy, the one who climbed up on the top of the Humvee, was making sure its turret gun was properly armed."

"So where's the team that's going to operate the Humvee?" Haley said.

Jeff said, "They're in an alternate universe."

"An alternate universe?" Haley said.

"What Jeff means to say is it's a drone Humvee," I said.

"You think Bowdoin, Liu, and Wellington have a drone Humvee?" Haley said.

"Why wouldn't they?" I said. "They seem to have access to anything NASAD makes. I agree with Jeff's instinct - if they can get hold of a stealth Black Hawk helicopter, and an army of weaponized flying drones, I don't see why they can't get themselves a drone Humvee."

"What are you going to do about it?" Haley said.

"Not sure yet," I said. "The question is, do we go charging in at them, or do we wait here to see what actually comes out of the room?"

Jeff said, "Since when do we start charging at what we don't know what we're charging at?"

Manu and Mosi again shared a look. I did my best to ignore them.

"Since never," I said. "That last Igla still ready to go?"

"Yes it is, massah," Jeff said.

I kept my binoculars trained on the French doors. The flames from the mini-mansion sites and the Black Hawk's carcass continued to blaze. The smoke around the compound grew thicker and the crackling and pop of burning wood louder. There was just enough smoke making its way through the Maybach's vents to sting my lungs and make my eyes water.

The French doors started sliding to the left, folding in on each other. I couldn't see the mercenary Haley said was in the room. I assumed he had taken cover behind the exterior wall and was using some kind of pulley or other mechanism to open the doors.

The doors continued to open, then suddenly stopped. The opening that had been created was wide enough to accommodate a Humvee. The room was too dark to see anything inside it, however.

"Adelaide and Jeff," I said into my headset, "can either of you tell what's going on in there?"

"Negatory," Jeff said.

Adelaide said, "I can't either."

Haley said, "The engine's heat signature just amped up to a whole new level and...whatever the object is it just started to move very fast and...it's coming right at you!"

"I can see that," I said.

CHAPTER 123

What was coming right at me was a big, heavily armored Humvee which would have been right at home on the killing boulevards of Kabul or Baghdad, but was then taking a joyride in the sunny environs of Southern California. The Humvee was tan in color. It looked like it was brand new, just out of the box, and never used before.

The Humvee was outfitted with an objective gunner protection kit, which is a fancy way to say its turret was also armored. That kind of turret is controlled by a joystick so the operator can rotate the turret in any direction on the turret ring he or she wants. The turret also had the optional overhead cover, which meant a gunner inside would be protected on top, bottom, and all four sides, and thus nearly impossible to hit. The turret had a fifty caliber machine gun too, which right then was facing straight ahead and aimed directly at the Maybach.

The Humvee's armor wasn't protecting any human beings, however. There was no gunner in the turret. There was no driver behind the wheel. In fact, there was not a single living soul anywhere on the outside or inside of the vehicle.

What the Humvee had instead of humans were laser remote sensing systems, miniature radar domes, and stereo cameras mounted on all its exterior sides and just below the turret. The sensing systems, domes, and cameras were very similar to the ones I had seen mounted on the artificial intelligence controlled sailboats at the NASAD lake. The devices' similarity to the NASAD sailboats also almost certainly meant the Humvee was a drone that was capable of thinking for itself and not dependent on a human pilot tucked away in a bunker thousands of miles away.

There was one key difference between the Humvee and the sailboats, though.

All of the Humvee's devices were shielded by thick Lexan plastic that was probably not just bulletproof, but bombproof as well.

The Humvee had accelerated rapidly out of the billiard room and had crushed the room's three front steps as it rolled over them. It had continued to accelerate and it was twenty yards out from the billiard room and already flying toward us at a high speed when it began to spit fifty caliber rounds from the machine gun in its turret. The rounds laid a trail of discrete explosions in the earth, violently kicking up rocks and dirt. The trail was zigzag and haphazard and missed us by a wide margin. I assumed that since the Humvee looked brand new, it had not been battle tested yet, and that its artificial intelligence had probably never been programmed to specifically deal with a high security Maybach either. But I also assumed its intelligence circuits would learn quickly and that those fifty caliber rounds would not keep missing for long.

Manu and Mosi stared at the Humvee, nearly frozen in panic.

"Wha...wha...what's that?" Mosi stammered.

"A self-driving drone Humvee," I said. "It's controlled by a computer running artificial intelligence software."

My words were calm, as if I saw self-driving drone Humvees every day of my life, but the truth was I had never seen one before. I was also thinking that it seemed like a cool device to have if it was fighting on your side. Unfortunately, it wasn't.

"Jeff, you got a line on that thing with the Igla?" I said. "I think the Maybach can withstand a few fifty cal rounds but I don't want to test it."

"Got a line," Jeff said. "But no go light."

"Funny," I said. "Take it down."

"Ain't no joke," Jeff said.

"Come on, buddy," I said.

"Hey, we got five out of six to work," Jeff said. "For Russian made hardware I bet that's some kinda record."

I hate to admit it, but for a brief moment I got mad at my beloved friend. Because what went through my head – even though deep down I knew there was no way I could blame Jeff for anything, as he was, after all, deeply ill – was that the Igla surface-to-surface missile wasn't truly defective, but that Jeff had fallen into a hallucinatory haze that had made him unable to fathom what to do with the weapon in his hands, a weapon he had wielded so expertly only minutes before. I got mad at myself too for ever thinking Jeff's damaged mind could hold up under the stress of combat, and for listening to my heart instead of my head and daring to believe my crazy friend wasn't crazy anymore. I also cursed myself for leaving the SSM with Jeff instead of taking it with me in the Maybach.

All those thoughts and feelings lasted no more than a second, however, as I quickly shunted them aside. They were, after all, not constructive in the then present situation.

The Humvee continued to close in on us, its machine mind seemingly learning with every passing millisecond. The sidewinder-like trail of bullets that had been failing to come anywhere near the Maybach narrowed its sinusoidal twists and turns and began to straighten out. A few bullets hit the earth only ten yards in front of us.

Manu and Mosi were in a cold sweat, their eyes fixed on the Humvee drone. The giant Samoans turned to look at each other and appeared to share some thoughts by ESP. They simultaneously broke eye contact and reached for their respective door handles.

"Don't you dare get out of this car," I said. "You get out, you die."

The twins froze in mid-reach.

"Manu, you were a linebacker, correct?" I said.

I think I saw a nod.

"That means you spent a lot of time studying the moves of opposing halfbacks, right?" I said.

Another nod, also nearly imperceptible.

"Well you're going to make like a halfback now," I said. "Get that Humvee to chase us, but keep zigging and zagging and do your best not to let it get a direct shot. You have to stay on the polo field because if we go back down the driveway we won't have anywhere to maneuver. And don't get between the Humvee and the ranch house - we don't want any fifty caliber rounds smashing through walls and hitting Dr. Lennon or Dr. Nimo."

Manu, seemingly not giving it even a moment's thought - I assumed he was more than happy to take any action that would take him away from the Humvee's hail of bullets - floored the gas pedal. We took off, racing toward the south end of the clearing. The Humvee followed, but Manu made moves worthy of Jim Brown and Walter Payton, and the Humvee's machine gun missed right and left, and up and down.

I figured our evasive actions might buy us at most another thirty seconds. After that the drone's artificial intelligence would probably gain enough proficiency to lace in some rounds that could test the Maybach's armor. The only way we were going to survive was if I could find a way to disable the Humvee. Since the Igla SSM was out of commission, that meant I had only Adelaide's, Jeff's, and my AK-12's to work with. I suppose I could have also counted the twins' Grach pistols, but doing so would've been well beyond even the wildest of wishful thinking.

It was highly unlikely we could take out the Humvee's cameras, lasers, or radar, protected as they were by the Lexan sheets. The Humvee's tires, like the Maybach's, were airless, so useless as a target. The only thing that might be vulnerable was the machine gun itself. It was protected on all sides, but there was a gap on either side of the barrel that allowed the gun to maneuver. I thought we might be able to get a round in the gaps and knock the belt off the machine gun's cam.

"Jeff, still a no go on the SSM?" I said into the headset.

"No go, no way, no how," Jeff said.

"Any way you can get a round on the belt feed?" I said.

"No harm in trying," Jeff said. "Send 'em my way."

"You understand why Jeff is asking us to do that, Adelaide?" I said.

"You think I'm an idiot?" Adelaide said.

"No, actually, I don't," I said. "You're unnecessarily difficult at times, but you're not an idiot."

"Good," Adelaide said. "Because I fully understand and appreciate that due to the Humvee's armoring the only way Jeff can get a belt shot is head on."

"Correct answer," I said. "We'll be coming your way at times too, Adelaide, as we have to change things up to keep the computer inside the Humvee guessing. I need both you and Jeff to please make the best of your chances since you're not going to get too many of them. And even if we keep the computer guessing, it isn't going to keep missing forever. When the Humvee's machine gun consistently starts hitting the Maybach, we may not last too long."

Jeff said, "I'm ready."

Adelaide said, "So am I."

I leaned forward into the driver's compartment and put my head next to Manu's ear.

"You know where Jeff and Adelaide are stationed, correct?" I said.

Before Manu could answer, a string of bullets from the Humvee's machine gun hit the Maybach's driver side window. Manu ducked and took the steering wheel with him, oversteering the Maybach and causing it to turn sharply right and nearly roll over. I grabbed the wheel with my right hand and straightened us out. I used my left hand to pull Manu back up into his seat.

All but one of the fifty caliber rounds had harmlessly bounced off, but the one that didn't had left a tiny crack in the Lexan. Manu turned his head and stared at the crack. I kept steering, weaving the car in as unpredictable a pattern as I could manage. I couldn't keep going that way, however, as without control of the brake or gas pedal, it would be nearly impossible to keep making the necessary maneuvers, let alone keep the Maybach from rolling if Manu suddenly decided to speed up when I didn't expect him to. I considered changing places with Manu, but knew we were likely to be shot to pieces if we slowed down or stopped to make the swap.

I needed to get Manu's head back in the game. I kept my hand on the wheel and, gesturing with my chin towards Manu's window, I said as calmly as possible, "See Manu, this stuff works."

Manu just stared at the window, seemingly studying the paths of the little spider cracks.

"Manu, I need you to get back in the saddle, okay?" I said.

Manu slowly turned his head to face me. His eyes looked glassy and far away and he said not a thing.

I steered right, then left, then right again. Luckily the Maybach seemed a bit more nimble than the Humvee, and I was able to keep us out of its path. The Humvee's computer also appeared to be having a hard time lining up anything but a straight shot directly over the Humvee's front end. The fifty caliber rounds kept missing, at least for the moment.

Mosi leaned forward so he could get his head around mine, but nearly knocked my arm off the steering wheel in the process. He grabbed Manu's shoulder.

"Hey bro, snap out of it," Mosi said. "Trust the man. We're safe."

Manu shifted his gaze to Mosi.

Mosi smiled a soothing smile. I had no idea how Mosi had suddenly summoned such seeming equanimity, but was thankful he had.

A dozen fifty caliber rounds raked across the Maybach's hood, sending sparks flying. The rounds left black trails of charred paint, but did no real damage. I whipped the car to the left and the next machine gun burst missed us by a big margin.

Manu kept looking at Mosi.

Mosi kept smiling.

There seemed to be a slight shift in the air molecules in the Maybach's front seat compartment which I assumed to be due to another telepathic brotherly moment.

Manu suddenly smiled, his face an exact mirror of Mosi's face. Manu gently removed my hand from the steering wheel, and took over control of the car.

Mosi sat back in his seat, nodded, and said, "That's the way to do it, bro."

Manu appeared to be fully back in the game. To say I was astonished by what had just occurred between the twins would be a vast understatement. I firmly believe in not looking a gift horse in the mouth, however, and I didn't.

"Thank you, gentlemen," I said. "Manu, you aim this beast right at Jeff, and then when you feel the Humvee is getting a bead on us, you evade. You then aim us at Adelaide until you feel the bead again, then you evade again. Repeat the pattern of aiming at Jeff, evading, aiming at Adelaide, and evading, until I say stop."

"I understand," Manu said.

Manu maneuvered the Maybach as directed, aiming and evading, aiming and evading, as if he was born to it. I watched out the back window as the Humvee lined up behind us. Each time we headed at Jeff or Adelaide, they each got off two or three shots. I saw the sparks their rounds made as they hit the Humvee. Most of the rounds hit the armor just to the outside of the gap surrounding the machine gun's barrel, but a few of the sparks came from inside the gap, so I knew Jeff and Adelaide had struck home. The fifty caliber gun, however, kept gunning.

"Jeff and Adelaide," I said into the headset, "they must have armor in front of the belt. We need a new plan."

"I'm all ears," Jeff said.

"No ideas?" I said.

"Hate to admit it, but not only do I see the Humvee, but also a hundred Somali gunmen running all over the polo field," Jeff said. "I take it as a good sign I know those Somalis ain't really there, but I'm using all my thinking energy to block them outta my mind while I'm shooting."

"Understood," I said. "Adelaide?"

"Why don't you just ram the damn thing?" Adelaide said.

"Hmm," I said. "That's not a terrible idea. I'll give you an 'A' for effort."

"You don't like it?" Adelaide said.

"Humvee outweighs us by about two to one," I said. "We're just going to bounce off."

Haley, who had been silent the whole time up until then, said, "Jack?"

"You have an idea, Haley?" I said.

"Wish I did," Haley said. "I just wanted to tell you the first fire engines have left the station. Their ETA is seventeen minutes."

"At least they'll be here a little later than we thought they would," I said. "Gives us some extra time to get this Humvee off our ass."

"I'll keep you posted on their progress," Haley said.

"Thank you," I said.

The Humvee got closer to us and let loose a sustained machine gun burst. The bullets missed, and Manu took off at high speed for a corner of the field. The Humvee zoomed past us.

Adelaide said, "Got another idea."

"Is it good?" I said.

"Of course it's good," Adelaide said. "I thought of it."

"What is it?" I said.

"You pull up alongside the Humvee," Adelaide said, "then open the Maybach's sunroof, climb up on the roof, jump onto the Humvee, open the Humvee's cabin door, get inside, and turn off the ignition."

"What if I get cut to shreds while I'm climbing out of the sunroof?" I said.

"Okay," Adelaide said. "Don't use the sunroof then. Just pull up close to the Humvee, and, at the last second, open your door and jump onto it from there."

"Jeff, what do you think of that?" I said.

"Got a ten percent chance," Jeff said.

"Which means I die ninety percent of the time," I said.

"One hundred minus ten is ninety," Jeff said. "So, yeah."

Ten percent wasn't good, but it wasn't zero either. And zero was how many other ideas I could think of to try at that moment.

"I'm gonna try it," I said.

"Why you gonna do a damn fool thing like that?" Jeff said.

The Humvee let loose with another burst of bullets, all of which missed.

"Because we're running out of time and it's the best idea we've got," I said.

Adelaide said, "I just thought of something."

"What?" I said.

"What if the Humvee's door is locked?" Adelaide said.

"The lock is probably the weakest link in the Humvee's armoring system," I said. "I'll blow the lock with the AK."

Jeff said, "You gonna die, Jack."

"We all die," I said.

"That's the dumbest thing you ever said and you've said a lot of dumb things," Jeff said.

"Thank you for your support," I said. I leaned forward into the front seat compartment and put my head next to Manu's. "Manu, circle around behind the Humvee, then make a run at it. I want you to get my door right up against the side of the Humvee."

Manu looked at me questioningly.

"Just do it, please," I said.

CHAPTER 124

As Manu began to circle the Maybach around the back of the drone Humvee, I held out hope that our plan would work and that we'd be able to get close enough to the Humvee so that I could jump aboard it and shut it off. After all, even plans whose odds of succeeding are only one in ten sometimes work. Of course they fail nine out of ten times...

The problem was that the odds of succeeding suddenly went to one in ten zillion. That was because the drone's computer brain suddenly got smart and did something I was afraid it might do all along.

What the computer did right then was stop the Humvee firmly in the middle of the polo field. From that position, the Humvee could just swivel the turret in any direction and fire. Rather than trying to hit us from a moving vehicle, which was hard, the Humvee's computer would be able to take aim from a stationary position and thus make the job of landing a round on the Maybach exponentially easier. Even if the bullets never hit us, the Humvee would still be able to keep us from getting to the ranch house and Kate and Dr. Nimo/Billy for as long as the Humvee wanted.

The high-speed circle into which Manu had already put the Maybach had so far kept the Humvee's machine gun turret from lining up on us. As dangerous as the Humvee's new positioning was, I thought we still might have a bit of time before its machine gun would be able to consistently hit us. That was because I had already formulated a new plan that involved a lot of zigging and zagging that was even more erratic than the zigging and zagging we had already done.

We would zig and zag for absolutely no discernible reason, evading an enemy that was purely imaginary, one that only we could see in our mind's eye and thus invisible to the Humvee. We would appear to the Humvee as completely batshit crazy.

I figured the plan would work, because even though the computer was learning quickly, I thought it would take a while for it to get adept at hitting a target that was moving in a wholly erratic and inconstant fashion. The reason behind my figuring was that most computer-guided military weaponry can have a hard time hitting targets that were purposely trying to avoid being hit and moved unpredictably in doing so. It was nearly impossible for a heat-seeking missile that had been launched from a drone to miss a car moving slowly along a highway. But a 'crazed' human fighter pilot could evade even the most advanced enemy missile.

There was one other thing besides zigging and zagging that would help us evade the Humvee's machine gun. And that was distance. Even small angles of aiming error are magnified greatly the farther the distance to the target. Keeping our distance from the Humvee and erratic movement were going to be my best friends in the upcoming moments.

"Manu," I said, "keep moving like that halfback and get to the edge of the field as fast as you can. Keep one eye on the turret. Your job is to make sure it never gets a solid bead on us. You're still going to have to turn around if you start getting between the turret and the ranch house, so vary your turning points as much as possible. Your cuts should appear to make no sense at all."

"No sense?" Manu said.

"Yes," I said. "Behave as if you're dodging a linebacker that only you can see. Otherwise the drone is going to be able to predict when you're going to turn and be able to lay some of those fifty caliber rounds into us. Got it?"

Manu nodded. The Maybach tore off to the northern edge of the polo field. The turret tracked us, but lagged just slightly behind us.

Jeff said, "I'm assuming now that the situation has changed, you're abandoning your crackpot plan of jumping aboard the Humvee?"

"I am," I said.

"What you going to do instead?" Jeff said.

"Not sure yet," I said.

"Well you better get sure," Jeff said. "You can't keep shucking and jiving forever. At some point that AI computer gonna make a lucky guess where you be turning around and then it gonna nail you."

"I know," I said. "Actually..."

"Actually what?" Jeff said.

"An idea just came to me," I said.

"What is it?" Jeff said.

"Maybe I can do what we did in the Korengal Valley when we were ambushed and ran out of grenades," I said.

"You talking about those Taliban machine gun nests that be raining death down upon us?" Jeff said.

"Yes," I said.

"We called in an air strike," Jeff said.

Manu made three hard cuts in a row with the Maybach. The cuts seemingly had come out of nowhere and they surprised even me. Manu, in other words, was doing his job perfectly.

"I'm going to do what we planned on doing if the F-16's didn't get there in time," I said.

"Oh man, I don't know if I like that idea," Jeff said.

Haley, who had continued to remain on the line, said, "What were you guys going to do?"

I said, "Put bullets down the centers of the barrels of the Taliban's machine guns and blow up their firing chambers."

"I think I'm with Jeff on this," Haley said. "I don't like that idea at all."

"Either of you have a better one?" I said.

Neither of them said anything.

"That's what I thought," I said.

A spray of bullets from the Humvee's machine gun hit the ground fifty feet behind us, ripping the grass and earth to shreds. The line of bullets moved rapidly towards us, tracking straight and true, leaving a trough-like path as it got closer and closer. Manu whipped the Maybach's steering wheel around. The Maybach made a one hundred and eighty degree turn while up on its two right side tires and zoomed off in the opposite direction. The Humvee's bullets tore into the earth right where we had been a moment before.

"Good job, Manu," I said. "Now, Manu, in order for me to get my shots off at the Humvee's machine gun, we're going to have to stop the Maybach and stay planted for a few seconds while I stand up in the sunroof. Adelaide and Jeff, I need you to cover the ranch house in case any of the mercs inside decide to start firing at me."

Haley said, "Jack, I really don't like this."

"You yourself said the fire trucks will be here soon," I said. "We're out of time. We don't have any other choice."

"You do too have a choice," Haley said. "You can abandon the mission."

"I'm not abandoning the mission," I said.

"Do you realize how hard it is to lace a bullet right down the center of a machine gun muzzle?" Haley said.

"Wouldn't that depend on who's doing the shooting?" I said.

"It would," Haley said. "And I'm going to grant you that you're one of the best shooters who ever lived. However, even given that, the odds of your plan working are practically zero. Which means you're going to die and take Manu and Mosi with you."

I knew Haley was probably correct. I truly wasn't worried about myself because I was pretty convinced if I didn't get in that ranch house soon, not only would Kate and Dr. Nimo/Billy die, but the Chinese war would start as well. Manu and Mosi were a different story, however. I'd struggled earlier with whether or not I should take the twins with us on the mission, but when I'd made the decision to allow them to come along the chance of their deaths was an abstract concept. Right then, the chance of their dying was very concrete and very real. It wasn't fair to force Manu and Mosi to take the risks I was willing to take.

"Manu," I said. "Head back to the driveway."

Manu made a series of four wild cuts in a row. He seemed to be enjoying himself.

"Why?" Manu said.

"Because we're going to drop you and Mosi off at the street," I said. "You're going to take the van and get out of here, and I'm coming back by myself with the Maybach."

"No," Manu said.

"That's a direct order," I said. "You can't say no."

Mosi said, "Yes we can. You are not our boss. We answer only to Dr. Lennon."

Suddenly there was a shrieking, ripping metallic sound. A fifty caliber bullet tore through the upholstery behind my right shoulder, zipped through the space between my upper arm and chest, continued on between the front seats, hit the interior of the front windshield with a dull thud, and clattered onto the dashboard. Manu, reacting seemingly instinctively, cut hard left, again bringing the car up on two wheels and evading the rest of the Humvee's machine gun burst.

Manu, Mosi, and I watched the bullet on the dashboard roll off the dash and onto the floor.

Haley said, "What was that?"

"That was the sound of level five armor failure," I said.

"Goddamnit Jack, you've got to get those boys out of there," Haley said.

Mosi said, "With all due respect, ma'am, we cannot leave. We must help General Wilder retrieve Dr. Lennon."

Manu cut hard right, but was a little late in doing so. There was another shriek and metallic rip as a bullet passed through the rear passenger door, smashed into the right side of Manu's seat, then continued on through and shattered the fine walnut facing of the glove box.

Manu and Mosi looked at each other. I detected no fear in their faces. What I did see was determination.

Haley said, "Was that another level five armor failure I just heard?"

"Yes," I said.

"Manu and Mosi, you realize there's a very good chance you're going to die if you stay in that car?" Haley said.

Mosi said, "We are okay with that, ma'am."

"How can you possibly be okay with that?" Haley said.

"It's Faaaloalo, ma'am," Mosi said.

"What's Faaaloalo?" Haley said.

Jeff said, "It's the Samoan code of honor. You should know better than to be messing with a soldier's honor."

"Manu and Mosi aren't soldiers," Haley said.

"Maybe so," Jeff said. "But they're men of honor."

"Jesus," Haley said. "Manu and Mosi, you sure you know what you're doing?"

"Yes, ma'am," Mosi said.

"There's absolutely nothing I can do to talk you out of this madness?" Haley said.

"No, ma'am," Mosi said.

"I guess I've said my piece then," Haley said. "Good luck and Godspeed."

Mosi said, "Thank you, ma'am."

I checked on the Humvee's turret. It was tracking us, but Manu was staying just ahead of the machine gun's barrel. Manu made three more wildly unpredictable cuts. The turret attempted to follow Manu's moves. Perhaps I was guilty of gross anthropomorphism, but the turret's motion appeared so discombobulated and jerky in that attempt that it seemed to me the Humvee was nothing if not confused.

I said, "Alright boys, here's what we're going to do. First, open the sunroof."

Mosi reached up and pushed a button on the ceiling of the car. The sunroof opened.

"Good," I said.

I tapped the AK's magazine to be sure it was in place, then double-checked there was a round in the chamber and that the safety was still off. Using the AK as a crutch against the floor of the Maybach, I slowly hoisted myself up on the back seat until I was standing on it, my head just below the opening of the sunroof.

I poked the barrel of the AK out through the sunroof and followed it with my head, shoulders, and arms. I braced my feet on the seat and my elbows on the roof and sighted the AK's scope on the Humvee's machine gun.

The timing of my shot was going to be tricky. I needed to get a round inside the Humvee's barrel and blow up its firing chamber, which meant I needed the Humvee's barrel to attempt to line up on me. But I couldn't allow the Humvee to get me squarely in its sights. If it did, the next shots the Humvee fired would cut me to ribbons. My plan was to follow the barrel on its sweep towards me - up or down, left or right - and then for me to squeeze off a round or two at just the right moment.

But it wasn't just the timing of the shot that was going to be a challenge. Aiming was going to be difficult as well. Since I had to shoot before the machine gun barrel was directly lined up on me, that meant I would be looking at the side of the barrel instead of straight down it. The muzzle opening, rather than being a hole, would be a sliver of a hole.

It was no different than trying to see the bottom of an opaque plastic water cup from the side of the cup. From the side, the rim of the plastic cup blocks not only a view of the bottom of the cup, but most of the cup's interior as well. When I aimed at the muzzle of the gun barrel without being directly in line with the barrel, the outer rim of the barrel's muzzle was going to occlude part of the muzzle's opening, just like the rim of the plastic cup would occlude a full view into the interior of the cup.

I found myself fleetingly wishing I had the CheyTac instead of the AK-12. The shot would have been a hell of a lot easier with the CheyTac, because its accuracy was probably at least six times better than the AK's. The CheyTac's accuracy, measured in minutes of angle or MOA, was well less than one, while the AK-12's MOA was likely closer to six. At a hundred yards, that meant the CheyTac would be accurate to under an inch, whereas the AK might miss by six inches. Wishing wasn't going to put a CheyTac in my hands, however. I was just going to have to do the best I could with what I had.

Manu continued to hug the edge of the polo field as he zigged and zagged. We were then about one hundred and fifty yards from the Humvee where it had planted itself in the center of the field. The ranch house was another hundred and fifty yards beyond the Humvee.

"Okay, Manu," I said, "on the count of three you turn this baby directly into the face of that goddamn Humvee and slam on the breaks. You keep us rock still in whatever position we come to rest in, but be ready to get instantly moving again on my command. Ready?"

"Ready," Manu said.

"One...two...three!" I said.

I braced myself with my elbows on the edge of the sunroof as the Maybach whipped around and skidded to a halt directly facing the Humvee. The Humvee's turret immediately swiveled in our direction and its machine gun began firing. Dozens of fifty caliber rounds cut up the ground twenty yards in front of us and slowly snaked their way towards us as the Humvee's barrel raised higher and higher.

I leveled the AK at the machine gun's barrel. The fifty caliber bullets smashed into the Maybach's grill. Below me, the interior of the Maybach sounded like the inside of a tin can in the middle of a hailstorm. The booming rat-a-tat-tat of the machine gun became deafening. The thickening smoke coming from the flames consuming the Black Hawk, mini-mansions, and many of the compound's trees made my eyes sting, and my lungs began to burn even more strongly than they had been burning before.

I had purposely forced myself not to blink in order to acclimate to the brightness of the sunlight after being behind the Maybach's tinted windows for so long, but that brightness, combined with the stinging of the smoke in my eyes, caused my vision to blur and made aiming the AK-12 a dicey proposition at best.

The Humvee's rounds climbed up the Maybach's grill and across its hood. I sighted the AK's scope at the hole in the machine gun's barrel as well as I could, braced myself even more firmly on the edge of the sunroof, took a deep breath, and held it. I focused on my heartbeat as I was only going to shoot between beats, the flow of blood with my heart's contraction being enough to throw my body off just enough to affect the flight of the bullet. I was ready to fire, but couldn't until the Humvee's machine gun barrel was aimed almost directly at me.

I waited.

The Humvee's rounds ascended up the Maybach's windshield.

I continued to wait.

The Humvee's rounds were just about to clear the edge of the Maybach's roof.

It was time.

I fired.

One shot.

Then another.

And another.

Three sparks flew off the steel rim of the Humvee's barrel muzzle.

None of the shots had hit the center of the muzzle.

I had missed my target.

I kicked my legs out from under me, began the three foot free fall to the Maybach's rear seat, my head clearing the sunroof opening as the Humvee's bullets penetrated the space my skull had just occupied. My butt landed with a thud on the fine leather, the shock of the contact sending cruel lightning bolts up my spine and down my legs.

"Go Manu!" I said. "Go now!"

The Maybach took off like a bat out of hell. Manu sped along the edge of the polo field staying just in front of the Humvee's tracking turret.

"Keep doing what you've been doing, Manu," I said. "Cut when you need to cut. Stop when you need to stop. Run when you need to run. We'll give it another try in a moment."

"Yes, sir," Manu said. He instantly cut off in another direction.

Jeff said into my headset, "Another try? Dude, this just ain't gonna work."

"I only missed by a millimeter or so," I said. "I know the AK's dispersion pattern now. I won't miss next time."

"What the hell are you talking about?" Jeff said. "The whole point of a dispersion pattern mean that it gonna disperse. You ain't any more likely to hit your target on the next try than on your hundredth one."

Jeff was probably right. But my only other option was to give up. I had already decided not to give up. With as much conviction in my voice as I could muster, I said, "I've got a feel for this rifle now. I won't miss next time."

"Why are you insulting me?" Jeff said.

"Insulting you?" I said.

"You don't think I can tell by the sound of your voice when you're mustering up conviction?" Jeff said.

"You're right," I said. "But again, unless you have a better idea, I'm going to give it a try."

Manu wheeled the Maybach around and headed for another corner of the polo field. The Humvee's turret was tracking us, but holding off on firing. Perhaps the computer brain was waiting for a better shot. Perhaps it was running low in ammunition. I didn't know.

Haley said, "Whatever you're going to do, do it soon."

"Why?" I said. "Are the fire trucks closing in faster than you expected?"

"No," Haley said. "I've got some stats on level five armor failure in Maybachs."

"You have stats on how Maybach level five armor does against fifty caliber rounds?" I said.

"Not actual stats," Haley said. "I was doing a simulation."

"What did you find out?" I said.

"It lasted a little longer than I thought it would," Haley said.

"What does that mean?" I said.

"From what I've been watching on the satellite video, the armor protecting the Maybach's engine compartment probably has at best ten direct hits left in it," Haley said.

Manu and Mosi had clearly heard what Haley said through their headsets. Neither of them showed any emotion. Manu kept to his driving, and Mosi's eyes remained firmly on the Humvee's turret. I was impressed. And proud too. To my mind, the twins were becoming fine soldiers.

"Thanks for the information, Haley, but, with all due respect, I'm not sure there's much I can do with it," I said. "Manu, ready to give it another go?"

"Yes, sir," Manu said.

"We're going to try something a little different this time," I said. "Last time we stopped, the machine gun moved vertically as it tried to sight in on us. I'm thinking I'd like to give it a go with the gun moving horizontally. As soon as we stop, I want you to both stay completely inside the car, but kick open your doors. Hopefully that will draw the Humvee's fire and I might have a bit better angle from which to shoot at the machine gun's barrel."

Mosi said, "That's what we'll do then, sir."

"On the count of three again," I said. "One...two...three..."

Mosi turned the Maybach to face the Humvee and slammed on the brakes. We skidded to a halt a hundred and fifty yards away from the Humvee.

"Open your doors now!" I said.

Manu and Mosi kicked open their doors and leaned into the center of the Maybach. The turret quickly aligned itself with Manu's door and commenced firing. The fifty caliber rounds ripped into the door, some of them piercing the steel with a sickening screech. Others pinged off the steel and gathered in a smoking pile beneath the door. The bullets' combined force caused the door to slowly rock back toward its closed position.

I again used my AK as a crutch, climbed back up on my seat, and pushed my upper body through the sunroof. It was hell outside the Maybach. The air was filled with the pungent smell of exploded gun powder from the hundreds of rounds the Humvee had fired. Towers of red and orange flames from the wreckage of the Black Hawk and the remains of the mini-mansions spread like tall fingers into the sky. The breeze had shifted and was blowing air that had been superheated by those towering flames into my face. Thick black smoke obscured the air above the ranch house.

I aimed the AK at the end of the Humvee's machine gun barrel. I waited for the Humvee's artificial intelligence computer brain to spot me and move the barrel in my direction. I had intermittently been looking out of the sunroof since my last failed attempt to take out the machine gun and believed my eyes were better adjusted to the sunlight for this next attempt.

Time would tell.

Dozens more fifty caliber rounds tore into Manu's door. Some of the rounds hit his window and made a strange clacking sound as they bounced off the Lexan.

The Humvee's sensors must have finally become aware of my presence, because the machine gun barrel moved up and away from Manu's door and slid across the roof towards me. I waited as long as I possibly could and again fired off three rounds at the center hole of the barrel.

Through the AK's scope, I saw two sparks flick off the rim of the barrel which meant two of my shots had missed.

But I had not seen a third spark.

Where had the third round gone?

Had it struck home?

The machine gun stopped firing.

The Humvee and its turret became completely still.

I waited and watched.

I needed to be sure the Humvee was dead.

After a few more moments of stillness, I said into my headset, "I think it worked."

Jeff said, "Get your head back in that car. I got a bad feeling about this."

"What're you talking about?" I said, keeping my gun aimed at the machine gun's muzzle. "That thing's deader than a doornail."

"My scope was locked in on that firing chamber when you peeled off those rounds," Jeff said. "You hit the chamber, there shoulda been an explosion. I didn't see no explosion."

Jeff had a good point. I again kicked out my legs from under me and began my free fall to the Maybach's back seat. It was lucky I did, since just as my chin cleared the edge of the sunroof, the Humvee's machine gun roared to life. Fifty caliber rounds whizzed directly over my head.

My backside hit the seat and more electric jolts shot up my spine.

"Shut your doors boys!" I said. "Manu, get us out of here!"

The twins reached out, grabbed their door handles, and slammed their doors shut. Manu floored the Maybach. I was thrown against my seat back by the car's acceleration and we were once again racing along the perimeter of the polo field.

"Shit," I said. "That thing was trying to trick me wasn't it?"

Jeff said, "Looked that way. If an AI computer can be learning how to beat those Russian chess dudes, don't seem much of a step to be figuring out how to run a bluff on a chucklehead like you."

"I'm a chucklehead now, am I?" I said.

"How else you explain what you doing?" Jeff said.

"Yeah, well, maybe I am," I said. "And maybe that AI monstrosity understands bluffing too. But you know what? I bet it doesn't know a damn thing about going for broke."

"Going for broke, huh?" Jeff said. "That the next part of your brilliant plan?"

"Like I said, unless you got a better idea...," I said.

"Just because I don't got a better idea right this very second, don't mean you gotta commit suicide," Jeff said.

Haley interrupted, "He's been committing suicide this whole goddamn time, Jeff."

"Yeah, but now it's worse," Jeff said.

"How can it possibly get worse?" Haley said

"Haley, you aren't here so you can't see," Jeff said. "But what Jack been doing is shooting at the last millisecond before that Humvee machine gun barrel line up directly on him. Make it a hard shot because he don't have an angle right down into the heart of the muzzle. Next time, he gonna line up right on it and dare the computer to outshoot him."

"How do you know that?" Haley said.

"Because I know Jack," Jeff said.

"Is he right, Jack?" Haley said.

I said, "What's the name of that guy who cut down the cherry tree?"

"George Washington?" Haley said.

"Yeah, him," I said. "Since, like our first president, I cannot tell a lie, I'll plead the fifth."

"I'll take that to mean Jeff is right, then," Haley said. "Which means it is worse. A lot worse. Jack, I'm ordering you to abandon this mission."

"That's sweet of you to say, my darling," I said. "But, unfortunately, I outrank you."

"I'm getting Hart on the line then," Haley said. "We'll see what he has to say about this."

"You gotta do what you gotta do," I said. "However, since I'm taking off my headset now, it's gonna be real hard to get ahold of me. Bye."

Haley started screaming, but I couldn't make out what she was saying as I had already taken the headset off. She kept screaming as I threw the headset onto the seat next to me, and even as far away as the headset was from my ears, her screams, though muffled, were still audible.

I unplugged the headset from my iPhone.

No more screaming.

I changed out the AK-12's magazine with a new full one, again checked to make sure there was a round in the chamber and that the safety was still off, then leaned forward into the Maybach's driver compartment and put my head between Manu and Mosi.

"Unplug your headsets boys," I said. "It's do or die time."

The twins nodded and did as they were told.

"We have to get closer this time," I said. "Manu, on my command you turn this baby right into the face of the Humvee again, but this time you go right at it. When we're fifty yards out, slam on the brakes, and then the two of you duck under the dash."

Mosi said, "Under the dash, sir?"

"We'll be taking a lot of fire," I said. "Engine block will protect you."

Manu said, "What about you, sir?"

"I gotta get up in the sunroof again," I said.

Mosi said, "If you are going to face death, sir, we cannot be cowering in fear while you do so."

"There's nothing you're going to be able to do while I'm up there," I said. "There's a difference between bravery and stupidity, men."

"It is Faaaloalo, sir," Mosi said.

"Come on guys," I said. "You can't be throwing out Faaaloalo as an excuse every time you want to do something crazy."

"Sorry, sir," Mosi said. "But we will not be hiding under the dash."

Mosi seemed quite adamant. I felt I needed to know the answer to one last question before letting the twins act so foolishly, however.

"Let me ask you something," I said.

"Yes, sir?" Mosi said.

"Is this Faaaloalo even a real thing?" I said. "It's not just something you made up, is it?"

"General Jeff Bradshaw knew of it, sir," Mosi said.

"Yeah, he did, didn't he?" I said. I sighed. "Well, then, I guess there's no arguing with Faaaloalo is there?"

"No, sir," Mosi said.

"One favor though, please," I said.

"What is it, sir?" Mosi said.

"If I get killed, take the Maybach and pick up Jeff," I said. "Despite his talk of suicide, I'm sure he'll want to give it a go in my stead."

"Understood, sir," Mosi said.

"One last time then, men," I said. "On my count...one...two...three!"

Manu ripped the steering wheel hard right, pointed the Maybach right at the Humvee, and shoved the gas pedal to the floor. We had a hundred yards to cross to get to within fifty yards of the Humvee and we covered those hundred yards in under three seconds. Manu slammed us to a halt. I jumped up on my seat and put my head and shoulders outside the Maybach's sunroof. I raised my AK, braced my elbows on the edges of the sunroof, sighted in on the Humvee's machine gun's muzzle, and waited for the turret to swing in my direction.

Time, as it had so many times over those last few days, instantly slowed down. The world outside the car was even more hellish than it had been before. The red and orange flames from the burning Black Hawk and mini-mansions seemed to have soared even farther into the sky. Loud snapping sounds came from the exploding gases within the burning trunks of the eucalyptus trees. The trees' leaves were also rapidly incinerating and they seemed to shriek in agony as they did so.

Winds that felt almost cyclonic in nature carried air past my face. The air felt like it had been birthed in a blast furnace. The odor of the dead mercenaries' burning flesh had added its scent to the pungent smells of burning concrete, helicopter fuel, and wood. The ranch house lay only two hundred yards away from me, but clouds of thick black smoke intermittently blocked out any view I might have had of it.

As the Humvee's turret turned inexorably toward me, I realized that the Humvee's artificial intelligence computer appeared to be changing its strategy. The computer had already lifted the Humvee's machine gun barrel to the height of my head, no longer seeming to have any appetite to waste its fifty caliber rounds on the Maybach's doors, hood, or windshield. The machine gun wasn't firing yet either, the computer apparently satisfied with waiting to unleash the fifty caliber rounds only when its gun had my skull firmly in its sights.

I also realized then, however, that I had a fighting chance in my seemingly suicidal battle with the Humvee's brain.

The hot, hellish winds were going to be my friend.

I knew how to adjust my aim for the elevated air temperature and the speed of the winds, but, after earlier watching the Humvee waste hundreds of rounds into the earth, I thought perhaps the Humvee's programmers had been more concerned with brute force than with the finer points of the sniper's art. I therefore doubted that the Humvee had any idea how to shoot in the conditions we both were facing. That is not to say I thought the Humvee's artificial intelligence mind wouldn't one day learn the appropriate adjustments. I just was going to do my best to be sure that that day wasn't *this* day.

The moment finally arrived.

The turret's swivel - which, though it had only taken seconds, had seemed like minutes - placed the machine gun's barrel directly in line with my face.

A relentless and vicious torrent of fifty caliber rounds was un-leashed, and the Humvee's bullets ruptured the air inches from my skull, their whistling echoing in my ears.

I took a deep breath that was more smoke than oxygen - a breath that seared my nose, throat, and lungs - and held it. With the sun's reflection off the Humvee's windshield both stinging my eyes and partially blinding me, I moved the sight of my AK-12 just up and to the right of the Humvee's machine gun's barrel muzzle to adjust for the wind and heat and distance.

Still holding my breath, I fired off a shot in the space between my heartbeats.

A spark flew off the front of the machine gun's steel barrel rim where the round struck, missing the center hole in the muzzle by less than a millimeter.

The fifty caliber bullets kept coming, their whistling growing louder and their air trails growing stronger as they moved closer and closer to my head. The Humvee's computer brain was learning, most likely through simple trial and error, and its aim was getting truer and truer. I adjusted my own aim, let out my breath, took in another deep one, held it, and once again fired off a round in the space between my heartbeats. Another spark, this on a spot on the rim exactly opposite from my first miss.

I had overcorrected.

I realigned my aim.

The Humvee's bullets grew ever closer. One of the rounds grazed the top of my skull and another nicked my ear. I felt the blood begin to flow down my neck from the ear wound. I took a deep breath, waited on my heartbeat, all the time thinking to myself this was probably going to be my last shot and I better make it good. I was just about to squeeze the AK's trigger again, when suddenly something completely unexpected happened and made me hold off...

I heard, and saw out of the corners of my eyes, the Maybach's two front doors open.

Manu and Mosi, gripping the Grach pistols Jeff had given them back at the fire road, leapt out of the car.

The twins ran away from the protection of the Maybach's doors and fired their guns at the Humvee seemingly as fast as they were able. After each of the brothers had covered about ten yards, they both dove to the ground, where, prone and facing the Humvee, they continued to fire.

Which, it turned out, was a damn good move on their part.

Because the Humvee's computer brain appeared to get confused for a moment.

Who, the brain seemed to be thinking, was the biggest threat?

Me and my AK-12, or the giant Samoans shooting at them nonstop?

The Humvee's machine gun paused as the computer apparently pondered the question.

I didn't know how long the pause was going to last.

Half a second?

Less?

It wasn't a question worthy of consideration.

Because there was only one answer.

Which was to take advantage of the pause to fire off more shots from the AK-12.

Which I did.

Three shots to be exact.

I kept my scope fixed on the machine gun's barrel muzzle after the shots had left my rifle.

This time there were no sparks anywhere near the muzzle's rim.

Either I'd missed completely, or I hadn't.

A flaming conflagration erupted out of the machine gun's muzzle hole.

The sudden materialization of the conflagration's flames was followed by a loud explosive sound. The machine gun's barrel shattered into seemingly a million pieces and shrapnel flew in all directions around the armor plate protecting the machine gun.

Explosions, flame, and shrapnel.

But no fifty caliber rounds.

I hadn't missed.

I had blown up the machine gun's firing chamber.

The Humvee's turret immediately started to violently rock back and forth. The AI brain probably thought the machine gun was jammed and was trying to clear it.

But it was not a jam and it could not be cleared.

The turret shook even more violently. The Humvee looked to me like a wooly mammoth in its death throes, the barrel its useless trunk.

I quickly realized my work in regard to the Humvee still was not over, however. It continued to present a danger to me, a danger I had to deal with. I needed to get inside the Humvee and I had to decide what would be the fastest method to cover the fifty yards to its shimmying hulk - running on foot or jumping behind the wheel of the Maybach and driving.

I chose running.

I dropped out of the sunroof and onto the Maybach's rear seat one more time. I quickly reattached the headset to my iPhone and put the headset back over my ears. I opened the right passenger door, and raced from the car.

I caught the looks on Manu's and Mosi's faces in my peripheral vision as I sprinted by them.

"Manu and Mosi, hold your fire, and get back in the Maybach," I yelled to them, then into my headset added, "Jeff and Adelaide, as you can see I've left the vehicle. Please provide cover fire for me as needed."

Haley said, "You've put your headset back on, Jack. How kind of you."

"I can be a good boy when I want to be," I said, already out of breath from my sprint towards the Humvee.

Haley said, "Why are you outside the Maybach?"

"Sorry, Haley, but it's better if Jeff explains," I said. "I'm in kind of a hurry right now."

Jeff said, "He blew up the firing chamber, Haley."

Haley said, "He did?"

"He most certainly did," Jeff said.

"Jesus Christ," Haley said. "That must have been some shot."

"It was," Jeff said.

I gobbled up the fifty yards between the Humvee and the Maybach in under five seconds. The Humvee's barrel-less turret interrupted its berserk boogieing and shifted towards me. The drone's AI brain should have been focusing its efforts elsewhere, however. The brain still had an effective weapon, but it apparently had played hooky the day it was covered in class.

I grabbed the Humvee's driver side door handle and yanked it. I had been prepared to shoot off the door's lock, but as I had expected, the door opened easily.

Neither the mercs nor the AI computer had thought to lock it.

I reached inside the door. The drone appeared to realize what I was doing and shifted the Humvee's transmission out of park and into drive. I turned the ignition key from on to off before the drone could apply the gas, however. I removed the key from the ignition, put it in my pocket, and climbed down off the Humvee.

I sprinted back to the Maybach, opened the rear passenger door, slid in, and closed the door behind me. Manu and Mosi had already retaken their seats in the front passenger compartment.

"Boys," I said, "you both just performed one of the bravest acts of heroism I've ever witnessed. Also one of the classiest diversions too. Good job."

Both twins beamed.

Mosi said, "Thank you, sir."

Manu said, "What next, sir?"

"Next we drive over to the ranch house and I go inside and get Dr. Lennon and Billy Einstein," I said. "Oh, and please put your headsets back on."

The twins put their headsets over their ears.

"Sir," Manu said, "if you don't mind my asking, why did you rush the Humvee after you had already destroyed the machine gun?"

I took out the Humvee's key and showed it to him.

Manu looked puzzled.

"The key?" Manu said. "Why did you want the key?"

"Think about it," I said.

Manu and Mosi looked at each other. Neither came up with anything. Since the clock was ticking, I cut the lesson short.

"The computer could have rammed us with the Humvee," I said.

"Oh," Manu said. "But shouldn't you have just taken the Humvee? Couldn't we use a vehicle like that?"

"I would have if I was sure the drone controls wouldn't override me," I said. "Last thing I want to do is be driven around here like I'm in some Disneyland robot car."

"Why can't I think like that?" Manu said.

"You will one day," I said. "I just happen to have about twenty more years of experience than you do right now."

"So you're saying that in twenty years I might be able to think like that?" Manu said.

"Yes," I said.

"I suppose that could be true," Manu said. "Just as long as I don't get killed along the way."

"There is that," I said. "You ready to go?"

"Yes, sir," Manu said.

"Good," I said. "Take it slow. Drive right up to the Suburbans and park next to them."

Manu shifted into drive, gently touched the gas pedal, and turned the wheel so the car was directly lined up with the ranch house.

"Jeff and Adelaide, we're going in," I said into my headset. "Have either of the two mercs inside the ranch house taken up a position in any of the windows or anywhere else from where they might be a threat?"

Adelaide said, "No. But I wish they would so I can blow their god-damned heads off."

"Hopefully you'll get the chance," I said.

The Maybach was then about two hundred yards from the ranch house. I watched the house for signs of movement as the Maybach rolled slowly forward. Was it really possible the mercs were going to let us approach without a fight? That didn't seem right. I began to get a bad feeling I was missing something. But I couldn't figure out what it was. Maybe I was just being paranoid. Maybe we were going to get lucky.

"Nothing's happening," I said into the headset. "ETA is fifteen seconds."

Jeff said, "Don't it bother you nothing happening?"

"I was just thinking that," I said.

"You're not also thinking we gonna get lucky are you?" Jeff said.

"What if I was?" I said.

"If you was," Jeff said, "then I suggest you stop."

Haley said, "Sorry boys, but Jeff took the words right out of my mouth."

I said, "You don't want me thinking we might get lucky either?"

"No," Haley said. "I want you to stop the car again. Right now too, please."

As I said before, when Haley says stop, she means stop. And right now means right now.

"Manu, do as the major says please," I said.

Manu stopped the Maybach. The ranch house was then about one hundred and fifty yards away.

"What's up Haley?" I said.

"Before I answer that," Haley said, "do me a favor."

"What's the favor?" I said.

"Please pull back farther, at least to the edge of the polo field," Haley said. "I know you're a macho dude and all, but I'll feel a lot better if you have some room to maneuver in case we're looking at what I think we might be looking at."

"You think they've got another Humvee?" I said.

"Please just do as I ask," Haley said.

If there really was another Humvee in the billiard room, Haley's request made sense. We could use some more maneuvering room.

"Manu, keep the Maybach's nose pointed at the billiard room so we can see if anything comes out of it, and back us up to the edge of the polo field, please," I said.

Manu started backing up the Maybach.

"What you got, Haley?" I said.

"The two mercs' heat signatures are leaving the living room again and appear to be heading back to the billiard room," Haley said.

"Maybe we should call it something else," I said. "I'm pretty sure by now it isn't really a billiard room."

"Considering what happened the last time the mercs did what they're doing now, I'm sure you can appreciate that I'm not really in a joking mood, Jack," Haley said.

The Maybach reached the edge of the polo field and Manu stopped the car.

"Fine, whatever," I said. "Will it make you happy if we wait here until we know what they're up to?"

"Very happy," Haley said.

Thirty seconds passed.

"Shit," Haley said. "The mercs just got back to the billiard room..."

"I thought we weren't going to call it that," I said.

"No," Haley said. "*You* weren't going to call it that. However, no matter what we call it, we've still got a problem."

"Another heat signature?" I said.

"Yes," Haley said. "And, it appears to be identical to the previous one."

CHAPTER 125

Manu stopped the Maybach near the edge of the polo field. We were then about three hundred and fifty yards from the billiard room. I grabbed my AK-12, climbed up on top of the Maybach's back seat, and poked my head and shoulders out of the sunroof.

"Adelaide and Jeff, please take a bead on the billiard room doors," I said into my headset. "Maybe we can nail the guy who tries to open them."

Adelaide said, "On it."

Jeff said, "Locked and loaded."

I lined up the scope of my AK at the spot behind the billiard room doors where I expected whatever was making the heat signature to exit.

Haley said, "Heat signature is increasing."

"Engine rev?" I said.

"Be my guess," Haley said.

"Where are the mercs?" I said.

"Looks like they're in, or on top of, whatever is making the signature," Haley said.

"Huh," I said. "You think they're coming along for the ride this time?"

Before Haley could answer, there was a thunderous crack and the billiard room's French doors exploded into thousands of wood splinters and glass shards. An armored Humvee burst out of the room, crushed whatever was left of the wood stairs at the base of the doors the first Humvee hadn't destroyed, and accelerated toward us. The new Humvee looked like an exact duplicate of the first Humvee, which appeared to have remained deactivated and continued to sit perfectly still in the middle of the polo field. The new Humvee had the same laser remote sensing systems, miniature radar domes, stereo cameras, turret, objective gunner protection kit, and fifty caliber machine gun, and was even the same tan color as the first Humvee.

I was fairly certain, however, that control of the new Humvee had been taken away from its artificial intelligence computer and turned over instead to sentient creatures of a more primitive nature. Because right then, what I saw through my AK's scope was a bearded, wide-eyed, long haired, teeth-bared, Afghan mercenary behind the Humvee's steering wheel and an equally bearded, wide-eyed, long haired, teeth-bared Afghan mercenary in the Humvee's rooftop turret. The Afghan in the turret had taken cover behind the transparent ballistic glass shields of the turret's protection kit. Those shields, combined with the kit's armored rooftop, would make it next to impossible for either Adelaide, Jeff, or I to fire a shot that would injure, let alone kill, the Afghan in the turret. The bulletproof glass of the Humvee's passenger cabin would keep the Afghan behind the wheel safe from any bullets fired by us as well.

It was bad enough we were going to have to face down another heavily armed and armored Humvee, but there was also something about the actions of the Afghan in the turret that filled me with a sense of unease far beyond what I normally would have expected in even so dire a situation. What the Afghan in the turret was doing was fumbling to control some kind of large device behind the turret's transparent ballistic glass. I couldn't quite make out what that device was, since much of my view was blocked by the anything-but-transparent armor of the Humvee's objective gunner protection kit. But whatever the Afghan in the turret was fumbling with, it wasn't the fifty caliber machine gun. The Afghan's hands were nowhere near the machine gun's trigger and the gun was completely idle.

A chill ran down my spine.

If the Afghan was fumbling with what I thought he was fumbling with, we were in a lot of trouble.

And it wasn't the kind of trouble we could run from.

Because running would only make it worse.

I fired off three rounds in quick succession at the Afghan in the turret.

I knew the shots were essentially a hopeless exercise, as the only way I was going to kill the Afghan was with a lucky ricochet.

But I had to try.

I watched through the AK's scope as the three rounds made tiny sparks on the turret's ballistic glass and steel armor.

The Afghan was unscathed.

The Humvee, which had already covered about fifty yards since it left the billiard room, kept coming.

Only three hundred yards then lay between it and the Maybach.

More sparks flew off the left and right sides of the turret.

I took those sparks to mean only one thing - Adelaide and Jeff were lacing their rounds into the Humvee's turret, also hoping for a lucky ricochet.

Their rounds left the Afghan unscathed as well.

The Afghan in the turret, apparently responding to our rounds, ducked down closer to the turret's floor. As he did so, more of the object he was fumbling with became visible. I couldn't see the entire object, but I saw enough of it to know my worst fears had been realized.

What the Afghan was holding in his hands, and just then shoving through the gap in the armor next to the Humvee's machine gun, was an Igla surface-to-surface missile. The Igla appeared to be identical to the Iglas Jeff and I had taken off the dead Kazakhs on Kanan Dume the night before and had fired at the Black Hawk and mini-mansions just minutes earlier.

If I had been the Afghans in the Humvee and had an Igla SSM, I would have just stopped the Humvee where it was and fired the missile at us. Hell, I would have fired it without even leaving the billiard room. But stopping seemed to be the last thing on the Afghans' minds. Perhaps the Afghans' bosses had struck the fear of God into the Afghans as to what would happen if they missed and they were waiting to launch until they were almost on top of us, or perhaps they were simply not confident in their own aim. Whatever the reason for the delay, it didn't change the fact that the Humvee continued to rapidly close in on us.

A high security Maybach can stand up to a lot of things - our hot off the presses experience with the previous Humvee's fifty caliber rounds was an excellent case in point. And I, more than just about anyone then alive, knew how damn hard it was to blow up a Maybach. It wasn't that hard, however, for an Igla, or any SSM for that matter, to blow up a Maybach. Truth be told, it was pretty easy, an SSM being essentially the weapon of choice for that particular job. The fact that the Afghan's Igla was then staring us in the face meant there was only one course of action open to us.

And it wasn't to turn tail and run.

If we did that, the Igla's heat seeker would lock onto the Maybach and destroy us.

I also couldn't try to shoot the Igla and blow it up like I had done with the previous Humvee's machine gun. Mainly because that would never work. The firing tube of the Igla SSM was too wide to jam with a bullet, and any round hitting the head of the missile would just bounce off the head and do no damage at all.

The only thing that could work, the only course of action that I could even consider, was for the Maybach to ram the Humvee at full speed and hope the collision would knock the Afghan in the turret out of commission before he had a chance to launch the Igla. It was a long-shot, but it was our only shot.

I ducked my head back below the sunroof.

"Buckle up your seat belts, boys!" I yelled. "And be quick about it! That clown in the turret has a missile aimed right at us!"

Manu and Mosi didn't hesitate in the slightest, just did as I had commanded.

"Okay, Manu, floor this puppy!" I said. "Ram that piece of shit before he blows us to kingdom come!"

I popped back out of the sunroof, firing more rounds at the Afghan in the turret, as Manu, again without the slightest hesitation, put the pedal to the metal. The Maybach's biturbo screamed to life and we took off like a rocket directly into the oncoming Humvee, the two vehicles then charging at each other like enraged water buffaloes, the gap between us only about two hundred and fifty yards and closing fast.

ETA for our head-on collision less than nine seconds and counting...

My latest rounds had failed to kill the Afghan in the turret, but I continued to fire. Adelaide and Jeff were also continuing to fire, and failing to hit the Afghan as well.

The Afghan behind the Humvee's steering wheel must have realized then that we were intent on ramming him. I watched as the Humvee's wheels locked and the Humvee began to go into a skid, slowing down as it did. The skid seemed to cause the Afghan in the turret holding the Igla to struggle to hold his balance.

Trying to stop the Humvee was a pretty good move on the driver's part. If he'd been worried about getting close enough to the Maybach so his compatriot could fire the Igla, that was no longer a concern - we were rushing at him and we'd soon get close enough on our own. Also, if the Igla failed to launch, slowing down would reduce the force of any collision between the Humvee and the Maybach.

With the Humvee slowing down, we could not afford to lose any speed. And, while I was certain that Manu's foot continued to lay heavy on the Maybach's pedal, I did not want to take any chances.

"Faster, Manu, faster!" I screamed into my headset.

Our collision with the Humvee was only seconds away.

I probably should have dropped down onto my seat then and buckled up just as Manu and Mosi had done, but I couldn't resist trying one last time to kill the Afghan in the turret.

I fired three more shots at him.

All three shots produced sparks on the Humvee's turret armor, but none of them ricocheted into the Afghan.

More sparks flew off the right side of the turret, sparks that were consistent with having come from rounds fired by Adelaide. Her rounds also failed to ricochet into the Afghan.

No sparks were coming from Jeff's side, however. I had a hard time believing Jeff would just give up, so I assumed he was out of ammo or his gun had jammed.

The Humvee loomed larger and larger in my rifle's sight. The Afghan in the turret appeared to have regained his balance and was sighting the Igla directly at us. We had at most five seconds left before we rammed into the Humvee, that is if we were able to ram the Humvee at all before the Afghan fired the Igla and turned us into rubble. It was time to get myself buckled in. I kicked my legs out from under me and began the free fall to my seat.

As I fell, time once more came almost to a standstill. Objects seemed to grow bigger, sounds louder, and colors brighter.

I heard Jeff's voice come in through my headset.

His voice was so heavy and garbled though that it was nearly unintelligible, as if his words were also being subjected to the laws of slow motion time.

All I could hear at that moment was, "I...got...a..." And nothing else.

I knew 'a' was unlikely to be the end of his sentence. Surely Jeff was about to speak more words...

We had maybe three seconds before we met either the Humvee or the Igla head-on, but the time distortion was making it seem like an eternity. And in that eternity, I suddenly had a strange premonition.

I somehow sensed - for reasons I cannot explain - that Jeff's next words would contain some deep underlying meaning.

Meaning of vital import.

But I began to fear their meaning would never be known to me.

Because Jeff's words, even though they kept coming, were getting lost in all the other sounds slowly bouncing around in the molasses-like time distortion...

- The sound of a single contraction of my heart echoed loudly in my ears, and, in the never-ending space before my next heartbeat, the echo seemed to travel into the cosmos and take up residence between the planets...

- The high-pitched winds outside the Maybach sounded like they were coming from the land of the dead or some other mysterious dimension...

- The hugely amplified sound of the twins' breathing, an exhalation of a solitary breath that seemed to come out of both their mouths at once.

My attempts at comprehension were also not helped by the sway of the Maybach on its suspension - which was being magnified so greatly that I felt every up and down or side to side movement of the Maybach's body - or that the arteries inside my skull seemed to be vibrating so strongly I thought my brain was about to explode, or that the flickering of the flames coming from the blazing forest on the edges of the polo field appeared to have slowed into a ghostly dance, as if beckoning us to our deaths...

With less than two and a half seconds before we rammed into the Humvee or the Igla blew us to bits, I finally landed on my seat, absorbing what felt like the hundredth lightning bolt of the day up my spine. I reached for my seat belt, my hands moving seemingly sloth-like in their slowness.

Finally, one more of Jeff's words somehow began to penetrate my consciousness with something remotely resembling intelligibility...

The word was but a vague reverberation, like a low sonar ping of a submarine, or the voices of whales beneath the sea, or the sound of a movie being run frame by frame...

The word was 'light'.

Light?

What light?

What was Jeff talking about?

I needed to know!

But with Manu, Mosi, the Maybach, and I continuing to move inexorably forward towards our date with destiny, a destiny that seemed certain to end in our annihilation, I doubted I ever would...

Then, in a way I can never explain, and can still hardly believe - was it a trick of my imagination? - my vision seemed to become superhuman and everything in sight became even more magnified.

As the Maybach still hurtled onwards, I watched as the finger belonging to the Afghan in the Humvee's turret slowly began to depress the firing button on the Igla SSM. I saw the Afghan's tendons contracting, the fattening of the finger's pad as it was squished in all directions by the pressure from the button, saw too the Afghan's aiming eye squinting and his mouth pursing in seeming concentration.

The smell of smoke suddenly became more intense, more acrid, more suffocating...

We had perhaps a hundred yards to go...

The Afghan's trigger finger continued to contract...

Manu, showing not even a hint of fear, kept to his task. His eyes were locked forward and his fingers were turning white, so strongly did they grip the steering wheel.

Seventy-five yards left...

The Afghan's finger had very little ways to go before it completely depressed the Igla's firing button...

The Maybach hit a bump and left the ground and I could feel its wheels spinning in midair. The wheels seemed to spin so slowly I could feel the slight side-to-side wobble their rotating mass imparted to the car.

Less than two seconds left until we rammed the Humvee...

Or the Igla got us first...

Which seemed more and more likely...

My superhuman vision took in everything on the Humvee, not just the Afghans - the one behind the wheel was grimacing as if dreading our impact and at the same time seeming to beg his comrade to launch the missile - but also the Humvee's tires, the space between the tires' treads looking like giant canyons and the pebbles stuck in those spaces appearing like boulders...

I finally managed to buckle my seat belt and braced myself for whatever was going to come next.

More of Jeff's words suddenly broke through.

Almost unbelievably, the words, though still coming slowly, were sharp and distinct.

"I...am...taking...the...shot...," Jeff said.

Shot?

What shot?

Why was Jeff wasting my time and his with such drivel at a moment like this?

Firing his AK couldn't possibly do any good.

The Afghan in the turret was behind the Humvee's impenetrable armor.

The Afghan's Igla was about to be launched...

My thoughts were interrupted by a flash of brilliant white light, like a shooting star or fiery comet, coming in from my left and passing through my peripheral vision.

As the comet flew by, my mind birthed a new thought amidst the vanishing phantom-like trails of the old interrupted ones...

It was a thought that intruded on my auditory and visual hallucinations, a thought that completely took over my mind, making every other sensation dampen and fade as I paid attention only to it.

The thought was clear, one that felt almost as if it alone was occurring in real time, while the rest of the world still moved slowly around me.

A simple thought spoken inside my mind.

'Thank you buddy,' the thought said. 'Thank you for saving my life one more time.'

One second - no, it was less - *milliseconds* before we would have met the Humvee or the Igla head on, the Humvee exploded into a mass of molten metal, white and red and orange, so that what had been there was simply, utterly, no more. The Humvee's mass moved out like an exploding star, and at the explosion's middle there was nothing but gas. The Maybach, Manu, Mosi, and I, rather than being crumpled like an accordion, sped rapidly through the Humvee's flaming debris. We were moving so incredibly fast all I felt was a momentary hot rush of air through the Maybach's sunroof and the thump of a few shrapnel-like pieces of blown-up Humvee as they bounced off the Maybach's high security steel plating.

I didn't know how Jeff had done it, but as we cleared the flaming gas cloud intact, I knew with as much certainty as I had ever known anything, that Jeff, against all odds, had finally gotten that one last Igla to work...

The onrushing billiard room was seventy yards ahead of us. I looked at the reflection of Manu's face in the rearview mirror. Manu still appeared not to have wavered his concentration in the slightest. He continued to white knuckle the steering wheel and his eyes continued to be fixed forward. Manu's eyes, however, were slightly glassy, possibly due to the beginnings of shock, and he appeared to be almost in a trance. I felt it likely he didn't realize what had just happened or perhaps even where he was.

Which was a problem.

Because if we kept traveling as fast as we were, we would fly into the billiard room and smash into its far wall in a matter of seconds.

I quickly unbuckled my seat belt and leaned forward between the twins. I turned my head to the left, placing it close to Manu's ear.

"Manu," I said, "stop the car."

Manu, still seemingly in that trance, slammed on the brakes. I was thrown against the back of the Maybach's front seat and the twins' massive bodies strained against their seat belts. We skidded to a halt inches from the billiard room's shattered front steps.

I took a moment to check that all three of us were in one piece.

We were.

I also took a quick look at the Maybach to try to discern what, if any, damage it had suffered due to the explosion. The exterior of the car didn't look much different to me, but it had already been such a shot-up mess before the explosion, it would have been nearly impossible to tell if any of its wounds there were truly new. There was one definite change in the car's condition, however. The right rear window had been reasonably intact before the explosion, but now was completely blown out.

"Good job, Manu," I said. "Now, men, we're all going to stay in the Maybach for a moment, while I decide on what we should do next. Understood?"

The twins nodded.

I checked the front of the ranch house for any signs of movement. There were none. Then, after taking a few deep breaths to calm my racing heart, I said into my headset, "So, General Bradshaw, I guess you finally got that last Igla to give you a light?"

"I did," Jeff said. "Ain't no way I was gonna let you do a damn fool thing like try to ram that Humvee."

"Ramming seemed like a good idea at the time," I said.

"Every idea you ever got seem like a good idea at the time," Jeff said. "That's what I'm here for. Save you from yourself."

"You're sorta like a preacher then?" I said.

"Yeah," Jeff said. "Or rabbi. I ain't prejudiced."

"What about witch doctor?" I said.

"Don't be making me sorry I done what I did, now," Jeff said. "I still got this here AK by my side, you know."

"For a man of the cloth, you're pretty quick to resort to threats of violence," I said.

"I am," Jeff said.

CHAPTER 126

It was close to 3:20 p.m. Only about two hours and forty minutes were left until the Chinese would begin their war in Saudi Arabia. The Maybach was parked directly in front of the billiard room, which meant the main body of the ranch house, including the front door, was to our left. My first scan of the front of the ranch house had been quick and somewhat perfunctory, so I had to scan again, this time more carefully. I looked to my left, my vision distorted by the smoke engulfing the compound and the multitude of cracks in the Maybach's windshield. There was no activity anywhere, the ranch house's windows devoid of even a whisper of movement.

I looked back right. I checked the inside of the billiard room through the ragged opening that had been created by the shattering of the room's French doors. Apparently, the billiard room really was a billiard room. A rack of pool cues was mounted on the room's right wall. The left wall had two billiard tables stacked against it - I assumed to make space for the Humvees. Multicolored billiard balls by the dozens lay scattered on the floor. Otherwise, the room was empty.

Outside the ranch house it was quiet other than for the crackling sounds made by the burning eucalyptus trees and the fires consuming the remains of the Black Hawk, Humvee, and mini-mansions. There were no sirens yet. The shadows on the compound had lengthened as the sun had continued its afternoon arc across the sky and sunlight glinted off the scarred surface of the Maybach's hood. I no longer heard the echo of my heart's contraction in the spaces between my heartbeats, nor felt any vibrations coming from the arteries within my head. I touched my ear where it had been wounded. The bleeding had stopped.

"Adelaide and Jeff, either of you see anything moving inside the house?" I said into my headset.

Adelaide said, "If I do, it's dead."

"That's fine," I said. "Just as long as what's dead isn't Kate or Billy Einstein."

"Ten four," Adelaide said.

Mosi squirmed around in his seat towards me.

"She's not supposed to do that," Mosi said. "If Adelaide can say 'ten four', why can't I?"

"Ten four," Adelaide said.

"She did it again!" Mosi said.

I said, "How about we let it slide for now?"

"But it's not fair," Mosi said.

Adelaide cackled.

"Mosi, I can hear you, you idiot," Adelaide said.

"I don't care," Mosi said. "Ten four, ten four, ten four!"

Manu reached over and gave Mosi a fist bump.

Adelaide said, "Was that a goddamned fist bump?"

Manu and Mosi looked shocked.

"There's no glass left in the rear window, you morons," Adelaide said. "I can see both of you perfectly through my scope."

Manu and Mosi both turned to look out the Maybach's empty rear window frame. It appeared they were trying to spot Adelaide where she was hidden in the brush along the canyon hillside. It didn't look like they were successful. They did, however, seem to exchange another telepathic moment, after which they smiled, shoved their arms toward the rear window, and gave Adelaide the finger.

"Screw both of you," Adelaide said.

Manu and Mosi fist bumped again.

I said, "Okay children, that's enough of that. We've still got work to do, and very little time to do it. Jeff, clear on your end?"

"The maiden be sleeping sound on the dank and dirty ground," Jeff said.

"'A Midsummer Night's Dream'?" I said.

"Uh huh," Jeff said.

"Haley, your infrared show anyone moving inside the ranch house?" I said.

"The five people we've been monitoring in the living room haven't changed their positions," Haley said. "We still have the two you've decided are Carter Bowdoin and Kenny Liu sitting across from the three you've also claimed are Dr. Lennon, Billy Einstein, and Bryce Wellington."

"You've decided? You've also claimed?" I said. "Am I detecting a hint of skepticism in your voice?"

"Perhaps," Haley said.

"Maybe you'd like to share your own views on the identities of the five mystery guests?" I said.

"Not in a million years," Haley said.

"That's what I thought," I said. "It's also a good move on your part, since I know I'm right. Now, according to my count, the two Afghans Jeff just vaporized in the Humvee with the Igla were the last of the fifty-nine mercs that came in on the Doctors of Mercy flights. Which means the only people left alive, other than us, on the entire Topanga compound are the five people in the ranch house living room. Do you agree?"

"I agree," Haley said,

"By killing all the mercs on the compound we also wind up with a little added bonus," I said.

"'A little added bonus'?" Haley said.

"I believe you previously advised us that there were fifty-nine mercenaries on the Doctors of Mercy flights, and that among those fifty-nine were three mercenaries who had each, independently and alone, visited the United States on an earlier occasion," I said.

"I did advise of that, yes," Haley said.

"You further advised us that you believe that during those visits each of those three mercs also caused the 'accidental' death of a NASAD drone sub engineer," I said.

"I advised of that as well," Haley said.

"Since those three mercs are currently among the fifty-nine dead mercs on the compound," I said, "three of the drone sub engineers can now be considered avenged."

"So you're saying the deaths of those three mercenaries are a kind of bonus?" Haley said.

"I am," I said.

"I like it," Haley said. She paused. "I suppose as long as we're on the topic of mercenaries and 'accidental' and 'bonus' deaths, I should also confirm we've now got a bead on the ten additional Heise De Shui mercenaries we spoke of earlier."

"Where are they?" I said.

"Kazakhstan," Haley said. "Each of them, just like the three you just mentioned, previously made short visits to the United States. Seven of the ten came separately and alone, and during their visits, Milt Feynman, Paul Lennon, and six of the twelve NASAD drone sub engineers died in 'accidents'. The three others came together, and were here during the time when the three drone sub engineers were executed in Las Vegas."

"I assume you've sent MOM agents to hunt them down?" I said.

"Yes," Haley said. "The agents have shoot to kill orders."

"That's my kind of order," I said.

Jeff said, "It is a nice order. But while you two be focused on the Kazakh mercenaries, and rightly so, I'd like to point out somethin' about the Afghan mercenaries, if I may."

"You may," I said.

"If no mercenaries be left alive on the compound," Jeff said, "it likely the Afghans that killed Sam and Lizzy all dead now too."

"Excellent point," I said. "Are you satisfied with that, however?"

"Satisfied?" Jeff said. "Of course I ain't satisfied."

"Is that because the mercs were just hired hands?" I said. "But you feel strongly the mercs' bosses still need a reckoning?"

"That's exactly how I feel," Jeff said. "Reckoning a good word too."

"Thank you," I said. "Haley, any suggestion Carter, Kenny, and Bryce have reinforcements on the way?"

"No," Haley said.

"When do you estimate the fire trucks will get here?" I said.

"Eleven, maybe twelve minutes," Haley said.

"I better get going then," I said. "What's the quickest route to the living room?"

"Quickest is through the billiard room," Haley said. "But then you'd have to navigate through the kitchen and a few hallways. It's more of a straight shot if you go in through the front door. I'd just do that if I were you."

"Front door it is," I said.

"Jeff and Adelaide, please cover me," I said. "Manu and Mosi, as much as I'd like to take Dr. Lennon home in this fine machine, I think it might be too conspicuous to travel any public highways in its present condition. Looks like one of those three Suburbans - the one in the middle - escaped our little firefight unscathed except for the tires Jeff shot out. What say you change out the flats on that one with spares from the other two and then we'll use it to transport Dr. Lennon and Billy out of here? If the keys aren't already in the ignition, I'll find them inside the house."

Mosi said, "What will we do with the Maybach?"

"We'll stash it on the fire road and come back and get it later," I said.

"Okay," Mosi said.

"Until we meet again," I said.

I adjusted my headset so that it was firmly in place on my head. I inserted a new magazine into my AK, then checked to make sure there was a round in the chamber and that the safety was still off. I put the AK's strap over my shoulder, slid across the seat to the right passenger door, grabbed the handle, and, keeping the door between me and the house as a shield, slowly opened the door.

I carefully stepped out of the Maybach, braced the AK against its shoulder strap, and lowered the AK in front of my chest at the ready. I once again swept the front of the house, my eyes, hands, and the barrel of the AK as one. Finding the front of the house still clear of any threat, I made a 360 degree turn and checked the terrain in all directions. It was clear as well.

I slowly walked towards the ranch house's front door.

Behind me, flames towered over the treetops and a half dozen plumes of smoke rose into the sky, twisting in the breeze like small tornadoes. Four of those plumes were nearly white, their smoke the product of the blazing funeral pyres that occupied the sites that had once held the mini-mansions. The plume over the Black Hawk was thick, black, and boiling. To my left, dozens of small orange and red fires consumed pieces of the exploded Humvee.

The heat from all the fires was almost unbearable, and the skin on my arms had turned red and dripped with sweat. A solitary turkey vulture floated on the thermals overhead, occasionally passing between me and the sun. Squirrels, jackrabbits, and quail suddenly burst from the burning forest and raced across the polo field. The fallen bodies of the sentries Adelaide and I had killed lay on the polo field's grass.

The stench of burning human flesh had grown greater over the last few minutes, nearly overwhelming the smells of burning helicopter and diesel fuel, molten metal, and timber that enveloped the entire area.

As I walked up the stairs to the front door, a flash of movement caught my eye. The movement had come from my left. I stopped in my tracks and quickly looked in that direction, my AK following in line with my gaze. A coyote appeared to have just come around the far left side of the ranch house and was running toward the small cinder block building that lay a few yards from the house. I remembered Haley saying the building had once been a recording studio. The coyote stopped a few feet away from the studio's front door, turned to face me, sat down on its haunches, and seemed to wink at me.

That was not the moment to start hallucinating.

I kept looking at the coyote, but shook my head and blinked a few times, trying to clear him from my vision.

He didn't budge.

The door to the recording studio began to open inwards. It was dark inside the studio, but I sensed movement somewhere in the gap between the doorjamb and the door. The door continued to open, and an arm took form in the gap. The arm was slender and beautiful and I instantly recognized it.

"Grace?" I said, under my breath.

Grace stepped out of the doorway. Her blond hair cascaded down around her shoulders. She was barefoot and wearing a summery white cotton dress that stopped above her knees. She held a golden lyre in her hands.

"Hello, my darling," Grace said.

"I've missed you," I said.

"I know," Grace said. "I've missed you too."

"I'm sorry I don't look so good," I said. "The last twenty-four hours have been pretty rough."

"I know," Grace said.

Haley's voice crackled in my headset, "Jack, who are you talking to?"

"Talking to?" I said.

"Yes," Haley said. "I thought I heard you say something about not looking too good."

"Must have been some kind of static interference," I said. I grabbed my headset's connector at the base where it entered my iPhone. I unplugged it and plugged it in a few times in quick succession. Each time I did that the headset made a high-pitched clicking sound. "That any better?"

"Not really," Haley said.

"This headset is pretty cheap," I said. "Must be going bad."

I unplugged the headset one more time and left it unplugged. I needed to be with Grace and I didn't want to be interrupted.

"Sorry, my love," I said to Grace. "That was Haley. You know how she is."

"I do," Grace said.

"Did you learn how to play the lyre?" I said.

"Yes," Grace said. "For you."

"That's wonderful," I said. "Are you going to play me a song?"

"We are," Grace said.

"We?" I said.

Grace put a finger to her lips. She began to play the lyre. I recognized the song. It was 'Time of Your Life', the Green Day song that had been playing in the background of Dr. Nimo's/Billy Einstein's voicemail to Kate. After the first few bars, the coyote started to sing the lyrics,

'Another turning point, a fork stuck in the road

Time grabs you by the wrist, directs you where to go

So make the best of this test, and don't ask why...'

I interrupted their playing.

"I don't think that's the coyote's song, is it?" I said. "Last time I saw him, the coyote was singing Rainbow's 'Long Live Rock 'n' Roll', the one that goes like this..." I began to sing,

'At the end of a dream

If you know where I mean

When the mist just starts to clear.'

Grace clapped. The coyote yipped in what sounded like approval.

"Very good," Grace said. "We're glad you can remember. What else do you remember?"

"Remember?" I said.

"Here's a hint," Grace said. "You like anagrams."

"I do," I said. "But what about them?"

"We'll keep playing," Grace said. "Give you a moment to think about it."

Grace strummed her lyre and the coyote sang once more,

'It's not a question, but a lesson learned in time

It's something unpredictable, but in the end it's right
I hope you had the time of your life.
So take the photographs, and still-frames in your mind
Hang them on a shelf in good health and good time
Tattoos of memories and dead skin on trial
For what it's worth, it was worth all the while
It's something unpredictable, but in the end it's right
I hope you had the time of your life.'
The world began to spin.

Grace, the coyote, the recording studio, and the ranch house blurred together into long, wide, rainbow-like swaths of bright colors that seemed to rotate all around me, as if they were splashed upon the walls of the vortex inside the eye of a tornado. My ears filled with the sound of a rushing wind that seemed like it would be more at home moving through the pines on my ranch in the Sierras. It was a sound light years different from the one made by the cyclones that had been created by the compound's fires. The smell of burning flesh, gasoline, and timber was replaced by the sickly sweet scent of incense. It was an incense that reminded me of the kind I had first encountered in Buddhist temples in Tibet, and it overwhelmed my senses.

Words and phrases suddenly began to mix with the sound of the rushing wind...

'Photographs'...

'Dead skin'...

'Still-frames in your mind'...

I then found myself somewhere else entirely, as if I had been transported body and soul without any effort of will on my part. The place I found myself in was the bunker that had been the home of the NASAD dark programmers, the NASAD war games' offensive team. I was surrounded by the dead, scarlet-faced programmers and I was staring at the movie posters above the desk I had presumed belonged to Dr. Nimo/Billy Einstein. The posters were the ones that had been created for 'The Conversation', 'Babel', 'Blow Up', 'Inception', 'Kill Bill', and 'The Matrix'.

The Green Day and Rainbow songs began to play simultaneously in my head.

"Oh my God," I said to myself, "it's not the songs themselves is it...?"

And with that thought, I was instantly transported to another place. That time I found myself inside Captain Nemo's 'Nautilus'. Nemo was standing on the control deck of the submarine next to the sub's pilot who had his hands on the ship's wheel. The submarine appeared to be deep beneath the ocean - perhaps even twenty thousand leagues! - and through the sub's window I could see it was being attacked by a horde of giant squid.

But I knew being in the sub was all wrong. My being there was just a taunt...

Because I had suddenly remembered that 'Gates of Babylon' was on the same Rainbow album as 'Long Live Rock 'n' Roll'...

And that the album that contained Green Day's 'Time of Your Life' was titled 'Nimrod'...

And I realized that the only movie poster that mattered was the one for 'Babel'...

And I knew with absolute certainty that Dr. Nimo was not, and never had been, a sea captain cruising beneath the sea in submarines...

Because Dr. Nimo was...

An anagram.

An ancient king of an ancient kingdom.

The son of Cush, grandson of Ham and great-grandson of Noah.

The founder of Shinar as recorded in the Book of Genesis.

Dr. Nimo was Nimrod.

Nimrod who ruled over Uruk, Akkad, Calneh, and Babel.

Babel, where King Nimrod caused his subjects to build a tower to show their defiance of the Lord, and the Lord was so affronted that He made sure they would never be able to understand each other again...

Whoosh!

I found myself back standing on the front steps of the ranch house in the middle of the swirling vortex. Everything was still a spinning blur, but my mind was clear...

Another whoosh!

The vortex disappeared.

The winds died down to almost nothing.

All was silent.

I turned to look at Grace and the coyote. The coyote seemed to smile, then trotted off into the brush.

Grace smiled too, and said, "You've done it my love. I'm very proud of you."

"Thank you, darling," I said.

"I have to go now," Grace said.

"I understand," I said.

"Be careful," Grace said.

"I will," I said.

Grace vanished. I was left staring into the empty darkness of the interior of the recording studio.

I reattached my headset to my iPhone and adjusted the earphones over my ears. Haley and Jeff were talking.

"What's he doing now?" Haley said. "His fight with the Humvees took almost ten minutes and we're running out of time. Those fire trucks will be there in maybe nine or ten minutes."

"He still just standing there staring into...no...wait," Jeff said. "Looks like he's fiddling with his headset..."

I said, "I can hear both of you. It's not polite to talk behind someone's back."

Haley said, "Well, it's not polite to just disappear like that on us either. Especially when we need you inside that house right now."

"I didn't disappear," I said. "I've been here all the time."

Jeff said, "We talking about your mind."

"Touché," I said. "But, now's not the time to quibble. Haley, I know where Dr. Nimo/Billy altered the software code. I can tell you where to look for it so you can figure out what he did."

"What?" Haley said.

"I can tell you where to look to find the software code Billy altered in order to create the insurmountable edge," I said.

"That's what I thought you said," Haley said.

"You don't believe me?" I said.

"I'd like to believe you," Haley said. "But given the fact that all you've been doing for the last ten minutes is either jousting with those two Humvees, or standing outside the front of the ranch house in a trance, you'll forgive me if I'm having a hard time accepting that you've magically come across such new and particularly vital information."

"It's not magic," I said. "I just happened to remember something when I saw the recording studio."

"The recording studio?" Haley said.

"Yes," I said. "That cinder block building next to the ranch house. You told me it was a recording studio."

"I did say that, didn't I?" Haley said.

"You did," I said. "And the thing I remembered made everything fall into place for me. Everything I've been thinking about ever since I heard Billy's original voicemail message to Kate suddenly made sense. I know what Billy was up to."

"Jeff, you listening to all of this?" Haley said.

Jeff said, "I am."

"What do you think?" Haley said.

"I think you should hear him out," Jeff said. "He sounds like he knows what he talking about."

"Crazy people sound like they know what they're talking about too," Haley said.

"He ain't crazy, Haley," Jeff said. "Not about this anyway. With all due respect, it ain't like you or anyone else at MOM making any real progress on this subject, is you?"

There was a moment of silence on the line. I supposed Haley was thinking about what she should do.

"Ah Jesus," Haley said. "I don't know why I'm going along with this. Those fire trucks will be here any minute, and what we really need Jack to do is get Kate and Billy out of that house...but...I'll bite. Jack, tell me what you think Billy was up to. Please be quick about it though."

Three mule deer ran out of the flaming eucalyptus grove next to the Black Hawk's carcass. The deer in the lead of the group of three was much larger than the other two and appeared to be their mother. The three of them raced across the polo field and seemed to be headed for the compound's driveway to the public street.

"I'll be quick," I said. "But before I start, can you please again confirm for me that, as far as we know, the military's computer systems are currently working without a hitch? It'd be embarrassing to go through the whole explanation and then have you tell me that the insurmountable edge has already turned on."

"I can confirm that the military's computer systems are working normally," Haley said. "There's no evidence the edge has turned on."

"Alright then, here is what Dr. Nimo/Billy Einstein was up to," I said. "The war game software code that Billy wrote completely destroys the ability of the U.S. Armed Forces to function. Because what Billy's code does is make it impossible for every one of our soldiers, machines, and computers to talk to each other."

"If you're right, and I'm not saying you are, that would certainly qualify as an insurmountable edge," Haley said. "How'd Billy do it?"

"I believe Billy probably messed with the encryption sequences," I said.

"The encryption sequences?" Haley said.

"Yes," I said. "Everything we've encountered about Dr. Nimo/Billy Einstein so far points to him having a keen interest in coded, secret messages and complex passwords. Example number one, there's the coded message that Billy sent to Kate that caused her to seek my help in the first place. Example number two, Billy set up the data on his phone so that it can only be unlocked using three of his fingers working in concert with an Enigma app. Hell, Billy even owns his own Enigma machine. Example number three is the over-the-top secret message Billy sent to Kate embedded in a Christmas catalogue. I mean, who *does* that? But Billy doesn't just have a keen interest in coded, secret messages and passwords, he also clearly has a keen ability to construct such messages and passwords. Just look at what you yourself are up against, Haley. You've got the best minds at MOM trying to crack the file Billy sent Kate and you can't do it. So, when you get right down to it, what else is behind the construction of those messages and passcodes other than the science of encryption? I think we can say, therefore, that Billy is obsessed with encryption, and it's not hard for me to believe that Billy's obsession with encryption is what drove the creation of his unique vision of an insurmountable edge." I suddenly realized I'd been speaking for quite a long time. "You still with me?" I said.

"Yes," Haley said. "Go on."

"If Billy, in the construction of that edge, did what I think he did - which is create a war game software weapon that disrupts the U.S. military's computers' encryption sequences - then I think there's two likely ways Billy might have constructed his weapon. One, Billy might have let the normal encryption sequences run and encrypt the data as the sequences usually do, but then he'd secretly re-encrypt the encrypted data one more time. He'd then throw away the new key that coincides with the newly encrypted data and pass on that newly encrypted data with the old key."

Haley must have been paying very close attention to what I'd said - and again, I'd said a lot - as she instantly chimed right in with, "And since the old key won't be able to decrypt the new data, that would, as you said, certainly make it impossible for every one of our soldiers, machines, and computers to talk to each other. What's the second way?"

"I actually like this way better since it's simpler," I said. "Billy allows the data to be encrypted normally, but then passes it on with either a new false key he creates, or so heavily corrupts the data's real key it can't be used. It's like I was explaining to Dr. Lennon the other day about Captain Midnight Decoder Rings. If you lose or damage the Captain Midnight Decoder Ring - or in this case, the software decryption key - God help you if you want to decode your message."

"Captain Midnight, huh?" Haley said.

"Yes," I said.

"Why would Billy let the encryption sequences run at all?" Haley said. "Wouldn't it be simpler just to stop the encryption process from the outset, rather than re-encrypting the data, or creating false keys, or corrupting the real key?"

"I think if Billy didn't let the normal encryption sequences run, it would be harder to get away with his war game attack on NASAD's military software systems," I said. "As a dark programmer, Billy would be intimately aware of those systems. He would surely know how heavily monitored the initial encryption is, since everyone from the most neophyte programmer at NASAD, on up to the top U.S. military brass, is scared to death about any breaches in data security. I figure Billy would look past the initial encryption steps to target a process people wouldn't have any reason to routinely look at. In Billy's war game situation, those people would be the NASAD programmers making up the defensive team in the NASAD Cyber Defense Hall. In the real world, now that Billy's software has gotten into the live U.S. military computer systems, those people would be the U.S. military's computer software engineers monitoring the performance of those systems."

"I can see that," Haley said. "If Billy did a good job of hiding whatever alterations he made to the computer software sequences that occur after the encryption portion of the software sequences, all a programmer checking on the software in real time would see is the encrypted data and its key flowing through the system. The programmer would have no reason to suspect the key, for one reason or another, didn't actually work with that data."

A flock of blackbirds raced over my head. They appeared to have come from the same part of the eucalyptus grove that the deer had run from only moments earlier. The blackbirds flew above the polo field for a short distance, made a sweeping, banked right hand turn, and darted straight up into the sky towards the top of the mountain ridge on the canyon's north side.

"Correct," I said. "And, if I'm right about what Billy did, then his insurmountable edge will be absolutely lethal to our Armed Forces. Because, as we all know, no one, absolutely no one, communicates in wartime via anything other than encrypted data. If Billy's insurmountable edge software gets turned on and begins to function at the commencement of a war with China - gets turned on and begins to function exactly as I believe Billy's insurmountable edge software would have turned on and begun to function at the time of his NASAD war games sneak attack - things will immediately start going haywire with all of the U.S. military's encrypted communications. We'll know that something is horribly wrong with our communications systems since we won't be able to understand any messages we receive, but the worst part is, since we won't be able to talk to each other, we won't be able to work together to figure out what it is that's gone wrong. We won't even be able to get to step one of a possible solution."

"We'd be in an impossibly bad situation if real war does break out and Billy's software becomes activated in the live U.S. military computer systems...," Haley said.

"Billy told me he never expected his software to get into the live systems, let alone become activated within them, and I believe him," I said.

"I believe Billy too," Haley said. "But if you're right about what Billy did - and even though everything is functioning just fine now as far as we know - if Billy's software is in the live systems and his software turns on at the commencement of a war with China, then what we'd be seeing at that moment of commencement is everything coming to a standstill. Not only voice communications, but GPS information, weapons commands - none of them will work without the correct decryption keys, because whatever coded data is sent will just be read on the receiving end as gobbledygook since the data can't be decrypted."

"Yes, that's exactly what would happen," I said. "And again, since we won't be able to communicate with each other to even take the first steps in fixing the problem, the war is lost almost immediately, and hundreds of thousands of our people will die."

There was silence on the line once more. I again assumed Haley was going over in her head everything we had just discussed.

"Damnit, Jack," Haley said. "You know this is a tough call don't you?"

"For you, maybe," I said. "But not for me. I know I'm right."

"You know, but I don't," Haley said. "And while I'm very tempted to believe you, I still need something else to go on. I mean, you're asking me to tell my people to stop looking for the insurmountable edge in the sequences of the integration section of the military operational software that I've already assigned them to review - software sequences that were determined after deep and careful consideration by all of us here at MOM to be the most likely source of the insurmountable edge - and start looking instead at the encryption and decryption sequences. Is there anything else you can give me so that I can have a bit more confidence I'm doing the right thing? Can you at least tell me why you're so convinced you're correct about all of this?"

A half dozen more squirrels fled the edges of the burning eucalyptus grove. They were followed by a more slowly moving possum. The turkey vulture continued to soar overhead. I looked back at the recording studio. The coyote had not returned.

"There is," I said.

"What is it?" Haley said.

"The Tower of Babel," I said.

"The Tower of Babel?" Haley said.

"Yes," I said. "Billy's weapon is very reminiscent of what happened at Babel."

"You're kidding, right?" Haley said.

"No," I said.

"What the hell, Jack?" Haley said. "Is this some kind of joke to you? The Tower of goddamned Babel? Here I was believing everything you said, but now you're scaring the shit out of me."

Jeff said, "He always scare the shit out of me."

I said, "The two of you seem to be inferring I've lost my mind. I assure you, I haven't. I'm convinced Dr. Nimo/Billy Einstein is heavy into the Tower of Babel."

Haley said, "Jeff, how quickly can you come down off that hill? I need someone who's not insane to get into that house right now."

Adelaide said, "Major Haley, you really should be talking to me then. I'm the only one of the three of us here that meets your qualifications."

I said, "Funny, Adelaide."

Jeff said, "Haley, I suggest we hear Jack out. He's starting to sound a little scary, but he still doesn't sound crazy."

"I agree with Jeff," I said.

There was another moment of silence on the line. I again assumed Haley was thinking things over.

Haley said, "Goddamnit, you two, I know I'm going to regret this... but go ahead, Jack. I'm all ears."

"At the Tower of Babel a person could speak and understand what they themselves were saying," I said. "But the person listening had no idea what the speaker's words meant. The listener, in effect, couldn't decrypt what the speaker was saying. All of which, in a nutshell, exactly parallels what I think Billy did."

"And because it happened at the Tower of Babel, that somehow gives more credence to your theory?" Haley said.

"Yes," I said. "Because it happened there, and also since Billy calls himself Dr. Nimo."

"What the hell does Dr. Nimo have to do with the Tower of Babel?" Haley said.

"Dr. Nimo was at Babel," I said. "Not only was Dr. Nimo there, but he built the tower."

"Billy built the Tower of Babel?" Haley said.

"No," I said. "Dr. Nimo. And the Dr. Nimo I'm talking about is the one spelled with an 'I' not an 'E'. Because that Dr. Nimo is an anagram."

"An anagram?" Haley said. "An anagram for what?"

"Nimrod," I said.

For a moment, no one said anything, and the line was completely silent. Then I heard what sounded like Jeff letting out a deep breath.

"Jesus, you're right," Jeff said "I don't know why I didn't see it before, but I see it now. You know, for a crazy, scary person, you pretty smart."

"Thank you, Jeff," I said.

Haley said nothing. I thought I heard her typing in the background, however.

I said, "Haley are you typing?"

"What if I am?" Haley said.

"What are you typing?" I said.

"None of your business," Haley said. "Alright. I buy your Nimrod anagram analysis. But I know you, Jack, and I know that an anagram isn't nearly enough for you to hang your entire hat on. There's something else you've got that's driving this cockamamie theory. What is it?"

I heard the sound of a loud explosion. I turned to look in the direction of the sound. A huge eucalyptus branch had just broken off its burning trunk and was falling to the ground. I assumed the gases from superheated sap within the trunk had built up so much pressure that they finally erupted with enough force to blow the branch from the trunk.

"The recording studio made me think of 'Time of Your Life', the Green Day song that had been playing in the background of the voice-mail Dr. Nimo/Billy Einstein had sent to Dr. Lennon," I said. "You remember, the one you told me had been on an album recorded at Conway Studios?"

"I remember," Haley said. It sounded like she was typing faster now.

"Well, then for reasons I can't really explain, it came to me that 'Nimrod' was the name of the album 'Time of Your Life' was on..."

"You're right," Haley interrupted. "I just looked it up."

"You did?" I said.

"Yes," Haley said. "You made me think of it when you mentioned the recording studio."

"Good," I said. "Then I started thinking about Nimo's/Einstein's desk in the bunker beneath the exploded crater and how I found the

Enigma machine there, and that on the wall above the desk was..."

"A poster for the movie 'Babel,'" Haley interrupted again.

"How'd you remember that?" I said.

"Please, Jack, give me a break," Haley said. "You know I remember everything."

"You do," I said.

"Jesus," Haley said. "It's been staring us in the face the whole time, hasn't it?"

"Well...it kinda depends what you mean by that?" I said.

"Cut the crap," Haley said. "Billy modeled everything he's done, including his code name, on Nimrod. Hell, maybe he even thinks he's Nimrod."

"Damn," I said.

"Why damn?" Haley said.

"Because that's exactly what I was thinking," I said. "But now that you just said it out loud, I gotta admit it sounds pretty crazy."

"It's not crazy," Haley said. "It makes perfect sense. And it all fits with Billy's profile too. I'm now completely convinced that messing with the encryption/decryption sequences is just the kind of thing that little squirt would do."

"Billy is actually a pretty big guy," I said.

"You know what I mean," Haley said. "Alright, it's almost 3:25 p.m. That gives us only about two and a half hours until war is set to commence. Let's gamble. I'll get the whole team working on the encryption/decryption sequences of the military's operating software right now. Maybe we'll find the insurmountable edge after all."

"You sure you want to do that?" I said. "What if you waste valuable time going on a wild goose chase?"

"As Jeff so politely pointed out a moment ago, we're getting nowhere doing what we're doing," Haley said. "The way I see it, we don't have much to lose."

"Okay, then," I said. "Go for it."

"I will," Haley said. "But Jack..."

"Yes?" I said.

"Our best bet is still to get Dr. Nimo/Billy Einstein out of there alive and have him tell us what the insurmountable edge is himself," Haley said.

"That's the goal," I said. "And barring that..."

Jeff interrupted, "We be beating it out of Dragon Man, Carter Bowdoin, or Bryce Wellington."

"Always an option," I said.

Adelaide said, "Can I help with the beating part?"

"Maybe next time," I said. "Haley, how long until the fire department arrives?"

"ETA is now eight minutes," Haley said.

"I better get inside the house then," I said. "Jeff and Adelaide, on the off chance the bad guys actually do have some reinforcements on the way, please be sure they don't bother me."

Jeff said, "Be my pleasure."

Adelaide said, "Ditto for me."

I checked on Manu and Mosi. They had already removed the spares from two of the Suburbans and were replacing the flats on the third one.

"Mosi," I said into my headset, "did you find the key for the Suburban?"

Mosi held up a set of keys.

"They were in the ignition," Mosi said.

I gave him a thumbs up.

I bounded up the ranch house's front porch steps and walked across the porch toward the front door. As I did so, I thought about how strangely the mind works at times. I had actually heard 'Time of Your Life' on Billy's voicemail, seen the 'Babel' poster above his desk, and unscrambled Billy's code name, 'Dr. Nimo', but where had the coyote's song, 'Long Live Rock 'n' Roll', come from? I suppose since somewhere in the back of my mind I had known all along that 'Long Live Rock 'n' Roll' was a track on the same album as 'Gates of Babylon', that that same back of my mind had been trying to make me see what I had not yet seen.

But then again...

What if the coyote was real?

That wasn't possible was it?

Better not to think about that.

Much better.

I opened the ranch house's front door and went inside.

CHAPTER 127

The ranch house's front door opened onto a small foyer. The bodies of the two Afghans we had killed earlier lay next to me. The foyer itself had been painted white. Two dark walnut wood doors with gold-plated knobs were on either side of the foyer. Both of the walnut doors were closed. The back of the foyer opened onto a hallway that ran for perhaps thirty feet before it appeared to end in a sunlit room. The sunlight was spilling into the room through a large, pane glass window. Everything I could see looked run down, but not nearly as decayed and neglected as the house's exterior. Maybe the roof and walls had protected the inside of the house from the ravaging effects of sun and weather.

"Haley, I just went in the front door," I said softly into my headset. "Is the hallway that's directly in front of me the one I take to get to the living room?"

"It is," Haley said. "The living room is at the back of the house, and the back of the house is at the end of that hallway. Assuming you're right about the identities of the people in the living room, Dr. Lennon, Billy Einstein, Carter Bowdoin, Bryce Wellington, and Kenny 'Dragon Man' Liu will be on your left as you enter the living room."

"Okay," I said. "I'm moving."

I walked down the hallway, my AK facing forward. There was dark walnut wainscoting on the lower halves of both of the hallway's walls. The upper halves of the walls were painted white and were decorated with prints of oil paintings in dusty, gilded frames. The prints depicted nineteenth century fox hunts in the English countryside and looked like they had faded over time. I assumed the scion who had once inhabited the house must have had eclectic tastes.

"Are you in the living room yet?" Haley said.

"I just started," I said. "I've got about twenty feet to go."

"Stop moving again then, please," Haley said.

Stop moving?

Again?

What was Haley worried about this time?

If there was another Humvee about to come charging down the hallway, I was going to be pretty pissed.

"You realize I'm in kind of a hurry, right?" I said, coming to a halt. "You said we've only got about eight minutes until the fire trucks get here."

"I do realize that," Haley said. "However, I need to warn you about something going on in the living room that we just picked up on infrared."

"What is it?" I said.

"There's no easy way to say this," Haley said, "but the heat signatures of the two people we believe are Dr. Lennon and Billy Einstein show their body temperatures have dropped below what we believe is compatible with human life."

"Repeat that, please," I said.

"The infrared techs believe Dr. Lennon and Billy are probably dead," Haley said.

I felt like I'd been punched in the gut.

Kate and Billy dead?

I'd come all this way, done all that I'd done, only to fail at this moment?

To let both of them down?

Haley couldn't be right, could she?

"How is that possible?" I said. "The techs have been monitoring the temperatures this whole time, and now suddenly the temperatures just dropped so quickly they think they're dead?"

"The techs have been watching the temperatures dropping slowly over the last half hour," Haley said. "But the techs weren't fully confident in the readings they were getting, so they've also been running calibration checks the whole time."

"So you're saying the techs are now feeling confident in their readings?" I said. "And that Dr. Lennon and Billy might be dead?"

"I'm sorry, but yes," Haley said. "I didn't want you to have an additional worry so I didn't mention it before as I thought it could all be a false alarm."

I didn't say anything to Haley.

But my heart rate skyrocketed...

Breathing felt nearly impossible...

I felt a burning behind my eyes...

Tears began to roll over the bottom rims of my eyelids.

I'd screwed everything up.

I'd had Billy in my arms earlier that morning but hadn't been able to save him.

I'd lost the only woman I'd really cared about since Grace died.

And in all likelihood, I was going to fail in the rest of my mission to prevent a war as well.

I felt as sad as I'd ever felt.

"Jack?" Haley said. "You there?"

I didn't respond.

Jeff said into my headset, "Hey old buddy, old pal, don't be getting so distraught you lose track of what we're doing here now."

I wanted to ignore Jeff, preferring to wallow in my sadness and self-pity, but for whatever reason - friendship? the call of duty? the realization I was on the verge of deeply embarrassing myself? - I found that I couldn't.

"Who says I'm distraught?" I said.

"I hear it in your breath," Jeff said.

"I'm not breathing," I said.

"Exactly," Jeff said.

I said nothing. There was no way I was going to give Jeff the satisfaction of having been right.

"I'll take your silence as assent," Jeff said. "Now, you be listening and listening good. I don't know what you think you heard Haley say, but what I heard her say is that those techs aren't absolutely sure what their readings mean. I say there's a chance Kate and Billy are still alive, so don't you be jumping to no conclusions."

Jumping to conclusions?

I had done that hadn't I?

It was never a good idea to jump to conclusions, was it?

And Jeff could be right, couldn't he?

For all any of us knew, Kate and Billy were still alive. It seemed unlikely, but it wasn't impossible.

"Fine," I said.

"Good," Jeff said. "Sound like you ready to get in there and do the right thing then."

I tried to take a deep breath in and surprised myself in succeeding to do so. I let the breath out. The sadness started to recede. My body, which had felt devoid of energy began to recharge.

"Yes, I am," I said.

"No, you aren't," Jeff said.

"What the hell, Jeff?" I said.

"You forgot the plan," Jeff said.

I said nothing.

"See? I'm right again, aren't I?" Jeff said. "You were just gonna wing it, weren't you? But I suggest that fifteen seconds of reviewing the plan we already come up with isn't gonna hurt none, since we still got seven minutes until those fire trucks get here."

Jeff, annoyingly, was right again.

My overwrought state had caused me to forget we'd actually discussed a plan when we were atop the boulders on the mountain ridge.

I *was* going to wing it, and winging it wasn't a good idea.

A moment of reflective thought was.

"Okay," I said. "Let's review the plan."

"Plan all depends on what you find in that living room," Jeff said. "If Kate and Nimo/Billy are being held hostage, but you can kill Carter Bowdoin, Bryce Wellington, and Kenny 'Dragon Man' Liu without harming Kate or Nimo, then that's what you do. If you can't be sure you can free Kate and Nimo without hurting either of them, then you gotta go with what we did in Kinshasa. If it's the worst-case scenario, and Kate and Nimo dead, just get Carter, Kenny, and Bryce outta there any way you can so we can torture them into telling us what the insurmountable edge is. After they tell us, we'll kill them."

"That really the plan we discussed?" I said.

"I may have made some minor modifications," Jeff said. "But they're for the better."

"Wasn't there something about shoving my gun in Kenny's face if I had to in order to keep Billy alive?" I said.

"There was," Jeff said. "You do that too if you need to."

"I will," I said. "Anything else you want to add?"

"Nope," Jeff said.

"Good," I said. "I like the plan. Hopefully it works."

I walked to the end of the hallway and stopped. I wanted to study whatever I could see of the living room before entering it.

The room was high-ceilinged and arched at the top. Sooty, thick, triangular pine buttresses suspended equally sooty, thick, pine cross-beams from the ceiling. The crossbeams and buttresses traversed the long aspect of the room and were fastened to each other by huge rusted steel bolts. A wooden chandelier in the shape of a spoked wagon wheel hung from iron chains that were attached to the ceiling's center. The chandelier's lights were disguised to look like giant wax candles.

The floor of the room was covered by pegged hardwood planks that were scuffed and discolored. A large fireplace made of granite boulders the size of wild boars lay against the far end of the room. Above the fireplace's iron-grated hearth was an oak mantel and above the mantel was a six-by-eight foot, washed-out, lusterless, oil painting of a red-kerchiefed cowboy in leather chaps riding a bucking bronco. The cowboy had one hand on the reins and the other waved a white ten gallon hat over his head. Around the cowboy's hips were two Colt six-shooters. A whoop seemed to be escaping from the cowboy's lips.

From my then present vantage point, that was all of the room I could see. But I needed to see more. Haley had told me the five occupants of the room would be found to the left of the hallway, so I pressed myself up against the hallway's left-hand wall, took out my iPhone, and carefully extended it, camera lens first, around the wall's edge. The part of the living room I hadn't yet seen appeared on my phone's screen.

A threadbare wool throw rug in browns and whites covered a large portion of the hardwood planks on that side of the room. Three dark brown leather club chairs were placed on one side of the rug and pointing towards me. Across from the club chairs and facing them was an eight foot long tan velvet couch with maroon velvet throw pillows. The chairs, couch, and pillows had gone to seed. Between the chairs and the couch was a piece of the trunk from a redwood tree. The redwood trunk, six feet in diameter, had been made into a coffee table by slicing its top and bottom into flat surfaces.

Kenny 'Dragon Man' Liu and Carter Bowdoin sat in two of the club chairs. Their heads were turned to their right and they were watching a large flat screen television mounted on the living room's interior wall.

They were both absorbed in the broadcast and didn't seem to notice my iPhone as it peered around the corner of the hallway into the living room.

The television was broadcasting CNN. The CNN war correspondent was at one of the U.S. military bases inside Saudi Arabia. It was the middle of the night in Saudi Arabia, but the base was lit up by giant lights mounted on tall, telescoping poles. Huge piles of sand, U.S. Army tanks, and large tents made of camouflaged canvas, surrounded the war correspondent. The sand was being whipped about by a strong swirling wind, and the sounds of helicopters taking off and landing could be heard. The announcer was saying war with China was imminent and that all diplomatic channels had failed.

Kate, Dr. Nimo/Billy Einstein, and Bryce Wellington were sitting on the couch across from Kenny and Carter. I couldn't see the faces of Kate, Billy, or Bryce, as they were pointed at Kenny and Carter and away from me. Kate and Billy were unmoving, and they were on either side of Bryce. I couldn't tell if Kate and Billy were alive or dead.

Bryce held two Glock 17's, one in each hand. The grips of the Glocks were duct-taped to Bryce's hands. His index fingers were wrapped around the triggers of their respective Glocks. One of the Glocks' barrels was taped to Kate's temple. The other Glock's barrel was taped to Billy's temple.

Carter and Kenny didn't appear to be armed and I was tempted to just put a bullet into Bryce Wellington's brain right then and there. But I knew doing so would just be too big a risk. Even if Wellington didn't have time to consciously fire the Glocks after I shot him, his fingers might still reflexively contract around the guns' triggers during his death throes.

A portion of the top of the redwood trunk coffee table was visible. I used my camera's extremely high-powered zoom lens to zoom in on that portion of the table and studied what lay there. There was no sign of any weapons, but there was an open bottle of Courvoisier Napoleon Cognac and an open box of Flor de las Antillas cigars. I didn't know much about cigars, but I was pretty sure the Cognac was top notch.

Next to the bottle of Courvoisier was a crystal decanter filled with amber liquid and three crystal glasses half-filled with the same liquid. A crystal ashtray held the remains of two stubbed out cigars. I made the brilliant deduction the liquid was Cognac, and that it, along with the cigars, had been part of a then defunct celebration. I knew it was probably me that had ruined the three men's party, but I felt not an ounce of remorse.

There were two used syringes and four small, empty medicine vials lying next to the cigar box. I zoomed in tighter with my iPhone's camera so that I could read the labels on the vials. If the labels were to be believed, three of the vials had contained Ativan, Valium, and Versed, while the fourth had been filled with something whose name was written in Cyrillic. I couldn't read Cyrillic so I didn't know what was in that vial, but I knew that Ativan, Valium, and Versed were benzodiazepines and, alone, or in combination, could be used as truth serum. I snapped photos of all the vials, then pulled my iPhone back in close to me and texted the photos to Haley.

"Haley," I said into my headset, "those photos I just texted you show vials that I believe would pretty much explain what killed Dr. Lennon and Billy, if they are indeed dead. If Dr. Lennon and Billy are still alive, however, then I'll need to know immediately what I can do to reverse the effects of whatever was in the vials."

"You can't tell if they're alive or not?" Haley said.

"No," I said. "But I should know in a few seconds. Please just get me the info on the vials, okay?"

"Will do," Haley said.

"Thank you," I said. "I'm going to switch to FaceTime so you can watch what's going on. Please make sure Adelaide, Jeff, and Manu and Mosi are also patched in."

"I will," Haley said.

I connected to Haley via FaceTime then put my iPhone into the left breast pocket of my shirt with the camera lens pointing out. Haley would be able to see what I saw and we could continue to talk to each other over my headset.

The question then facing me was whether to enter the living room with my AK leveled and at the ready, or take a somewhat less confrontational approach and leave the rifle slung over my shoulder.

Arguing for a less confrontational approach was the fact that the only guns I had so far seen in the room were taped to Kate's and Billy's heads and so were absolutely not a danger to me. My impression of Kenny and Carter was that, again, they most likely considered themselves members of a ruling elite - in whatever way the two assholes would have defined such an elite - and my experience was that most people who looked at themselves in that way considered the taking up of arms with their own hands beneath them. Even if it turned out Kenny and Carter were armed, I was sure I was much quicker than they were, and was confident that I could kill the two of them well before they could take any kind of bead on me - even with my AK draped over my shoulder.

Arguing in favor of a strongly confrontational approach was that having my AK pointed out straight in front of me, and with my eyes behind its scope, would make it a lot easier for me to quickly blow off Kenny's, Carter's, and Bryce's goddamned heads.

Except...

One, if Kate and Billy were still alive and I blew off Bryce's head, again, even in death, Bryce's fingers might contract around the Glocks' triggers and Kate and Billy would be killed.

Two, blowing off Kenny's, Carter's, and Bryce's goddamned heads would be too easy a way for them to die. Sam and Lizzy, who were always on my mind - even during all the most stressful moments of the last few days - deserved, and would get, better.

And three, if I killed Kenny, Carter, and Bryce, there would be no one left alive to torture to find out what I could about the insurmountable edge. I was extremely doubtful that torture would work, but if it came down to torture being my only option to stop the war with China, then I had to give torture a try.

Patience, I counseled myself, patience.

The only problem with patience, however, was that I couldn't afford too much of it. I needed to know as quickly as possible if Kate and Billy were still alive. If they were, and needed some kind of antidote, minutes, if not seconds, could make a difference.

Besides being patient, I also needed to be calm. I couldn't afford to startle that damn fool Bryce Wellington and cause him to accidentally put a bullet into Kate's and/or Billy's heads.

I therefore had to try to strike a balance somewhere between patience and calm, and quick, brutal action.

Which is just as hard as it sounds.

Heaven help me!

Hitching the AK tightly against my shoulder, I adopted an outward air of professional insouciance, focused my inward self on being ready at all times to slay the three assholes if things went in a direction that warranted such action on my part, and entered the living room.

CHAPTER 128

I closed the gap between Kate, Billy, Kenny, Carter, and Bryce and me as quickly and silently as I could. Kenny, Carter, and Bryce, who had their backs to me, seemed fixated on the television and had not yet shown any evidence that they were aware of my presence.

I got up within a few feet behind of where Kate, Dr. Nimo/Billy, and Bryce were sitting on the couch. I studied Kate and Billy from that distance, wary of startling Bryce and having him firing off the Glocks that were taped to his hands and Kate's and Billy's heads.

Both Kate and Billy seemed to be breathing.

Breathing very shallowly, but breathing.

Kate's and Billy's skin tones were incredibly pale, but not blue or purple. I also detected the faintest of pulses in their necks.

All of which, of course, meant that Kate and Billy were still alive.

Haley, who could see what I could see as the scene was being broadcast to her via the FaceTime connection on the iPhone in my pocket, said into my headset, "It looks like they might be alive, Jack. Maybe we'll get them out of there after all."

I couldn't answer Haley without risking revealing my presence in the room to Kenny, Carter, and Bryce, so I said nothing.

But the notion that Kate and Billy were alive had been getting me more and more excited by the second.

So excited, I was afraid I might lose control of my emotions.

Which wouldn't have been good.

Because if I lost control of my emotions I wouldn't be able to think straight.

And I needed to think straight.

Think straight and make sure that whatever choice I made in terms of what I would do next was the best possible choice I could make.

I took deep, quiet breaths to calm myself.

I resisted a sudden overwhelming desire to go up and hug Kate and Billy.

I resisted a sudden, even more overwhelming desire to kill Kenny, Carter, and Bryce.

And I forced myself to keep thinking.

What my thinking came up with was that I had some time.

Kate and Billy were alive, and from what I could see, there was a good chance they were going to stay alive for at least a little while longer.

A little while longer that I hoped would allow me to get a handle on the mindsets of Kenny, Carter, and Bryce.

A little while longer that might also allow me to get the Glocks off Kate's and Billy's heads and get Kate and Billy some medical help so that they would survive and live long, happy lives.

A little while longer that meant I could proceed with calmness, coolness, and methodicalness, and switch to lethal brutality only if it became absolutely necessary.

I took another deep, quiet breath.

I deemed myself ready for whatever might come.

Let the games begin...

"Gentlemen, my apologies," I said. "It looks like I've interrupted some kind of board meeting. You wouldn't perchance have a need for an outside director would you?"

Carter, Kenny, and Bryce swiveled their heads in my direction. None of them seemed surprised to see me, though each of them appeared to react in his own unique way to my presence. Bryce Wellington looked worried, Carter Bowdoin was poker-faced, and Kenny Liu/Dragon Man seemed positively happy, even ebulliently so.

"General!" Kenny said. "So good to see you!" Kenny spoke English with a Chinese accent, which was the same accent Timmy had described the man in the dragon mask at the stoning site had. Kenny's accent was also overlaid with the barest hint of a New England accent, a fact I chalked up to his Yale schooling. With a wide, welcoming sweep of his arm, he added, "Come in, come in."

I tipped my head, as if grateful for the invitation.

"Kenny, Carter, Bryce," I said. "Good to see all three of you as well."

"Ha ha!" Kenny said. "You know my name and we have not even been introduced. Carter, how wonderful is that?"

Carter said, "I don't know, Kenny. Is it wonderful?"

"Don't be such a grump, Carter!" Kenny said. "General, it's so good of you to come to our rescue! As you can see, Bryce and his terrorist friends kidnapped us and now the terrible man is holding the lovely Dr. Lennon and Billy Einstein, or should I say Dr. Nimo, hostage."

I wasn't surprised Kenny knew Billy's code name. If the three men had known his code name before the mercenaries had taken Billy from Kate's estate, it explained why they had made such an effort to go after Billy in the first place. And in the unlikely event they hadn't known it at that time, the empty vials on the coffee table would most likely have caused Billy to reveal everything he knew about anything.

Bryce said, "Goddamn it, Kenny. Don't you think he sees right through your bullshit?"

"I don't know if he does or not, Bryce," Kenny said. "Let's ask him. General, what say you?"

I held off on answering Kenny and instead took a few seconds to study the little Chinese man more closely. Kenny looked almost exactly like the photo of him that Haley had shown me. The photo hadn't done justice to the aura of ferocious energy that completely enveloped Kenny, nor to the savagery that animated his features when one viewed him up close and personal.

Kenny's skin, which was mahogany colored, clung tightly to his fiercely angular cheek and jawbones. His skin was also so closely shaved it glistened. Kenny's thin lips were pulled back in a wide smile over perfect white teeth. His deep set eyes were opaque and dark, so dark there was no demarcation between the pupils and the irises. The only color in his eyes was a slight yellowing of his sclera. Kenny's hair was jet black and hung straight down off his skull in a razor cut that left the ends of his hairs hugging the edges of his smaller than expected ears and barely touching the top of his shirt collar.

Kenny was not more than five foot six, but with a wiry and muscular body that was well outlined by a tightly tailored blue silk suit. His shirt and tie looked to be silk too, as did the pocket square neatly folded in his jacket breast pocket. The shirt was white with impossibly fine yellow stripes, and the tie and pocket square were solid yellow. He had on black alligator shoes with yellow socks, and a matching alligator belt. A gold, diamond encrusted Rolex watch was on his left wrist. A dragon-shaped gold ring with diamond eyes, ruby nostrils, and jade teeth was on his left ring finger.

Carter and Bryce were also well dressed. Carter had on a white linen shirt, blue blazer, tan pants, and brown Louis Vuitton shoes with gold buckles. Bryce was wearing what looked to be a very expensive blue suit and black leather loafers.

"Sorry, Kenny," I said when I was done with my studying, "but I think Bryce is correct. I sorta do see through your bullshit."

"Really?" Kenny said, looking and sounding as if I'd hurt his feelings. "How come?"

"Well, first off, I know that your so-called terrorists flew in on a plane owned by Pennsylvania Avenue Partners," I said.

Kenny gave Carter a sharp look.

"I thought you said the ownership couldn't be traced?" Kenny said.

Carter shrugged.

"Someone screwed up," Carter said. "What can I say?"

Kenny shook his head sadly.

I said, "And second off, there's the duct tape." I gestured toward the Glocks taped to Bryce's hands and Kate's and Billy's heads.

Kenny instantly brightened. He smiled widely again and clapped his hands.

"Bravo!" Kenny said. "Bryce couldn't possibly have taped those guns to his hands and Dr. Lennon's and Dr. Nimo's heads by himself, could he?"

"I don't believe so, no," I said.

Bryce Wellington said, "Damn right, I didn't. The goddamned asshole jabbed me with one of those syringes and filled me with Versed. When I woke up, this is how I was."

Kenny narrowed his eyes. He hissed his reply to Bryce through his thin, tight lips.

"Not sure I'd be calling the man who is going to save your life a goddamned asshole, General Wellington," Kenny said.

"Screw you," Bryce said.

Kenny turned to me, and all smiles again, said, "I don't think it's any secret, General Wilder, that General Wellington is a somewhat stupid man, is it? So sad that he was the best we could find for our purposes."

"Screw you, and screw your...," Bryce said.

Carter Bowdoin interrupted Wellington before he could finish his sentence.

"Put a lid on it, Bryce," Carter said. "We lost this round, okay? Take it like a man. I can't stand your goddamned whining."

Kenny clapped again.

"Spoken like a true gambler, Carter!" Kenny said. "One bet gone, and on to the next one. Is it any wonder I love you?"

"I love you too, Kenny," Carter said. "But please. Cut the crap and get this over with, okay?"

I snuck a glance at Kate and Billy. My heart sank. It seemed to me that their breathing had become more shallow, their skin more pale, and their pulses weaker than when I had first walked into the room. I did my best to hide the feelings of despair that were growing within me, as my instincts told me that Kenny, Carter, and Bryce might try to use those feelings against me in the negotiations that were sure to come.

Despair or no despair, if Kate's and Billy's lives were now at greater risk, I needed to know about it. Keeping my face a mask, I said, "I hope you boys won't think me rude, as I really do find all your bickering quite amusing, but I need to interrupt. I'd like to take a look at Dr. Lennon and Billy, if you don't mind?"

Kenny said, "Mind? Why would we mind? We understand. You need to check the quality of the product to be purchased. Go right ahead."

Product to be purchased?

Purchased as in a trade?

Was Kenny's plan to bargain Kate's and Billy's lives for Carter's, Bryce's, and his own?

If that really was what he was planning, it seemed to be a big gamble, didn't it? What would Kenny do if Kate and Billy died? Didn't Kenny see what I saw, that both Kate and Billy appeared to be on death's door?

Jeff's voice crackled in my headset, "Kenny just say what I think he say?"

I didn't want anyone in the room seeing just then that I was talking to someone, especially not about what Kenny had just said. But if I didn't respond to Jeff, I was afraid he might keep talking, which would make it hard for me to concentrate. So, without moving my lips and as quietly as possible, I said into my mouthpiece, "Um-hmm."

"Damn," Jeff said.

Haley said, "Jeff, come on. Jack needs to focus."

"Oops, sorry, you right," Jeff said. "I'll be quiet. But if Kenny thinking he can make himself some kind of deal for Kate and Billy, that not only be wonderful news, but it also mean maybe Kinshasa on the table now. And if Kenny be selling *us*, that also mean we don't have to be selling *him*."

Wonderful news if Kate and Billy lived, yes. Jeff was also right to be focused on selling. Because Kinshasa was, at its heart, a deal. A deal wherein the hostage takers negotiate their freedom and a plane ride to wherever they want to go - or at least believe they are negotiating their freedom and that plane ride - in exchange for their release of the hostages.

Any deal demands a certain amount of selling by both parties to the deal, but I always had found it was easier to sell a deal if the other side made the first move. Which was because I always found it easier to sell someone on an idea if they thought the idea was their own idea in the first place. Kenny appeared to have made that first move, and if I could just massage him into thinking the key components of the Kinshasa scenario were also his idea...

But I was getting ahead of myself.

Keeping Kate and Billy, Kenny's so-called product, alive was my first priority.

I said, "Thank you, Kenny."

I took a few cautious steps toward the couch on which Kate, Billy, and Bryce were seated.

Kenny said, "Hold on General! Stop right there please! I almost forgot. I have something for you."

I didn't have any idea what Kenny was up to, but in an abundance of caution, I did as he asked and stopped my approach towards the couch.

Kenny 'Dragon Man' Liu lifted an iPad off the redwood coffee table and repeatedly tapped its glass surface with his index finger.

"The news is so boring, don't you think?" Kenny said.

CNN and the China war news vanished from the television screen and were replaced by a grainy, out of focus video. The video slowly came into focus, but not enough to make out what it was depicting.

Carter said, "Kenny, what the hell are you doing?"

"Shhh, Carter," Kenny said. "The General is going to love this."

"Turn it off Kenny!" Carter said.

"Didn't I just say Shhh?" Kenny said.

Three human forms began to take shape in the video. I got a sickening feeling in the pit of my stomach. My right hand moved as if on its own for the butt of my AK.

The three human forms became clear.

The forms were three Afghan men.

The men were tall and thin with black hair and beards and dressed in baggy clothes. The men's faces were dark, and they looked uncannily alike, as if the Afghans were brothers. The men appeared to be standing over a hole. There was sandy earth around the hole.

The video slowly zoomed out.

I discerned some low mountains behind the men. I recognized the mountains as the ones that could be seen in the distance from Sam and Lizzy's stoning site.

The sickening feeling in my stomach grew stronger.

My right hand gripped the butt of the AK harder.

A shovelful of earth flew out of the hole.

Jeff said into my headset, "Dragon Man showing us what I think he showing us?"

I said nothing.

"Don't let him get to you, dude," Jeff said. "Stay professional."

I again said nothing.

A shovel blade sliced through the air above the top of the hole. The shovel blade whacked into one of the Afghans' knees. The Afghan grabbed his knee in apparent pain.

A little girl suddenly appeared at the top edge of the hole. It looked like someone was pushing her out of the hole. She scrambled onto the sandy earth and began to run away from the Afghans. A little boy quickly followed the girl out of the hole and ran after her.

The three Afghans gave chase.

The little girl wasn't running as fast as the little boy. The boy caught up to the girl and grabbed her hand and tried to pull her along with him.

I recognized the boy and girl from the Lancaster morgue and the photos I had seen of them in their home.

They were Sam and Lizzy.

Kenny 'Dragon Man' Liu said, "Watch carefully, General. Here comes the best part!"

The video must have been edited, as it quickly cut to a shot of a man wearing a tuxedo and a dragon mask. The man was holding a cinder block and standing over the grave. The dragon mask looked exactly like the mask that Bobby and Timmy had described to me, and was also the same mask I had seen on the cracked screen of the Kazakh's cell phone at the NASAD drone submarine manufacturing site. Who else could the man in the tuxedo and dragon mask be but Kenny Liu?

The lifeless, mutilated bodies of Sam and Lizzy lay on the grave's floor. The man in the tuxedo and dragon mask raised the cinder block over his head and, seemingly with all his might, threw the block down on Sam's skull.

Kenny, his eyes still focused on the television, clapped his hands and cackled with glee.

Bile rose in my throat.

My eyes felt molten with anger.

I whipped the AK off my shoulder and fired a dozen rounds into the television.

The television shattered into a thousand pieces of metal and plastic.

I pointed my AK at Kenny's head.

Kenny cackled again.

"Now, now, General," Kenny said. "Don't you think that was a dangerous move? You could have spooked Bryce. He's the skittish type, and those Glocks have hair triggers."

Bryce said, "Shut up, Kenny."

Carter said, "Shutting up is good advice, Kenny. Or don't you see where Wilder is pointing that rifle of his?"

Kenny cackled again and stuck his tongue out at me.

"Goddamnit, Kenny!" Carter said.

I sighted the scope of my AK between Kenny's eyes.

I felt my finger begin to curl around the rifle's trigger.

Jeff said into my headset, "I can see through your iPhone camera you're lining up on that piece of shit. Don't do that. Not now. Take a breath instead."

I truly wanted to squeeze the AK's trigger as much as I'd ever wanted to squeeze anything in my life.

But a small voice deep in my head said,

'Listen to Jeff...

Jeff is right...

Not now...

Later.'

My blood was at an absolute boil, but somehow my finger began to let up on the AK's trigger.

I took a deep breath.

"That's it," Jeff said. "I can hear you breathing. Breathe some more."

I took some more breaths.

"Put that AK back on your shoulder," Jeff said.

I did as Jeff said.

"Good work," Jeff said. "Now get back to business."

"Okay," I whispered into my headset, again not moving my lips. "Okay."

My breathing began to dissipate the fury that had consumed me.

I slowly regained my composure.

I resumed my air of casual insouciance and acted as if nothing had ever happened.

Kenny cackled.

Kenny said, "See, Carter? I knew he wouldn't do it!"

Carter shook his head in disgust.

I ignored both of them and checked on Bryce Wellington. Bryce had sweat streaming down both sides of his forehead.

"You alright, Bryce?" I said.

Bryce said, "Do I look okay?"

"Not really," I said.

"I guess that's why you're a hero, Jack," Bryce said. "Because you're so goddamned astute."

"I'm sorry about the television," I said. "I probably should have found an easier way to change the channel. If I promise not to do any more shooting, do you think you can control those fingers of yours, Bryce? No accidental firings?"

"Honestly, I don't know," Bryce said. "But I do know that if I don't control them, you're going to kill me. So the sooner you get me out of this goddamned mess, the better."

Had Bryce really just said 'me'? That could be interesting. It had already been clear to me that there was some serious division in the ranks between Kenny, Carter, and Bryce, but maybe it was more serious than I had thought. Divide and conquer was a time-tested strategy and one that worked well. If they were already dividing themselves and I could further widen that gap...

Before I could complete that thought, I was interrupted by Jeff's voice crackling in my headset.

"I like the way you talking to Bryce," Jeff said. "You're sounding like you back to your old self. Is you?"

"I is," I said softly without moving my lips.

"Funny," Jeff said.

"Um-hmm," I responded nearly inaudibly.

"You be comprehending the full meaning of what Bryce just said?" Jeff said. "That he seem like he itching to sell his boys down the river?"

"Um-hmm," I responded softly.

"It's pretty choice stuff," Jeff said. "Of course, it's not unexpected. Considering Bryce such a goddamned coward."

"Um-hmm," I responded once more.

Haley said into my headset, "Jeff, I think Jack understands your point. How about you let him do his job now?"

"Jack, you ready to do your job now?" Jeff said.

"I am," I said.

"Bye," Jeff said.

I agreed with Jeff. It really was pretty choice stuff. But I also began to think that it all seemed too good to be true.

Bryce already wanting out?

Kenny already proposing a deal?

There was no way things were going to be that easy, were they? I had to be missing something. What was it?

I said, "Bryce, believe me, I'd like nothing better than to get you out of this mess, as you put it. But remember, what goes on here in the next few minutes is pretty much up to the three of you and whether or not you all make the right choices, not me. And the choices you have to select from will be much, much better if Kate and Billy remain alive. So I need to take a close look at both of them, okay?"

Bryce said, "Okay."

"I'm going to start moving again," I said. "You want me to stop, just say stop."

I began to slowly approach the couch once more.

Kenny, cackling, said, "You listen to the man, Bryce. He's giving you good advice. Especially if you feel those trigger fingers getting twitchy."

Carter said, "Kenny, you aren't helping. You know that, right?"

"Carter, who is it that always says, 'A life without risk is not a life worth living'?" Kenny said. "Wait! It's you, isn't it?!"

"There's risk, and then there's risk, Kenny," Carter said.

"Not in my book," Kenny said. "Let's go, General Wilder. Hop to. Time's a wastin'. General Wellington isn't going to shoot anyone. He's too big of a coward."

Jeff said into my headset, "Huh. Guess all of us, both good guys and bad guys, in agreement about Bryce being a coward."

Haley said, "Jeff, come on! These comments from the peanut gallery are really not helping."

"Peanut gallery people generally not be making such wise observations as me," Jeff said.

"Ah, Jesus," Haley said.

I said, again softly and without moving my lips, "It's okay Haley. There's nothing you can do to make him stop anyway."

Jeff said, "See how well he know me? Haley, how come you don't know me as well?"

Haley said, "I do know you. I just must have lost my head there for a moment."

"It back now?" Jeff said.

"Yes," Haley said.

"Good," Jeff said. "Because it a good head and we still be needing it on this mission."

Bryce Wellington himself had said nothing. But he appeared to be growing more and more agitated. I stopped my approach to him once more, afraid that if I got any closer to him he might completely lose control.

I said, "Bryce, I know you're not a coward." I was lying, of course, but under the circumstances I thought lying was a good idea. "You were a general in the United States Army and U.S. generals are not cowards."

Bryce said, "Kenny doesn't understand that."

"He doesn't, but I do," I said. "Listen, I'll make you a deal. Tell me how to stop the insurmountable edge, and promise me you won't hurt Dr. Lennon or Billy Einstein, and I'll make sure you get out of this scot-free."

Bryce looked like he was about to cry.

"I'm sorry, Jack, I can't do that," Bryce said. "Carter and Kenny didn't tell me what the insurmountable edge was."

"But you were sitting here while Carter and Kenny were interrogating Billy Einstein, weren't you?" I said. "I can't believe Billy wouldn't have revealed everything he knew about the edge, given the fact they injected him with those drugs on the table."

"Carter and Kenny never asked Billy about how the edge worked," Bryce said. "They just wanted to know if Billy told anyone else how it worked."

I studied Bryce's face. There was nothing in it that said he was lying.

"Did Billy say he told anyone else?" I said.

"Billy swore he didn't," Bryce said. "He said he sent a coded message to Dr. Lennon, but she swore she never was able to decipher it."

"Did Carter and Kenny have plenty of time to ask Billy how the edge worked before Billy became unconscious?" I said.

"Yes," Bryce said. "Carter and Kenny didn't seem worried about how it worked."

"Don't you think they'd want to know?" I said. "Unless, of course, the reason they didn't ask how it worked was because they already knew how it worked."

"I don't know what Carter and Kenny know or don't know," Bryce said. "All I know is they never discussed how it works in front of me."

I still hadn't heard or seen anything that led me to believe Bryce was lying. I glanced at Carter and Kenny. They were both stone-faced.

"Alright, Bryce, if you can't tell me how to stop the edge, I'll settle for you freeing Dr. Lennon and Billy," I said.

Bryce seemed to be unable to hold back his tears any longer. He began to cry.

"I'm sorry, I can't do that either," Bryce whimpered.

"Why not?" I said.

Before Bryce could answer, Kenny raised his right hand high above his head. As he did so, the sleeve of his jacket pulled away from his wrist and revealed what looked like a small wireless remote-control device taped to his forearm.

"Oops," Kenny said. "What is it the magicians say? There's nothing up my sleeve? But lo and behold...there is!"

I quickly releveled my AK at him.

"Don't move, Kenny," I said.

Kenny smiled, then shuddered in what appeared to be an over the top display of mock fear.

"Don't worry, General, I wouldn't think of moving!" Kenny said. "But, if you shoot me, my arm might just fall like this and hit the arm of my chair..." He made a sharp jabbing downward motion halfway to the arm of his chair then quickly brought it back up. "And if that happened, there's no telling what Bryce might do."

Bryce said, "He put a dog shock collar on me, Jack. You can't see it because it's hidden under my shirt collar."

"Woof, woof," Kenny said, cackling gleefully. Then, turning to Carter, he added, "You see Carter? I was right about our not being able to trust Bryce. Not only is he a coward, but he's so weak that he was quite willing to give all of us up at the drop of a hat! Aren't you happy now that I made him our pooch?"

Carter said, "It does look like you made the right call, Kenny."

Bryce said, "Both of you can go to hell!"

Glocks taped to the heads of Kate and Billy. A shock collar on Bryce. It was all decidedly low tech, but there wasn't much I could do about it. I still couldn't shoot Bryce since his fingers might involuntarily contract and he would wind up killing Kate and Billy. If I shot Kenny and the button on his remote control hit the chair's arm and caused the dog collar to shock Bryce, then Bryce's fingers could just as easily involuntarily contract from the shock as well. If I could take any consolation in what I'd just learned, it was that I'd been right in assuming there was no way things would go as smoothly as it had first appeared they might.

But that wasn't really any consolation at all.

I said, "Alright, Kenny, I get it now. You're a certified madman, aren't you?"

"No, no, no," Kenny said. "You have me all wrong. I'm not mad, I just like to think out of the box. Plus, of course, I don't like leaving anything to chance. Now please, may we get on with this? We have a transaction to conduct, and I think we both know we need to get it done before your authorities get here."

I stared blankly at Kenny. It was true I wanted to get out of there before the authorities arrived just as badly as he did - and I certainly wanted to finalize a negotiation that would save Kate's and Billy's lives as soon as possible - but I felt it best not to reveal anything to him about what I was thinking on those topics at that moment. I figured the more things Kenny was uncertain about - and the more things he had to worry about - the easier it would be to negotiate with him.

I turned away from Kenny and faced Bryce.

"Bryce, hold still, buddy," I said. "I'm comin' at you again."

I walked around the end of the couch. As soon as I had done that, I saw that Kenny had a dragon mask - the mask was identical to the dragon mask the tuxedoed man was wearing in the video that Kenny had just shown me - sitting at his feet. The mask had been hidden from my view before by the redwood coffee table.

Jeff, who must have seen the mask broadcast over FaceTime, said in my headset, "If there any question before - which there weren't, but if there was - ain't no question now. We found our Dragon Man. Asshole."

I stepped between the front of the couch and the redwood coffee table. I moved in close to Bryce Wellington. Kate and Billy were on either side of me. I could see a thin strip of the dog shock collar Kenny had put around Bryce's neck peeking above Bryce's shirt collar. Carter and Kenny were behind me on the other side of the coffee table.

I took a quick look over at Kate. She had obviously been through hell, but still looked beautiful, at least to me. Her chest was moving only slightly though, her skin color was becoming ashen, and I could no longer see a pulse in her neck.

I wanted to go to Kate right then and there, but the professional thing to do would be to check on Billy first, as Billy's value to my mission was, at least in theory, higher than Kate's value. Love or professionalism - it was definitely a close call. In the end I chose Billy, but I'm not sure I would have done so if I wasn't painfully aware my actions were being broadcast back to Haley and Jeff.

Keeping a watch on Kenny and Carter out of the corner of my eye, I moved to get myself in front of Billy. I felt Billy's carotid artery. There was a pulse, but it was very, very slow - perhaps under thirty beats a minute - and thready and weak. Billy was also breathing very shallowly - the expansions and contractions of his chest were nearly imperceptible - and his skin was as ashen as Kate's.

Kenny said, "Oh, we have guests do we?"

I said, "Come again, Kenny?"

"Your iPhone in your pocket," Kenny said. "I hadn't noticed it before. You're sending a video feed, aren't you?"

"What if I am?" I said.

"Doesn't matter to me," Kenny said. "As you saw earlier, I love videos!" Kenny cackled again.

I ignored him.

I turned my attention to Billy's eyes, both of which were closed. I pulled open Billy's left eyelid. The pupil was pinpoint, but it moved ever so slightly smaller when the light hit it. I put my hand on his forehead. Billy's skin felt a lot colder than normal.

My iPhone broadcast no longer a secret, I moved my lips and spoke at a normal volume into my headset. "You getting all this, Haley?"

"Yes," Haley said. "I'm sharing the feed with the medical staff. The docs want to know what Billy's pulse and respiratory rate are."

"Pulse about thirty, breathing maybe four times a minute," I said. "Forehead feels very cold. What do the docs think is going on?"

"The Cyrillic writing on that vial translates to RZ 119," Haley said. "It's a Russian truth serum made out of barbiturates, benzodiazepines, narcotics, and scopolamine. The doctors think Billy is most likely suffering from an overdose of RZ 119."

"What do they want me to do?" I said.

"They say he is probably stable for the moment," Haley said. "They want you to check on Kate."

Probably stable?

For the moment?

That didn't sound so great.

"Okay," I said.

I stepped between Bryce's knees and the redwood coffee table and moved next to Kate. I wanted to lean in and kiss her and wake her up and make everything alright. But, again, I stayed professional. I reached for her carotid and felt it.

I almost fainted.

Kate's pulse couldn't have been more than twenty beats a minute.

Haley said, "You okay? Looked like the camera was pretty unsteady there for a second."

I was afraid if I answered Haley my voice would crack and Carter and Kenny would know how badly Kate's condition was affecting me. So, I said nothing, just struggled to continue my exam. I counted Kate's breaths at less than three a minute. I touched her forehead and it felt like ice. I peeled back the closed lids of her right eye. The brilliant blue irises that I had so lovingly gazed upon were dull and grey. Her pupil was pinpoint and fixed. Light did not affect the pupil at all.

My body began to shake and it took every ounce of self control I had to not just turn around and blow Kenny and Carter away.

Kenny said, "It must be hard, yes General? You like the woman very much, do you not?"

I spun on my heel and shoved the barrel of my AK in Kenny's face. It was an impulsive act, and a dumb act as well, but I couldn't control myself. My feelings in regard to Kate, which I'd tried to keep hidden, were now completely out in the open.

"Shut the hell up, Kenny," I said. "One more word and I'll..."

"Please calm down," Kenny said. Kenny seemed to be trying to appear calm himself, but I was pretty sure I detected a look of fear flitter across his face. He also shuddered slightly, though, unlike last time it didn't look at all voluntary. The flitter and the shudder, if they'd actually been present at all, promptly disappeared however, and Kenny quickly looked like his old self again. Smiling, he turned his face towards the dog collar remote that he was still holding over his head, and added, "We don't want Bryce to come in for a shock do we?"

I jammed Kenny's head back with the AK's barrel. I thought about blowing off Kenny's arm, or at the very least grabbing his arm and keeping him from pushing the remote's buttons, but decided it was too big a risk. I had no idea how sensitive the buttons on the dog collar remote were, and I couldn't rule out the possibility the device could be set off even if I just took hold of Kenny's arm in the wrong place.

I realized then, however, that Kenny's comments - far from what Kenny had intended, I'm sure - had actually had a surprisingly positive effect on me. The blood rage he had caused me to feel, had driven away, at least for the moment, the queasiness that had come over me due to Kate's condition. I slowly refocused on the job at hand. A few seconds later, I felt I could even keep things together when I reported what I'd found out about Kate back to Haley.

But before I reported back to Haley I thought it would be a good idea to get Kenny off his high horse. He seemed to be feeling pretty good about having once again manipulated me into a rage, and I didn't want him to get the idea he could do it another time, or that he might have gained the upper hand in the negotiations in which I'd soon be engaging with him, and possibly also with Carter and Bryce.

I pulled the AK back to my side and smiled my best Kenny smile.

"Jeez, Kenny," I said. "You should've seen the look on your face."

"What are you talking about?" Kenny snapped.

"I thought you might shit your pants," I said.

"Fine, I admit it," Kenny said, somewhat testily. "You got a rise out of me. Don't think you can do it again, though." He suddenly smiled, then turned to Carter and added, "Maybe I pushed the general a bit too far that time? Mentioning his feelings for the lady was perhaps unnecessary? Did I, as you and your poker playing buddies like to say, go on tilt?"

Carter said, "That was way beyond tilt."

"Did it scare you?" Kenny said.

"Nothing you've ever done has ever scared me, Kenny," Carter said.

"Good," Kenny said. "General, aren't you going to advise your friends on the other end of your iPhone connection of the good Dr. Lennon's condition?"

Kenny's voice was as gleeful as it had been earlier, maybe even more so. I got the distinct sense that Kenny thought he knew something

- something important - that I didn't. I can't explain exactly why, but I also got the feeling that Kenny believed that knowledge allowed him to toy with me in a way he had not yet toyed with me, and that toying with me in this new fashion was exactly what he was doing at that moment.

What was it Kenny thought he knew?

My instincts told me it had to be something to do with Kate's condition, but what was it?

I tried to look at things from his perspective.

Kenny had to think that I thought Kate was going to die at any moment, didn't he?

Wasn't that what anyone would think looking at Kate just then?

Which meant...

That if Kenny thought that I thought Kate was going to die...

And Kenny believed he knew something I didn't...

Then the thing Kenny knew was...

That Kate wasn't going to die?

That had to be it, didn't it?

It wasn't just wishful thinking on my part, was it?

The asshole had something else up his sleeve and it wasn't another remote for a dog shock collar.

The only thing I could think that something else might be was...

Something I should have thought of earlier but had not...

And then kicked myself for having failed to do so...

Kenny had some kind of antidote for whatever he had given Kate and Billy!

He couldn't afford for his hostages to die, otherwise he'd have nothing to trade for his own life.

Kenny hadn't been gambling that Kate and Billy would stay alive long enough to trade his life for theirs.

Kenny had known all along he could keep them alive, that they wouldn't die unless he let them die...

A solitary red blood corpuscle of hope winged its way through my heart.

I quashed it.

Hope wasn't going to help me then.

But right action might.

CHAPTER 129

I played out the next few moments trying not to give Kenny the slightest hint that I thought he might have the antidote for Kate and Billy. I behaved exactly as I believed Kenny expected me to behave - as a man whose true love was surely about to die, but who was doing his best to keep his feelings under control.

I said, letting my voice crack just a little, "Thank you, Kenny. Indeed I was just about to advise my friends of Dr. Lennon's condition. I beg your pardon while I do so."

I said into my headset loud enough to be sure Kenny heard every word, "Haley, Dr. Lennon's pulse is under twenty, respiratory rate is three or less per minute, the pupil is pinpoint and unresponsive to light, and her forehead feels like ice."

Haley didn't respond immediately. Instead, I thought I heard her draw in a deep breath, as if she was trying to calm herself.

Haley said, "Okay."

"Okay, as in it's not as bad as it looks?" I said.

Another pause.

If I hadn't convinced myself Kenny had an antidote, I would have taken the pause as a bad sign.

"I know you have feelings for Dr. Lennon," Haley said. "So I need you to stay calm."

"I am calm, Haley," I said. "I won't stay calm, however, if you keep beating around the bush. Give it to me straight."

"None of the docs here have any idea how Kate is still alive," Haley said. "They think she could go at any second."

"Understood," I said, forcing my voice to waver slightly. "What do we do to reverse the RZ 119?"

"We can't," Haley said.

"What do you mean we can't?" I said. "I'm very familiar with each and every one of those component drugs that you told me were in RZ 119. They all have reversing agents."

"I'm sorry," Haley said. "What I should have said was we can't do it in time. The antidote is at Fort Detrick. It will take us five hours to get it to you."

"Fine," I said. "Those fire trucks are, what, about five minutes out? They've got to be traveling with a paramedic. We'll keep her on life support until the antidote gets here."

Haley took in another deep breath.

"The docs say RZ 119 is unique in that at a certain point its effects on the brain literally fall off a cliff," Haley said. "Once it does that, the brain is irreversibly damaged and death is inevitable. They think that Dr. Lennon may have already reached that point. If she hasn't, then the only thing that can stop it is the antidote."

I tried to make myself look as worried as I possibly could.

Kenny cackled loudly.

"You think my face looked bad, you should see yours!" Kenny said. "Your friends must have told you about RZ 119's point of no return, I presume?"

I shifted from fake worry to fake anger and raised my AK until it pointed directly at Kenny's face again.

"I'm tired of you, you little shit," I said. "Get ready to die."

Kenny cackled even more loudly.

"You know you're not going to kill me, General," Kenny said. "One, nothing's changed - even in death I can still shock my little puppy Bryce. Two, I'm sure you still harbor some silly notion that you might be able to torture the insurmountable edge out of me if all else fails - which of course you can't do if I'm dead. And three, the only thing that can keep someone from going past RZ 119's point of no return is RZ 119's antidote. Which I just happen to have some of..."

Kenny opened his mouth. There was a small vial of liquid lying under his tongue.

"Think of me as Charon," Kenny said. "Only I can escort Dr. Lennon in the opposite direction. From Hades, across the rivers Styx and Acheron, and back to the world of the living." Kenny made a quick snapping motion with his mouth. "Or, I could bite down on the vial right now and swallow its contents, and all is lost. So, who is the little shit now? It's you, wouldn't you say? Therefore, let's stop screwing around. Let's make a deal so that we can all get the hell out of here before your authorities arrive."

Kenny 'Dragon Man' Liu cackled again.

I could have patted myself on the back just then, but didn't. I was almost certain he was telling the truth about the antidote. But I needed to be sure. I put the AK down at my side again, lifted my iPhone out of my pocket, and zoomed the iPhone's camera in on Kenny's mouth. Kenny, seeing what I was doing, opened his mouth even wider for me.

"Can you tell all my teeth were capped, General?" Kenny said. "It was a very expensive job, too. I used the top cosmetic dentist in Manhattan."

"Haley, can you read what's on the vial?" I said into my headset.

"Hold on," Haley said.

The line went silent for a moment, then Haley came back.

"The docs say it looks like the vial contains the antidote for RZ 119," Haley said.

"Is there enough in it to reverse the amount of RZ 119 Dr. Lennon and Billy appear to have been given?" I said.

"They say there's enough to get started," Haley said.

"Get started?" I said.

"Assuming Dr. Lennon and Billy haven't already gone over the cliff into irreversible brain damage," Haley said, "giving each of them half of what's in the vial could keep them from doing so. But it would only hold them for about forty-five minutes. After that you'd need more."

"Would it wake them up?" I said.

"Jack, they may never wake up," Haley said.

"Is that a 'no' then?" I said.

"I'm sorry," Haley said. "I should have answered more carefully. What I should have said, is if they wake up at all, it won't be for at least forty-eight hours."

"Which means we can't question them before war breaks out in regard to the insurmountable edge," I said.

"Correct," Haley said.

"Thanks," I said.

I studied Kenny for a moment. What he'd done was actually a good move on his part. He knew he had to keep Kate and Billy alive to use them as hostages, but he also knew he had to keep them from talking about the insurmountable edge before war broke out. As Kenny also knew there was no way I'd risk not getting Kate and Billy the antidote, I was sure he had also calculated that the antidote was his ticket for safe passage off the compound and out of the country.

My gut also told me Kenny had more antidote somewhere other than in his mouth. Logic told me that too. As the initial dose of antidote was only effective for forty-five minutes, Kenny couldn't possibly expect me to make a deal that didn't include the chance that Kate and Billy could survive after that initial dose wore off.

Yes, Kenny had done well.

But he also might have sealed his own fate...

Because I only had less than two and a half hours left to learn what I needed to know about how the insurmountable edge worked so that I could stop the war with China from commencing. And the way I saw it, I had only three options left to gain that knowledge -

One. Awaken Kate and Billy and ask them about the edge. I was fairly certain though, that even if I could awaken them, it would be only Dr. Nimo/Billy who would have had any useful information. Unless Bryce had lied about Billy not saying anything about how the insurmountable edge worked when Carter and Kenny were interrogating Billy, it was unlikely Kate knew anything of value she would be able to impart to me. All of that seemed moot, however, since Haley had said neither MOM nor I would be able to wake up Kate and Billy in time.

Two. Haley's team working on their own found the edge in time within the military's software code. Given everything Haley had said about how difficult that task was, it seemed highly improbable she would be successful.

Which left only option three. Torturing Kenny, Carter, and Bryce to get the information I needed about the insurmountable edge.

I still believed Bryce when he said he didn't know anything about the insurmountable edge, as I was fairly certain that Bryce, in order to save his own life, would have told me whatever he knew about the edge when I had asked him about it a few minutes earlier.

But I was going to torture Bryce nevertheless.

Th.... was always the chance Bryce had lied to me, and I couldn't discovering anything he might know that was of potential

hich one of you knuckleheads came up with the brilliant

idea of using the antidote as a bargaining chip?" I said.

Kenny said, "I wish I could say it was mine. But actually it was Carter's idea. I approved it however!"

Kenny smiled widely, as if he was proud of himself.

"It's a pretty big gamble, isn't it Carter?" I said. "The timing's tight. Dr. Lennon and Billy Einstein need to get the antidote within a very limited window, or they die."

Carter nonchalantly opened his palms and spread them skyward.

"Gambling is what I do," Carter said. "I thought it was the best solution to our problem. We needed Dr. Lennon and Billy alive if they were to be effective as hostages for us, but we also needed them to be unconscious as we couldn't afford to have them talking to you. It's now clear to us that there's nothing Dr. Lennon could have told you, but we weren't able to confirm that until after we had already given her the truth serum."

"You do realize you might have forced my hand, however?" I said. "What's to say I won't beat the crap out of all three of you to find out what I need to know?"

Carter shrugged.

"Kenny and I long ago decided never to know exactly how the insurmountable edge works, since we can't reveal what we don't know," Carter said. "Our reason for kidnapping Billy and Dr. Lennon was not to get information about the insurmountable edge itself. What we needed to find out was whether or not either of them had leaked what they knew about the edge to anyone else. Clearly any such leak could have thrown a serious wrench into our plans. We've monitored NASAD very carefully for any leaks, but the only hard evidence of a leak actually occurring involved Billy..."

"I assume you're talking about Billy's calls to Eric Beidermann and Dr. Lennon?" I said.

"I am," Carter said. "We did not feel Eric purposely gave away any information to Billy, but whether it was on purpose or not, that is exactly what he did do, and we felt he might do it again. We didn't believe any of the other dark programmers had leaked or would leak, but in an abundance of caution, we made sure that neither Eric, nor they, could do so."

"Made sure that neither Eric, nor they, could do so?" I said. "Why don't you just say what you did? You murdered them."

"We murdered them, yes," Carter said. "But let's get back to your primary concern at this moment, shall we? Do Kenny or I know anything about how the insurmountable edge works? The answer to that is, again, a resounding no. Kenny and I stayed true to our decision not to know anything about the edge when we interrogated Billy. As Bryce reported to you, Kenny's and my questions during that interrogation focused solely on finding out whether or not Billy and Dr. Lennon had told anyone else about the insurmountable edge. If you have any doubts about how worried Kenny and I were about Billy and Dr. Lennon, or need any proof about how far we were willing to go to allay those worries, all you need to do is look outside at the smoldering remains of those little houses and the stealth Black Hawk, or remind yourself of all the mercenaries you've killed over the last few days."

Carter was poker-faced when he spoke. It was impossible to tell whether he was lying or not.

"Not that I don't already have enough evidence to hang every one of you," I said, "but I suppose you're admitting to the additional crime of murdering the dark programmers so I'll believe that you're being completely honest and upfront with me, especially about your claim that you and Kenny know nothing about how the insurmountable edge works?"

"I am being completely honest and up front with you," Carter said.

"And I'm a monkey's uncle," I said. "The edge hasn't been yours and Kenny's only concern though, has it?"

"I'm not sure what you mean?" Carter said.

"Maybe this will help you think about it," I said.

I shoved the barrel of my AK-12 up against Bowdoin's forehead.

Bowdoin's eyes went wide, but then he instantly appeared to do his best to hide his emotions. Which he seemed to do pretty well. Because for the next few moments, even though I was pretty sure he was in a full-blown panic, Bowdoin didn't reveal any further signs of emotional distress. He did seem to be thinking hard, however. His thinking was followed by what looked to me like a flash of recognition.

"You're talking about the children Sam and Lizzy, yes?" Carter said.

I said nothing.

"You probably aren't too happy about what was done to their mother or grandparents either?" Carter said.

I still said nothing.

"I'm sorry about what happened," Carter said. "All of it was Kenny's misguided revenge fantasy. I argued against it."

"Argued against it, but didn't actually stop it, you piece of shit," I said. Carter didn't say anything.

I was sorely tempted to blow Carter's head off.

Should I or shouldn't I?

That was the question.

Did Carter know that was the question too?

I couldn't be sure.

While I further pondered that question, Carter continued to do a good job of hiding his emotions. Carter also seemed to be thinking hard again. I was reasonably certain I could detect indications of complex calculations going on behind his eyes.

Did Carter's new calculations have something to do with his poker player mind reading tricks?

I didn't know.

I used the AK's barrel to viciously jam Carter's head back far as I thought I could go without breaking his neck.

Then I did some mind-reading tricks of my own.

I became pretty convinced Carter was sure I was going to kill him. Which was fine with me.

Because I was pretty convinced of the same thing.

I held Carter's head back for a few more seconds, my index finger slowly squeezing the AK's trigger.

But in the end, the more rational part of my brain got the better of me.

That part of my brain knew that time was running out for stopping the war with China, and that MOM and I needed Carter alive in case torturing him turned out to be our best option for determining the true nature of the insurmountable edge.

I pulled my AK away from Carter's forehead and pointed it at the floor. Carter's chin sagged and his shoulders dropped. I also heard a loud, sustained breath escape from his nostrils.

Carter's efforts to hide his emotions from me had apparently run out of steam.

Jeff said over my headset, "I knew you ain't be shooting Carter.

That's why I didn't say nothing."

"You must know me better than I know myself," I said softly back to him.

"I probably do, yes," Jeff said.

I positioned myself so that I could address Carter Bowdoin, Kenny Liu, and Bryce Wellington all at the same time.

"I'm holding all three of you accountable for the deaths of Sam and Lizzy and the countless others who died as a result of your actions," I said. "Tell me how the insurmountable edge works, or none of you are going to get out of here alive."

Bryce said, "But I told you I don't know anything!"

I said nothing.

Kenny shook his head sadly.

"Please General, don't waste our time with threats," Kenny said. He glanced down at his watch. "By my estimate we have only three minutes until your authorities arrive. Once they do, I will turn this into a full-scale hostage situation and we will simply hold off the authorities until Carter's and my little war has begun. As said war will begin in about two and a half hours, Dr. Lennon and Billy Einstein will die since the dose of the antidote that I have will last at most an hour. Ultimately Bryce, Carter, and I will be taken to prison, but just as ultimately, Carter and I will be released due to our formidable political connections. Bryce will either go to prison for life for treason or be executed, but I couldn't care less about that." Kenny glanced at Bryce, gave him a big smile, then continued, "Carter's and my release will take time however, and I have no interest in spending even a day in a cell. So would you like to hear our deal or not?"

Kenny's analysis of what the future might hold for him, Carter, Bryce, Kate, and Billy if we didn't leave the ranch house compound within the next few minutes was probably not too far off the mark. The most interesting thing Kenny had said, however, was his comment about the antidote. The comment seemed to reconfirm for me that Kenny fully understood Kate and Billy's situation, and that Kenny was going to have to offer a way for them to live longer than just the forty-five minutes provided by the single dose of antidote he had in his mouth.

Still, that was not the time to let Kenny think I had even the slightest interest in whatever he was going to propose. The longer I held out, the more Kenny would feel like he had to sweeten the pot in order to get me to go along with him, and thus the better the terms I would get in the end.

"Not really," I said.

"I'm going to tell you anyway since I think it is in your best interest if I do," Kenny said. "As I'm sure your people have informed you, we have a jet at the Van Nuys Airport. The six of us in this room will go to the jet and fly to Beijing. Once there, Carter, Bryce, and I will deplane. The jet will then leave Beijing and take you, Dr. Lennon, and Billy Einstein wherever you want to go."

Jeff said into my headset, "That's pretty close to Kinshasa, but don't be too quick in proposing our alternate destination. Kenny might get suspicious."

I said, "I know that, Jeff."

Kenny said, "Are you talking to your friend, the negro general?"

"If you mean, Jeff, yes," I said. "And he's not a negro. He's an African American. Jeff says the only way you'll fly out of here on your own jet is over his dead body."

Kenny said, "My, my, my. I assume he has a different plan in mind?"

"Yeah, he does," I said. "Jeff said I should stop being so sentimental and just let go of any hope that Dr. Lennon and Billy are going to live. He said I should just let Bryce fire away and then drag the three of you assholes up into the hills above the ranch house and beat you all to death."

I stole a glance at Bryce. He looked like he was about to pass out.

Jeff said, "Ooh, that beating them all to death a good line. I like it. But then again, Dragon Man is smiling, isn't he?"

"He is smiling," I said.

"Why you think he's smiling?" Jeff said.

"Because Kenny's a nut job," I said. "To tell you the truth, I wouldn't have expected him to do anything else."

Kenny said, "I'm not a nut job. But I do see your point. You've seen through the flaw in my plan, haven't you? Nothing in my offer actually guarantees that you will ever leave China once we land. Since you have turned down my first offer, I would like to give you another one."

"Sorry, no deal," I said. "I kinda like Jeff's plan." I raised my AK and pointed it at Kenny. "All of you on your feet, now! We're getting out of here."

Kenny put his hands out in front of him.

"You're not serious are you?" Kenny said. "I can offer you a solution that will save both Dr. Lennon's and Billy Einstein's lives and you are going to refuse it?"

Instinct continued to tell me that it still had to appear as if no matter what Kenny offered I would find his offer unacceptable. I didn't want to risk Kenny becoming suspicious I had something up my own sleeve - Kinshasa, of course, being that something - when I ultimately did accept his offer.

I figured the best way to get Kenny to believe I was serious about rejecting any offer he might make was to shoot a bullet at him. There was a risk that firing off another round might upset Bryce Wellington enough to involuntarily fire one or both Glocks. Bryce's trigger fingers had remained steady, however, when I'd vaporized the television, so the risk seemed low and worth taking.

I squeezed the trigger on the AK and let loose a bullet that ruffled the hair above Kenny's left ear, but otherwise did no damage.

Bryce's upper body flinched, but his fingers moved not at all.

Kenny stared at me in disbelief. He reached up and touched his ear and scalp with his hand, then brought his hand down in front of his face and studied it. I assumed he was checking for blood. Apparently satisfied there wasn't any, Kenny smiled and turned towards Carter.

"I told you I couldn't be killed," Kenny said to Carter.

Carter said, "I think the general hits what he's aiming at."

"Is that true, General?" Kenny said. "You missed on purpose?"

I said, "I don't miss."

Kenny cackled.

"No, of course you don't," Kenny said. "My mistake."

"Get up," I said. "Or the next round goes right between your beady little eyes."

Kenny didn't get up.

"I just need ten seconds," Kenny said. "How can that possibly hurt?"

I grimaced, then pretended to give some thought to what Kenny had said.

"Fine," I said. "Ten seconds. But not a second more."

"There's another country fairly close to us that both the U.S. and

China have good diplomatic relations with," Kenny said. "I believe you and I can trust that country to let us go our separate ways after we land within its borders."

Jeff said into his headset, "He say Costa Rica, it gonna be me who shits his pants."

I said to Kenny, "This country have a name?"

"Costa Rica," Kenny said.

I looked as skeptical as I could manage.

"Jeff, you hear that?" I said into my headset.

"Looks like you got him in the palm of your hand," Jeff said. "However, I do want to be clear. I was speaking metaphorically when I say I be shitting my pants."

I nodded my head as if Jeff had said something important. At that point I probably could have agreed to Costa Rica with Kenny, but I still felt I needed to hold off, if only for a few more moments. Kenny had to believe he had won a hard-fought battle, and not suspect for a moment that when I agreed to his plan that his plan was also my plan, and exactly what I had wanted him to do all along. I decided my best bet to prevent any such potential suspicion was to hit him with a one-two punch.

I delivered punch number one by saying, "Sorry, Jeff says no go to Costa Rica. He continues to insist we're just wasting time since Dr. Lennon and Billy are probably already as good as dead." I then put my eye against the sight of my AK, which I had kept pointed at Kenny's forehead, and added, "Now, get the hell up."

Kenny acted like he hadn't heard me. He remained in his seat and appeared to be continuing, now somewhat desperately, to try to come up with an offer he could sell me on.

I delivered punch number two by pretending to be receiving some additional communication over my headset.

"Repeat that please, General," I said. I shook my head. "This Liu guy is a piece of shit. I don't trust him farther than I can throw him...Uh huh...Uh huh...Sorry, sir, but I can't do that."

Bryce Wellington, who had been listening intently to my every word, said, "Jack, who are you talking to?"

"None of your goddamned business, Bryce," I said.

"It's Hart, isn't it?" Bryce said.

Hart was exactly who I had hoped Bryce would think I was talking to.

Kenny said to Bryce, "Is Hart the man you said was Wilder's commanding officer?"

"Yes, Kenny, he is," Bryce said.

I said, "Shut up, Bryce."

"Let me talk to Hart, please," Bryce said. "Kenny's an asshole, but he's also a man of his word. I'm sure I can convince Hart of that."

"What the hell do you know about being a man of your word, Bryce?" I said. I pretended to be listening to something else coming through my headset. "No, sir. I would not disobey an order, sir. But, with all due respect, I think it would be a bad order, sir."

I continued to listen some more to the nonexistent voice coming over my headset. Out of the corner of my eye, I noticed Carter studying me as if I was some opponent sitting across a poker table from him. I had expected him to do that and had been keeping my best poker face on. Whether it would turn out to be good enough, I'd know soon enough.

"Alright, sir, I'll ask him," I said into the headset. I turned to Kenny. "My superior says we might be able to make a deal to get you to your plane and then on to..."

Carter interrupted, saying, "Kenny, something's wrong here. Whatever they're offering, I wouldn't take it."

Kenny said, "And you know this how, Carter?"

"I can tell Wilder is lying," Carter said.

I suddenly heard the sound of approaching sirens. Kenny, Carter, and Bryce turned their heads in the direction the sirens were coming from, so I assumed that they had heard them too. The sirens' sounds seemed to push Bryce into a desperation bordering on hysteria.

Bryce screamed, "How can you possibly know that Carter?! Are you a mind reader? Don't you hear those sirens? Don't you understand we need to get out of here?!"

"Calm down, Bryce," Carter said. "If we make a mistake now, it could be fatal."

"Staying here until the cops get here is what will be fatal!" Bryce said. He turned to Kenny. "Please Kenny. I know Hart. He's an honorable man. He'll do what he says."

Kenny said, "Be quiet please, Bryce." Kenny seemed to go into a trance and his face became almost inscrutable. He actually looked for a moment - I hate to say it - like I imagined an ancient emperor might have looked. He put a hand up to his ear and seemed to be listening to something. Whether it was to the sirens, to the voices of his ancestors, or both, I'll never know. Finally, he faced Carter and said, "Unfortunately, Carter, I think we are just about out of time. I trust your judgment, my friend, but unless you have a better idea, I think we have to listen to what General Hart has in mind."

Carter said, "I don't have a better idea."

Bryce said, "Thank God!"

Kenny said, "Alright, please General, please tell us what your commander said."

I said, "First off, give both Dr. Lennon and Billy the antidote, right now."

"I'd like to hear the rest of the deal first," Kenny said.

"My superior's terms are non-negotiable," I said.

Kenny appeared to study me. He looked very much like a man caught between a rock and a hard place. I thought for a moment Kenny might kiss off my imaginary General Hart's terms and take his chances with the Los Angeles Police Department. But then, with a nearly imperceptible grimace, Kenny got up out of his chair, took the vial of antidote out of his mouth, and grabbed a syringe off the redwood coffee table. He inserted the syringe's needle into the vial's rubber needle port, injected air into the vial, tapped the vial to send the bubbles to the vial's bottom, and withdrew all the vial's contents. He walked over to Kate, jabbed her upper arm with the needle, injected half the syringe's contents into her arm, and then did the same with Billy.

"Thank you," I said. "I next need to have your assurance that you have access to additional antidote for the RZ 119."

Kenny cackled.

"General Hart is clearly much smarter than you Wilder!" Kenny said.

I didn't say anything.

"There, there, little man," Kenny said. "Do not sulk. I was only referring to the fact that you never thought once to mention the problem of additional antidote - without which of course both Dr. Lennon and Billy Einstein would die - yet your commanding officer instantly hit upon the issue. You were born to be a subordinate, Wilder!"

Jeff said into my headset, "Kenny saying you were born to be subordinate to an imaginary General Hart you just cooked up on the other end of the phone line?"

"Looks that way, Jeff," I said.

"That's actually an interesting idea," Jeff said. "How that be working going forward?"

"I don't have a clue," I said.

"It kinda like that Jimmy Stewart film, 'Harvey,'" Jeff said. "The one that got the talking rabbit."

"I could see that," I said.

Haley said into my headset, "Would you guys mind focusing on the job at hand? We really are running out of time."

Adelaide said into my headset, "As I said before, Major Haley, they're incapable of focusing on anything. It's the bane of my existence."

"Mine too, Adelaide," Haley said. "Mine too."

Kenny said, "Are you talking to your negro friend again?"

"You're a slow learner, aren't you Kenny?" I said. "Like I told you before, Jeff's an African American. And Hart says cut the shit. Do you have the additional antidote or not?"

"It's on our plane, General," Kenny said. "But do not think for a moment that you can access it on your own. Only I can open the case that holds the additional vials of antidote. If anyone else tampers with the case in an attempt to open it, the case will destroy the vials."

I rolled my eyes.

"Where'd you get that idea?" I said. "From a James Bond movie?"

"Yes," Kenny said. "I happen to like James Bond movies."

"I guess that explains a lot," I said. "Hart has one additional term."

"Yes?" Kenny said.

"This little vendetta of yours against Paul Lennon stops," I said. "No going after Dr. Lennon, her kids, or Paul Lennon's sister, Professor Margaret Lennon, at any point in the future."

"Not sure I can agree to that," Kenny said.

"No deal then," I said.

Kenny appeared to think. He put his hand up to his ear. Unlike the previous time Kenny had done that, this time I was sure he had no interest in the sirens, and was, indeed, almost certainly listening to the voices of his ancestors. After a moment, Kenny put his hand down.

"Fine, fine," Kenny said. "My illustrious brother advises me he is very proud that I will soon fulfill my destiny as emperor. He says Lennon's relatives are not worth any more of my time."

"Good, your brother sounds like a smart guy," I said. I pretended to listen to my headset for a few seconds, then nodded my head as if I was acknowledging what the imaginary person on the other end of the line was saying to me. "Hart says we've got a deal. We'll leave for the airport immediately. I should warn you, though, that if you don't give Dr. Lennon and Billy the antidote the moment we get on the plane, I've been ordered to shoot all three of you."

Bryce appeared to shudder.

"General, I am not an idiot," Kenny said. "Do you think I don't know that once we leave here I will still need living hostages in order to continue to effectuate my escape?"

"I don't know what you know, Kenny," I said. "Now, let's get moving." Into my headset I added, "Manu and Mosi please come into the living room as fast as you can. We're leaving with Dr. Lennon and Billy and I'll need some help carrying them."

Mosi said into my headset, "On our way. Ten four."

Adelaide said, "Goddamnit!"

I said, "Kenny and Carter, please take the cartridges out of those Glocks, then remove the tape holding the guns to Dr. Lennon's and Billy's heads."

Kenny said, "That wasn't part of the deal."

"Don't screw around, Kenny," I said. "It's too dangerous to move Dr. Lennon and Billy with the guns in place."

"You should have thought of that before we closed the deal, then," Kenny said. "Those Glocks were a key component in my decision making. An extra bit of insurance that you will do as I say."

"But you control the antidote with your goddamned James Bondian villainous booby trap for Chrissakes," I said. "That should be plenty of insurance."

"No Glocks, no deal," Kenny said.

I didn't say anything. Transporting Kate and Billy with the Glocks taped to their heads and Bryce Wellington's hands was extremely dangerous. But, with the fire trucks' sirens growing louder with each passing second, I didn't feel like I had any time to argue with Kenny.

Seemingly reading my mind, Kenny put a hand to his ear as if listening for something.

"Hmm," Kenny said. "What's that I hear? Sounds like those fire trucks are getting very close..."

"Fine," I said. "Either one of those Glocks goes off though, Kenny, the shot is the last thing you'll ever hear."

"Anyone ever tell you you have a flair for the dramatic, Wilder?" Kenny said.

I said nothing.

"Have trouble taking a compliment, do we?" Kenny said.

I still said nothing.

"Alright, be that way," Kenny said. "I'm ready to go if you are. You will advise your negro friend Jeff and the girl sharpshooter not to fire once we get outside?"

"I will," I said. "However, if you keep calling Jeff a negro, I'll tell them both to blow your goddamned head off."

CHAPTER 130

Kenny 'Dragon Man' Liu, Carter Bowdoin, Bryce Wellington, and I, along with Manu and Mosi assisting with Kate and Billy - Kate, Billy, and Bryce still linked together by the Glocks duct taped to Kate's and Billy's heads and Bryce's hands - exited the ranch house's front door and then immediately headed for the Suburban that would take us to the Van Nuys Airport. The Suburban was sporting the fresh spares that Manu and Mosi had used to replace its shot-out tires. Haley had said we had at most sixty seconds before the first fire trucks arrived, and the sound of blaring sirens grew louder and louder by the moment.

The Suburban's windows were heavily tinted so no one would be able to see inside the SUV while we were driving to the airport. I also didn't want anyone to see the Glocks that were taped to Kate, Billy, and Bryce when we transferred the three of them from the Suburban to Carter and Kenny's jet. I'd taken three blankets from one of the ranch house's bedrooms to cover up their heads and shoulders during the transfer.

Kenny Liu had also taken something with him when he had left the house. His dragon mask. He was cradling it under his left arm as he climbed into the Suburban's front passenger seat. If it hadn't been for the fact that Kenny still had Bryce's dog shock collar remote taped to his forearm, and that Kate and Billy still needed the antidote once we got to the jet, I'm sure I would have killed Kenny the moment he'd picked up the mask from the living room floor.

Cradling the blankets, and with my AK's strap draped over my shoulder, I scrambled in through the Suburban's rear doors. I then climbed over the tops of the seats in the middle row and into the SUV's back passenger compartment. From there I would be able to keep a watch on everything that went on in front of me, and hopefully be able to control Kenny, Carter, and/or Bryce if they should decide to misbehave.

Carter jumped behind the wheel of the Suburban. Manu and Mosi gently lifted, pushed, and pulled Bryce, Kate, and Billy into the middle seat. When Manu and Mosi were done, I shouted, "Close those doors, men, then get into the Maybach and hightail it up to the fire road where you'll meet up with Adelaide and Jeff. All four of you will stay there until Haley gets someone to pick you up, which should be very soon. My main concern now, however, is that you two get out of here before the firemen arrive and notice that the Maybach looks like someone used it for target practice. If they do, they'll tell the cops what they saw, and the cops will feel a need to investigate. That's something we don't want." I paused, then added to Haley, who I was sure had heard everything, as I was still connected to her, along with Adelaide, Jeff, and the twins via my headset and cell phone, "Haley, I'm correct in saying you'll have someone at the fire road very soon?"

"Everything has already been arranged," Haley said. "ETA less than fifteen minutes."

"Thanks," I said. "Manu and Mosi, since there won't be anything you need to hear on the conference line from now on, please disconnect yourselves. Haley will contact you directly on your cells."

The giant twins nodded, slammed shut the SUV's middle seat doors, and ran for the Maybach.

"Adelaide and Jeff, you heard all that too, correct?" I said into my phone.

Jeff said, "Loud and clear. I'll be at the fire road when Manu and Mosi arrive."

Adelaide said, "How do you want me to get to the fire road?"

I said, "Move down off your perch, circle around the back of the ranch house, and then scramble up the other side canyon to the fire road."

"Got it," Adelaide said.

"Good," I said. "Also please stay under the cover of the brush the whole time, because I don't want any firemen or policemen to see you."

"Duh," Adelaide said.

Carter put the Suburban into gear and we took off across the polo field towards the compound's driveway. Carter drove fast, but not recklessly. He dodged the flaming Humvee, Igla SSM debris, and the carcasses of the dead mercenaries strewn across the surface of the field, all the while seeming to take care not to jolt the car in any way that might upset Bryce Wellington's trigger fingers.

Outside the Suburban, the fires continued to rage on the polo field's perimeter. The searing heat from the fires radiated inward from the

Suburban's windows. The fires' smoke, which was seeping in through the Suburban's air vents, continued to reek of a strange brew of eucalyptus oil, human flesh, and diesel and jet fuel.

I looked behind me. Manu, with Mosi riding shotgun, was keeping the Maybach close to us as he navigated the bullet-ridden car through the debris strewn polo field.

When our Suburban reached the compound's driveway and its relatively smooth surface, Carter gradually increased the SUV's speed and we rapidly moved away from the polo field and down towards the public street fronting the compound. Upon reaching the street, Carter turned left and we headed in a direction that would take us back to Topanga Canyon Boulevard. Manu and Mosi turned right, taking the route that would return them to the fire road.

We saw the first fire truck when we were about a hundred yards away from the compound. Siren raging and lights flashing, it flew by us, the firemen inside it barely paying us any heed. Four more fire trucks quickly followed in a line. There were as yet no police cars in sight, but I was sure there would soon be an armada of such cars racing to the compound.

It was then 3:38 p.m. Only a little more than two hours and twenty minutes were left before war with China was set to break out. The drive to Van Nuys Airport would take about forty-five minutes. Assuming all went well, the freeing of Kate and Billy and the completion of the entire Kinshasa process would take at least another hour after we reached the airport. Best case scenario then was going to be that I would have about thirty-five minutes left before the war started to try to beat out of Carter Bowdoin, Kenny 'Dragon Man' Liu, and Bryce Wellington whatever they knew about the insurmountable edge.

I continued to believe that beating them wouldn't do much good, however. I had three good reasons to back up that belief -

One, torture was a tricky proposition at best when it came to producing any intel of value.

Two, based on the three men's statements and behavior back in the ranch house living room, there was a reasonable chance that none of them knew much about the way the edge actually worked.

And three, for an interrogation to be effective, days, if not weeks, are often needed. The odds were that thirty-five minutes wasn't going to cut it.

The Suburban reached Topanga Canyon Boulevard and blended into the flow of traffic. We headed north towards the San Fernando Valley, retracing the path Adelaide, Jeff, and I had followed in the Kazakhs' van about two hours earlier. Carter, Kenny, and Bryce, perhaps consumed by their own internal thoughts, hadn't spoken since we left the compound.

Adelaide, Haley, Jeff, and I hadn't communicated to each other either. If we had, it would have been by text, however. All three of us knew it was possible, due to the close quarters within the Suburban, that Carter, Kenny, and Bryce might be able to pick up on any voice communications coming over my headset's earphones. That was something we didn't want to risk happening, and was why I had already taken off my headphones and tossed them in the Suburban's rear storage space.

The three of us had also decided to limit our texts to only absolutely essential communications. The fewer texts I saw, the less chance there was for their content to play across my features. Carter had gotten a great read on me in the ranch house living room and still appeared to be studying me - he spent almost as much time looking at me in the rearview mirror as he did keeping his eyes on the road - and I didn't trust myself to maintain a perfect poker face for the entire trip.

A text, however, was coming in right at that moment.

I waited until Carter turned his attention back to the road, then glanced down at my iPhone's screen.

"Carter and Kenny's normal flight crew will greet you upon arrival at Van Nuys Airport. Mechanics are ours. I'm texting copies of the diplomatic passports to you now," Haley's text read.

All of which was good news.

It meant Kinshasa was proceeding as planned.

I watched as the passport copies arrived on my phone, then looked up at Carter. He was still looking at the road and appeared not to have noticed me reading the text. I tried to keep a stone face despite the good news, but had no idea if I had been successful or not.

I had also kept an eye on Kate and Billy ever since we had left the compound, but had not checked their vital signs as I was afraid of what

I might find. Not checking was a coward's way out, however, and not in any way consistent with what I thought of as my duty. Unable to abide such a weak version of myself any longer, I leaned my head next to Kate and put my cheek next to hers.

Kate's skin was still cold as ice.

I gently placed my finger on her neck and felt for her carotid.

Her pulse was eighteen beats a minute, which was slower than before.

I fought off a feeling of rising panic and counted her breaths.

They were still three a minute.

The world seemed to begin to violently spin around me. My heart raced and I felt like I was gasping for air. I began to think there was no way I could survive unless I was somehow able to get out of the Suburban and into the fresh air.

Another part of me knew there wasn't anything wrong with me, however, and that was the part to which I listened. Breathing as deeply as I could, I forced myself to do the right thing, which was to check on Billy next.

I touched his forehead, then took his carotid pulse and counted his breaths. Billy was still cold, and his heart rate and respiratory rate were as horribly slow and weak as they had been in the ranch house.

I noticed Carter looking at me in the rearview mirror. His face betrayed nothing, but how could he not see my distress? Fine, I thought to myself, good for him. He'd reaffirmed that I cared about Kate and Billy and that they both were in terrible shape.

But in the end, whatever he believed he knew wasn't going to make a whit of difference, was it?

Kinshasa was still in store for the asshole, no matter what happened to Kate and Billy.

I suddenly felt like I desperately needed to contact Haley again. If only to give me hope that things weren't as bad as they seemed for Kate and Billy. Since my emotions were already on my sleeve, there wasn't anything left to hide from Carter.

What harm could contacting Haley do?

As long as I was contacting Haley, shouldn't I also include Adelaide and Jeff in my message to her?

The more minds, the merrier, right?

My hands shaking, I texted Haley, and included Adelaide and Jeff, "Haley. Dr. Lennon and Billy are unchanged. Does that mean antidote failed? Are they going to die?"

I knew as I wrote the words that I was being completely unprofessional - acting like an idiot, even - but honestly, right then, I didn't care. I was scared to death. I continued to breathe deeply as I waited for Haley's response.

After what seemed like eons, but in reality couldn't have been more than a minute, Haley texted back, "Docs are uncertain what it means. Antidote can take some time to work. Hang in there."

Hang in there?

How the hell was I going to do that?

Another text came in, this one from Jeff -

"They ain't gettin' worse. I take that as a positive. Keep breathing... And stop actin' like an idiot. You the greatest soldier who ever lived. Just do your thing."

I stared at the words. Greatest soldier who ever lived? That was laying it on a little thick wasn't it? And if Jeff felt he had to say that, didn't it mean Jeff had to think that I'd completely lost it? That I'd passed from the realm of the presumably somewhat sane to the land of the entirely unhinged?

Was I really that bad?

I looked down at my hands.

They were still shaking.

I tried to steady them.

If anything they shook more strongly.

Oh my God!

Jeff was right.

I'd completely lost it.

"Was this it?" I said to myself.

Was I really down for the final count?

Just one more beaten, barely conscious fighter sprawled on the canvas mat in a boxing ring, the referee shouting nine, the fighter knowing full well that the next number about to come out of the ref's mouth was ten, the doomed, immutable, unredeemable sentence bestowed upon all of the world's wretched losers?

I looked back up at Carter.

He was smirking.

Carter thought he'd won.

He'd beaten me, and he was on top of the world.

Somewhere deep inside me, my blood began to boil.

Who the hell did Carter think he was?

Did Carter actually believe he could defeat the greatest soldier who ever lived?

Strike that.

The two greatest soldiers who ever lived?

The second one being Jeff, of course.

I may be acting like an idiot, but Carter *was* an idiot.

An idiot who clearly had never been a student of the sayings of Yogi Berra, the immortal Yankee manager, and a man who had far more valuable things to say about the art of war than that other idiot, Sun Tzu.

My hands still shaking, I texted, "It ain't over 'til it's over."

"When you come to a fork in the road, take it," came the text back from Jeff.

"Baseball is ninety percent mental and the other half is physical," I texted back.

"Always be goin' to other people's funerals, otherwise they ain't be goin' to yours," Jeff answered.

Which wasn't quite the exact quote, having been altered by Jeff-speak.

It was good enough for me, however.

My confidence had reawakened.

I felt a smile start to form on my lips.

But I suppressed it.

I was Mr. Poker Face again.

No reason to let Carter have any idea that the reawakening of my confidence, and indeed, the rejuvenation of my brutal, fighting spirit, made me feel like I'd drawn to, then hit, an inside straight.

True, there was nothing I could do then until Kinshasa had been fully implemented, but when it was...

BAM!

Carter Bowdoin was a dead man.

BAM!

Kenny 'Dragon Man' Liu was a dead man.

BAM!

And, yes, even the ever-pathetic Bryce Wellington was a dead man.

BAM! BAM! BAM!

Still, there wasn't any reason to get *over*-confident. I knew I was so mentally weak that I could be blown back down to the depths again by even the slightest negative thought wafting through my mind. I needed to keep my internal ruminations away from a world in which Kate no longer lived. I came to the realization that what I really needed to do was concentrate all my energy on keeping Kate alive rather than on my own selfish fears about her possible death.

Given the deadly, powerful nature of the drugs that were in Kate's system, I knew there wasn't much I could do for her other than pray. I was about to start praying, but then remembered something I had tried on my wounded battlefield comrades who had fallen into unconsciousness on the battlefield and were near death. It was something I had tried after reading that people in comas could at times respond to words of loving encouragement whispered in their ears. Those comatose people responded to the words despite the seeming impossibility of them comprehending anything being said to them, respond so positively in fact, they occasionally even woke up. It seemed to have worked on some of my dying comrades - they awakened and went on to survive against what had appeared to be insurmountable odds.

I leaned forward once again, and, not giving a damn if anyone heard me, whispered into Kate's ear, "I love you. You're going to be fine and we're going to have a long and happy life together. A very long and very happy life."

Which, of course, were not the exact words I said to my dying comrades, but they weren't that much different either.

I swear I think Kate stirred, if only for a second. I said the same three sentences over and over to her ten more times. Kate did not stir again, but I convinced myself that first stirring meant there was hope.

I put my mouth close to Billy's ear. I whispered, "Stay with me buddy. I'm gonna get you out of this."

Billy didn't move at all, but I repeated that phrase to him ten more times, just like I had done for Kate, then sat back in my seat. Time would tell what each of their fates would be, but for the moment, it was time to start praying for them.

And pray is what I did.

I was still praying when we crested the Santa Monica Mountains and began the long downward slope along Topanga Canyon Boulevard as it headed into the San Fernando Valley. I checked the time on my iPhone. We still had about thirty minutes before we arrived at the airport. I watched Carter as he drove. He was moving the Suburban smoothly through the winding curves of the boulevard. He seemed to be enjoying himself, as if driving was what he was born to do. Carter also seemed not to have a care in the world.

We came to a particularly sharp bend. To navigate the bend, Carter had to turn the steering wheel in a larger arc than he had so far been required to do. In turning the wheel he had also had to extend his arm farther than he had previously extended it. The sleeve of his blue blazer pulled back off his wrist to reveal he was wearing a watch.

It was a different watch than I'd seen Carter wearing before.

The watch was a gold racing watch, with multiple interior dials on its face that could keep track of lap times. The watch also had a black band.

Hadn't Bobby and Timmy said the Caucasian man driving Dragon Man's party bus at the stoning site had been wearing a watch?

A gold racing watch with lots of big dials and a black band?

I felt sour bile rise in my throat.

Carter had to have been Dragon Man's driver, didn't he?

Wasn't it also likely then that the second 'American' man Bobby and Timmy said had stayed within the bus was Bryce Wellington?

Which meant Carter and Bryce had been there when Sam and Lizzy were killed.

Carter Bowdoin and Bryce Wellington had watched Sam and Lizzy being stoned, their tiny bodies ripped apart, and their faces mutilated almost beyond recognition.

That sudden realization nearly catalyzed me beyond my breaking point. It took every bit of self control I had to keep myself from leaping across the seats and strangling both Carter and Bryce right then and there. I once again took deep breaths to try to calm myself, just like

I had done only minutes earlier, and countless other times over the course of those past few days.

Patience, I counseled myself as I breathed. What did the Sicilians say? Revenge was a dish best served cold? I could lower the temperature at least for a little while couldn't I? Carter and Bryce would soon get theirs if all went according to plan, wouldn't they? And as for Carter, if he loved to drive so much, I could let him have this last little driving adventure, couldn't I? After all, it was only going to be the driving equivalent of a condemned man's last meal, wasn't it?

My breathing and those cheering thoughts had the desired effect.

I began to relax.

But then I started wondering about how Carter could be as calm and cool as he appeared. Kenny had made it clear that Beijing was the ultimate destination of his and Carter's jet after it stopped in Costa Rica to drop off Kate, Billy, and me. I had believed Kenny about that final destination, as, after all, where else in the world would he, Carter, and Bryce be safe once the U.S. government learned of what the three of them had done?

Didn't Carter have to know that once he arrived in China the odds of him ever returning to the United States were practically zero? What kind of life was he planning to live in China? Did he really trust Kenny not to betray him once he got there?

I supposed Bryce Wellington was in the same spot as well. I knew the three of them would never get to China if Kinshasa went as planned, but I suddenly had an overwhelming need to know what they were thinking. And so driven by my curiosity, I, perhaps cruelly, and also perhaps against my better judgment, asked.

"Carter," I said. "There's something I don't get."

"Yes, General?" Carter said, his voice sounding as merry as he looked. "What is that?"

"Your final destination is China, correct?" I said.

"Yes," Carter said. "I certainly can't come back to the States, not for a while anyway."

"What makes you think you can trust Kenny to keep you safe in China?" I said. "I mean, there must be a lot of money at stake. Why would he share?"

Kenny cackled and turned around in his seat to face me.

"Trying to divide and conquer, are we General?" Kenny said.

"Would you begrudge me such a time-honored tactic, Kenny?" I said.

"Time-honored as it may be, it won't work here," Kenny said. "Carter, you agree, don't you?"

Carter said, "Yep."

"Why not?" I said.

Kenny said, "Because, as we very clearly told you before, Carter knows I am a man of my word." He looked at Bryce Wellington, and laughing, added, "Of course in Bryce's case I might make an exception."

Bryce said nothing. He appeared to quietly fume.

I said, "If you're such a man of your word, why did Carter need you to make a special trip with him all the way to the Banco Mundo de Panama in Panama City to sign a contract between your company and his?"

Carter laughed.

"Kenny, it looks like your super secret Panamanian connection wasn't so super secret after all," Carter said. "Guess that makes us even in the screw-up department."

Kenny shrugged his shoulders.

"C'est la vie," Kenny said. "Banco Mundo de Panama for me, Doctor of Mercy jet for you." He paused, seeming to think about something for a moment, then added, "General, it's really none of your business, but rather than bear the pain of having to be on the receiving end of any gloating on your part, I feel I must inform you that you have entirely misread that contract."

"How so, Kenny?" I said.

"That contract was a demand made upon me by my mother and father, who as I am sure you know, since you seem to know everything else, are the major shareholders in my company, the Golden Dragon Fund," Kenny said. "And the reason they wanted it," he paused again - I supposed for dramatic effect - then waved his hand in the air like an impresario, "was because they did not trust Carter!"

Kenny cackled again.

"Is that the same father who was one of Mao's right-hand men?" I said.

"Of course!" Kenny said. "I don't know about you, but I only have one father." Kenny laughed so hard I thought he might choke to death. Which wouldn't have been a bad thing, but it's not what happened. Instead, Kenny seemed to regain control of himself and continued, "You must not say anything against my father, as that would make me very angry. He, or should I say, his relationship with Chairman Mao, is after all the reason I am a princeling. True, some may use that phrase in a derogatory fashion, but I am proud of it, especially as I am a princeling soon to become an emperor in his own right." Kenny paused. "By the way, General, do you know how old the Kingdom of Saudi Arabia is?"

"I don't know," I said. "Ninety years?"

"Close enough," Kenny said. "Do you know how long the Great House of Qin Shi Huang has been in existence?"

"Why don't you tell me?" I said.

"For over two thousand two hundred years," Kenny said.

"Your point being?" I said.

"My point being," Kenny said, "that the so-called kings of Saudi Arabia were busy riding around on disgusting camels and pitching filthy tents in the desert until ninety years ago when someone told the foolish clowns they were sitting on a few hundred billion barrels of oil. If the Saudis hadn't been told about the oil, they wouldn't even have known the oil was there, and they'd still be living in filthy tents and riding around on disgusting camels. In all the time the Saudis have existed, that's all they have ever contributed to the world - camels, tents, and oil. On the other hand, The Great House of Qin Shi Huang has for the last two thousand two hundred years been a beacon for all of mankind in the fields of mathematics, medicine, philosophy, science, and the arts."

"I'm surprised you didn't bring up Sun Tzu," I said.

"Sun Tzu was before Qin's time," Kenny said. "Sun Tzu was also an idiot."

"You'll get no argument from me there," I said. "So you're saying the Saudis are essentially nobodies when stacked up against the Qins?"

"Correct," Kenny said. "The Saudis are an abhorrent aberration, a mere speck of history. The entire lot of them will be obliterated at 6:00 p.m. tonight."

"And following such obliteration, his heavenly ordained highness, Kenny Liu, direct descendant of the great Emperor Qin Shi Huang, will be installed as the Emperor of Saudi Arabia?" I said.

"Exactement," Kenny said. Kenny looked down at his watch. "Now, as I calculate it will take us about half an hour to reach the airport, and another six and a half hours to fly to Costa Rica, I suggest you shut your goddamned peasant mouth and simply enjoy basking in the presence of my very royal highness for the next seven glorious hours. I am quite sure it is an opportunity you will never get again."

"From your mouth to God's ears, Kenny," I said. "From your mouth to God's ears."

PART VIII

KINSHASA

CHAPTER 131

The Suburban arrived at the Van Nuys Airport at 4:21 p.m., one hour and thirty-nine minutes before the war with China was scheduled to commence. We stopped at an automatic steel gate that was next to a private terminal building. The terminal building was made of white stone and red glass. Passengers were waiting inside the building for their flights. Private jets were being readied for takeoff on the tarmac on the other side of the steel gate.

Carter Bowdoin rolled down his window and seemed about to speak into a microphone at the gate - I assumed to ask someone to open the gate for the Suburban - but he stopped and turned towards me instead.

"General," Carter said, "before we get on that plane I need you to confirm one thing."

Kenny Liu said, "Carter, can't it wait? The sooner we get airborne, the better I'll feel."

"That's exactly what my question for the general is about," Carter said. "I want to be sure we're actually headed for Costa Rica."

"Where else would we be headed?" Kenny said.

"May I ask my question, please?" Carter said.

Kenny rolled his eyes.

"Fine, whatever," Kenny said.

"General, I assume you know that in order to land in Costa Rica we will need some kind of visa?" Carter said.

Carter's question was exactly the one Jeff had predicted Carter would ask.

"My team did inform me of something along those lines, yes," I said. "But they didn't say visas. They said diplomatic passports."

"Thank you," Carter said. "I stand corrected. Did your team send you those passports?"

"They did," I said.

I took out my iPhone and pulled up the copies of the diplomatic passports Haley had texted me. I extended my arm across the middle seat and pointed the phone's screen toward Carter. Carter shifted around in the driver's seat, leaned his head toward the phone, and looked very closely at the passports. Kenny, who still seemed annoyed at Carter for wasting time by inquiring about the passports, didn't bother to look. A moment later, Carter grimaced and pulled his head back. Kenny shot him a glance.

Kenny said, "You don't seem happy, Carter."

"I'm not," Carter said.

"The passports didn't look real?" Kenny said.

"Oh, they look real," Carter said. "I just still don't trust this whole thing."

"What's there not to trust?" Kenny said.

"I don't know," Carter said. "But it sure seems like they're letting us off the hook too easy after everything we've done."

"You're misanalyzing the situation, Carter," Kenny said.

"I am, am I?" Carter said.

"Yes," Kenny said. "One, they're not letting us off the hook, since we were never on. Two, they know who our families are, so they know there is nothing they could have ever done to us. Three, they know there is nothing they can do about the insurmountable edge, so right now all they're concerned about is cutting their losses."

"You mean Dr. Lennon?" Carter said.

"Love is a powerful thing, Carter," Kenny said. "If we don't go to Costa Rica, Dr. Lennon doesn't get the antidote. If she doesn't get the antidote, she dies."

"You think Wilder loves Dr. Lennon that much that he'd let us go in order to save her life?" Carter said.

"I thought you were a master reader of human character, Carter," Kenny said. "Do you really need to ask me that?"

Carter didn't say anything. Instead, he turned towards me and stared at me long and hard. I kept my best stone face on. Carter broke his stare and emitted a loud sigh.

"I hope you're right about this, Kenny," Carter said.

"I am right, Carter," Kenny said. "We have nothing to worry about."

Carter leaned out the window and spoke into the gate's microphone. The gate swung open and we drove across the tarmac, coming to a stop when we were within twenty yards of Pennsylvania Avenue Partners' Gulfstream G650 jet. The Gulfstream was parked among half a dozen other private jets.

Overhead, the blue sky was filled with clouds that were light and wispy. A flock of seagulls passed under the clouds. The gull's high-pitched squawks filtered into the Suburban's cabin. Heat waves rose from the asphalt beneath the Gulfstream G650's wings, and the late afternoon sun threw long shadows off both the jet and the Suburban. The scent of jet fuel was heavy in the air.

A few mechanics were at work in the large hangars lining the east side of the airport, some cars were scattered near the hangars, and a security guard was patrolling the hangars' entrances. A Lear business jet was taxiing to the north end of the airport's concrete runway in preparation for takeoff.

Nothing looked out of place, nothing was out of the ordinary, nothing called attention to itself.

Which was the way things would be if all was well with Kinshasa.

But it was also the way things would be if Kinshasa had not proceeded as planned either.

Haley must have been reading my mind. She texted me right at that moment.

"Everything is ready," the text said. "Have a nice flight."

The everything ready part of her text was fine. But have a nice flight? There were still too many things that could go wrong that would have the potential of making the flight anything but nice.

A pretty blond-haired, blue-eyed female flight attendant in a tight fitting, blue and white uniform whose skirt ended above a pair of very fine knees exited the door of the Gulfstream G650 and descended the jet's boarding staircase. She was followed in close order by an equally pretty brown-eyed, brown-haired female flight attendant with equally fine knees, who herself was followed in turn by two men in black pilot uniforms. The pilots' shirts were starched and white, their ties thin and black, and their black hats had gold braid on the brims and gold wings on the crowns.

The flight attendants and pilots approached the Suburban. I hurriedly placed the blankets I had brought with me over the heads and shoulders of Kate, Billy, and Bryce Wellington. Kenny and Carter got out of their respective doors. A blast of hot air shot into the car.

The first pilot to reach the Suburban shook Kenny's hand.

"Good to have you back, sir," the pilot said.

"Nice to be back, Captain Korok," Kenny said. "I assume our flight plan has been approved?"

"Yes," Korok said, "Costa Rica, and then on to Beijing."

"Excellent," Kenny said. "We have three very sick passengers in the back of the car. We will need you to assist in their boarding."

"We were told there would be six passengers, sir, but no one said anything about anyone being sick," Korok said.

Kenny glared at Korok.

"Your point being?" Kenny said.

"Well, sir, it's a long trip," Korok said. "Are you sure they'll be able to make it through the entire flight without having a problem?"

"You'll have to talk to General Wilder about that," Kenny said.

"General Wilder?" Korok said.

"The big guy dressed in the filthy clothes who's in the back seat," Kenny said.

Korok appeared to be about to say something, but held his tongue. Kenny squeezed Korok's cheek.

"That's better," Kenny said. "Now, please load up your passengers. I'd really like to get out of here."

Kenny grabbed his dragon mask. He and Carter strode up the landing stairs and disappeared into the Gulfstream's cabin.

Korok opened the Suburban's right rear door, and keeping a respectful distance as if he was afraid of contracting whatever disease Kate, Billy, and Bryce Wellington were suffering from, looked into the passenger area. Korok appeared to study the odd trio, though such study was complicated by the blanket obscuring everyone's features. Korok's gaze seemed to finally settle on Wellington.

Bryce said, "What are you staring at Korok?"

Korok appeared to startle.

"General Wellington?" Korok said.

"No, it's the Easter Bunny," Bryce said.

"Sorry, sir," Korok said. "Mr. Liu didn't tell me you would be joining us today."

"Mr. Liu didn't tell me you would be joining us today," Bryce said in a whiny, high-pitched imitation of Korok. Then, shifting into his own voice, Bryce continued, "What kind of kiss-ass candy-ass are you anyway, Korok?"

Kiss-ass candy-ass? I'm not sure if I'd be calling the pilot of a jet I was about to board a kiss-ass candy-ass. Call me crazy, but I think I'd like the guy to be calm, confident, and focused on flying the plane and not potentially dwelling on issues of his own self-esteem.

"Sorry, sir," Korok said.

"Please just shut up and help me get these two on the plane," Bryce said. "It's goddamned hot in here."

"Are they asleep, sir?" Korok said. "It might be easier to move them if we woke them up."

"Do they look like they're asleep?" Bryce said.

Bryce appeared to be getting more and more agitated. I spoke before Korok had a chance to answer, afraid that whatever Korok might say could push Bryce over the edge.

I said, "Captain Korok, I'm Jack Wilder. I apologize for my companion's poor manners in failing to introduce us. The woman and the young man on either side of General Wellington are my prisoners, hence the need for my weapon."

Korok's gaze shifted to my AK. His eyes went wide.

"W...w...weapon?" Korok said.

"I assure you Captain Korok I am very experienced with this rifle and you have nothing to worry about," I said. "As I'm sure you noticed, the prisoners are unconscious at the moment. However, they are not sick. We had to give them a sedative to make sure they behaved themselves until we were able to get them onto the plane."

Korok said, "But Mr. Liu said they were quite ill."

"You know Mr. Liu loves to jest," I said.

"Why do they have blankets over their heads if they're not sick?" Korok said.

"The blankets are there in order to avoid prying eyes," I said.

I gently pulled back the portion of the blanket that was covering Kate's head to reveal the Glock taped to her and Wellington. Korok's eyes went wide again.

"General Wellington was kind enough to assist me in guarding the prisoners," I said. "We did not anticipate General Wellington having to keep his arms elevated as long as he has, however, and I'm afraid he has grown a bit testy." I rubbed the top of Wellington's head. "You're a real trooper, Bryce."

"Screw you, Jack," Bryce said.

"You see, Captain Korok?" I said. "Very testy indeed. The sooner we get General Wellington on board and give him a nice stiff drink, the better off we'll all be."

Korok seemed to relax a bit. Perhaps it was because I had given him an assignment that was more in line with his normal duties. He turned to Bryce and said, "Will it be the usual, sir? Glenlivet 25 on the rocks?"

Bryce said, "Goddamnit Korok, just get us out of here!"

"Yes, sir," Korok said. "Sorry, sir."

I said, "Captain, please advise your crew to be very careful not to jostle General Wellington. We don't want those Glocks going off, do we?"

"No, sir," Korok said. "Absolutely not, sir."

"And please keep the blankets in place," I said. "I'd prefer it if no one outside of our little group sees what is going on."

"Understood, sir," Korok said.

Korok and the other pilot helped get Kate, Billy, and Bryce out of the car, then carefully began to assist the trio up the jet's stairway. The two flight attendants, who had been silently watching the proceedings until then, moved to help the pilots, but Korok gestured with his chin towards the Suburban, and the flight attendants remained in place. I supposed that gesture meant Korok wanted the flight attendants to attend to any boarding needs I might have. I didn't have any such needs, but I did decide it was time for me to get moving.

I climbed over the middle seat and out of the car. I saw that the flight attendants were wearing name tags. The blonde's tag said 'Sally' and the brunette's 'Lorna'.

"Good to meet you, Lorna and Sally," I said giving them a big, friendly smile.

The flight attendants didn't seem to notice my smile, however. They appeared fixated instead on my AK-12. Their eyes had opened even wider than Korok's eyes had opened when he first saw the rifle.

"I see you're interested in my gun," I said. "It's a Russian-made AK-12. The AK stands for Avotomat Kalishnikova, which means automatic

Kalishnikov. The Kalishnikov is for Mikhail Kalishnikov who designed it." I paused. "But what am I saying? I'm sure you both already knew that."

Lorna and Sally said nothing.

"Go ahead, keep looking at the rifle all you want," I said. "It's no problem for me. By the way, my name is Jack Wilder. I'm a general in the U.S. Army and I assure you, just as I assured your captain, that I know what I'm doing with this firearm and that you have nothing to fear."

Again not a peep from Lorna or Sally. If I'd had to guess, I would have said that the flight attendants were none too keen on flying with a heavily armed passenger who looked like he had just come from a war zone. I felt my best course of action was to keep smiling and act as if nothing out of the ordinary was going on, so that's what I did. I gestured to the Gulfstream's open door.

"Looks like our friends have boarded," I said. "What say we join them?"

Sally and Lorna didn't move. I got the sense that they were both getting ready to bolt to the parking lot.

Kenny suddenly appeared in the doorway.

"Girls!" Kenny said. "What's the holdup? Get your asses in gear. I really need a drink."

The flight attendants looked at each other. They seemed to share a telepathic moment similar to the ones I had seen Manu and Mosi share. The moment must have led to some kind of unspoken agreement, as, without even a glance at me, they both instantly turned on their heels, went up the jet's stairway, and disappeared into the cabin.

I gave one last look around. The airport appeared to be continuing to function normally. Nothing out of place, nothing out of the ordinary.

Which, again, is exactly how things should have looked if Kinshasa was proceeding without a hitch.

But, again, it would also look exactly the same way if there had been a hitch.

Even though Haley had only a moment ago assured me everything was fine, with so much at stake, I was very tempted to contact her to see if she had encountered any problems with the plan since she had last texted me. I reached for my phone, but didn't complete the motion. I saw that Carter was intently peering at me from one of the plane's windows. As I still couldn't afford for Carter to get a read on what Haley and I were up to, I stuck with my no contact with Haley and MOM protocol.

But just thinking about contacting Haley, along with the uncertainty of my situation, had produced within me an extremely uncomfortable level of anxiety.

I told myself to shut up and stop being a weenie.

I had to do that three times before I had sufficiently calmed myself enough to be able to start climbing the jet's stairs. Upon reaching the G650's doorway, I ducked my head below its arched top, and entered the cabin.

The air inside the cabin was cool and dry and filled with the airplane chemical smell of freshly cleaned carpet and upholstery. Soft lighting came from LED bulbs. There were eight elegant, wide, white leather passenger chairs on swivels - four in the back of the plane and four in front. Placed between the sets of chairs was a white leather couch that could hold four additional passengers. Across from the couch was a teakwood entertainment unit with a large flat screen television. A full wet bar was just in front of the entrance to the cockpit. A plush, deep pile, beige carpet that looked like it had been hand woven ran the length of the cabin's floor. The lavatory was at the rear of the plane behind a teakwood bulkhead.

The pilots were helping situate Kate, Billy, and Bryce onto the white leather couch. Lorna and Sally were already at the bar preparing drinks and pouring mixed nuts into a large silver bowl. Kenny 'Dragon Man' Liu and Carter Bowdoin were in two of the seats at the back of the plane. Both men were reclining and had big smiles on their faces as they watched the goings-on in front of them. Kenny's dragon mask sat in one of the other two seats next to them.

I needed to be sure that the Gulfstream didn't contain any unexpected occupants. I checked the cockpit first. The cockpit's avionics were awash with blue, green, red, orange, and yellow lights but there weren't any people sitting in the cockpit's seats. I walked to the back of the cabin and checked out the lavatory and the baggage compartment. No people there either. I was then confident Kate, Billy, Bryce, Carter, Kenny, Captain Korok, the copilot, and the two flight attendants were the only people on board the Gulfstream besides myself.

I returned to the cabin, walked past Kenny and Carter, and stood next to where Kate, Billy, and Bryce were sitting. I watched the pilots snap Kate's, Billy's, and Bryce's seat belts into place. When the pilots were finished, they went forward and into the cockpit.

I turned to Kenny.

"Kenny," I said, "aren't you forgetting something?"

Kenny wagged a finger at me and laughed.

"No getting anything by you, is there, General?" Kenny said.

I said nothing.

Kenny closed his eyes, leaned farther back in his chair, crossed his right ankle over his left, put his hands behind his head, and spread his elbows wide.

"I'm not saying I won't get the vials of antidote out of their box," Kenny said, his eyes still closed, "but what would you do to me if I decided to take a nap instead?"

I knew what I wanted to do. I wanted to stroll down the aisle and smash the butt end of my AK-12 into Kenny's teeth. But I didn't think that would go over too well with the pilots and the flight attendants, especially since I assumed all of them were probably already on edge due to the curious, dare I say, frightening, spectacle of Kate, Dr. Nimo/Billy, Bryce, and the Glocks. Of course it was also likely my AK wasn't inspiring feelings of good cheer either.

"I'm not going to do anything to you, Kenny," I said, "because I'm expecting you to keep your word. Unless of course all that stuff Bryce and Carter said about you being a man of honor was just a bunch of bullshit."

Kenny smiled.

"Yes, well, I didn't say *when* I'd give the antidote, did I?" Kenny said.

"No, you didn't," I said.

"It seems a grievous error, doesn't it?" Kennys said. "But then again, I'm not surprised. The need to clarify such an important point as when was just too much for your tiny brain to comprehend. I understand how you could make such a mistake, however. You simply assumed logic would dictate that I would provide the antidote as soon as we were on the plane, as to do otherwise, would most likely kill your two friends."

"I wasn't relying on logic, Kenny," I said. "I was relying on self-interest."

"Self-interest?" Kenny said, his eyes still closed.

"Yes," I said. "As it is in your self-interest to keep my friends alive, otherwise I'm going to blow your sorry ass to kingdom come."

"My, my, General," Kenny said. "Sometimes you are so vulgar."

"I'm sorry," I said. "Does my vulgarity disturb you?"

"Not really," Kenny said. "I wouldn't expect anything else from a heathen such as yourself." Kenny opened his eyes and sat up. "Be that as it may, I do see how you could be confused about the timing of my providing the antidote. So, rather than risk you twisting your confusion into some kind of proof that I'm untrustworthy, and then going around badmouthing me with your wholly mistaken impression, I will get the antidote now."

Kenny moved towards the front of the cabin, bent down next to the television, and opened a drawer under the television. The drawer contained a small top-opening safe. Kenny leaned his face in close to the safe - which I assumed was to allow his retina to be scanned - and the safe's door sprung open.

Kenny reached inside the safe and took out a syringe and a vial. The vial looked exactly like the vial that had contained the antidote that Kenny had had in his mouth in the ranch house living room. I could see about eight more similar vials lying in the safe. Haley had said each vial was good for about 45 minutes, so there were more than enough vials to last until Haley obtained more of the antidote from Fort Detrick.

Kenny closed the safe. He took the cap off the syringe's needle, held the vial with its rubber stopper down, inserted the needle, and withdrew about half of the vial's contents.

"I know what you're thinking, General," Kenny said.

"What's that, Kenny?" I said.

"I wish he didn't have that dog collar remote still strapped to his wrist, as otherwise I could rush him right now, take the antidote, and be done with him," Kenny said.

"Close enough," I said.

Kenny cackled.

"We could have been great friends, General," Kenny said. "If only you weren't such a goody two shoes."

Kenny walked over to Kate, jabbed the syringe's needle in her upper arm, and injected its contents. He withdrew the rest of the antidote from the vial, injected Billy as well, put the cap back on the needle, and put the syringe in his jacket coat pocket.

"My honor remains intact," Kenny said.

Sally, the blond flight attendant, approached Kenny. She was carrying a tray which held a glass of amber liquid - which I assumed to be Bryce's Glenlivet - two martinis, and the silver bowl of mixed nuts. Sally handed one of the martinis to Kenny. Kenny took a sip and pointed at the glass of the presumed Glenlivet.

"What's that?" Kenny said.

"General Wellington's drink," Sally said.

Kenny turned to Bryce.

"Are you kidding, Bryce?" Kenny said. "Do you really think I'd let you get drunk with those Glocks taped to your hands?"

Bryce said, "Come on, Kenny, I'm ready to jump out of my skin here."

"And what happens to us if you accidentally kill the hostages, Bryce?" Kenny said. "Have you even given that notion a moment's thought?"

"I can hold my liquor, Kenny," Bryce said.

"Maybe you can and maybe you can't," Kenny said. "I'm not willing to experiment, however. General Wilder, would you like Bryce's Glenlivet?"

"Goddamnit!" Bryce said.

I said, "No thanks, Kenny."

Kenny said, "A Macallan man are you? We have some of that too if you'd like."

"I think I'll wait until we land, if you don't mind," I said.

"Alright," Kenny said. "It would be a shame however to let this fine substance go to waste."

Kenny grabbed the glass of Glenlivet with his free hand, downed the drink in one gulp, and gave the empty glass to Sally.

Bryce said, "Shit, shit, shit!"

"Sally please hand me the tray," Kenny said. "I'll bring Carter his martini and the nuts while you get General Wellington a Coke."

"I don't want a goddamned Coke!" Bryce said.

"Fine," Kenny said. "Sally, forget the Coke."

Sally said, "Yes, sir." She walked back to the galley area.

"What say we get this show on the road, Wilder?" Kenny said.

"That sounds like an excellent idea, Kenny," I said.

Kenny took his seat next to Carter. The two of them toasted each other with the martinis and ate some nuts.

I sat down in a seat on the right side of the aisle and near the cockpit. I swiveled the seat to face the center of the cabin so that I could keep everyone in sight.

Kenny and Carter made another toast, this one directed at me, then snickered, and gave each other a high five.

I imagined I heard Jeff's voice in my head. The voice said, "The truest characters of ignorance are vanity and pride and arrogance."

"Samuel Butler?" I silently answered.

"Uh huh," Jeff's imaginary voice said.

I basked in the glow of getting the correct answer, but then almost immediately found myself wondering if I really could give myself credit for the answer, since it seemed like there was something not quite fair about me answering myself. I decided, however, that the question of whether or not it was fair was potentially a particularly thorny one, both logically and philosophically, and was certainly much too complicated to explore at that present moment. I tabled it for later consideration.

I waited as the pilots went through the last of their checklist before taking off. Through the cabin windows across the aisle from me I could see the homes that dotted the foothills of the San Fernando Valley's northern border. I also watched the comings and goings of flight crews, mechanics, and passengers in the area surrounding the private terminal.

A young man in white overalls climbed into the Suburban we had arrived in, started it up, then drove it out through the automatic steel gate and into the airport parking lot. I presumed he was going to park the Suburban in the lot where it would wait for our return. If all went well with Kinshasa, it was going to be a very, very long wait.

Sally walked up to me and said, "What can I get you to drink?"

Up close I could see her eyes were sapphire blue and that her fine blond hair was her natural color. She stood so close to me I could feel the heat radiating off her body. She appeared much more relaxed around me than she had outside on the tarmac.

"I'm fine, thank you," I said.

"Well, I'm always here if you change your mind," Sally said and smiled. "Oh, and please buckle up. We're about to depart."

"Can't wait," I said.

Sally winked at me and turned on her heel, her very well constructed backside gently brushing my shoulder as she did. The brush almost made me sorry Kinshasa was in play and that I wasn't actually going to be traveling to Costa Rica with her.

Sally and her backside made their way to the cabin door. Sally retracted the staircase, closed the door, and sealed it shut. She took a jump seat outside the cockpit entrance and belted herself in. Lorna quickly joined her.

I heard the engines start up, first one then the other.

Kenny shouted across the cabin.

"Don't feel bad, General," Kenny said. "You almost made it. You did the best you could under the circumstances."

I ignored him.

"You were just overmatched from the start," Kenny continued. "An intelligent man will beat a violent one every time."

I ignored him some more. Kenny chuckled and downed the rest of his martini.

The pilots started to pressurize the cabin and Kinshasa began. I then leaned back in my seat and thought about how I was going to give up control to get control. It sounded very Zen, but it was anything but Zen. The Kinshasa process was very scientific, very technical, and had been rehearsed in training sessions countless times.

As the cabin continued to pressurize, the air coming from the vents became thick and misty, almost fog-like. The fog-like mist was something any veteran air traveler had seen many times and knew that the mist formed when the air outside the plane was humid. Such veteran travelers might have paid the mist heed the first or second time they had seen it, but by the third time, and all times beyond, I doubted anyone even gave the mist a passing thought. Certainly no one on the Gulfstream G650 appeared to pay the mist any heed - not the flight attendants, not Kenny 'Dragon Man' Liu, not Carter Bowdoin, not Bryce Wellington.

I breathed in the mist and slowly started fading. I saw Kenny's head droop and wondered what he would have to say about intelligence when he woke up.

The last thing I did before losing consciousness was text Haley to tell her about the method Kenny had used to open the safe that contained the antidote.

CHAPTER 132

I came to slowly, rising out of a dream in which Grace and the coyote were singing to me. They were singing 'Long Live Rock 'n' Roll', the Rainbow song I had sung to them outside the recording studio. Grace and the coyote had altered the lyrics, however, dropping some and repeating others. What they sang was,

At the end of today

I can feel the sound of writing on the wall...

Like a spiral on the wind...

It was simple but strange...

Simple but strange...

Simple...

I said, "Simple?"

Grace and the coyote nodded.

"You're talking about Billy Einstein, aren't you?" I said.

They both nodded again.

"Yeah, simple is what I was thinking too," I said. "Billy's a genius, and probably really good with the complicated stuff, but he's young. If he made a mistake it would be something simple. What was it?"

Grace and the coyote smiled mysteriously and disappeared.

"Hey, where you guys going?" I said. "Come back!"

They didn't come back.

"Alright, be that way," I said. "I'll figure it out on my own. You'll see."

And then just like that, I was awake, the dream vanishing to wherever dreams go. I was in my seat in the Gulfstream, my head twisted to the right and leaning against the seat's white leather, the leather flattening my right cheek. My mouth felt like it was stuffed with cotton. The only things I could move, and those just barely, were my eyelids and my eyeballs. The air blowing through the cabin's ventilation vents was cool and dry and the fog-like mist had completely vanished. I could hear the hum of the Gulfstream's jet engines and some strange noises coming from behind me. The noises sounded like the muffled guttural intonations of a very angry human.

Someone had reclined my seat after I had fallen asleep and turned it to face forward as well, so that I was then looking out the cabin window on my right side. We were flying on a level course over the Pacific Ocean, perhaps thirty thousand feet above its surface. The sea was a deep ultramarine and the waves were rolling in huge swells with white caps at their crests. The sun was a ball of yellow fire perched in a cloudless azure sky. I estimated by the sun's angle over the horizon that I must have slept for almost an hour. Which would have made the time close to 5:30 p.m. War with China might be only half an hour away.

My sleeping for an hour had been consistent with my exposure to the gas that had come over the vents masquerading as the fog-like mist. The Kinshasa hostage rescue protocol demanded the bad guys holding the hostages be put to sleep quickly and without fail. If even one of the bad guys didn't immediately go to sleep and realized what was happening to them, they could wreak incredible havoc - including possibly killing every hostage and potential rescuers such as myself - during the few seconds they stayed awake before finally succumbing to the gas. The gas used in Kinshasa therefore was both very reliable and very strong. One of the gas's side effects, however, was that it was not easily reversible and that it generally lasted for at least an hour. Of course that side effect affected everyone on board the plane - bad guys, good guys, and hostages alike.

I took the fact I was alive and sitting unbound in my seat to mean Kinshasa had gone at least pretty much as planned. If Kinshasa had gone as planned it also meant I wouldn't be seeing Captain Korok, his copilot, or Lorna and Sally anytime soon. Members of MOM, dressed as paramedics, would have cleared every last bit of sleeping gas from the Gulfstream's cabin while the jet remained parked on the tarmac at the Van Nuys Airport. Then, MOM's team, using a cover story about food poisoning, would have taken Kate, Billy, and all four of the unconscious crew members in ambulances to a local hospital.

The four former Gulfstream crew members were most likely awakening safe and sound at the hospital right at that moment. Billy and Kate, if they ever awakened at all, wouldn't do so for at least forty-eight hours according to what Haley had told me. I gave a silent prayer that 'if they ever awakened at all' would ultimately turn out to have been a meaningless qualifier as it related to Billy's and Kate's fate, and that Billy and Kate would not only awaken soon, but live long and prosper.

Though I couldn't turn my head to verify it, I assumed the guttural noises coming from the back of the plane were being made by either Kenny 'Dragon Man' Liu, Carter Bowdoin, or Bryce Wellington. The three men, unlike me, would be tightly bound.

I slowly rotated my eyes to the left until I was looking at the open cockpit door. The sun's rays shone through the cockpit's windows and reflected off the top of the plane's control console. I couldn't see the pilots' seats, but I did catch a glimpse of a dark hand moving to turn a switch mounted on the cockpit's ceiling.

I took some deep breaths to try to clear the cobwebs from my brain. I moved my tongue around inside my mouth to get rid of the cottony feeling. I struggled to bend and unbend my fingers to get the blood circulating in them. With each passing second I grew more alert and more capable of controlling my movements. I finally was able to slowly rotate my left forearm so that my watch was visible. It was 5:37 p.m. The good news was that I had been close in my estimate. The bad news was that war was then only twenty-three minutes away.

Using all the energy I could muster, I said, "Jeff!"

But it came out as a whisper and I got no response.

I tried again.

"Jeff!" I said.

Louder, but not much, and still no response.

I took in as deep a breath as I could.

"Jeff!" I said.

Jeff's head, a pilot's black cap atop it, suddenly appeared through the open cockpit door. His head was at about waist height - I assumed because he was leaning out of the left pilot's seat - and he smiled broadly at me. Adelaide's head, a set of heavy earphones over her ears, then appeared on top of Jeff's head, so that the two of them looked like a human totem pole. Adelaide was also smiling.

Jeff rose out of his cockpit seat and came towards me. In addition to the cap, he was still wearing the blue jeans, t-shirt, and combat boots he had been given by the hazmat team earlier that morning. As he drew closer, I realized the cap, with its gold braid and wings, looked suspiciously like Korok's.

"Where'd you get the hat?" I said, the strength of my voice having returned nearly to normal.

"Borrow it," Jeff said.

"From Korok?" I said.

"That his name?" Jeff said.

"Doesn't borrowing imply the asking of permission before one takes something?" I said.

"How I be asking permission if he be asleep?" Jeff said.

"Good point," I said. "Anyone else up there in the cockpit besides Adelaide?"

"Nope," Jeff said.

"She's not flying the plane is she?" I said.

"Autopilot," Jeff said.

"Wise," I said. "Did MOM's team get the antidote from Kenny's safe?"

"Uh huh," Jeff said. "They put ol' sleepyhead Dragon Man's eye up to the scanner."

"So the antidote went with Kate and Billy to the hospital?" I said.

"Yep," Jeff said.

"Has the hospital been giving it to Kate and Billy whenever they need it, and does the hospital have enough antidote to last until Haley gets more from Fort Detrick?" I said.

"They have, and they do," Jeff said.

"How are Kate and Billy doing?" I said.

"Haley says they're stable," Jeff said.

"Are they going to live?" I said.

"Look that way," Jeff said.

A wave of relief washed over me. I felt a tear form in the corner of my eye.

"That's great," I said. "I suppose they're still not waking up anytime soon, though?"

"No," Jeff said.

"So unless Haley and her team can find the insurmountable edge in Billy's code, we're going to need to get it out of Kenny, Carter, or Bryce?" I said.

"'Fraid so," Jeff said.

"I assume the three of them are behind me?" I said.

"Uh huh," Jeff said.

Jeff swiveled my seat around to face the rear of the plane.

Kenny 'Dragon Man' Liu, Carter Bowdoin, and Bryce Wellington were sitting next to each other on the couch. Duct tape covered their mouths, lashed their forearms to their thighs, and bound their ankles together. A big swath of duct tape encircled their combined chests and constrained their upper bodies to the couch. A second similar swath constrained their lower legs against the couch as well.

Kenny and Carter were staring at Jeff and me. They appeared relatively calm. Bryce was grunting, looking down at his feet, and struggling mightily against his restraints. I assumed Bryce was the one who had been earlier making the angry human sounds.

"Enjoying the flight so far boys?" I said. "Anything I can get you? Coffee, tea, or me?"

Bryce, upon hearing my voice, instantly raised his face towards Jeff and me. His eyes were wild with panic and he continued to struggle and grunt.

"Bryce, calm down buddy," I said. "I'm afraid you might hurt yourself."

I unbuckled my seat belt and got up out of my chair. I was weak, but felt myself growing stronger with each passing second. I carefully made my way rearwards in the cabin and stood in front of Bryce. He was whipping his head back and forth, and jerking his arms and kicking his legs against his duct tape bindings.

"Dude, we only have about twenty minutes until that war you and your two idiot friends here are trying to instigate breaks out," I said. "I need you to focus so we can stop it, okay?"

Bryce kept whipping, jerking, and kicking.

I drew my right arm back and hit Bryce with a backhand across his face. His head snapped to the side and his body slumped in his seat. He began to whimper.

Carter and Kenny looked at each other and rolled their eyes.

Jeff said, "Dang. How in God's name this piece of shit ever be making it to general in the U.S. Army?"

"I think it had something to do with his father," I said.

"Yeah," Jeff said. "I forgot he were a general too."

"In the loosest sense of the word," I said.

Jeff seemed to think about something. He looked at Carter, then Kenny, then back again at Carter.

"You know," Jeff said, "I'm beginning to see a pattern here I didn't see before."

"Nepotism?" I said.

"Yep," Jeff said. "Bryce's daddy a general, Carter's daddy used to be president of the good ol' USA, and Kenny's daddy why Kenny be a princeling in some kind of quasi-royal Chinese family."

"That's Emperor Kenny to you, General Bradshaw," I said.

"Emperor sans empire," Jeff said.

"'Sans' a good word," I said.

"It is," Jeff said.

I turned to face Kenny, Carter, and Bryce.

"Alright, gentlemen," I said. "I'm going to remove the tape from your mouths now. Anyone misbehaves, it goes right back on."

I tore the tape from their mouths.

Kenny said, "I can't tell you how disappointed I am in you, General Wilder."

"I can't imagine why," I said.

"I thought you were a man of your word," Kenny said.

I felt the floor of the Gulfstream angle slightly downward and to my right. I looked out one of the cabin windows. We were no longer horizontal to the horizon and we were gently moving more westward in relation to the sun. I assumed the autopilot was making a small course correction.

"I believe I am," I said.

"You promised me, that if I gave you the antidote, you would allow me to take our jet to Costa Rica and then on to Beijing," Kenny said.

"No, Kenny, that's not accurate," I said.

"It's not?" Kenny said.

"No, it's not," I said. "I clearly remember you talking a lot about your jet, and where you wanted to go on it, and how if I tried to open the case that held the vials of antidote without you, the case would explode. But all I agreed to do was to get you to the airport without Jeff and Adelaide shooting you as long as you gave Dr. Lennon and Billy the antidote as soon as we got on board your jet."

Kenny didn't say anything. He seemed to be thinking over what I had just said.

"You replaying our conversation in your head?" I said.

"Quiet, please," Kenny said.

A moment later, Kenny nodded.

"It seems I've made a mistake," Kenny said.

Carter Bowdoin said, "That's a pretty big goddamned mistake, Kenny. You screwed us, didn't you?"

"You were there Carter," Kenny said. "You could have said something."

Carter appeared to consider what Kenny had said.

"You're right," Carter said. "Sorry. I take back what I said."

Bryce Wellington looked bewildered.

"What does all this mean?" Bryce said.

I said, "It means I don't owe any of you anything. And that if you want to still be alive at one minute past 6:00 p.m. this evening, you better start telling me how to defeat the insurmountable edge and telling me fast."

"But I don't know anything about the insurmountable edge!!" Bryce said.

"Then you better hope your friends do," I said.

"Carter! Kenny!" Bryce said. "Tell him!"

Kenny said, "Bryce, please shut the hell up."

"But Wilder will kill us!" Bryce said. "I told you! He's an animal!"

I said, "Thank you, Bryce. That's very kind of you to say."

A shadow entered the Gulfstream and passed from one side of the cabin to the other. I looked out one of the plane's windows. A solitary cloud floated in the sky and was partially blocking the sun. The cloud moved beyond the sun and the cabin shadow disappeared.

Kenny said, "Bryce, we're not telling anybody anything, okay? General Wilder is on the wrong side of history. There will be a war and there is nothing he can do to stop it."

Bryce seemed confused.

"There isn't?" Bryce said.

"No, there isn't," Kenny said. "General Wilder is bluffing. He's out of time and as long as we keep our mouths shut, we win. Got it?"

"But he's going to kill us," Bryce said. "I know him."

"He's not going to kill us," Kenny said.

I said, "I'm not?"

Kenny laughed.

"No, you're not," Kenny said. "You can't afford the diplomatic stink that would come from killing Carter and me."

"Because Carter is the son of a former president of the United States and you're a princeling?" I said.

"Correct," Kenny said.

"What about Bryce?" I said.

"What about Bryce?" Kenny said.

"No one's going to care about him?" I said.

Kenny shook his head and laughed.

"Please, General," Kenny said. "Let's be serious."

"Fine," I said. "I'll grant you that. No one is going to care about Bryce."

Bryce said, "What?!"

Jeff said, "Bryce, you best be quiet now."

"But there's a lot of people that are going to care about me," Bryce said.

"Maybe they is, maybe they ain't," Jeff said. "But it isn't material to the problem at hand and you just wasting our time, okay?"

I said, "Jeff's right Bryce. It's in your best interest to be quiet at this time."

Bryce studied me for a moment.

"It is?" Bryce said.

I nodded.

"Okay," Bryce muttered.

"Now, Kenny, getting back to this diplomatic stink," I said. "How can there be a stink if no one knows you're dead?"

Kenny said, "While you were outside the jet helping to remove Bryce, Dr. Nimo, and Dr. Lennon from the SUV, I called my family and told them about our flight plan. When this plane arrives in Costa Rica, I better be alive or they'll know what you did."

"Jeff," I said, "is this plane headed to Costa Rica?"

"Depend on your point of view," Jeff said. "If you're an air traffic controller, radar station, or satellite, then yeah, it be headed to Costa Rica for sure."

"How about from my point of view?" I said.

"From your point of view, I do believe it be headed into the middle of the Pacific Ocean," Jeff said.

For only the second time that day, I noticed a crack begin to appear in Kenny's aura of invincibility.

"Something wrong, Kenny?" I said.

Kenny didn't say anything.

Carter Bowdoin said, "Shit."

Bryce Wellington looked confused.

"Carter? Kenny?" Bryce said. "What's going on?"

Carter said, "Are you really that stupid, Bryce?"

"Why are you calling me stupid?" Bryce said. "I haven't done anything."

"They're using the same technology that was used when someone took down Milt Feynman and Paul Lennon's plane, you moron," Carter said.

"*Someone?*" I said.

Carter ignored me.

Bryce said, "But, but...they're on the plane with us. That doesn't make any sense."

"Good point, Bryce," I said. "You're right. On the surface it doesn't make any sense. We need to dig a little deeper."

"Deeper?" Bryce said.

"Adelaide," I called out loudly toward the open cockpit door, "would you mind showing our friends here one of those green things you brought on board?"

"Sure," Adelaide said.

Adelaide removed her headphones and exited the cockpit. She walked the length of the cabin and entered the aft baggage compartment. A moment later, she came out of the compartment carrying a large green backpack. Adelaide held the backpack out to me.

"This what you're talking about?" Adelaide said.

"Yes, thank you," I said.

Bryce said, "Is...is...is that a parachute?"

"Well done, Bryce!" I said. "Adelaide, how many parachutes do we have?"

"Three," Adelaide said. "We also have three life jackets to go with each of the parachutes."

"Three?" I said. "But there's six of us."

"Major Haley didn't tell me to bring any for those assholes," Adelaide said.

"How silly of me," I said. "Of course she didn't. It wouldn't have been part of the plan. You may return the chute to the baggage compartment, please."

Adelaide nodded and took the parachute back to the compartment.

Bryce said, "How are we going to get off the plane then?"

Jeff and I shared a look.

Jeff said, "That nepotism must be a really powerful thing."

"Powerful indeed," I said.

Bryce said, "Excuse me. You can insult me all you want, but you still haven't told me how we're getting off the plane without parachutes."

"You're not," I said.

"But we'd have to," Bryce said. "If the three of you get off, there will be no one to fly the plane and it will crash."

"Yes, it will crash," I said. "And it will do so in the middle of the Pacific Ocean. Since everyone will be looking for the plane somewhere between Van Nuys and Costa Rica, no one will ever find it, you, Carter, or Kenny."

"Oh my God!" Bryce said.

"Of course if you tell us what we need to know, we'll turn this puppy around and make a beeline for San Jose," I said.

"San Jose?" Bryce said.

Jeff said, "San Jose be the capital of Costa Rica, Bryce."

Kenny said, "General Wilder, please cut the bullshit. You're not going to ditch this plane. You know full well that doing so would cause an international incident."

"Why is that?" I said.

"Because, while we may not really be going to Costa Rica, I also told my family that you're traveling with me on the jet," Kenny said. "If the jet disappears, and you show up alive one day and I don't, they'll know you murdered me."

Adelaide walked past me on her way back to the cockpit from the baggage compartment. Another shadow made its way across the cabin. I again looked out the cabin window. Another solitary cloud had just passed in front of the sun.

"Sorry, Kenny, but that's not correct," I said. "At some time prior to the Gulfstream taking off from Van Nuys you may have told your family you were on your way to Costa Rica with me, but I'm quite sure you haven't communicated with them since we put you to sleep. Captain Korok, the copilot, Lorna, and Sally will be told when they wake up that I got off the plane with Dr. Lennon and Billy and that you continued on with a different crew. So, as far as anyone will ever know, I'm not on this plane."

Bryce said, "What if we pay you?"

"Pay me?" I said.

"To turn this plane around and go to Costa Rica," Bryce said. "Carter and Kenny can pay you a lot of money."

"How much?" I said.

"One hundred million dollars," Bryce said. "You'd do that wouldn't you, Carter and Kenny?"

Carter and Kenny said nothing.

"That's a lot of money," I said.

Bryce, apparently believing I was considering his offer, looked like he was getting very excited.

Bryce, nodding vigorously, said, "Yes, it is."

"What would I do with all that money?" I said.

"Whatever you want," Bryce said. "Houses anywhere in the world. Cars, women, your own jet. You could even have your own chef."

"I have to speak to my financial advisor," I said. "Jeff, what do you think of that offer?"

"We got a house," Jeff said.

"Women might be nice," I said.

"Women never been a problem," Jeff said. "And I like to cook, so don't need no chef."

"Jet sounds good though, doesn't it?" I said.

"I'm happy with the Cub," Jeff said.

"Sorry Bryce, it's very generous of you, but I guess we don't need the money," I said.

Carter said, "Kenny, I think it's time to bail."

CHAPTER 133

The Gulfstream G650 continued on its westerly course away from Costa Rica. We hit an air pocket and the plane shook slightly. The afternoon sunlight glared off the sea below. I checked on Adelaide. She was in her seat in the cockpit but had turned her head around to face us. She seemed to be listening intently to everything that was being said in the cabin.

Kenny said, "Carter, don't you dare tell them anything. In fourteen minutes, the plan you and I have worked so long and hard on will come to fruition. The heavenly soldiers of the People's Liberation Army will begin their glorious conquest of Saudi Arabia. The U.S. forces will be incapable of offering any resistance and they will be completely crushed. When the war is over, you and I will own a very large portion of Saudi Arabia. That's trillions of dollars, Carter. So stay the course, my friend. Because in fourteen minutes, we win."

Carter said, "What good does that do us if we're dead?"

Kenny shook his head sadly.

"You aren't thinking straight, Carter," Kenny said.

I said, "He seems to be thinking pretty straight to me."

Jeff said, "Me too."

Kenny cackled.

Kenny said, "Of course that is what both of you would say! Whether or not you believe what you are saying is an entirely different matter, though isn't it? So, let's be real here. For someone who claims to be an expert in game theory, Carter's thought processes in regard to our current situation leave a lot to be desired."

Carter said, "I assume that means you don't believe they're going to kill us?"

Kenny smiled.

"Of course not!" Kenny said. "What do they have to gain by it? Killing us would be an unnecessary risk they have no reason to take."

"What's their risk, Kenny?" Carter said.

"They know that even with their crap about radar evading technology, satellites, and whatnot, there's still a chance that someone will find this jet even if it is in the middle of the Pacific Ocean," Kenny said. "When that happens, they're up shit's creek."

"It's a risk they're willing to take," Carter said.

"And you know this how?" Kenny said.

"I don't know how I know," Carter said. "I just know."

"And I don't know how I know, but I know they won't take that risk," Kenny said.

"You're misreading them, Kenny," Carter said. "You're assuming they'll play their cards like you would, but they don't think like you."

Bryce Wellington screamed, "That's what I've been trying to tell you! They're savages! Barbarians!"

"Bryce, please let me finish," Carter said.

"You've got to make Kenny understand!" Bryce said.

The Gulfstream hit another air pocket. The plane shuddered briefly and wobbled from side to side, then quickly stabilized itself.

"I'm trying to," Carter said. "But I can't do it unless you shut up."

"Okay, Carter, I'm sorry," Bryce said. "I'll shut up. I promise. I'm just very, very stressed!"

"Trust me, Bryce, we're all fully aware of how stressed you are," Carter said. "Kenny, we've discussed it many times. Play the man, not the cards."

Kenny said, "That's true. We have discussed that."

"I submit to you then that these two men, Wilder and Bradshaw, are very angry at us for what we've done," Carter said. "They'll kill us to assuage their anger."

I said, "Vengeance too. Don't forget vengeance."

Carter and Kenny both ignored me.

Kenny said, "They don't have any proof we've done anything."

Carter stared at Kenny for a moment.

"You're kidding, right?" Carter said.

"No, I'm quite serious," Kenny said.

"What about all the Afghans and Kazakhs lying dead on the polo field?" Carter said. "What about that goddamned video of the kids being stoned? What about the burning hulk of the Black Hawk outside the ranch house?"

"They know we brought the Afghans and Kazakhs into the country, but who's to say that once the Afghans and Kazakhs were here they didn't act on their own?" Kenny said. "Just because I have a copy of the video doesn't mean I had anything to do with the actual filming. The Afghans could have shot it themselves and given it to me. And I don't see how it was a crime for us to hitch a ride on the Black Hawk."

Carter looked like he was having a hard time believing Kenny had actually responded in that fashion. He seemed about to speak, but I cut him off.

"Hold on there, Carter," I said. "Kenny is making a very good point. Jeff, is it possible we made a mistake?"

Jeff did an excellent job of pretending to give my question some serious thought before he answered.

"Well," Jeff said, "I suppose it's possible the Afghans and Kazakhs that come over here on Carter's plane killed everyone without Carter's or Kenny's knowledge or permission. Afghans could have made that video too. It's also possible the twelve dead NASAD engineers die in accidents, and all the NASAD dark programmers at the bottom of that crater actually killed by terrorists. And maybe Carter, Kenny, and Bryce know all about that NASAD radar evading and mislocating technology, but they had nothing to do with murdering Milt Feynman and Paul Lennon. It's even possible that Kenny don't know nothing about what Heise De Shui done to me in the Sudan even though he own the damn company, and it's also possible Bryce Wellington got all that money in his secret bank accounts because he gone and won the lottery. And Kenny probably right there nothing wrong with taking a ride on a Black Hawk." Jeff paused. He pointed at the dragon mask sitting on one of the four seats at the back of the plane, then continued, "But, how do you explain that?"

"The dragon mask?" I said.

"Uh huh," Jeff said. "Far as I remember, it exactly match Bobby and Timmy's description of the mask that guy wearing who stoned Sam and Lizzy to death, and it also be the mask the guy who done the stoning wearing in that video Kenny showed you in the ranch house."

I went to the back of the cabin, picked up the dragon mask, strolled back to the couch on which Carter, Kenny, and Bryce were sitting, and put the mask on Kenny's head. I stepped back to admire my handiwork.

"What do you think?" I said.

"I think that him," Jeff said.

"The Dragon Man?" I said.

"Yep," Jeff said.

"Me too," I said. "So, Carter and Kenny. Bryce claims to know nothing about the insurmountable edge, which means the choice is up to the two of you. Either you tell us how we can stop the edge, or we're going to kill you."

Bryce said, "What about me?"

"We're going to kill you too," I said.

"Oh God!" Bryce said.

"God's not going to help you, Bryce," I said.

Carter said, "That's it, Kenny. I'm going to tell them. The money isn't going to do me any good if I'm dead."

Kenny, from under the dragon mask, said, "Please, Carter, don't do that. They're bluffing. They won't touch us. I'm sure of it."

"They're not bluffing," Carter said. "General Wilder, if I tell you what I know about the insurmountable edge, you'll let us go? No strings attached?"

"No strings attached," I said. "We'll let you off in Costa Rica like Kenny originally proposed."

Carter said, "Even if what I tell you doesn't allow you to stop the war? Because I can tell you how the insurmountable edge works, but I really don't think it can be stopped."

"Even if it doesn't allow us to stop the war, yes," I said. "I should warn you that if I find out later that you did know how to stop the edge and didn't tell me, I'll hunt you down to the ends of the earth and kill you. Bryce and Kenny too. Not that you care about Bryce."

Kenny said, "Carter, we've been friends a very, very long time. We're on the verge of making a vast fortune. I can't believe you're doing this to me...to us."

Carter said, "I'm still your friend. I will always be your friend."

"With friends like you, I don't need enemies," Kenny said.

"Please Kenny, don't be like that," Carter said. "You know how much I care about you."

"Hmmph," Kenny said. "That's a joke."

"You make it sound like I'm betraying you," Carter said.

"You are betraying me," Kenny said. "I don't know why I ever trusted you in the first place."

I was pretty surprised by what happened next. Carter's face fell and he looked like he was having second thoughts. It seemed likely that Carter and Kenny must have had a much deeper and more complex bond than I had imagined, otherwise why would Carter have reacted the way he did? After all, didn't Carter have to know he was facing certain death at Jeff's and my hands despite all of Kenny's attempts to convince him Jeff and I were bluffing? In any event, I couldn't afford to let Carter go where he seemed he might be going.

I said, "Come on Carter, time's a wastin."

Carter said, "I'm sorry. I just need another moment."

"It's your life," I said.

My iPhone rang. It was Haley. She was able to connect with me because the Gulfstream had a satellite uplink for cell phone calls.

"We found the insurmountable edge in Billy's code!" Haley said through the phone.

"You did?" I said.

"Yes!" Haley said.

"How confident are you?" I said.

"Very," Haley said.

"Great," I said. "Hold on a second." I covered my iPhone's microphone and spoke to Jeff. "Jeff, Haley says she's found the insurmountable edge. Please do me a favor and tape those assholes' mouths shut until I can assess what she's got. I don't want them trying to claim credit if they try to tell us what they know about the edge after we don't need them anymore."

Jeff took some duct tape out of his pocket and sliced off a piece with his knife.

Carter screamed, "But I was going to tell you!"

"He who hesitates is lost, Carter," I said. "Jeff, please do Carter first, then Kenny, then Bryce."

Carter started wildly jerking his head from side to side, seemingly trying to avoid the tape in Jeff's hand. Jeff steadied Carter's head by grabbing hold of Carter's hair, then taped Carter's mouth shut. Bryce began to whimper again, but no sound came from behind Kenny's dragon mask. Jeff covered Bryce's mouth with tape. Jeff took off Kenny's mask, taped Kenny's mouth as well, then put the mask back on.

"Alright, Haley," I said. "What do you have?"

CHAPTER 134

"Sorry, I need you to hold on for a second," Haley said through my iPhone. "Hart just called in. He wants to go to FaceTime with us."

"That's pretty good timing on Hart's part," I said. "What was he doing, spying on you?"

"I tried to reach him before I called you, but he wasn't available," Haley said. "He just called me back."

"You called him before you called me?" I said. "I guess I know where I stand."

"Stop being a baby," Haley said. "Give me a moment while I patch him in."

I waited for Haley to get back to me. The Gulfstream G650 continued its high altitude course over the Pacific Ocean. The jet's wings caught a rising thermal and we were gently lifted upwards and floated equally gently down. Through the cabin window behind Carter Bowdoin's head, I could see a squall far off in the distance to the north of us. The squall's clouds were black and sheets of dark grey rain were falling out of them. The sheets looked like a wall connecting the clouds to the surface of the sea. On either side of the wall, the sky was blue and bright and sunny. The wall itself was impenetrable.

Fifteen seconds after Haley had asked me to give her a moment, she and General Hart appeared in split screens on my phone. Hart was still at the Army's desert headquarters in Saudi Arabia, the nighttime Saudi sky lit by harsh overhead lights. Haley hadn't moved from her post at NORAD. She looked fresh as a daisy.

Hart said, "Jesus, son. You look like something the cat dragged in."

"I've been in kind of a rush since we left the Topanga compound," I said. "I haven't had time to shower yet."

"I guess that's a good enough excuse," Hart said. "Where are Bowdoin, Liu, and Wellington?"

I pointed my iPhone camera at the three men.

"We're in close quarters, sir," I said. "I want to warn you all three of them can hear what we're saying."

"Doesn't matter to me," Hart said. "Matter to you?"

"There's nothing they could do with anything they learn, so no," I said.

"Good," Hart said. "That Liu wearing the stupid mask?"

"Yes, sir," I said.

"They tell you anything we can use?" Hart said.

"Bowdoin appeared like he might be about to, but then Haley called," I said. "I taped his mouth shut so he wouldn't be able to claim credit for something Haley might tell me on her own."

"What was Carter Bowdoin hoping to earn with his credit?" Hart said.

"His life, sir," I said.

"Which you are quite willing to take?" Hart said.

"Nothing would make me happier," I said.

"God willing we won't need Carter's help after we hear what Haley has to say, then," Hart said.

Carter, who had been listening keenly to our exchange, struggled against his bindings. His nostrils flared and the veins in his neck engorged.

"Appears Carter's not too keen on dying," Hart said.

"He should have thought of that before," I said.

"Yes, he should have," Hart said. "Haley, tell us what you know."

Haley said, "Thank you, sir. We've determined the insurmountable edge is in the communication encryption sequence and it works pretty much as Jack predicted."

I said, "Excuse me, Haley, but did you just say it works pretty much as Jack predicted?"

"Yes, I did say that," Haley said.

"Goddamn, I'm good," I said.

Hart said, "Jack, please shut the hell up and let Haley continue."

"Yes, sir," I said. "Of course, sir."

Haley said, "As I was saying, the insurmountable edge works pretty much as Jack predicted. I should note, however, that Jack presented two possible options to me that Dr. Nimo/Billy Einstein might have used to construct the insurmountable edge, and that it was Jack's less preferred option that Billy chose."

"My aren't we picky?" I said.

Hart said, "Jack, what did I just say?"

"Are you talking about the part about shutting up," I said, "or letting Haley continue?"

"Both," Hart said.

"Understood, sir," I said. "Haley, please go on."

Haley said, "As we all know, encryption/decryption coding systems rely on both parties having access to the same key. Mary Queen of Scots had to have the same key as Babington in order to decipher Babington's communication regarding their plot to assassinate Queen Elizabeth. Users of the Enigma machine had to have one machine for the sender and one for the receiver, with each machine being set up exactly alike. Even for Captain Midnight Decoder Rings - Jack's favorite - both parties need to have the same ring."

"Those rings actually work pretty well, I might add," I said.

Hart rolled his eyes. Outside, a ray of sunlight glinted off the waves and shot skyward. It seemed like the entire cabin of the Gulfstream was suddenly brighter.

Haley said, "Billy Einstein's insurmountable edge lets the normal encryption sequences run, including the sequences that form the key, so that everything appears to be working as it should. But hidden away in a completely different area of the software, in a way that no one would ever find unless they knew exactly what they were looking for, let alone had reason to look for it in the first place, is a re-encryption system."

"*Re-encryption*, huh?" I said. "Who could've possibly predicted Billy would do that? Oh, wait...me."

Hart said, "Please, Jack!"

Haley said, "Billy's software re-encrypts the original enciphered message with his own new key before the message is sent to the receiving entity. After the re-encryption, Billy sends the new, re-encrypted message to the receiving entity, but with the old key, not the new key. The receiving entity, having the wrong key, can't possibly decipher the message."

"What does Billy do with the new key?" I said.

"He throws it away," Haley said.

"Imagine that," I said. "Just like I said he would."

Hart said, "Goddamnit, Jack!"

"Sorry, sir," I said. "I can't help myself, sir."

"Can't or won't?" Hart said.

"That's very deep, sir," I said. "Actually, I'm not sure."

"You're such an asshole," Hart said.

"Thank you, sir," I said. "Now, Haley, I want to be certain I have this straight. Billy's insurmountable edge works because it makes it look like the entire encryption and decryption system is working perfectly, but what it is producing is completely unusable. Is that correct?"

"Yes," Haley said. "Billy's entire system is quite elegant and quite deadly."

The Gulfstream passed through another thermal. The plane once more gently floated up, then down. I checked on Adelaide again. She was still in her seat in the cockpit. She seemed to be continuing to pay keen attention to everything that was transpiring in the cabin.

"It certainly seems that way," I said. "But I'm surprised there's not some system in place within the software that re-verifies the integrity of the encryption. Something that would provide a form of double-check that would ensure things actually had worked as expected."

"A double-check system does exist," Haley said.

"Why doesn't it catch Billy's re-encryption and keep it from doing any harm then?" I said.

"All the bells and whistles were built to alert the users to failed encryption and/or failed key delivery," Haley said. "Since Billy's design allows the original encryption to run, and the original key to be delivered, the bells and whistles never go off."

"So even though the original key is delivered, the re-encrypted message is unreadable since it requires the new key to decipher it?" I said.

"Correct," Haley said. "The new key, the one that is created at the time of the re-encryption and would actually work to decrypt the re-encryption of the original encrypted message, has been thrown away. The receiving entity just gets the old key. The receiving entity can try to decipher the re-encrypted message with the old key a thousand times, but the result will be the same - the message cannot be read without the new key."

"Which means satellites, computers, and people can send whatever message they want," I said, "but anything on the receiving end - weapons systems, airplanes, naval ships, other people - will never be able decipher any of the messages? GPS, guidance systems, telecommunications, none of it will work?"

"Right," Haley said. "Which essentially means nothing in all of the

U.S. Armed Forces will work."

I looked down at my watch. It was 5:51 p.m. War was nine minutes away.

"I suppose there's no way to fix or override the insurmountable edge's code in the next nine minutes?" I said.

"We're working on a patch for an override," Haley said. "We think we can get it done within about six hours and then another four to get it installed in our most important systems."

Hart said, "Which gives the Chinese ten hours to shoot at us without us being able to shoot back. Haley, has your team run an assessment of the predicted damage that will inflict?"

The jet passed through one of the few clouds in a sky, that other for the distant squall, was otherwise cloudless. The cabin's windows were momentarily shrouded in a misty, white curtain.

"We have, sir," Haley said. "We believe that in the next ten hours our combined Armed Forces will lose over two hundred thousand men and women, along with sixty percent of our tanks, planes, ships, and fixed artillery that are stationed in the Middle East."

"Which means we lose the war," Hart said.

"Yes, sir," Haley said.

I caught movement out of the corner of my eye. It was Kenny. He was snapping his fingers, tapping his toes, and humming. He was also rhythmically rolling his shoulders and rocking his head beneath his dragon mask in a way that could only be construed to be dancing. I walked up to him, tore off the mask, and punched him in the face. Kenny stopped dancing. I shoved the mask back over his head.

I said, "Haley, we have to be missing something."

"If we are, I don't know what it is," Haley said.

"It has to be something simple," I said. "There's no way an eighteen year old kid, no matter how smart he is, thought of everything."

Hart said, "I agree with you, Jack. But we're just about out of time. I think we're going to lose this one."

I looked over at Carter Bowdoin.

"Damn," I said. "I hate to say this, but I think I'm gonna have to give that asshole Bowdoin a second chance."

I walked over to Carter and stood in front of him. I ripped the duct tape off his mouth.

"You heard everything that we've been saying, correct?" I said.

"Yes," Carter said.

"The deal remains the same," I said. "You tell us how to stop the edge, you live. Otherwise, you die."

Carter shook his head sadly.

"I could lie to you and make up something, but I don't know what good that would do me," Carter said. "Bottom line is that woman on the phone exactly described the edge. I don't have any more idea how to stop it than she does. And, honestly, from what I know, it can't be stopped."

I slapped the duct tape back over Carter's mouth. I turned to Kenny, took his mask off, and tore the tape off his mouth.

"What about you?" I said.

"Moi?" Kenny said, smiling.

"Yeah, you asshole," I said.

"I can sum up what I have to say in four little words," Kenny said. "I win. You lose."

Kenny started laughing hysterically. I punched him in the face again. This time his eyes rolled back in his head and his chin sagged to his chest. I resealed his mouth shut with the duct tape, then threw the dragon mask on the floor in disgust.

I turned to Jeff.

"You have any ideas?" I said.

He shook his head.

I felt as low as I ever had in my life. Every part of my body that had been damaged over the last few days screamed in pain. Exhaustion seemed about to completely overtake me. I closed my eyes and took a deep breath, trying to will myself to think of something, anything, to stop the insurmountable edge before the war started. I let my hands fall to my sides, my phone going with them.

A veil seemed to pass behind my eyes, separating me from the outside world. I felt like I was falling into some kind of trance. Everyone around me appeared to grow smaller and smaller. I saw myself floating away from them and moving into outer space. The earth receded below my feet, and I passed deep into the nether regions of the Milky Way. The Milky Way then slowly began to disappear, and it seemed like I had entered another dimension, one outside space and time.

And then...

I don't know how or why...

An idea began to form in my mind.

The idea didn't feel like it was coming from my own mind, however, but rather as if it was being planted in me by some ineffable being.

At first, I resisted the idea.

It didn't seem like it could possibly be true.

But the more I tried to push the idea away, the more the ineffable being seemed to keep it in the forefront of my mind, as if the being was forcing me to consider the idea and give it credence.

Finally, I could resist the being no longer, and I began to examine the idea.

The more I examined it, the more sense the idea seemed to make.

But even then, I pushed back.

"The idea is too simple," I said to myself, "too simple to be believed."

But wasn't simple what I had been looking for?

Somewhere behind me, as if from very far away, I thought I heard Jeff speak. I was, however, unable to make out his words. I turned to face Jeff, my mind seemingly still millions of light years away.

"Did you just say something?" I said.

"Go with it," Jeff said.

"Go with it?" I said.

"I know you," Jeff said. "You there."

"I am?" I said.

"Uh huh," Jeff said. "Come on now. Don't be letting me down."

I took a deep breath. I felt the veil behind my eyes slowly begin to dissolve.

"Yeah," I said, nodding. "Can't let you down. Can't ever let you down."

I was distracted for a moment by the view out the cabin window. The sun had moved lower in the west. Its rays were spreading across the surface of the Pacific and making the waves ripple with golden light.

I looked away from the light. I pointed my phone's camera directly at my face. Haley and Hart were still on the screen.

Haley said, "Where were you? You disappeared and left us looking at the floor."

"Well, I'm back now," I said. "Listen, I need to confirm something with you. The last time we spoke about the operational status of the military's computer systems, you said the systems were continuing to function in a completely normal way. Is that still the case?"

"It is," Haley said. "There is absolutely no evidence that Billy's re-encryption sequence has activated yet. Everything is consistent with Billy not wanting any of his NASAD war game opponents in the NASAD Cyber Defense Hall to have even a hint of what was about to come before he sprang it on them."

"And those NASAD war games are the war games that Billy would have started by launching a sneak attack exactly at 6:00 p.m. Pacific time tonight, yes?" I said.

"Yes," Haley said.

"Which would mean that the Chinese war, if it begins as we believe it will at 4:00 a.m. Saudi time, will start at exactly the same time, after correcting for time zone differences, as the NASAD war games would have started, assuming Billy followed through with his sneak attack?" I said.

"You already know that Jack," Haley said. "We've gone over it many times."

Jeff said, "Stay with it, buddy. You're almost there. It ain't over 'til it's over."

I looked at Jeff.

"And it hasn't begun until it's begun," I said.

I checked my watch. 5:52 p.m. Eight minutes left.

"Haley," I said, "how does Billy's re-encryption sequence know when it's time to start?"

"Start?" Haley said.

"You said Billy's NASAD war game re-encryption sequence isn't running yet," I said. "How does it know when to start running?"

"It's called up in the software code," Haley said.

"What does the code say?" I said.

"I don't have it in front of me," Haley said.

"But you saw it, didn't you?" I said.

"Yes," Haley said.

"Tell me whatever you remember," I said.

Haley seemed to think for a moment. I could tell she was struggling to stay calm even though time was running out. She breathed heavily out through her beautiful mouth.

"The code was pretty simple, I think," Haley said. "It said something like, if the time is 18:00 Pacific time or greater, and if the date is today's date or later, go to this sequence."

"By 'this sequence', you mean the software sequence that re-encrypts everything and throws away the new key?" I said.

"Yes," Haley said.

"By today's date, you also mean this actual day we are on, June seventh of this year?" I said.

"That's what it said," Haley said.

"And according to your team, until Billy's sequence is put in play, our entire military software should just keep doing what it's doing?" I said. "Will work just like we would expect it to? Just like it's working without a hitch at this moment? Every machine understands every other machine? Everyone understands everyone else?"

"Yes, Jack," Haley said. "I told you. Everything is working just as it is supposed to right now."

"Well, then it's simple isn't it?" I said.

"It is?" Haley said.

Hart said, "Son, you're scaring me. You sure you're okay?"

Jeff said, "He more than okay."

I said, "General, I assume you have a backchannel open with one of your Chinese counterparts in the People's Liberation Army? And that you can get him or her to get the Chinese to stand down if you can convince him or her we've overcome their insurmountable edge?"

Hart said, "I have a channel open."

"Okay," I said. "Get ready to use it."

And then I told Haley and Hart what to do to stop the insurmountable edge.

CHAPTER 135

Haley and Hart got off the line to do what I had told them to do, which was to set all the clocks in the U.S. military back twenty-four hours. I figured if Billy had written his software to start the insurmountable edge at 6:00 p.m. Pacific time, and that time never came, then maybe the edge would never start up and things would keep working just as they had been.

Turning the military's clocks back wasn't going to be as complicated or as hard as it might sound. The systems for synchronizing the military's clocks were as tightly honed and up to date as any in the military. The reasons those systems were so tightly honed were as old as war itself.

Military commanders throughout history have recognized the necessity of coordinating combat operations in regard to purpose, location, and time in order to achieve maximal combat effect. Everyone in the military needs to know exactly what they are expected to do and precisely where and when they are expected to do it. The faultless coordination of the 'when' portion of any military's combat equation can only be accomplished with absolutely surety if everyone's clocks are synchronized. Without such synchronization, targets are missed, drop-offs and pickups blown, and soldiers die.

In the United States military, all clocks are set to the same time by issuing a system-wide time synchronization command. Once the command is issued, all the clocks in the military's computers will line up to the split second.

I wasn't sure how long it would take Haley and Hart to accomplish their assignment and get back to me, but whether it was seconds or minutes, I couldn't bear the idea of spending even an iota of that time in the company of Carter Bowdoin, Kenny 'Dragon Man' Liu, and Bryce Wellington.

"Jeff, let's go the the cockpit," I said.

Jeff and I entered the cockpit and I shut the door behind us. Adelaide was in the right pilot seat, so Jeff took the left. I sat down on the edge of the center console that was between their seats, careful not to touch any buttons, dials, or levers. With the cabin door closed, the cockpit air grew suddenly very cold.

The Gulfstream's engines continued to hum. Outside, lightning bolts shot through the clouds of the squall that lay to our northwest, the bolts' brightness almost blinding against the dark rain curtain. A violent updraft nearly knocked me from my perch on the console.

"I'll say this for you," Jeff said. "It's a simple idea."

"You sound skeptical," I said.

"Maybe it's too simple," Jeff said. "I'm afraid Billy might have put in some other code that blocks your plan."

"Adelaide, you heard everything we talked about in the cabin, correct?" I said.

"Yes," Adelaide said.

"Do you have an opinion about what Jeff just said?" I said.

Adelaide seemed to think for a moment.

"Well, you guys have been saying all along that Billy is a genius, but that he's young and inexperienced right?" Adelaide said.

"Correct," I said.

"If I put myself in Billy's shoes," Adelaide said, "and I really believe that I'm going to have surprise on my side, and that the insurmountable edge is going to start up before the NASAD defensive team knows what hit them, then..."

"Yes...?" I said.

"Then, I don't think I would have thought to build in any code that would counteract what you told Major Haley and General Hart to do," Adelaide said. She paused. "However..."

"However?" I said.

"I'd still rather be young and inexperienced, than an old fart like you," Adelaide said.

I stared at her.

"You do realize your last statement isn't really on point, don't you?" I said.

"Yes," Adelaide said. "But I liked saying it."

"I'm sure you did," I said. "Jeff, do Adelaide's comments alter your thinking at all?"

"If you're asking me whether I agree with her that you're an old fart,

I have to say yes," Jeff said.

"I meant about the code," I said.

"You want me to be honest?" Jeff said.

"Yes," I said.

"It's a coin flipper," Jeff said.

"So you think it could go either way?" I said.

"Yep, either Billy done it or he not done it," Jeff said.

"That's quite an analysis," I said.

"You asked me to be honest," Jeff said.

"Every man has his fault and honesty be yours?" I said.

"Couldn't have said it better myself," Jeff said.

"Neither could William Shakespeare," I said.

It was then 5:54 p.m.

Six minutes left until Billy's software turned on and the entire U.S. military shut down.

Or not.

For the next few moments, neither Adelaide, nor Jeff, nor I, said a word. Alone with our thoughts, we stared out the cockpit windows and waited for Haley and Hart to call us back. More lightning bolts crackled through the squall's grey curtain. Billowing cloud banks as tall as skyscrapers floated far above our heads and intermittently blocked out the sun's rays. The shadows created by the clouds swept across the ocean's surface, breaking up what only moments before had been endless swaths of golden sunbeams dancing on the rolling waves.

I looked down at my watch.

5:55 p.m.

Five minutes to go.

My iPhone rang.

It was Hart and Haley on FaceTime.

I answered their call and held the phone far enough away from me so that Adelaide and Jeff could look and listen in.

Haley said, "Well, 6:00 p.m. Pacific Standard Time, Wednesday, June seventh, and 4:00 a.m. Arabia Standard Time, Thursday, June eighth, is not going to come."

Hart said, "At least not for our guys. As far as the U.S. military is concerned, it's 12:00 a.m. Pacific time, January first of this year."

I said, "But I just said to set the clocks back twenty-four hours."

"A bit of overkill can be a good thing sometimes, son," Hart said.

"Did you contact your backchannel counterpart in the People's Liberation Army?" I said.

"I did," Hart said. "His name is General Chiang."

"Did you get him to stand down?" I said.

"Not exactly," Hart said.

"What does that mean?" I said.

"Chiang wants to talk to you," Hart said.

"Me?" I said. "Why me?"

"Chiang seems to think you might be able to put him in touch with Kenny Liu," Hart said.

"You didn't tell him I'm on Kenny's plane with him, did you?" I said.

"Of course not," Hart said. "Kenny is going down and we don't want you tied to that in any way. Everyone still thinks you got off in Van Nuys before the jet took off for Costa Rica."

"Why does Chiang want to talk to Kenny?" I said.

"Chiang's superior refuses to believe that what I told Chiang about the insurmountable edge not turning on unless our clocks reach 6:00 p.m. is true," Hart said. "Chiang says the only way he can get his superior to believe me is if Kenny Liu personally confirms I'm telling the truth."

I thought for a moment.

"I suppose we could tell Chiang that you were mistaken, that I'm actually on the plane with Kenny and that Kenny is willing to talk," I said. "But even if we allow Kenny to talk to Chiang, Kenny will just lie and say the edge is working fine. Kenny's deal with Carter Bowdoin ensures that he profits no matter who wins the war. All Kenny cares about is that the war starts."

"You think Kenny would lie, even if you offer him his life in exchange for telling the truth?" Hart said.

"I've already gone down that path with Kenny," I said. "There's no question he'll lie."

"That forces our hand then, doesn't it?" Hart said.

"If you mean no Kenny, then yes," I said.

"That is what I mean," Hart said. "You got any other ideas?"

"Maybe Chiang will settle for Carter or Bryce?" I said. "They'll tell

Chiang the truth if it means saving their own necks."

"Worth a try," Hart said. "I'm patching Chiang in now."

"Hold on," I said. "You're not putting Chiang through on FaceTime, are you?"

"Yeah," Hart said. "That way Chiang will see you're on the Gulfstream."

"But...," I said

Hart rolled his eyes.

"Jack, do you really think Haley and I are idiots?" Hart said.

Haley said, "No FaceTime, Jack. Chiang is on a landline."

I heard a hiss on the line and a couple of pops.

"General Chiang," Hart said, "you're on the phone with Jack Wilder."

A voice said in English, "It is an honor to meet you, General Wilder. You are quite a legend in the world within which we all operate."

The voice had been clear and crisp. Every word had been carefully and completely enunciated and spoken in what sounded like a California accent.

I said, "It's an honor to meet you too, General Chiang. You speak English very well."

"I went to college at U.C.L.A.," Chiang said. "It was a very enjoyable time in my life. However, that is not what we are here to discuss is it?"

"I hope not," I said.

Chiang laughed.

"General Hart told me about your discovery of a weakness in the insurmountable edge," Chiang said. "I have no reason to doubt General Hart, but, unfortunately, despite my best efforts to convince my superior otherwise, he remains quite skeptical any such weakness actually exists."

Hart said, "The superior General Chiang is referring to is the current chairman of the Central Military Commission, Wei Hsin. Chairman Wei, like your good friend Kenny Liu, is a princeling."

"A princeling, yes," Chiang said. "A horrible concept, but one we must live with, I'm sad to say. In any event, it was Kenny Liu who assured the politburo that the plan was foolproof. Most of the members of the politburo are also princelings and they all stand to do quite well financially if China wins the war. There is a lot of pressure to forge ahead."

"Even if it means you're going to be fighting a real war?" I said. "The losses suffered on both sides will be extraordinary."

"Again, thanks to Mr. Liu, the politburo believes the losses will be one-sided," Chiang said. "A belief that will, of course, turn out to have been well founded if the insurmountable edge works as Mr. Liu said it would. Not only will all of your weapons be useless, but you will not even be able to talk to each other." Chiang paused. "The only chance I have of preventing this war is if Kenny Liu can confirm what General Hart has told me about the software not activating the insurmountable edge if your clocks never reach 4:00 a.m. Saudi time. Is there any way you can put us in touch with Mr. Liu?"

"I don't know where Liu is," I said. "But I might be able to track down Carter Bowdoin and Bryce Wellington."

Chiang chuckled.

"No one on the politburo will give a rat's ass what Carter Bowdoin or Bryce Wellington say," Chiang said.

"What about your own programmers, then?" I said. "Can't they look at the code and confirm what General Hart said?"

"Our programmers are at this moment studying the specific sequences General Hart pointed out to us," General Chiang said. "But even if they confirm what General Hart said, it won't matter. The politburo has utter confidence in what Kenny Liu told them. The politburo will say there must be fail-safes built into the code that we have not found yet, fail-safes that would prevent such a simple thwarting of our edge."

Another downdraft nearly knocked me from my perch atop the cockpit's console again. A half-dozen lightning bolts streaked in quick succession across the squall's curtain.

"Does the politburo know that the guy who designed the edge is an eighteen year old boy?" I said. "That its intended use was for a war game, and that the boy never expected his war game opponents to have any idea the code even existed before the edge was activated?"

"The politburo knew that the edge was designed for a war game," Chiang said. "But they did not know the age of the programmer. Personally, I can see how one so young could make a mistake, but the politburo will not care." He paused. "Excuse me one moment, please."

It sounded like General Chiang had covered his phone's microphone. I could hear a discussion going on, but it was very soft and I could not make out anything being said.

I checked my watch. 5:57 p.m. Three minutes left.

The disconcerting idea that Billy might have put fail-safes into the insurmountable edge that would override our attempt to defeat the edge by pushing the U.S. military's date and time back to the beginning of the year once again passed through my mind. I shoved the idea aside.

Chiang came back on the line.

"That was our programmers," Chiang said. "They confirm the edge will not turn on if your clocks never reach 4:00 a.m. Saudi time on June eighth."

I said, "You're absolutely sure you can't get Wei or anyone on the politburo to listen to them?"

"It will not happen," Chiang said. "Greed is clouding their vision."

"There has to be something we can do," I said.

"If there is, it will have to come from you," Chiang said. "I have considered all my options and determined that there are none that will work."

"Major Haley and General Hart, I assume you don't have any ideas either?" I said.

Haley said, "I wish I did."

Hart said, "It's tragic. But I think we're going to war."

I turned to Adelaide and Jeff.

"What about you two?" I said.

Adelaide and Jeff shook their heads.

I looked down at my watch. Two and a half minutes left.

Outside, the squall's dark curtain grew almost black as thick sheets of rain pummeled the sea below. Jagged lightning bolts crisscrossed the curtain in every direction. The Gulfstream rocked from side to side as we were buffeted by high winds. I gripped the cockpit console, struggling to keep from being tossed to the floor.

It was clear everyone around me was certain war was inevitable. But I refused to accept that was the case. I had no idea what to do, but after coming as far as I had, there was no way I was going to give up.

I thought.

I thought some more.

And then I thought again.

I got an idea.

It wasn't a great idea, but it was the only idea I had.

"General Chiang, your bosses know the insurmountable edge is supposed to turn on at 6:00 p.m. Pacific time, 4:00 a.m. Saudi time?" I said.

"They do," Chiang said. "That's why our forces are set to commence our assault at exactly that time."

"Would your bosses go to war if we could prove to them the insurmountable edge didn't turn on?" I said.

"I'm sorry, you're losing me, General Wilder," Chiang said. "If the edge is supposed to turn on at exactly 4:00 a.m. Saudi time, and that is also the time we begin our assault, how do we prove to my superiors the edge did not turn on before we're already at war?"

"I think we can do it if you can get your forces to hold off for a few seconds while our two militaries conduct a test," I said.

"What kind of test?" Chiang said.

"The test I have in mind would require you to fly one of your unmanned drones over the Saudi border at exactly one second past 6:00 p.m. Pacific time, 4:00 a.m. Saudi time," I said. "Can you make that happen?"

"What would that accomplish?" Chiang said.

"If we shoot the drone down, it will accomplish a lot," I said. "Shooting a drone down is a complex task. It requires the coordination of multiple computer systems, none of which will be working if the insurmountable edge turns on."

"So you are saying, that if you do indeed shoot down our drone, then the insurmountable edge did not turn on?" Chiang said.

"I am," I said.

Chiang said nothing for a moment.

"It would be a very elegant and very simple proof, wouldn't it?" Chiang said.

"I believe it would be, yes," I said.

"Of course, if you do not shoot the drone down, the obverse would be true," Chiang said. "The edge did turn on."

"That's correct," I said. "And we'd be screwed."

Chiang chuckled.

"Screwed would be an understatement," Chiang said. "However, your test is an excellent idea, General Wilder. I think we should go with it. If you will please hold on while I discuss your suggestion with

Chairman Wei. As he is right now meeting with the standing committee of the politburo, we should be able to get a quick answer."

Chiang left the line. I again checked my watch. 5:58 p.m. Two minutes left.

Hart said, "You think Wei and his masters will go for it?"

"They should," I said. "They shoot at us, and we shoot back, it will be massively embarrassing for them."

Haley said, "They'll go for it. They've got nothing to lose by holding off for a few seconds."

Jeff said, "They're going for it. They don't, I eat my hat."

I said, "Need I remind you that hat you're wearing isn't yours? It belongs to your predecessor, Captain What's-his-name."

"Korok," Jeff said.

"Yeah, Korok," I said.

"I'll eat Korok's hat, then," Jeff said.

Chiang came back on the line. It was 5:59 p.m.

"The test is approved," Chiang said. "The drone is already moving into position and will cross the Saudi border in approximately sixty seconds. You may of course not fire at the drone until after 6:00 p.m. Pacific time, 4:00 a.m. Saudi time, and we will allow you one full minute to successfully shoot it down. If you do not shoot the drone down, then war will commence."

I said, "One minute? You're kidding, right?"

"That is not enough time?" Chiang said.

"It's too much time," I said. "Your drone will be dead meat in under twenty seconds."

"We shall see," Chiang said.

I checked my watch. We were forty-five seconds away from 6:00 p.m.

"Haley, I assume you've already patched yourself in with the commander of our anti-aircraft missile batteries?" I said.

"I have," Haley said. "I'm on the line with Colonel Pete Kantner right now.

"General Chiang, do you have someone reporting to you on the drone's status?" I said.

"I do," Chiang said.

"How about we put everyone in on this?" I said. "Then we can all hear what's going on in real time?"

"Fine with me," Chiang said. "I'll reroute our drone battalion commander, Lieutenant Chun-lin, onto my line as well."

I heard a couple of clicks and whooshes on the line.

Haley said, "Colonel Kantner you are on the line with Generals Wilder and Hart, and their counterpart in the People's Liberation Army, General Chiang."

Colonel Kanter said, "It is an honor to meet you all."

Chiang said, "Thank you, Colonel Kantner. The honor is mine. Lieutenant Chun-lin, our drone battalion commander, is also on the line with us now."

I checked my watch again. Thirty seconds to go.

I said, "Colonel Kantner, I assume all your systems are running smoothly?"

Kantner said, "Yes."

"You understand that any drone that invades Saudi airspace is to be immediately shot down?" I said.

"I do, sir," Kantner said.

"Lieutenant Chun-lin, your drone is aloft?" I said.

Chiang said, "Excuse me, but Lieutenant Chun-lin does not speak English. I have to translate your question and his answer."

I heard some muffled words in Chinese.

"Lieutenant Chun-lin says he has many drones aloft," Chiang said.

Kantner said, "Forty-three to be exact. All just outside the Saudi border."

More mumbled Chinese, followed by a chuckle which sounded like it had again come from General Chiang.

Chiang said, "Colonel Kantner is correct. We have forty-three drones hovering in position along the Saudi border."

Looking at my watch, I said, "Okay, then, twenty seconds left. Fifteen...ten, nine, eight, seven, six, five, four, three, two, one, zero..."

We were all silent. The silence seemed to last forever, but in reality lasted no more than a second. It was Kantner who broke it.

"We have an intrusion by an enemy drone aircraft into Saudi airspace...," Kantner said. "Damn."

Damn?

That couldn't be good.

I said, "Is there a problem, Colonel?"

"More than one drone has intruded," Kantner said.

"How many?" I said.

"Twenty-five of the forty-three," Kantner said.

"Are you tracking all of them?" I said.

"Yes," Kantner said.

I breathed an inward sigh of relief. I knew our systems had to be working normally and that the insurmountable edge had not turned on, because if the edge *had* turned on, we wouldn't have been able to track the drones. But shooting down all twenty-five drones was going to be a difficult task even if all our systems were working perfectly. Twenty-five drones were also twenty-four more than we had agreed to.

"Chiang, what's up?" I said.

Chiang chuckled again.

"We thought we'd give you a real test," Chiang said.

"Understood," I said. "But the fact we're tracking every one of the drones means the insurmountable edge didn't turn on. Should we abort the test?"

"Let's let it continue," Chiang said. "Tracking is one thing. Destroying is another."

Kantner said, "Missile guidance has acquired all twenty-five targets and missiles are locked on."

I said, "Last chance, Chiang. Do you want us to abort? It'll save you the cost of a lot of expensive hardware."

"Please proceed," Chiang said. "Chairman Wei and the politburo still do not believe they could have been so badly misled by Comrade Jinping 'Kenny' Liu."

"I guess they don't know him as well as we do," I said. "Colonel Kantner, if you would be so kind as to knock those birds out of the sky."

"Yes, sir," Kantner said. He paused momentarily, then continued. "We have missile launch for all twenty-five missiles...the missiles are currently tracking their targets."

"All twenty-five are tracking properly?" I said. "Not a single tracking failure?"

"No, sir," Kantner said. "No failures."

"How long until your first missile makes contact?" I said.

"Six seconds, sir," Kantner said.

"And when will the last missile make contact?" I said. I asked as I knew, that due to the varying distances between the Chinese drones and our missile batteries firing at them, it would take varying degrees of time for each missile to reach its drone target.

"Twelve seconds, sir," Kantner said.

If Kantner was right, it would mean we would shoot down all twenty-five Chinese drones in line with my original estimate of twenty seconds to destroy the single drone that had originally been contemplated. Such thinking, however, was not only quite petty, but also meant I was getting way too far ahead of myself. With twenty-five drones to deal with, a miss, or even two or three misses, was more than likely.

"One second until the first missile makes impact, sir...," Kantner said. He paused. "First drone destroyed."

"One for one, Colonel," I said. "Keep it up."

"We're trying, sir," Kantner said. He paused again. "Seven more drones destroyed, sir."

"No misses, yet?" I said.

"No, sir," Kantner said. Another pause. "Sixteen more drones destroyed, sir."

"Still no misses?" I said.

"No, sir," Kantner said.

"That leaves one drone left, correct?" I said.

"Yes, sir," Kantner said. "Impact in four seconds, sir, except..."

"Except?" I said.

"The drone is taking evasive action," Kantner said.

"Drones can take evasive action?" I said.

"I should have said 'attempting' to take evasive action, sir," Kantner said. "The drone has just been destroyed."

My watch said it was nineteen seconds past 6:00 p.m.

I again heard some muffled voices speaking in Chinese on the line. I assumed Chiang and his drone battalion commander, Lieutenant Chun-lin, were conversing.

I said, "Please God, tell me we got all of them, General Chiang?"

Chiang chuckled.

"You got all of them," Chiang said. "Lieutenant Chun-lin reports all our drones are, as you say, dead meat. Very impressive too that you did it under twenty seconds, just as you said you would. Congratulations."

I laughed.

"Thank you, General Chiang, and congratulations to you as well," I said. "Please also accept our heartfelt thanks for your assistance in this matter."

Outside, the squall's downpour suddenly ceased, and the clouds appeared to be breaking apart. The lightning came no more.

"You are most welcome," Chiang said. "Well everyone, it's been wonderful spending this time with you and I congratulate all of us on successfully keeping our two countries from going to war. However, I'm afraid I must be going now. If any of you see Kenny Liu, you might want to suggest to him that he stay away from China for a while. I'm sure there are a number of people who aren't very happy with him at the present moment."

"If we see Kenny, we will definitely do that," I said. "Goodbye, General."

"Goodbye," Chiang said.

General Chiang and Lieutenant Chun-lin left the line.

I heard then a lot of clapping, hooting, and hollering going on in the background of the call.

"That your men, Kantner?" I said.

"Sorry, sir," Kantner said. "They're a little excited."

"No need to apologize," I said. "Tell them they did a great job. Drinks on me tonight."

"There's a lot of men here, sir," Kantner said.

"No problem," I said. "General Hart will reimburse me."

Hart, who had been silent since shortly after introducing me to Chiang, said, "Hold on there. Who said anything about reimbursing anyone?"

"Ignore him, Kantner," I said. "You're excused now. Go ahead and get those drinks flowing."

Hart laughed and Kantner left the line.

Adelaide, Jeff, and I gave each other high fives, then slapped high fives on my iPhone's camera for Haley and Hart.

Haley looked like she was about to wipe a tear away from her eye.

"Thank you," Haley said. "Your congratulations are much appreciated. But I'm a little embarrassed it was you, and not my software team, that came up with the solution for stopping the insurmountable edge, Jack."

"Nothing to be embarrassed about," I said. "You guys were focused on complex programming issues and reams of code. I, on the other hand, have a very simple mind."

Hart said, "You can say that again."

"I'll pretend I didn't hear that," I said. "And Haley, don't you ever forget we're all just one big happy family. None of this could have happened without everyone at MOM pitching in. This was a group effort, and any words to the contrary are strictly prohibited."

Haley said, "Alright. I can't argue with that."

"Now, I hate to switch gears," I said, "but is the pickup team ready?"

"Yes," Haley said. "They're expecting you in forty-five minutes. Jeff has the coordinates."

I looked at Jeff. He nodded.

"Major Haley, General Hart," I said. "If you'll both excuse us, please. We need to take care of a few issues with Carter Bowdoin, Kenny 'Dragon Man' Liu, and Bryce Wellington before we get to the pickup zone."

Hart said, "You didn't change your mind, did you? You're not thinking of bringing them home with you, are you?"

"Heaven forbid," I said.

CHAPTER 136

I got up off my cockpit center console seat, fully prepared to rid the earth once and for all of Carter Bowdoin, Kenny 'Dragon Man' Liu, and Bryce Wellington. I reached for the handle of the cockpit door but before I could grab hold of it, I felt a tug on my arm. I stopped and turned around. It was Adelaide who had tugged. Behind her head, and through the cockpit windows, I could see that the squall had continued to break up. The surface of the sea was like a flat blue plain.

"I have a question before we go out there," Adelaide said.

"Ask away, Adelaide," I said.

"General Hart is okay with us killing those assholes?" Adelaide said.

"You heard what he said," I said.

"I would've thought someone like him would've wanted them to stand trial or something," Adelaide said.

Jeff said, "General Hart wants justice. We bring them home, Hart know there won't be no justice. Kenny probably be getting off due to some kind of diplomatic immunity. Carter's pappy and his friends gonna do everything they can to be sure Carter don't pay for his sins. No one in Washington got the balls to be hanging Bryce either, considering he be a United States Army general."

Adelaide looked questioningly at me. I assumed she wanted me to validate Jeff's statement.

"Jeff's right," I said.

"Have you done this kind of thing before?" Adelaide.

"What do you mean by 'this kind of thing'?" I said.

"Execute prisoners without a trial," Adelaide said.

"We have," I said.

"A lot?" Adelaide said.

"No," I said. "Not a lot."

"You only do it when you don't think you'll get justice if you bring them back home?" Adelaide said.

"Or if transporting them would compromise our own safety," I said.

Adelaide nodded.

"I want to help execute them," Adelaide said.

"That wouldn't be a good idea," I said.

"Why not?" Adelaide said. "They deserve to die. I want to be a part of it."

"I respect that," I said. "You've certainly earned the right to be a part of it, especially considering how well you performed at the tunnel and the ranch compound. But this is an entirely different thing. It's going to be hard enough for Jeff and me do to what we have to do, let alone you."

"That's a lie," Adelaide said. "You want to do it. You hate them for what they did to everyone, especially those kids."

"Sam and Lizzy," I said.

"Yeah, Sam and Lizzy," Adelaide said.

Adelaide was right, of course. I did hate the three men tied up in the back of the Gulfstream's cabin. And I looked forward to killing them and making them suffer while I did so. It wasn't very professional of me, but it was the truth.

"Okay, Adelaide," I said. "You got me. I'm not going to have any problem killing those pieces of shit. But neither Jeff nor I ever did anything like what I'm going to do to them until we were much older than you. I'm not sure it's safe for a mind as young as yours to have that kind of experience."

Jeff said, "You ain't even eighteen yet, girl."

Adelaide seemed to think about what we had said. She appeared to be unhappy we wanted to keep her from participating in the executions of the three men, but at the same time I sensed that somewhere deep down she knew we were right. She probably could have continued her internal struggle for quite a while, but we didn't have the time for it. I decided it would be best to give her a different option.

"How about this, Adelaide?" I said. "You watch this time. If you're okay with it, I promise you can help next time."

"What if there isn't a next time?" Adelaide said.

Jeff said, "World full of assholes, Adelaide. There gonna be a next time."

Adelaide looked at me, again as if seeking confirmation.

"Past is prologue," I said.

Jeff grimaced.

"That ain't what that quote mean," Jeff said.

"Not in the context of where it was originally said, perhaps," I said. "But you know what it means here."

"Yeah," Jeff said. "I do."

Adelaide said, "So do I."

I said, "What does it mean to you, Adelaide?"

"It means I'm going to get my turn," Adelaide said.

I smiled.

"Let's go join our guests," I said.

CHAPTER 137

Adelaide, Jeff, and I stood in front of Carter Bowdoin, Kenny 'Dragon Man' Liu, and Bryce Wellington. The Gulfstream continued to fly west, headed for the center of the Pacific Ocean. The wind had suddenly picked up again and below us the surface of the sea was roiling. The squall had reformed and lightning tore through the squall's dark curtain of brutal rain. The plane fell suddenly into a downdraft and Adelaide, Jeff, and I had to steady ourselves. Carter Bowdoin, Kenny 'Dragon Man' Liu, and Bryce Wellington, constrained as they were against the couch, bobbled and swayed, but the duct tape did all their steadying for them.

"Well, boys, it hasn't been a good day for you," I said. "Not only is this plane not going to Costa Rica, but that insurmountable edge of yours proved to be not so insurmountable after all."

Jeff said, "Ain't gonna be no war, either."

"No, there is not," I said.

"We do, however, have some business need attending to," Jeff said.

"You're referring to their unpaid debts?" I said.

"I am," Jeff said. "Time for them to be giving back what they took."

Carter's, Kenny's, and Bryce's eyes darted from Jeff's face to mine and then back to Jeff's.

"Seem like Carter, Kenny, and Bryce unsure what we're talking about," Jeff said. "Perhaps you'd like to explain it to them?"

"Be my pleasure," I said. "The three of you took a lot of lives. You're going to be paying for those lives with your own."

"He means he's going kill ya all," Jeff said.

"Correct," I said. "I'm also going to make your deaths as unpleasant as possible."

Bryce Wellington struggled mightily against his bindings. He violently shook his head from side to side. Carter Bowdoin appeared to be trying to digest what I had said. Perhaps he thought I was bluffing. Kenny 'Dragon Man' Liu glared at me, his eyes seeming to burn with an angry fire.

"Adelaide, earlier you were kind enough to show me the parachutes I asked Haley to tell you to bring aboard for us," I said. "There was another item I asked Haley to tell you to bring aboard as well. Did she remember to do that, and do you have it?"

"You're talking about the hammer?" Adelaide said.

"I am," I said.

"Would you like me to bring it to you?" Adelaide said.

"Yes, please," I said.

Adelaide nodded. She slipped past me and moved towards the rear of the cabin. The eyes of Carter, Kenny, and Bryce swiveled to follow Adelaide as she went. Bryce bucked even harder. Carter appeared to be catching on to what was in store for him and his face began to fill with dread. Kenny seemed to be trying to keep up the intensity of his glare, but he was failing badly. Was it possible even the great Emperor Liu was succumbing to so common a human emotion as fear?

As I watched Adelaide enter the aft baggage compartment, I remembered I had promised Kate that she would be with me when Carter met his fate. Obviously, due to Kate's incapacitation, and the situation then confronting me on the plane, I was going to have to break that promise. I sincerely felt bad about that. I also believed, however, Kate would forgive me as she would understand circumstances had forced my hand.

Adelaide exited the baggage compartment carrying a sledgehammer. The sledgehammer had a three foot long ash wood handle and a polished steel head in the shape of a rectangular block. The head weighed at least fifteen pounds.

Upon seeing the sledgehammer, both Bryce and Carter appeared to have been overcome with terror. Kenny started breathing very rapidly. His jaw muscles contracted and the rest of his face went into weird contortions. It looked like Kenny thought that somehow his breathing and weird facial movements would help him fight off the horror that had to be growing inside of him.

Good luck with that, I thought.

Adelaide handed me the sledgehammer.

"Thank you, Adelaide," I said.

I set the hammer's head on the cabin floor and held the handle upright with my left hand. I began to rethink my decision to allow Adelaide to watch the coming proceedings. I'm not sure why I did that. I assume it was probably that the feel of the hammer in my hand had made me fully confront for the first time the reality of what was about to happen. But whatever the reason, the more I thought, the more convinced I became that what I was about to do was definitely not appropriate for Adelaide's still young eyes and ears.

"I'm sorry, Adelaide," I said. "I know I said you could watch, but I've changed my mind. I think it might be best if you wait in the cockpit with the door shut until Jeff and I have finished what we need to do."

"Why?" Adelaide said.

"Because you're too young to witness what's going to happen to these three assholes," I said. "It might have a bad effect on you."

"You're kidding right?" Adelaide said.

"No, I'm not," I said. "Please go to the cockpit."

"I'm not doing that," Adelaide said.

"Please, Adelaide," I said, "I'm not in the mood for an argument."

"There's nothing you could do that could have a 'bad effect' on me," Adelaide said. "I can't believe you don't know me better than that."

"Like I said before, this is going to be a much different situation than anything you've ever experienced," I said.

"Different from what?" Adelaide said. "Different from yesterday when I did everything you asked in regard to the dark programmers in the bunker? Different from when I helped save Professor Margaret's life, or from when I rammed the Kazakhs at the tunnel? Rammed them twice, I might add."

"Yes," I said.

"Will it also be different from what I did this morning when I tried my best to get Billy and Kate to safety while we were being shot at and gassed the whole time?" Adelaide said. "Different from when I blew the heads off five of those goddamned mercenaries in Topanga Canyon?"

"It will," I said.

Adelaide seemed to think for a moment.

"Okay, I guess I believe you," Adelaide said.

"Good," I said. "Please get back into the cockpit. I'll tell you when everything is over."

"I said I believed you, not that I agreed with you about what I should do," Adelaide said.

"Please Adelaide," I said. "You're making this much harder than it needs to be. Just go to the cockpit."

"Let me ask you a question," Adelaide said. "Did anything I've done over the last twenty-four hours seem to hurt me in any way?"

I took in a deep breath and let it out.

"Not that I could see," I said.

"Do I look like I'm suffering from some kind of trauma right now?" Adelaide said.

"No," I said. "But the stress of combat can do weird things, Adelaide. There could be a delayed reaction."

"If there is one, I'll deal with it," Adelaide said. "Just like you and Jeff deal with it. I was born to do what I'm doing, and I've earned the right to be here while you do whatever it is you're going to do."

I turned to Jeff.

"You want to help me out here?" I said.

"Adelaide making some good points," Jeff said.

"So you think it's okay if she sticks around?" I said.

"I don't know about that," Jeff said. "What I do think is she a lot tougher than I be at seventeen. Probably you too."

"Hmm," I said. "You could be right about that."

Adelaide said, "He is right about that. Now, let's get on with this."

I studied Adelaide for a moment. She truly did look like she wasn't suffering any deleterious effects from our recent activities. I compared the way she was behaving to how I'd seen my comrades behave immediately after brutal combat. I then compared my comrades' immediate post combat behavior to how those comrades had fared over the following days, weeks, and months. Adelaide looked and acted like my comrades who had come out fine, and nothing like the ones who had been felled by PTSD. Rightly or wrongly, my gut said Adelaide would be fine too. I also felt Adelaide's heroic actions had earned her 'the right to be here'.

"Okay," I said, "you can stay. But promise me you'll leave the moment you start to feel even the slightest bit uncomfortable."

"I promise," Adelaide said.

I turned to Kenny, Carter, and Bryce. Bryce seemed bewildered, as if he had been trying to follow Adelaide's and my conversation but couldn't quite make sense of it. Carter looked like he was slowly coming to terms with the fate that awaited him. Kenny was still ferociously glaring at me like some rabid dog on the verge of ripping my throat out.

"Gentlemen," I said, "I'm sure that the three of you felt that all of the actions you took in pursuit of your goal were justified. I'm here to tell you that they weren't justified, and also to administer justice. Justice for Sam and Lizzy Lennon, for their father Paul, their grandfather Milt Feynman, and the crew of their Otter, for Sam and Lizzy's mother, Sarah, and Paul Lennon's parents, for General Jeff Bradshaw's Sudan fire team, some of the greatest warriors this planet has ever known, for the twelve NASAD drone sub engineers, for the fifty-five young NASAD men and women known as the dark programmers, their boss the Vice President of Dark Programming Rick Benavidez, and for countless coast guards-men and FBI agents, good men all."

I grabbed the sledgehammer with both hands and raised it above my head.

"Hold on," Jeff said. "You including Agent Burnette as one of them good men?"

I set the hammer back down.

"You think we should?" I said.

"I believe he was dumb and misguided," Jeff said. "But he wasn't so bad if you be comparing him to these assholes."

"I guess the same could be said for Freddy Feynman, couldn't it?" I said.

"Yeah," Jeff said. "Freddy deserve justice too."

I raised the sledgehammer over my head again.

"Alright," I said, "for all the innocent souls we have just named, and for Freddy Feynman and Agent Burnette as well, I do hereby administer this good and righteous justice."

I paused.

I had remembered there was another item of business I needed to bring to the attention of everyone in the cabin. I again put the hammer down on the cabin floor.

"Sorry," I said. "One more thing before we begin. I feel like I really should mention why I chose this particular sledgehammer for the task at hand. The reason is that the shape of this sledgehammer's head reminds me of the stones that were used to murder Sam and Lizzy. True, the head is much larger than those stones, but I still feel it can serve as an appropriate stand-in for those stones."

"You're saying the hammer is a metaphor?" Jeff said.

"A metaphor, yes," I said.

I lifted the sledgehammer, then smashed it down on Bryce's left knee as hard as I could. There was a sickening crunching sound as his femur and knee cap shattered. A high-pitched scream that sounded like a wounded elephant came out of Bryce's nose. I then took out Bryce's other knee. Bryce screamed louder.

I paused for a breath and put the hammer down.

Carter Bowdoin was shaking so hard I thought he might be having a seizure.

"What the hell is wrong with you Carter?" I said. "You weren't shaking like this while Sam and Lizzy were stoned to death, were you?"

Jeff laughed.

Jeff said, "You know he weren't."

I lifted the sledgehammer above my head.

"Yeah," I said. "I guess I do."

I smashed Carter's left knee as hard as I could. I felt the bones shatter beneath the hammer's head. Carter's bones made more of a cracking sound than the crunching sounds that Bryce's bones had made. The high-pitched screams that came out of Carter's nose, did, however, sound remarkably similar to the screams Bryce was continuing to make. I smashed Carter's right knee.

I rested the hammer's head on the floor and paused for another breath. I moved over in front of Kenny. He was still breathing hard, and he was continuing to make those odd contortions with his face. I also got the impression Kenny was trying to give me the evil eye.

"Jeff, is this anything to be concerned about?" I said, pointing at Kenny's eyes.

"You think it's some kinda bad voodoo?" Jeff said.

"It could be, couldn't it?" I said.

"Nah," Jeff said. "I never met no Chinaman could do voodoo worth a shit."

"Good," I said. "I won't worry then."

I raised the sledgehammer over my head and fiercely brought it down on Kenny's left femur, aiming for the center of the bone rather than the knee cap. Kenny's femur snapped in two. The fracture caused sharp, bloody bone spicules to form at the end of the lower half of the broken femur, and the spicules punched through the pants of Kenny's fancy suit. I delivered the same blow to Kenny's right femur. Spicules from the femur's lower half also knifed through Kenny's pants. Kenny groaned loudly through his nose and breathed in even faster and shorter breaths.

"You didn't go for the kneecap," Jeff said. "Think this way hurt more?"

"I think it probably hurts about the same," I said. "But this way looks better after you do it."

Jeff nodded.

I set the hammer down and took some more deep breaths. I studied the three men. They all appeared to be in agony. They continued to sound like it too. Good. I figured I'd let them stay that way for a while before I added to their misery by smashing their collarbones, a maneuver that would be particularly painful.

I looked over at Adelaide and Jeff. They were both observing the three men. Adelaide seemed to be fine with what she had seen, perhaps even pleased. Jeff seemed pleased as well, and yet there was a look in his eye that made me take pause. I studied the look. It was a look that seemed to say, whether Jeff was aware of it or not, that he wanted to join in, to be a part of what I was doing.

I began to feel I was being selfish.

Selfish, and also perhaps missing an opportunity to help my friend.

Over the course of the last few days, I'd come to believe, rightly or wrongly, that Jeff's participation on the mission had been an overall plus for him. It seemed his taking part in combat-like action had actually calmed his PTSD, and dare I say it, even begun to retrieve his soul. I began to think that as good as it had felt for me to hammer on the three evil shits in front of me, it might be better if I turned over some of the responsibilities to Jeff. I also had an idea how those responsibilities might take shape.

"Your turn," I said to Jeff.

"My turn?" Jeff said.

"I think these boys are learning pretty well what it must have been like to be Sam and Lizzy during their last moments on earth," I said. "But there are also some men, men you and I hold particularly near and dear, who might appreciate us handing out a somewhat different, though equally instructive lesson."

Jeff at first seemed unsure of what I had been talking about. But realization appeared to dawn on him. He smiled.

"You full of good ideas, ain't ya?" Jeff said.

"I try," I said.

CHAPTER 138

Jeff slipped his combat knife out of his pants pocket, held up the blade in front of his face, and studied it as the Gulfstream's cabin lights danced on its polished surface.

Carter Bowdoin's and Bryce Wellington's eyes grew very wide. Their breath came rapidly through their noses in fast, harsh, grating bursts, and they fought hard against their restraints. Kenny growled somewhere deep inside his throat. His eyes took on an almost otherworldly, evil glow, and he continued to appear to be trying to kill us with his gaze.

"I'm not sure what the hell is going on inside Kenny's head," I said. "But it looks like Carter and Bryce know exactly what we have in mind."

"It do," Jeff said. "Who should I start with?"

"With all due respect," I said, "I'd be looking at it from the other direction."

"You saying I should be thinking about who be last?" Jeff said.

"Uh huh," I said. "Let him get a taste of what's coming for him."

Jeff smiled.

"You cooking on all cylinders today," Jeff said.

"Thank you," I said. "Who you want to be last?"

"General Bryce 'Shit-For-Brains' Wellington," Jeff said.

"Excellent choice," I said.

"Next question be who gonna go first," Jeff said. "I think it best I make that decision scientifically."

Jeff pointed his index finger at Carter, then at Kenny, then wagged his finger back and forth between them, saying as he did:

"Eeny, meeny, miny, moe,

Catch a tiger by the toe,

If he holler, let him go,

My momma tol' me

Pick the biggest asshole

And that be Y...O...U..."

The finger had stopped on Kenny.

"Another good choice," I said.

Jeff walked over to Kenny and stood directly in front of him. Jeff turned the palm of his hand to the sky so that the combat knife's blade faced skyward as well. He drew his hand back, then effortlessly, and with lightning speed, plunged the knife deep into Kenny's belly just above the beltline. He ripped the blade upward until it hit Kenny's breastbone, then pulled the knife back out again even faster than he had put it in.

Jeff dropped the knife on Kenny's lap. As blood poured out of Kenny's gaping wound, Jeff put both his hands into the open space, turned his palms outward, grabbed the muscle and skin on both sides, and ripped the wound wide open. Kenny's intestines fell out of the hole that was created. Jeff shoved his right hand deeply into Kenny's abdomen, grabbed some more intestines, and yanked them out so that they splayed over onto Kenny's lap. Jeff reached under the guts, pulled out his knife, stepped back, and admired his handiwork.

"I think that's how it's done," Jeff said. "Only got to see it once."

"It's a really nice job for only seeing it once," I said. "But then, you've always been a fast learner."

Kenny's face had grown pale, but he still appeared to be trying to throw murderous eye beams at us. The beams seemed much weaker, however, and Kenny's eyes were becoming glassy and unfocused. The breaths coming out of his nose became less harsh sounding and less frequent.

Jeff moved to his left and stood in front of Carter Bowdoin. Carter's head jerked from side to side. Blood vessels were bursting in Carter's bulging eyes, the sinews in his neck were popping out, and the muscles in his legs and arms were straining so hard I thought he might actually rip his lower limbs from his already weakened knee joints.

Jeff plunged his knife into Carter's belly, entering nearly the exact spot as he had in Kenny. He ripped the blade upwards, tore open Carter's abdominal wall with his hands, and yanked out Carter's intestines. Carter looked down at the intestines fanned outside his body, then immediately jerked his head back up and looked at the ceiling. His eyes seemed to be pleading to a higher source, as if doing so would somehow fix his slashed open abdomen and make it go back the way it was.

Jeff sidestepped over to stand in front of Bryce Wellington. Bryce pressed against his tape restraints far more desperately and violently than he had before. He was still screaming through his nose.

"Jesus, Bryce," Jeff said. "I ain't even touched you yet."

Bryce froze when Jeff said this. He stopped screaming and stared into Jeff's face, his eyes pleading.

"What kinda look is that?" Jeff said. "You killed my men and you was hoping tens, maybe hundreds of thousands more good American soldiers would die today. You a treasonous piece of shit. There be no mercy for you."

Jeff twisted his palm and the knife blade skyward again, pulled back his arm and shoulder, then thrust mightily forward.

He stopped just before the tip would have entered Bryce's belly.

It had been a feint.

Bryce appeared bewildered and confused. His eyes made erratic, rapid circling motions in their sockets. His screams no longer sounded like a bull elephant, but rather more like the death chirps made by a squirrel caught in a hawk's beak.

I gave Jeff a questioning look.

"This asshole deserve to die more'n once," Jeff said.

"A coward dies a thousand times before his death, but the valiant taste of death but once?" I said.

"Uh huh," Jeff said.

"Not sure we have time for a thousand more," I said.

"One more be plenty," Jeff said.

Jeff again spun the knife in his hand so that the blade was skyward. He thrust the knife into Bryce's stomach above his beltline and ripped the blade towards Bryce's breastbone. Jeff reached into the wound, pulled back the wound's edges, then grabbed fistfuls of Bryce's intestines and dumped them outside his abdomen.

I took a quick look at Bryce, Carter, and Kenny. They were all breathing shallowly and slow. The only noises they were making were low murmurs. I knew all three men would be dead soon.

That knowledge should have made me happy.

But I wasn't happy.

A sudden rage had arisen within me, a rage accompanied by the images of Sam and Lizzy's mutilated faces flickering in front of my eyes. I felt as if that rage would cause me to explode if Bryce, Carter, and

Kenny lived even a moment longer. And yet, as much as I wanted to kill all three of them right then and there, a small voice in my head stopped me from doing so. The voice said it would be unprofessional to act while under the influence of so brutal an emotion. How would it look to Adelaide and Jeff? the voice said.

Needless to say, I didn't like the small voice. I wanted to crush it as much as I wanted to crush Carter, Kenny, and Bryce. I came up with a plan. I would couch my wishes in a way that would make them seem completely reasonable...

Doing my best to contain myself and appear utterly calm, I said to Jeff, "I'm afraid they could linger for a while."

"They could," Jeff said. "But we're fixing to throw them in the sea, aren't we?"

"What if they float?" I said.

As soon as I said those words, I realized how stupid I sounded, and how dumb my plan had been.

Jeff stared at me.

"What if they what?" Jeff said.

"Forget it," I said.

Jeff appeared to study my face. I was pretty sure he was seeing right through my attempt to hide my rage. I looked over at Adelaide. She was studying me too. She seemed worried.

Jeff said, "I guess it's a lot harder than I thought it was."

"What are you talking about?" I said.

"I'm talking about you seeing the way Sam and Lizzy looked in that morgue," Jeff said.

I didn't say anything.

"It's okay, buddy," Jeff said. "You're human."

Again I didn't say anything. I felt tears welling up in my eyes.

"You know what I'd do if I be human?" Jeff said.

I shook my head.

"I'd take that sledgehammer and I'd send those pricks back through the same gates of hell from whence they came," Jeff said.

"Right now?" I said.

"No time like the present," Jeff said.

I nodded.

I picked up the sledgehammer and took a wide stance in front of Bryce. I raised the hammer high over my head.

"Bryce," I said, "this is for Sam and Lizzy."

There seemed to be a flicker of recognition in Bryce's eyes.

I brought the hammer down on Bryce's skull as hard as I could. His skull shattered and the hammer kept on going, deep into Bryce's head, so deep in fact, it actually got stuck. I wriggled the hammer free. A fountain of bright crimson blood shot out of Bryce's brain and up to the ceiling. The hammer itself was covered with blood and bone shards.

I looked down into Bryce's head. Some of the brain arteries were still pulsing as Bryce's blood continued to flow through them. I lifted the hammer again and I smashed it down as far as I could into Bryce's skull. I lifted and smashed, lifted and smashed, over and over, until the only part of Bryce's skull left above his neck was in the shape of a very shallow, very empty, crater-like bowl.

Jeff said, "Don't think you got to worry about Bryce doing any lingering now."

I moved over to Carter Bowdoin.

"For Sam and Lizzy," I said.

Carter's eyes seemed to flicker with recognition, just as Bryce's had.

I brought the hammer down on Carter's head. A fountain of Carter's blood shot to the ceiling from Carter's shattered skull. I kept hitting Carter until I had created another low-rimmed skull bowl.

Jeff said, "You getting good at this."

I nodded, then moved to Kenny 'Dragon Man' Liu.

"You still with us, Kenny?" I said.

Kenny's head turned ever so slightly. He made a guttural noise that sounded like a dying crocodile.

"You remember Sam and Lizzy, Kenny?" I said.

Kenny's eyes narrowed infinitesimally. They seemed filled with hate.

"Looks like you do," I said. "I'm glad about that. Means you understand why this is happening to you. Goodbye, Kenny."

I hit Kenny's skull with the hammer harder than I had hit either of the other two men. Another bloody fountain spattered the Gulfstream's ceiling. Kenny's skull didn't just shatter like Carter's and Bryce's had, however. Rather, it split in two jagged-edged halves, like two halves of a watermelon that had been sliced by a ragged machete. Using both of my hands, I scooped one half of Kenny's brain, then the other, out of their shell-like casings and threw the halves on the cabin floor. I stomped Kenny's brain halves with my foot. I stomped hard and repeatedly. I completely lost myself in what I was doing. I didn't stop until nothing was left of Kenny's brain other than a thin, bloody, gelatinous film smeared all over the Gulfstream's floor. I was out of breath, sweat was dripping off my brow, and my hands and feet were covered with blood, but I felt a hell of a lot better than I had only a few moments before.

I looked up to find Adelaide and Jeff staring at me.

"What?" I said.

Jeff said, "I've seen a lot, but I don't believe I've ever seen nothing like that."

"In a good way or a bad way?" I said.

"Good," Jeff said. "Real good."

Adelaide said, "That was *so* cool!"

I said, "So you're okay? No ill effects?"

"Are you kidding?" Adelaide said.

"Great," I said. "I'm glad you enjoyed it then."

I noticed the dragon mask lying on the floor next to the couch.

"Oops," I said. "I almost missed something."

I kicked the mask to the center of the cabin aisle and stomped it to pieces.

I checked my watch.

"We only have about thirty minutes until our pickup," I said. "What say we dump these sacks of shit and slip into our chutes?"

CHAPTER 139

We couldn't use the Gulfstream's forward cabin door to dump the bodies of Carter Bowdoin, Kenny 'Dragon Man' Liu, and Bryce Wellington into the sea. If we used the forward door, we risked having the men's bodies sucked into the Gulfstream's engines and crashing the plane. We also couldn't parachute out of the forward door without risking being sucked up into the engines ourselves. What we could use, though, for both dumping the bodies and our parachute jump, was the aft baggage compartment door.

The aft baggage compartment door couldn't be opened, however, until the air pressure inside the jet was equal to the air pressure outside the jet. There were two reasons for that. One, the inside pressure of the cabin was much higher than the pressure of the outside air. That higher pressure essentially created a vacuum seal. In order to overcome that seal and open the baggage door, we would need to exert almost 24,000 pounds of pull on the door. Exerting that much pull was not a doable task. Two, even if we did somehow succeed in overcoming the vacuum seal and opening the baggage door, the rapid decompression of the plane that would occur as the air inside the cabin rushed out to join the air outside the jet would cause the jet to break apart.

We chose eight thousand feet to be the altitude at which we would equalize the inside and outside air pressures. That was because eight thousand feet was not only a safe altitude for that purpose, but since we had regular parachutes and not HALO equipment, it would also be a safe altitude from which to jump.

For safety, we also needed the jet to be going as slow as possible when we jumped out of it. The autopilot could be programmed to achieve the safe speed we required. The autopilot could also control the Gulfstream's descent to the appropriate altitude. Jeff and I, however, decided it was better if he was personally piloting the Gulfstream for those maneuvers in case there were any unexpected complications. Jeff left Adelaide and me in the cabin and went to the cockpit.

While Jeff did his job, Adelaide and I did ours. Together we cut the duct tape off the dead bodies of Carter, Kenny, and Bryce, then hauled them to the aft baggage compartment and stacked them there. Once we were done with the stacking, we prepared all three parachutes. Adelaide and I put on our life jackets and then slipped into our chutes.

Fifteen minutes later, we were cruising at about eight thousand feet and moving at about one hundred and twenty miles per hour. Jeff exited the cockpit and joined Adelaide and me.

"Everything where we need it to be and we now on autopilot," Jeff said. "Pickup zone in seven minutes."

Jeff put on his life jacket.

"What about after that?" I said.

"Jet fly on for another hour or so, then land," Jeff said.

"Land?" I said. "I don't want anybody finding this thing."

"It landing in the middle of the ocean, fool," Jeff said. He put his parachute on over his life jacket.

The Gulfstream would most likely break up when it hit the water. Even if it didn't, it would quickly sink since water would rush in through the open aft baggage compartment door.

The jet's supposed flight path to Costa Rica was over the Gulf of California and well off the Mexican coast, so the NASAD radar evading and mislocating technology would trick anyone who was watching into believing that the jet had crashed in the gulf. The plane's EPIRB unit had been removed before we had taken off from Van Nuys. An Air Force jet would soon be dumping the EPIRB in the Gulf of California. The EPIRB would go off when it hit the water. The jet would never be found.

"Middle of the ocean's good," I said. "How about the two of you hold on to me while I open this door?"

Adelaide and Jeff each linked an arm under the baggage compartment's heavy-duty netting, then grabbed one of my parachute's shoulder straps. I leaned forward and opened the door. I was buffeted by a cold wind, but it was nothing worse than what I had experienced many times standing in the open hatch of an Army jump plane.

I moved back from the door and picked up Bryce's body. Adelaide and Jeff held on to my parachute's shoulder straps again and I shoved Bryce's body out the door. We did the same with Carter and Kenny. I took particular pleasure in leaning out the door and watching Kenny's headless form tumble to the ocean below.

I stepped back out of the doorway and rubbed my hands together.

"Alrighty, then," I said. "I believe we can now consider this mission successfully concluded. Jeff, how much longer to the drop zone?"

Jeff said, "Three minutes."

"Everyone ready?" I said.

Adelaide and Jeff nodded.

"Very good," I said. "Jeff will you be so kind as to give us a count when we are thirty seconds away?"

"Be my pleasure," Jeff said.

The three of us looked out the baggage compartment door as the plane continued its journey. The winds had died down once again and the ocean surface was glass-like with nary a wave in sight. The sun, which had fallen in the sky, was a glowing orange as sunset approached in the Pacific. The sound of the Gulfstream's engines roared in our ears.

Six miles away from our then present location, a Zodiac that had been dispatched from a Navy destroyer would be waiting for us. The Zodiac would be carrying a Seal team. The pickup spot had been carefully chosen to be free of all sea traffic and was more than a hundred miles in all directions from the nearest shipping lanes.

Our cover story was that Adelaide, Jeff, and I had been on a round-the-world sailing trip when our boat had taken on water and we had been forced to abandon ship. The Zodiac would take us back to the destroyer where it would be waiting in a location ten miles away from the pickup zone. Ten miles was sufficient to put the destroyer in a spot far enough over the horizon so as to prevent both our parachute jump and pickup from being seen by any prying sailors' eyes.

Since we would be making our jump into the ocean's cold water without the benefit of wetsuits, the Seal team would be carrying a change of clothes for all of us. The change of clothes would not only keep us warm, but allow us to discard the bloody garments we were then wearing. The Seal team on the Zodiac would also all be members of MOM. Since the sailors on the destroyer would only know us by the false names we would give them, no one other than members of MOM, Adelaide, Jeff, and I would ever know the three of us had been on board the Gulfstream.

"Thirty seconds," Jeff said.

I said, "Adelaide you go first, then we'll follow. Be sure to pull the ripcord no more than twenty seconds after you clear the plane."

Adelaide said, "I've done this a thousand times before. I know what I'm doing."

"From the ranch's jump tower," I said. "This is a little different."

"Not in my book," Adelaide said. "And I'm pulling the cord at forty seconds, not twenty. Twenty would put me at five thousand feet. Two thousand is fine."

"Five thousand is safer for your first real jump," I said.

Adelaide rolled her eyes.

"Okay, whatever," Adelaide said.

Jeff said, "Ten seconds."

The Zodiac came into view on the surface of the sea.

"Five, four, three, two, one...," Jeff said.

Adelaide jumped.

Jeff and I watched her fall through the air.

"You know she ain't pulling that cord until she's at two thousand feet, right?" Jeff said.

"Yeah," I said. "I only bothered to tell her to pull it at twenty seconds so that I won't feel guilty when she kills herself."

Jeff laughed.

I bowed and made a sweeping gesture with my arm towards the open baggage door.

"After you, my dear Alphonse," I said.

Jeff bowed back.

"Don't mind if I do," Jeff said.

He jumped.

A moment later, so did I.

PART IX

ECLIPSE

CHAPTER 140

A little less than two months later, it was early August, and I found myself in San Mateo, California. The day was bright and sunny, the sky cloudless, and there was just a hint of breeze coming in over the coastal foothills. The temperature was in the low seventies.

Every year around that time the locals hold the Sonoma County Fair. As part of the fair, the locals also hold a horse racing meet, which is why I was there. Jeff had gotten Eclipse ready for his comeback and had entered him in the fifth race that day. It was ten minutes before post time for Eclipse's race.

I sat in the grandstand facing the track. The track had two big ovals, one within the other. A turf course made up the inside oval and a dirt track surrounded it. Both racing surfaces were bordered by gleaming white rails. Kate sat next to me on my right, and on my left were Adelaide and Billy Einstein.

Billy and Kate had completely recovered from the physical effects of their overdoses of RZ 119 truth serum. Kate was still in mourning over the loss of her brother Freddy, though her sadness seemed to lessen day by day. Billy and Kate, along with Kate's children, and Manu and Mosi, had spent the last week at the ranch as my guests. Along with Jeff, Adelaide, and Eclipse, we had all made the six hour trek to San Mateo by Maybach, pickup truck, and horse trailer. I still didn't like Maybachs, but I'd made an exception for the new Maybach Kate's insurance had paid for. After all, Kate's old Maybach had performed admirably well when I had needed it to.

There was a loud roar overhead and the sky darkened for a moment. I looked up. A U.S. Department of Justice helicopter was making a beeline for a landing zone that had been reserved for it in the fairground parking lot. I knew that Vandross, Ray Carpenter, and Bobby and Timmy would be aboard the helicopter. It looked like they might make it just in time for Eclipse's race.

General Hart and Major Haley had planned on coming to Eclipse's race as well. Hart, however, had suddenly been called upon to deal with an incident on Ukraine's border with Russia, and Haley had stayed underground in one of her bunkers to assist him. I told them I would text them with the results of the race.

Kate looked especially beautiful that day. Her blond hair was swept fully off her face and her turquoise eyes were sparkling. She was dressed in a crisp white blouse and exceptionally well-fitting jeans. Kate's children, Carolyn and Dylan, sat next to her, both wearing San Mateo County Fair caps and eating cotton candy. All of us had had a wonderful time at my ranch over the last week, and Kate and I had discussed the possibility of her and the children moving to live on the ranch with me. Grace had communicated to me her approval of such a move.

Adelaide and Billy were studying the 'Daily Racing Form', analyzing Eclipse's chances in the race. The two of them had taken a liking to each other. My thoughts about that potential relationship could be summarized in three words - Heaven help Billy.

"I like Eclipse's chances," Billy said.

"Have you ever seen a 'Racing Form' before in your life?" I said.

"No," Billy said.

Adelaide said, "Billy's good with numbers, Jack."

"I know that," I said.

Billy said, "We should bet. Eclipse is ten to one. That is way over his odds."

Ah youth, I thought.

"How much?" I said.

"Twenty should do it," Billy said.

I fished out my wallet, extracted a twenty dollar bill, and handed it to him.

"You better hurry," I said. "You only have six minutes left."

Adelaide and Billy ran off to the betting windows.

The Department of Justice helicopter had just then landed in the parking lot and I watched as Vandross, Carpenter, and Bobby and Timmy dashed down its ladder.

Jeff, after saddling Eclipse in the paddock fifteen minutes before, had disappeared. Jeff said the anticipation of the race had made him nervous and he wanted to walk off the excess energy. Manu and Mosi had followed him.

The three of them suddenly reappeared at that moment. They were standing next to the rail that circled the dirt track and were about fifty yards in front of me. Jeff was looking through a pair of binoculars. He seemed to be following Eclipse as Eclipse warmed up on the track. Jeff had purchased a new Willie Shoemaker t-shirt especially for the occasion.

Kate spotted Jeff at about the same time I did. She squeezed my arm and pointed at him.

"There's Jeff," Kate said.

"Uh huh," I said.

"He still looks very nervous," Kate said.

"He'll be okay," I said.

"How do you know?" Kate said.

"I know," I said.

She studied my face for a moment, then sighed.

"I guess if anyone would know, it would be you," Kate said. "Jeff's been a lot better lately, hasn't he?"

"He has," I said.

"He's probably not cured, and maybe never will be, but it's good he's better," Kate said.

She paused.

"I think you did the right thing asking him to come along and help you on the mission," Kate said. "Most doctors would have said it would have been a big mistake."

"What do doctors know?" I said.

"Hey, I'm a doctor," Kate said.

"Oh, yeah, I forgot," I said.

Kate leaned over and kissed me on the cheek.

The track announcer's voice boomed over the loudspeakers.

"The horses are at the gate!" the announcer said.

Adelaide and Billy sat down next to me. They were both out of breath.

"We placed the bet," Billy said.

"Did you bet it all to win?" I said.

"Of course," Billy said. "The payoffs to place and show aren't as good."

"What if he doesn't win?" I said.

"Trust me," Billy said.

I looked over at him. I guess if anyone had earned the right to be trusted in my book, it was Billy.

"Okay," I said.

I don't know how they did it, but Vandross, Carpenter, and Bobby and Timmy had found Jeff and the giant Samoan twins and joined them at the rail.

The announcer's voice boomed, "The flag is up!"

A bell sounded, the gates opened, and the horses bounded forward. The crowd began to cheer.

Eclipse had come out fastest of all and led the field down the back-stretch by two lengths. He entered the far turn three lengths in front, and rounded into the stretch five lengths in front. At the rail, Jeff had put down his binoculars and was jumping up and down, windmilling his right arm, cheering Eclipse home. Manu, Mosi, Bobby, Timmy, Carpenter, and Vandross were doing the same. All seven of them were yelling so loudly, I could hear them over the roar of the crowd.

By mid-stretch, Eclipse was ten lengths in front.

"He's going to win!" Billy screamed.

"Was there ever any doubt?" I said.

Printed in the USA
CPSIA information can be obtained
at www.ICGtesting.com
LVHW051059300124
770355LV00024B/200/J